SUMMONED

SUMMONED

M.B. THURMAN

This book is dedicated to you.

You are the real magic.

Many a strange occurrence has come to pass, but none so strange as the discovery

that you are not at all who you thought yourself to be.

PART ONE:

A JOURNEY BEGINS

CHAPTER ONE

A rooftop in Paris seemed an unlikely place for our overdue reunion. I pulled the mysterious note from my pocket, scrutinizing the words that summoned me across the Atlantic, as though I didn't know them by heart.

Meet me next Friday at 6pm – the top of Notre Dame. Don't tell anyone. I'll adjust your travel arrangements.

I turned to the sweeping view, the full grandeur of the city visible. Block after block of historic architecture lay on either side of the Seine, down to the Eiffel Tower, and beyond toward the high-rise skyline – surely a mesmerizing scene under different circumstances. A faint chill crawled the length of my spine, rattling my already growing nerves. My eyes glanced over each shoulder, answering a compulsion that bordered on habit. Familiar, shallow bursts of energy coursed through me, vibrant and sure. It had been above a year, but I couldn't ignore the gnawing sign of being watched. Eyes landed sporadically on mine as I scanned the bustling, historic attraction. Tourists spread thickly in every direction, but it wasn't *their* eyes I sought.

Not for the first time, I considered perhaps the note wasn't from Fitz. My left hand involuntarily reached for my right, needing to feel the smooth surface of the moonstone, the ring I couldn't remove. I closed my eyes, anticipating the deepened state of awareness brought on by the stone, my thoughts churning, my senses heightened.

I checked my watch – an hour past our intended meeting time. The low setting sun and my fading optimism tempted me to trade stone gargoyles for dinner. Maybe my nerves would steady over a glass of wine. I meandered around tourists lingering in the waning daylight, many excited by the prospect of golden hour photos and sunset views, but only one person truly captured my attention. A tall, well-dressed man stood casually near the stairwell, gazing at me above a mischievous smirk. Staring into his lively, bright eyes, the breath caught in the back of my throat.

"Fitz."

"I swear, you haven't changed a bit," he nearly whispered, shaking his head lightly.

"You came."

I couldn't recall the witty lines I rehearsed to my bathroom mirror, all of that practice lost somewhere in the back recesses of my mind. He laughed softly, and between my rising nerves and the infectious sound of his laughter, I did the same. The eyes that held mine were a mesmerizing emerald in color, set in an oval face, and below a tousled head of chestnut hair.

My heart pounded as Fitz met me in an embrace. An unmistakable shock radiated softly through my body, an odd reaction between the two of us that we never could explain. I found my composure, sliding my arms around him just before he gave a tight squeeze and released me, the scent of oak and whisky dissipating with the warmth of his touch. Though his mouth twisted into a smile, his wide eyes communicated the answer I sought – the shock also registered in his body.

My thoughts flooded with questions, suddenly racing from mind-numbing shock to hungry curiosity, before recalling it was neither the time nor place for an inquisition, annoying as that might have been. The man disappeared once before; I didn't want him to change his mind before I found my answers.

"Hadley." He smiled. "I'm sorry I'm late."

"Fitz," I replied, painfully aware his name escaped my lips twice in a minute's time. "I just can't believe you're here."

"Aye... a bit surreal, isn't it?" he asked, his Gaelic dialect thick on his tongue.

Though he seemed confident in speech and action, his eyes followed my movements warily. He was uncertain – *probably waiting for the shock to wear off before I slapped him right across the face*, I mused, and not without satisfaction.

"Why *are* you late?"

"I was," he trailed off, registering the people surrounding us, before dropping his voice. "I was followed."

"By?"

"No idea – not the usual folks."

"We need to talk. Somewhere else."

"Let's go to dinner."

He mistook my pause for disinterest.

"I mean, no pressure, it's just…"

"Okay."

"Okay?"

I laughed. "Let's get dinner."

"I thought you'd never ask."

We wound through the thick crowd waiting just outside the cathedral. Fitz turned his body toward mine, placing his hand on the small of my back to prevent our separation in the chaos – or at least, that's what I told myself. The gesture felt comfortable, like we were assuming our previous roles. A twinge of apprehension hit the pit of my stomach, warning me to act with caution.

A couple of streets over, the sidewalks were free of crowds, and I released a bit of my mounting tension through a deep sigh. The wind blew gently across the Seine, which served as our guide toward the café, granting us the opportunity to focus on something other than navigation. But between the sights of Paris and Fitz's abrupt re-entry into my life, I didn't know where to begin. We walked in silence only a moment before Fitz provided a much-appreciated glimpse into his thoughts.

"If I'm being honest, it's kind of overwhelming to see you," he said, a slight edge in his voice.

Perhaps he was overwhelmed; nervous – definitely. The last

time I saw him, we stood in his parents' cabin in Washington State, while he explained that we couldn't see one another for some undetermined amount of time, though he promised we would see each other again. I didn't take the news well, to put it mildly.

"Yeah, I know the feeling."

He nodded, a taut smile on his face.

"When did you arrive?" I continued.

"Wednesday. You made it on Tuesday?"

I halted, eyeing him suspiciously.

"I have to keep tabs on things like that."

"Fitz! It's just not normal."

"Neither are we."

He was right, and I couldn't dispute that fact. He and I possessed strange abilities, and there were people who somehow discovered what Fitz could do. He and I remained apart to keep me safe, though that was never something I wanted – and it nearly broke the two of us.

"Why did you move your travel up?"

"I wanted more time to sightsee." I shrugged. "You know I haven't been here before."

"Things aren't that simple, Hads. I need to know where you are – just in case."

"I couldn't exactly call you at the time, now could I?"

"Point taken."

"I had a feeling you'd catch it anyway. And when I checked into the hotel early, and a burner phone was sitting on my bed…"

"One I'm assuming you didn't bring with you tonight, since I couldn't reach you."

I felt my expression darken.

Fitz smirked. "Anyway, I had to stick to the plan. I couldn't get here early, but Henry took care of it."

"Your mysterious best friend, whom I've still not met."

"Soon."

"Are we safe here? You said someone was following you."

"We're safe. No one is tracking us. But let's keep moving? I feel like a sitting duck."

I nodded, resuming our previous pace.

"Look, we have a lot to dig into, but I'd like to just have dinner and catch up first."

I scoffed.

"Aye, it's a tall order, but... there's a lot we haven't covered, even in our letters. I'll have information to discuss soon. I promise."

Stepping into the café, the conversation paused. It couldn't be helped, as we drank in the charm of the small space. The host led us to a back corner, navigating mismatched, antique tables – the products of a bygone era still serving as a catalyst for food and conversation, even in our modern age. They looked at home amongst the maroon walls, which were covered in eclectic, vintage wine bottles. Although the restaurant was filled with patrons, the hum of conversation was soft, giving an intimate feel to the place.

Fitz pulled out my chair and proceeded to his seat. My eyes flickered across the table, wondering what it was about him that made every bit of my soul so incredibly aware of his presence. Though the awkwardness of our reunion lingered, a long-forgotten voice demanded to be heard – begging me to recall our previous chapters, reminding me of the trust we placed in one another. His lips curved into a soft smile.

"What?" I asked skeptically, realizing my eyes lingered far too long on my dinner partner.

"You. I forgot how observant you are... about everything."

"And you find it amusing?"

"I find it endearing."

I shook my head, butterflies dancing in my belly.

"Your mind is my favorite thing about you. There's always so much going on up there," he trailed off, searching my eyes. Silence fell, neither of us sure what to say, and I would've felt embarrassed had it been anyone else.

The moment dissipated with the waiter's arrival at our table. We ordered a bottle of wine, and I suggested Fitz use his discretion to select food for the table. As I'd been in Paris only two days, it seemed wise to allow the veteran to take the wheel, and Fitz was enthusiastic about sharing a couple of his favorite dishes with me.

With food and drink sorted, Fitz leaned forward, and in his most studious voice – "Now, where were we? Oh yes, your question about who's following us."

"It wasn't your gaze I felt at Notre Dame, was it? It didn't feel right."

"No. I had just climbed the steps when we met near the

door."

"So, someone else *was* watching me."

"Aye, but Hadley, you know how this works. Sometimes it isn't bad intent."

"You think someone was watching both of us at the same time, and it's just a coincidence?"

Fitz gasped playfully. "Did you just roll your eyes at me?"

I grinned. "Yes. But the question still stands."

"No."

"I don't think so either."

"But it wasn't the government."

"And how do you know that?"

"I just do."

Though Fitz and I both possessed the ability to perceive when we were under watch, he could also identify the source – to a certain extent.

"I'm telling you this is different."

"Why did you decide on Paris?"

"I didn't want to meet you in London – just in case Big Brother sorted out that you were headed there next week. It's a close enough pit stop. And they think I'm in Budapest," he offered through a smile.

"You don't think they've figured out we're here?"

"They've likely figured out I'm not in Budapest, but they have no trace to Paris."

"Nice." I smirked.

"I needed to get away anyway, and Paris was a good place for it. You have impeccable timing."

"Get away from what?"

"My latest project. Shall I bare my soul to you?"

I grinned, nodding in encouragement.

"I'm deep into a side project right now, but this one is personal, and I've hit a dead end. I just needed to get away from everything for a few days. Paris usually does the trick. I'm distracted by all the culture and get the break I need from my own thoughts."

"This personal project…"

"Go ahead."

"Who's helping you? It's nearly impossible to remain objective when it comes to something personal."

"No one," he admitted. "I haven't trusted anyone. I'm trying to solve a mystery surrounding my ancestor – a great-grandfather – and an object he lost in 1662."

The look on my face must have betrayed my confusion.

"There are individuals who don't need to know my family ever had possession of it, and I'm honestly not sure who I can trust."

His candid response surprised me. But why would it matter to anyone outside of his family if his ancestor lost something hundreds of years ago? I'd spent far too much time on the mysteries of Fitz MacGregor and his family, and it seemed that pattern would continue.

"You're telling me about it now?"

"Aye."

"Why?"

"Because I trust you."

As the waiter delivered our wine, his request for Fitz to approve the *Chateau de Ferrand* broke our gaze, along with the intensity of the moment. We often locked eyes and could barely look away, as though we became vividly aware of each other for the first time, recognizing the magical, invisible thread connecting us. It seemed to be some sort of communication we didn't yet understand – we inexplicably developed the ability to feel each other's emotions and physical pain. I felt his nerves across the dinner table even then, and I innately knew he felt mine. I was aware it would sound crazy to anyone else, but luckily no one else needed to know.

The waiter poured the beautiful, deep burgundy liquid into my glass. After a brief swirl, I took a small, tentative sip, allowing it to trickle smoothly across my tongue.

"That's delicious," I exclaimed, before taking another sip.

Fitz chuckled at my response and raised his glass in turn. "What do you taste?"

I closed my eyes, pulling another slow sip from the glass. "Dark fruit – black cherries. Spice. It'll open up nicely."

"Aye, and a bit warm, which I fancy. You're right – it does want oxygen. I'm glad you approve. Wine tasting has been a bit lackluster without you." He deftly swirled the dark liquid, opening its full possibilities, as he lost himself deep inside his own thoughts. There was something playful and unassuming in his manners. I could've argued that in his features I found both a man to leave you breathless and a boyish countenance to put you at ease.

"You trusted me enough to talk about your secret project, so… let me help you."

"I'd like that. But not today. I want to talk more about you."

My eyes narrowed to slits.

"Come on, Hadley. Let's save this conversation for another day."

"Another day?"

"Yeah, I mean… my intention is to see you again. I was hoping we could sightsee tomorrow."

"You'd better ask then," I countered, slowly regaining my footing.

"I'm thinking of touring Musee Rodin tomorrow morning. Join me."

I smiled but offered no reply. He needed to work a little harder than that.

"I'd like to see you tomorrow, Hadley. I'd like to show you Paris if you'll allow me to do that?"

I shrugged, smirking. "I think I'm free."

As the food was served, we spoke about my career as a public relations consultant in Boston. When I first met Fitz, I was earning my master's degree after a few years of working in the industry. Most of my weekends were spent at my parents' house on the Olympic Peninsula, especially after my dad's cancer diagnosis. Fitz's parents owned a cabin next door, and the rest was history, as they say.

"I hinted at this in my last letter, but I've got a bit of breaking news for you."

Fitz smiled. "Breaking news about what?"

"I made a pretty big decision about my career, and honestly my life in general."

"Do tell," he encouraged.

"The real reason for the London trip is because I'm interested in moving there. Seems reasonable, right?"

"Perfectly reasonable I'd say, though I've never been the foremost scholar in reasonable."

I laughed knowing he was absolutely right, which I considered a mark in his favor.

"Why London?"

"The culture, the history, the architecture… it has always interested me, and I thought, why not live in Europe for a while? London has great career options – companies, museums, universities. I feel like it would be a good next step for my career."

"Sounds like a good idea."

"This world is so beautiful and fascinating. I just can't imagine living in one country my entire life."

He beamed as he found his response. "Right. I couldn't agree more. Not everyone understood my family's decision to move to the States, nor my decision to move back to this side of the water. You have to take those chances, though, and see where they'll take you."

"You've been cryptic about your exact location – where's home at the moment?"

"Edinburgh."

"Hold on."

"I'm holding."

"Are you teaching at the University of Edinburgh?" I asked, slightly in awe.

"Aye."

"Impressive."

Fitz smiled, clearly gratified by my response. From an early age, he wanted to become a professor, just like his father. The university was consistently ranked as one of the top in the world, and Fitz was only in his early thirties.

"I should have picked up on that. Your accent is stronger," I teased, pulling a laugh from him. Though he spent many of his formative years in Washington, between his parents' thick Highlander dialects and the amount of time the family consistently spent in Scotland, he carried some of the Scottish accent in his speech – which I loved. Obviously, after his return to Scotland, the accent only grew stronger – which I also loved.

"I'm jealous. I can't wait to see Scotland. There's so much I want to explore, especially in the Highlands."

"You're going to love it. Actually, we'll have you over here in no time."

"Ha! Always so confident, Fitz."

A smirk rested on his lips. "Maybe, but I know you'll fall in love with Europe."

"I already have."

"Let's keep that sentiment alive tonight."

"I just might agree to that. What do you have in mind?"

Fitz requested the check, a gleam in his eye.

CHAPTER TWO

L uckily, lines at the Eiffel Tower were relatively short for September, and I soon found myself ascending the Parisian staple with my adventurous escort. My breath was short once we reached our destination, but not only from the exercise. I'd seen countless photos of the historic landmark, but nothing prepared me for the grandeur of the experience. We gazed at the countless lights of the city, the cool, evening air granting us vitality, as we created a memory I would always remember. People tell their grandchildren about such moments, eyes closed, recalling how alive they felt.

We shared more about our time apart, both hungry for details of each other's lives, completely lost in the stories only we could tell. I don't know how long we stood there, suspended above the city, reveling in the rediscovery of our long-lost companionship. But at some late hour, we paused to appreciate the light show sparkling all around us, before descending the tower in search of a sweet bedtime snack.

We were close to abandoning our search when we finally happened upon a closing shop. The owner was pleased to pause his closing tasks, supply us with end-of-day croissants, and bid us adieu as we wandered back into the dim evening streets. We ate in comfortable silence, happy to stay in that moment as long as it would allow, until the gold and maroon hallways of our hotel welcomed us home. And just like all unforgettable nights, ours ended, coming to a close as I leaned against the outer door of my room.

"Are you going to tell me the rest of it?"

"The rest of what?" I whispered back, aware of the neighboring rooms.

"What's drawn you to London? It's a proper Hadley story, with the positive spin and all, but there's more to it."

"What makes you think there's more?"

"Because I know you, and I know when you aren't telling me something."

"Maybe you don't know me so well anymore."

"I'll always know you," he responded, the soft smile fading from his face.

"You left, Fitz. I'm sure we've both changed. I know I have."

"I didn't leave. You did."

"I moved, but I didn't end things."

"I didn't either."

"Okay, fine. You left things open, and we haven't seen each other for over a year."

"You know that was for your protection."

"Do I?"

"Wow, Hadley. That's *really* unfair."

I exhaled sharply.

"I don't want to argue right now. I just asked a simple question."

I closed my eyes in an effort to think clearly. "Truthfully, I thought about coming over here a couple days early, even before your note. I need to… wrestle with my thoughts, and process the past couple of years before jumping into interviews. With Dad…" I trailed off, willing the tears to stay in.

"When you lost your dad."

"You know, I told you my dad died, and it changed nothing."

"It was for your own good."

"I don't know if I believe that anymore."

"You will."

"How can you be so sure?" I challenged.

"I'll explain that part, but not now. It's late, and we'll both say things we don't mean."

"You summon me halfway across the world, and then you don't even want to talk about the issue that's kept us apart?"

"You know that's not true."

"Fine."

"So… your dad," he nudged.

"It's nothing you don't know. He was my best friend – one of the few people who understood me – and I lost him. I haven't been able to talk about it. I haven't processed that he's gone. I need to face the tough things that happened in the past couple of years, and let go of what I can. I already gave my notice at work – I'm done with Boston."

"There's more."

"That'll have to do for tonight."

"Fair enough," he returned, his hand taking hold of mine, giving it a squeeze.

"I *will* actually see you tomorrow? You're not going to disappear, are you?"

"I'll be here tomorrow morning at ten. And Hadley… I promise we'll get into everything soon. Really soon."

He smiled, but his nerves resurfaced in *my* body. My mind was spinning, as we both danced around the things we needed to say, but didn't yet know how.

"Okay," I returned simply. "Tomorrow then."

"I'm looking forward to it."

Instinct smothered my rationale as I planted a soft kiss on his cheek and turned to walk through the door.

CHAPTER THREE

I sat on the edge of the bed, staring at the cream-colored walls of my hotel room, my thoughts returning to the last time I saw Fitz. His parents hosted a going-away party for me before I left for Boston, where my first job out of graduate school awaited. Fitz gifted me a moonstone ring, before sharing that we couldn't see one another for a while.

"Why?"

"If I'm being honest, I'm not supposed to tell you why. I'm supposed to tell you something… anything rather than the truth, but I care too much about you to lie about it."

"I don't understand – are you calling things off?"

"No, of course not… I know this doesn't make sense. I don't want things to happen like this, but it isn't my choice."

"Who says we can't talk?"

"I can't tell you that either. I know that's difficult to accept, but I'm already breaking the rules by being honest with you."

"I don't understand any of this."

"I know you don't understand it right now, but I promise you will one day. You and I will see each other again."

"When?"

"I don't know exactly. It won't happen for a while, but it will happen. I swear."

"This is ridiculous."

"Look," he began, pausing briefly. "I wish I could explain it all to you right now, but you have no idea what this is doing to me. I have no choice. Please just try to trust me."

I reached for his hand, holding it in both of my own. The pain of contact returned, before falling into a dull roar, and I wondered if my touch was adding to his discomfort. Our emotions were muddled, and I could only guess we were intensifying the pain the other felt. I released my grasp, feeling like I was letting go of more than his hand.

"You know what? Screw this."

"Hadley."

"No. Maybe we haven't talked about what this is lately, but you and I both know damn well what it is."

Fitz took my arm and led me onto the back deck, away from the questioning glances of our friends and family. The wind tore through my loose hair, sending strands of strawberry blonde floating all around me. I couldn't convey the right amount of anger with nature obscuring my vision. I tore my hair away from my face, the act further incensing me, as Fitz turned on his heel, rage burning through his green eyes.

"I didn't say a bloody thing about not knowing what we have," he *growled.*

"Then how can you expect to tell me something like this and then it's just supposed to be okay?"

"I know it's not okay! I know it's going to suck for you, okay? It's going to suck a lot more for me, trust me."

"How am I supposed to trust you?"

His eyes widened, their anger fading with my freshly delivered blow, before he turned toward the lake.

"Don't you dare turn away from me."

"I know you're pissed. And that's okay. I would be, too…" He paused, turning to face me once again. "I've already said too much, and that's because I care about you."

"I need more."

"You're observant, Hads. You're different, and so am I… and so is my family."

"Come on. Don't give me this crap, Fitz."

"No, you need to listen. The things we can all do — that's why we'll be apart for a while. When I can come to you again, I promise I won't waste a second."

"Is this… stuff… with your family the reason we have this weird connection?"

"Yes and no."

"Real helpful, Fitz."

"Damnit, Hadley," he muttered under his breath.

"What? Give me something."

"Aye, it has something to do with it, but our connection isn't exactly

normal. It's special to you and me. That's it, okay? You have no idea how much trouble you're getting me into."

"Except that no one knows about this conversation other than us, right?"

"Come here," he said, pulling me into him. "I love your curiosity… your love for learning. But it's going to drive you crazy in this instance, and get us both into trouble."

He didn't want to tell me. But eventually, I wore him down. The situation had something to do with the government. Someone knew about his abilities. He wanted to keep me safe, and he was under strict instruction not to contact me, at least for a while – they hadn't yet discovered that I, too, harbored strange gifts. Fitz and I kept in touch through burner phones that showed up at my apartment – and letters I mailed to various locations around Europe after the addresses came inexplicably into my possession.

I considered walking away countless times, but I knew Fitz held the answers I needed to finally understand myself – to understand the things I was able to do. I could only guess at the information he gathered during our time apart, but regardless of his need to protect me, he was about to share everything he knew – and soon.

CHAPTER FOUR

The next morning I ordered room service and prepared for my outing with Fitz. I knew there was something about the French I admired, and sitting at my desk devouring a chocolate croissant, I recalled what it was. Even with the vast societal contributions the French made to art, architecture, and music, having perfected both the croissant *and* the macaron was what I considered their most commendable accomplishment to date.

I caught a glimpse of myself in the mirror, coffee cup in hand, and reflected on my differences since first meeting Fitz. My unruly hair had thickened, cropped just below my collarbones. As the strawberry blonde grew more brilliant, my skin developed a smoother complexion. I no longer needed contacts, which was a complete mystery to the physicians I consulted. The changes occurred around the same time that I felt a necessity for exercising more frequently, and I noticed the way men's eyes lingered. But Fitz saw the person I truly was, my inner appearance – and he loved me nonetheless.

My greatest secret was my greatest mystery. I heard the thoughts of others and by no desire of my own. In the beginning, the information registered randomly, and I had no control over it. And then things changed. Instead of merely acquiring information, I heard others' thoughts clearly, thinking they shared information with me aloud. I would respond, only to their surprise or confusion. As a result, I became increasingly paranoid in my conversations with others.

I slipped up during the previous evening at the café. The dessert offerings weren't listed on the menu, but I was positive the waiter told us about them, and I ordered the special, sharing that his spiel about it was too tempting. Apparently, we hadn't discussed dessert, which was an abrupt transition for the waiter, especially after I mentioned that, like his wife, it was one of my favorites. I recovered by saying I overheard him relay the information to others, which I knew wasn't true, but could have been. The waiter decided to be incredibly awkward about it, but Fitz graciously asked the waiter to make that two clafoutis and quickly changed the subject, along with the waiter's focus. He was like his sister in a few respects, and their ability to redeem an awkward situation was one of them.

I was picking blackberries for my grandmother the day I met Fitz's sister, Izzy. The morning was cool and rainy, and for a moment I thought I'd get out of the task. I didn't mind helping Gram, but for the previous two days, I felt I was under watch.

I had just finished picking the berries when a splash in the creek startled me, loosening my grip on the bowl and sending blackberries scattering through the blades of grass. Izzy ascended from the creek bank, her long, auburn hair hanging loosely down her back, complementing her tall, slender figure. As she faced me, I felt the full intensity of her emerald eyes and would have been more in awe of her flawless, milky skin had those eyes released me from their spell. I recalled the unsettling feeling sweep over me when she called me by name, knowing I hadn't yet shared it with her. Just another MacGregor family oddity.

I was slipping on my shoes when someone knocked, the vision of Izzy dissipating along with it. My heart rate quickened, and I opened the large, wooden door to find Fitz leaning against the doorframe. Dressed in dark jeans and a gray sweater, he looked as handsome as ever. This guy would be the death of me, with his casual way of making my heart stop.

"Hi, I'm Fitz. I'll be your tour guide today."

I laughed, the previous night's tension dissipating with the touch of our hands. He held my hand for a moment and laughed softly in turn. The shock registered again, but I noticed, as with the kiss after dinner, that the initial jolt was lessening.

As we walked the city, Fitz did qualify as my tour guide. We talked about architecture, history, art, and our love for the city while we slowly meandered to the museum. The tour was a good distraction, and the conversation lively as we discussed the magnificent pieces we encountered along the way. Post-tour, we found an unoccupied bench in a large courtyard, as I pressed Fitz to share more about his career. He demanded we talk about me the previous day, but it was my turn to learn the real details about his life since we last met.

"I focus primarily on early Scottish history and spent time studying the witch trials. I was so fascinated by the subject, I traveled to the towns in Scotland where accused witches were tried and murdered. Now, I teach classes on early witchcraft and religion in Scotland, mostly focused on the 17th century."

"What piqued your interest in that subject?"

"My family tree. My father and I even traced back to a grandmother who died in the witch trials in Forfar in 1662."

"I can't fathom the way people must've lived in fear. It's extraordinary you were able to trace back to her. It must've been shocking to discover your ancestor was executed in a witch trial."

"When we made that discovery, I was horrified. It disturbed me to know she died like that. Yeah, it was a long time ago, but it felt personal. From there, I learned as much as I could about who she was and about the time period."

"It changed the trajectory of your career."

"Yeah, I guess you're right. I was a freshman in college when we got our ancestry sorted, and I changed my major."

His eyes bore into mine. There was something unspoken in the air – I felt it, but whatever it might be, I couldn't quite grasp it.

"I never knew that…why you changed your major."

"I guess I never talked about it."

"You've always seemed guarded with real details about yourself. Why is that?"

"Honestly, I don't know. I guess I don't think I'm that interesting."

"I'm interested."

"Thank you," he returned, laying his hand briefly on mine.

I closed my eyes for a second, taking in the warm, fuzzy jolt. My mind wasn't the only thing that had missed Fitz. Our bodies were falling back into sync.

"It was obviously a good decision for you – changing your major and all. I can understand why you became so entwined with the subject."

"It just felt right at the time, and looking back, I'm happy about the path I took."

"So, this is how you landed back in Scotland?"

"A friend of mine lectures at St. Andrew's but has a lot of connections at UE. I loved UE when I was studying for my master's, and he thought I'd be a good fit for the history faculty, so he invited me over for a visit. I took him up on the offer, and two days later I applied for an open position."

He told the story nonchalantly, in his quintessential Fitz style, but it required hard work to secure his current position, and I sensed the pride he took in his work.

"You seem happy."

"I'm happy with my career, and it's been nice to spend time in Scotland again. Catching up with family is great, too."

I opened my mouth to respond, but I couldn't seem to find the words. A prickle worked its way up my spine, like an assault of hundreds of tiny needles. Fitz's eyes widened before he regained his composure.

"Let's get out of here."

CHAPTER FIVE

"We need to drive toward Sacré-Cœur, but without taking a direct route."

Our driver glanced suspiciously at Fitz in the rearview mirror.

"We're being followed. If that makes you uncomfortable, we'll call another car."

The driver hesitated briefly, before tossing a smile in our direction. His foot slammed on the gas, and we sped away from the museum.

"What are they driving?" the driver questioned, a heavy accent rolling from his lips.

"The silver Peugeot," I answered, garnering a raised eyebrow from Fitz. "What? You think you're the only observant one in this car?"

"Can you make that turn?" Fitz questioned.

Our driver laughed, shaking his head. "Can I make that turn?

Of course, I can."

And indeed he did – at a record speed, I was sure. I slid across the seat and into Fitz, his head nearly hitting the window.

"Hell yeah!" Fitz shouted, laughing.

After countless turns, crisscrossing our previous paths and meandering down nearly every street in the 17th and 18th arrondissements, we lost our pursuers. Adebayo, our fearless driver, turned down a narrow alleyway and positioned the car out of sight.

"We lost them. But you should walk through this building, and call a different car to pick you up on that next street."

I smiled, impressed.

"Adebayo, my friend. A job well done," Fitz exclaimed.

He grinned. "It's been a while since I had excitement like that. Just like James Bond."

They shook hands warmly before we followed his instructions and requested a new driver to take us back to our hotel.

We entered the hotel through a back entrance, making our way quietly to my room. I pulled the curtains closed, as Fitz took a seat at the desk.

"We shouldn't go out tonight."

"What? That's ridiculous."

"Hadley, we just had a tail follow us around half of Paris."

"Yeah, I was there."

"Check the attitude, Hads. You really think we should go back out there and risk it?"

"I thought these weren't the people who normally follow

you."

"Right, and that scares me."

"I get that. But if it's the same person who watched us at Notre Dame, then they likely know where we're staying anyway. I don't think being out in public puts us at more risk."

"I don't know."

"I'm not saying this doesn't worry me – it does. But we're probably safer out in the crowds than sitting in this room."

Fitz nodded slowly.

"Tell me what you know," I demanded.

"All I know is that these people are different."

"What about the government people – you're certain it isn't them?"

"I lost them when I left Edinburgh. They haven't found us."

"What happens now?"

"I'm not sure."

"Fitz. What are you not telling me?"

He sighed. "I talked to my dad this morning. He's been in contact with the officials. He works with them. They still don't know where I am."

"Wait… your dad works with the government people?"

"Aye. That part is harder to explain, but he's worked closely with them on various projects for years. Even Dad doesn't know where we are."

"You still have a lot to tell me. But I guess we need to focus on finding out who's following us here first."

"I think you're right about being just as safe out as we are in here. Though I'm going to have the hotel move our rooms next to one another."

"Good idea – see if they have adjoining rooms with a door in between."

"And we'll go out tonight. If they're watching, we'll throw them off. I think it'll confuse them if we just go back out and sightsee. I bet they're waiting for us to run."

"Eventually, though… that's what we'll have to do, isn't it?"

"I don't know. I truly don't. I'll have more information from Dad soon. Then I'll tell you everything I know, and you and I will sit down and make a decision together."

I nodded, reaching for his hand.

"I'll go get our rooms sorted."

CHAPTER SIX

Fitz would only share that we'd dine at a Parisian staple that evening – and he planned to wear a suit. It took longer to dress than I cared to admit. I wore comfortable clothes romping around Paris, but practicality had no place at our dinner. A deep desire bubbled inside me. I needed to show Fitz a different part of myself. Throughout our past relationship, we were in the middle of the Olympic National Park – hiking, biking, canoeing, and swimming – but Fitz had never even seen me in a dress.

I studied my reflection in the bathroom mirror, nervous about my newly acquired little, black dress that fit snugly against my body. I wondered if we were making a mistake. A deep breath escaped my lips as I tugged at the sleeves around my wrists and the hemline hugging my thighs, knowing the longer I sat idle, the higher my anxiety would flare. I slipped on the black heels I packed for job interviews, and touched up my eyeliner and lipstick, keeping both my hands and mind occupied. The knock at the door almost startled me.

"Wow. You are… *stunning.*"

I was gratified by the dumbfounded look on his face. "Thank you. You look pretty good yourself."

And he did. His gray suit and black cashmere sweater were flattering, and the perfect complement to my attire. *In sync*, I thought to myself.

Soon we were again exploring the streets of Paris, the lights of Rue de Rivoli guiding us toward our destination. We first walked in companionable silence, taking in the bustling streets saturated with happy tourists and well-dressed diners. The night was intoxicating with the hum of activity, the sights around the Louvre, the cool breeze against our skin, and no signs of being under watch. Fitz took my hand, placing it in the crook of his arm and offering an unsure smile in my direction.

"Gentleman," I said, shooting him an encouraging smile.

Dinner was more adventurous than our previous meal, but I was thrilled to be seated across from Fitz at Maxim's, a Parisian staple indeed. I looked around distractedly, finally viewing a restaurant I dreamed about for years. Beautiful murals decorated the walls, intricately detailed columns and molding adorned the dining rooms, white tablecloths spread across small tables… all cast in a dim haze of soft crimson. It was nearly overwhelming to sit down in such a famed restaurant.

Our waiter pointed out the table where President and First Lady Kennedy dined during their visit, and he shared stories about everyone from Grace Kelly to Marion Cotillard, all of whom dined in the magnificent establishment. A tuxedo-clad man crooned classic jazz tunes, and soon enough, the music of Frank Sinatra and the Rat Pack morphed into the soundtrack of our evening. Food and wine were plentiful on our table, the experience of tasting new food and drink steering the conversation in a lighter direction. But once we ate our way to the dessert menu, I decided to delve back into Fitz's work, curiosity taking root.

"How did you learn that the ring your grandfather lost was your grandmother's – the one who died in the witch trials?" I asked, reaching for another... whatever that was at the center of the table.

"I never told you the object was a ring, or where it came from."

I froze. I was certain he told me of the ring when he first spoke on the subject. My mind raced through what I thought I remembered, stunned that I messed up over something like this.

"I..." I honestly had no idea how to explain it.

"Just tell me the truth. I can obviously be open-minded, but there's no room for lies – not between us."

"You probably won't even believe this one."

"Hadley, have you met us? There's absolutely nothing normal about either one of us."

I hesitated still.

"I'm not going anywhere, so you might as well be straight with me. Did the information come to you like it has in the past?"

I looked tentatively around our table, but our neighboring diners appeared preoccupied in their own conversations. "I can hear people's thoughts now," I whispered shyly. "But it's not all of the time. It just comes and goes."

My eyes darted nervously around the nearby tables, anticipating horrified expressions, but no one paid us any mind. I braced myself before meeting Fitz's gaze. My hands fumbled with each other, cold and restless as they were. His hand reached across the table, steadying mine, and nodded his head. His encouragement pushed me onward in my explanation.

"So, the random information I used to know about people?" Fitz nodded.

"Now I can actually hear them thinking. I don't know what's wrong with me." My voice shook, releasing a pressure that threatened to consume me, finally sharing what I'd kept carefully hidden.

"There's nothing wrong with you. Please don't say that," he implored, his fingers sliding through my own, finding a firmer grip.

I nodded, not believing him, but unable to find the words I wanted to say. He rubbed the base of my thumb with his own, sending my feelings into battle with one another — pain, joy, anxiety, peace.

"When did it start?"

"Actually hearing thoughts? That started I guess about six months ago."

"Did anything else change around the same time?"

I rambled about the physical changes I encountered, the words tumbling out after my prolonged secrecy. "I know this sounds crazy, but it did happen all at once. I've been trying to find a connection, but it's difficult to research something most people don't even believe is real."

"I know that must be difficult."

"Honestly, I feel completely alone. I haven't talked to anyone about the changes."

"Why didn't you tell me this earlier?"

"I don't know. Our conversations are always brief. I definitely didn't want to put information like this in writing. I guess I just wasn't sure how to share it."

Fitz nodded, his eyes soft in understanding.

"You know I talked to my parents about the random information, but that was as a child. And Jordan, but we haven't really talked about it since we were, I don't know… teenagers? She just cuts me a look occasionally." I smiled, thinking of my best friend. "But she doesn't know about the change either."

"Thank you for trusting me."

"I feel like an idiot. I mean, what is wrong with me?"

"You're not an idiot. Don't say things like that."

"It's how I feel."

"You've just harbored this secret for too long. Everyone is born with different gifts. Somehow this is yours."

I shook my head.

"I know hearing people's thoughts must feel weird. But, Hadley, you and I both have unique abilities. This isn't all that strange. Look at the story of my grandmother. She was different from the 'norm,' too. Humanity doesn't have a lot of tolerance for those whose strengths are unique, but you have a gift, Hadley. You just need to use it wisely."

"I can't seem to do that, though. I think people have told me things they haven't, so I accidentally tattle on myself. I see the confusion set in with some people – they're racking their brains thinking they're crazy for not remembering conversations. Others look at me like I'm the crazy one, which isn't far from the truth."

"Your gift seems to be evolving, and you've had no help. We can work on that. I think there are cues you're missing, but with the right training, you could hone these skills into something manageable. I want to help if you'll let me."

I simply stared, searching for the right response. Finally, I managed a simple thank you and squeezed his hand.

*   *   *

As we arrived at my room, a soft smile blanketed Fitz's features, and I wondered how he was so calm after learning the information I dropped on him only an hour before.

"You amaze me. You tell me you have the most amazing skill tonight, and you sit there waiting for me to cut and run. I'm not going to." He took my hand in his. "I care about you, Hadley. I always have. You're the most amazing woman."

Disbelief undoubtedly registered on my face.

"This is difficult, I know that. Last time nearly broke both of us. I don't want to stop seeing you. I didn't then, and I don't now."

"But you did then."

"Aye, because I didn't have a choice. I do now."

"And that's not going to change like it did before."

"No, it won't. You and I are drawing a line in the sand right now. Being here, together – this changes everything."

"You're ready for this?"

"I've been ready for this since the beginning. But we weren't prepared. And I couldn't bring myself to put you in danger."

"I'm ready, too. I'm exhausted from the secrecy – from being apart."

"I still have no way of knowing the consequences."

"I don't care about the consequences."

"It's easy to say that now."

"Maybe. But this phase of our lives is over. It has to be. Whatever the next one brings, we sort it out together."

Fitz's features grew stormy, and he pulled my body closer to him, one hand resting on my waist, as the other cradled the base of my skull. My arms slid across his back, and instead of the jarring shock I anticipated, warmth pulsed through my veins, like life-giving energy channeling between the two of us, granting us peace. My heart raced as his eyes searched mine. He slipped a finger under my chin and dipped his head slowly and deliberately, as though he knew the prolonged moment would only make me want it more. To his credit, it was working.

As his lips found mine, electricity quivered through my body, sending chills across my skin. My eyes popped open and found that his had done the same, wide with shock. Our grip tightened, and we continued to search one another a few moments longer. His lips were imploring, as though they could find the answers he sought in my kiss. He drew back as gently and deliberately as he came toward me in the beginning, eyes closed, drinking in the last intimacies of the moment.

"Who's the mind reader now?" I laughed, fully drunk on something other than the wine.

He laughed deeply and planted a quick kiss on my forehead.

"Goodnight. I'll see you in the morning."

CHAPTER SEVEN

The next morning over breakfast, I allowed Fitz to put me through what I described as an interrogation. When I shared the sentiment with him, he boomed with laughter, and I could only summon the energy to roll my eyes. He could at least wait until I was through my first cup of Earl Grey before hounding me with questions.

Encouraged by the lack of observance the previous night, we ventured out for breakfast. Seated in an open-air café, we casually worked our way through breakfast, watching passersby stroll along the old stone street, and – oh yes, contemplating the complexities of my mind.

"Okay, but focus: did anything odd or, I don't know, noteworthy, happen when things started shifting? Was there an important life event or something of the sort?"

I thought hard but couldn't come up with anything other than, "I guess it was shortly after my dad died, but I don't see how that would be related."

Fitz nodded his head thoughtfully.

"How about a trigger? Do you notice a pattern in what people are thinking?"

"No. It truly is all over the map. Just in our time together here, it's been the detail about your grandfather and your research and the dessert menu. No connection at all."

"Give me other examples."

"How much my car repair would cost, how old someone was, or even what the gender of a child is while it still grows in its mother's belly."

"These are all things that you've been curious about."

"…Yeah."

"There's a connection between them all."

"What do you mean?"

"You wanted to know something. That's the connection. Every instance you can recall is because you wanted to know the answer to an internal question. Random information isn't just coming to you – you're controlling the answers you receive. We just need to figure out how you're summoning them."

"The thought crossed my mind, but how can that be? It would have to be completely unconscious. I'm not asking for this information, Fitz. That's what I'm saying. I'm not controlling this."

"You can hear people's thoughts, actually hear them. You hear information you're curious about – is it so hard to reason that your brain is asking for the information? It seems logical to me."

"Yeah, I see what you're saying. It makes sense; I just didn't think it would be that simple."

"Right. You're close to the problem, so you're probably overthinking it. As you said, it's difficult to remain objective when something is too personal."

I nodded, considering the new possibilities.

"If you aren't calling up thoughts and information all the time, it must happen when you're more than mildly curious about something."

"Also makes sense."

He took a sip of coffee, his face scrunched in deep thought. He was awfully cute.

"That still leaves us with the biggest problem, though. I have no clue how I'm calling this information to me. I have no memory of infiltrating anyone else's mind."

"Think of it like breathing. You don't think about it most of the time, but your body is busy at work. If you need more air, or let's say you're at the doctor, and they ask you to take a deep breath, you can command your body and mind to make that happen. I think it's the same for mind reading."

"I need to figure out how I even have this ability. I need to understand how it works if I'm going to control it."

"I'm going to help you figure that part out relatively easily," he reasoned, albeit a bit nervously.

"How are you going to do that?"

"Because I'm a witch. And so are you."

The words hung in the air, which suddenly seemed lifeless and stale. My stomach turned. Witches and witchcraft didn't exist. They were the ideas created from the back of someone's mind many years ago. They were fabricated excuses used to persecute the innocent. They were Halloween stories and the substance of books and films, but they weren't real.

I looked at Fitz, a man I knew to be truthful. He wasn't always forthcoming, but I'd never caught him in a lie. The man who sat before me was not a storyteller, nor a lunatic. He was a lucid, intelligent man who held an esteemed position at one of the foremost learning institutions in the world. This was the man who showed me care and support, even when no one else knew how. He couldn't be lying, but he also couldn't be telling the truth. My mind wouldn't allow it.

"Fitz, do you realize what you just said to me?"

"Of course, I do. I think you're in shock. Here, drink some of your water," he countered, sliding the glass closer to me.

"I'm just fine, and I don't need water. You can't say something like that and then tell me how to respond. You can't just show up to breakfast on a Sunday morning and casually throw out to your breakfast date, 'Oh hey, I'm a witch, and so are you.'" I paused. "On second thought, do you want to take it back?"

"No, I don't. You *are* a witch."

"Yes, I heard you. Loud and clear."

He leaned back in his seat, an arched eyebrow the only sign that he was listening.

I looked around us, hoping to God no one was eavesdropping.

"Don't worry about them. No one can hear us." Fitz smiled coyly. His eyes were wild, full of something bordering excitement.

"You say that so confidently."

"Oh, aye."

"How can you possibly know that?"

"That's not important right now."

"Oh, Fitz," I nearly whispered. "Listen, I just… my parents aren't witches. There's no way I wouldn't know if they were. And I don't have some magical powers, okay? I can read minds. I know it's strange, but not strange enough to call me a witch."

"You're right about your parents not being witches. Your mom can't know about this at any point. Do you understand?"

I found myself nodding before I realized the insanity of playing along.

"Good. And there's nothing strange about mind-reading. Or witches."

I let out a slow, loud sigh, wondering how I was even supposed to approach a conversation like this. Fitz seemed to be discussing something he found completely normal.

"Please don't be crazy," I whispered under my breath.

Fitz stifled a laugh. I was borderline angry, and he was amused. It would've been just another day for us, had he not uttered those unbelievable words only moments before.

"I'll explain everything to you. I understand it's a lot to take in after living twenty-nine years believing witches are just made up stories. But this is no fabrication, and whether you want a role in it or not, you're part of this now."

I thought about standing up and walking out of the restaurant. This was lunacy. But something seemed to hold me in my seat as curiosity took over.

"For argument's sake, let's say that I believe witches exist. Which I don't," I clarified. "And that I believe I have my abilities because I am… one. How could I be a witch if my parents are human?"

"Traditionally, witches are born into families of witches. That was the circumstance of my birth. It's easy to feel normal when you're surrounded by a large family just like you. However, there's an occasional witch born into a family of humans. And you've felt the difference your entire life. It's one of the reasons it's so easy for you to be around me."

He gauged my expression before continuing. "We're not sure why it happens, but it appears to be some sort of genetic anomaly showing itself after years of human ancestry. Somewhere down the line, there was a witch in your family tree. It's not allowed, but that family member must've mated a human."

"I see," I returned skeptically. "What happens with these witches?"

"When they first show a sign of harboring powers, other witches are assigned to look after them until their powers are mature enough to begin accessing them. At that point, we're allowed to mentor them as their power develops."

"So, you've what? Followed me?"

"Everyone in the family has an avid interest in keeping you safe. We watch you through spells, not in a constant, creepy way. We use spells that reveal where you are and how you're doing, but we're not always physically present. If you were to run into trouble, we'd know immediately and could react. Witches developing their powers tend to get themselves into some interesting and sometimes dangerous situations."

"So your family was assigned to babysit me?"

"We were assigned to help you."

"Why were you assigned to me?"

"My dad really is a college professor, but he also receives monitoring assignments from our council – our government – to monitor witches developing their powers. Izzy and I have trained with him, and we work with him from time to time."

"I don't feel like I'm just some project to you." My voice faltered as I searched for any indication that what Fitz and I had was real, that I hadn't been completely wrong about everything. I didn't want to believe it was only about evaluating my powers. My powers… did I just say that? My heart sank and my mind raced. He was in the process of explaining impossible things, things I couldn't fathom to be true.

"Of course you aren't. That's ridiculous. The reason I'm the only family member involved at this point is because I truly care for you. I told you, even my dad has no idea where we are right now."

I could've discerned his anger from his tone of voice alone, even if I hadn't already felt it radiating through my body. Regardless of whether I believed what he was saying, I felt his belief in it. Things were far more complicated than I realized. I wasn't sure if I wanted to throw my arms around him or punch him square in the face.

"I don't need your protection."

"Where are you going?"

"The hotel," I hissed and then froze.

"Oh, come *on*," Fitz spit out.

"Perfect timing."

"You're not walking back alone."

CHAPTER EIGHT

Fitz tossed enough euros on the table to cover our meal, and we hit the sidewalk with purpose.

"If we walk around long enough, they'll lose interest. I think," Fitz began.

"And if they approach us?"

"I don't know. I don't think they will, though."

After a few moments, I broke the silence.

"You said 'our government' back there…"

"Aye, we have our own government in witchkind. I can explain the structure when we have more time, but they're the ones who mandated we stay apart."

"Why?"

We turned down a less trafficked alleyway and picked up our pace, noticing the lack of witnesses.

"They were uncertain your full set of powers would materialize. They told me to stay away from you unless things developed."

"Because?"

"Because humans aren't allowed to know about us. Until we knew you'd come into your full powers, they thought I was putting witchkind at risk."

"That's ridiculous." I panted, our pace making conversation difficult.

"I'm fully aware, trust me."

Rounding the corner into a bustling street, we tucked ourselves into a doorway, pretending to be otherwise engaged. The seconds ticked by slowly, and I questioned if we lost our pursuers – until the man and woman in question passed our shelter. Fitz's breath caught in the back of his throat. We stepped out, prepared for whatever followed, meeting the gaze of our stalkers. Their faces were impassible, but not their minds. My lips slowly curled into a mocking grin. They weren't anticipating a standoff, and we claimed the upper hand for ourselves. They held our gaze for mere seconds before sprinting off.

"That was… easy."

"Too easy," Fitz said. "I don't suppose your mind heard anything useful?"

"Not really. They were surprised and thought they couldn't risk a confrontation, but I have no idea why – my reception got a little fuzzy."

Fitz nodded thoughtfully. "So, they don't want us to know who they are, or what they're up to."

"I don't know if that makes me feel better or worse."

"Me neither. Something's not right about it."

"Either way, let's get out of here."

Fitz reached for my hand, and I felt the surge of the unspoken connection flowing between us.

"Seriously, Fitz, why do we feel this energy? And don't you dare tell me you don't know."

"You won't like this," he began, his lip twitching. "But I don't know for sure. Usually, when you come into contact with another witch, you feel it. You feel the difference in the air, and your chemistry reacts in a different way than when you interact with a human. When I make contact with you, it's electric."

"I remember the first time it happened."

"In the barn. At my parents' place."

It was a late December morning, and I was walking the stables with Fitz at his parents' house when I tripped over a rake that was left in the walkway. As I tumbled backward, Fitz caught me in his firm grasp just before I would have hit the ground, one hand sliding under my clothing and across my bare back. A shock registered with his touch – not a great jolt, but a tingling of electricity pulsed through my back, slowly traveling to every nerve ending in my body.

"Why do you think we didn't feel the shock before that day?"

"I think it had to do with your powers beginning to stir. Suddenly our chemistry was different, and our bodies recognized and reacted to that."

"I can't even begin to process any of that."

We walked the final stretch to the hotel in silence, allowing me to think through the bombshell Fitz dropped. I knew his words were truthful. Over the years, I witnessed friends, family, and even strangers lie to me, from small fibs to intricate webs. But I always knew the truth. I felt the lies hanging heavily in the air. Was that another innate witch power Fitz would eventually explain? This left me wrestling with the breathtaking conclusion that he was telling the truth, and that truth would mean I was a witch. I wondered my entire life why I was different. Did Fitz finally give me the answer?

CHAPTER NINE

"Tell me everything," I demanded, holding the door open for Fitz to enter my room. I spent all night tossing from side to side, praying I'd finally find relief from my stunned mind by falling asleep. Between lack of sleep and a rattled mind, I certainly wasn't on my best behavior.

"Okay, what do you want to know?"

"Anything, Fitz. Everything. What am I?"

He paused momentarily, allowing enough time for me to change my mind again.

"Actually, wait. Show me magic first. I want to see it. I *need* to see it."

"You believe me, then?"

I struggled with the words but finally nodded.

He looked satisfied. "What do you want to see?"

"What can you do?"

"Levitate something. Call forth an object from the air. I don't know? I don't know what you want to see," he explained flatly.

"Okay, any of that's fine."

He looked toward the small, built-in desk in the corner of the room, his eyes resting on a half-peeled orange. With his thumb and first two fingers slightly extended from the others, he flicked his wrist, and the orange hovered in the air. A brief intake of air was all that betrayed my surprise – I felt the blank expression still resting on my face. He looked at me from the corner of his eye and then returned his focus to the orange. With another flick, the peel removed itself, as if it were the work of invisible hands, and floated into the trash can. And with one final flick, the perfectly peeled fruit floated across the room, arriving in front of me.

"Hold out your hand," Fitz nearly whispered.

I followed his direction, and the orange dropped into my open palm.

"Good God." When I looked up, I was met by an unreadable expression. "Now tell me everything."

He sighed, struggling with his words. "Let's go for a walk. I can't concentrate in here. Did you even sleep? Your energy is *everywhere*."

It was my turn to sigh. I grabbed my coat and headed for the door.

We spent much of the morning discussing life as a witch in the human world, and the complications created by remaining secretive your entire life. After wrestling with myself for much of the evening, I decided that despite the lack of a true scientific explanation, everything pointed to Fitz being truthful. Rather than wasting time in angst, I wanted to spend my last day in Paris learning. Plus, there were a few things I knew for certain. I would know if Fitz lied, due to my lifelong ability. I was gifted with abilities that made no sense in the human world. My intuition – my gut – pointed in the direction of this being the truth. It told me I could trust him. And if that hadn't been enough, the man levitated, peeled, and dropped an orange in my hand without even touching it.

*   *   *

I snatched another croissant from the center plate and leveled my gaze at Fitz. My stomach was in knots most of the morning, but after a few hours of walking and talking with Fitz, I was ravenous. Consequently, we found a tiny café for lunch and settled at an outdoor table in petite wicker chairs. The warmth of the sun cut the crisp air, and I tilted my face toward the sky, knowing I would miss the energy of Paris when we left.

"I can't believe my time here is over. I board the train tonight to London and have my first meeting in a couple of days."

"Right. I'd like to travel with you and begin your training if you're comfortable with that arrangement?"

I didn't welcome demands, especially when it came to important matters – and he knew it. Most of the morning's conversations occurred in Jardin des Tuileries, and at some point, spread out on the grass, I realized I'd have to reach a decision about all of this. Countless questions arose when Fitz shared that our witchkind government, whoever they were, kept us apart. There was still so much to discuss, so much I wanted to understand, but there was only so much I could take in at one time. Even through my many questions, I knew almost instantly what I would choose.

"Yeah. I'd like that."

My simple answer surprised him, but during the sleepless night, it wasn't only my belief in the supernatural that I struggled with. I considered my relationship with Fitz, and what this new information meant for us. I needed to better understand who I was becoming, and I clearly needed someone to teach me how to utilize and control my powers. I was comfortable with Fitz; I didn't want anyone else as my guide, or at least not during the immediate future. And the thought of being apart again did nothing to quell my anxiety.

"I have a question, though," I added.

"Shoot."

"How are you able to take time off like this during the semester?"

"I'm not teaching this semester. I'm working on a research project, so I have to be physically at uni for certain things, but I'm also doing a lot of field research in the Highlands, working from there or from home. Or Paris, as it were."

"Makes sense. You'll have to tell me more about this later."

"As you wish."

"Time is running short. What else do I need to see in this city before we leave tonight – let's get moving and do some Q&A along the way."

"You're a bit bossy today," he observed through a mischievous grin, knowing I hated the word.

"You ruined my day of sightseeing yesterday with the 'you're a witch' bomb-dropping you did. Although you did redeem yourself slightly this morning with the whole magic orange peeling thing. That was pretty cool, and this afternoon's going to be even better, right?" I returned his mischievous grin.

"I'm in for it," he replied, grinning, and signaled to the waiter for our check.

*   *   *

Roughly a thousand questions and a few Parisian sites later, I was seated next to Fitz somewhere high above Paris. The Eurostar was my humble suggestion, but a friend of Fitz's lent us his family plane. Though it felt extravagant, it provided Fitz with the means to lose the witchkind spies in Edinburgh. Whoever was following us in Paris was about to receive the same treatment.

Sipping whisky on our brief path over the English Channel, thoughts darted around my exhausted mind. I felt so divided. I worried about this new chapter – I was nervous to open my eyes and see the world for what it truly was, and not for what I previously believed it to be. But another feeling beat fiercely against the first for control. It bubbled up, refusing defeat.

I was excited.

I vividly recalled dressing as a witch every Halloween. I was obsessed as a child, and my parents grew concerned when they realized it wasn't a phase. Somewhere in my teenage years, I came to believe it was a mere fantasy – a little girl's fascination with something that didn't exist. I needed to search inside myself to uncover that little girl and her unwavering belief.

Fitz leaned over, whispering. "You're going to be unstoppable."

"Stop doing that! It's so unnerving when you're in my head like that. You said you can't read minds."

"I can't. But I can sense your feelings and read your facial expressions. You smell doubtful, and you look like you're trying to solve a puzzle that's got the best of you."

"You can smell me thinking?" I asked, my face scrunched in full disbelief.

"Oh, aye. It smells a lot like smoke right now."

I punched his shoulder playfully, though I was grateful for the comedic relief.

His expression grew serious as he read a text on his phone. "What now?"

"No, it's nothing bad. Dad said the council called him this morning asking for any information he might have on our whereabouts."

"So, they don't know we're headed to London."

"Which means we were successful in keeping things quiet when we booked your travel."

"And you were right about the Parisian spies – they definitely weren't linked to the witchkind watchers."

Fitz nodded thoughtfully.

"They're smart enough to suspect we're together, though," I observed.

"They suspected this would happen from the beginning. At least we're ahead of them."

"And our Parisian stalkers think we're headed to Beijing – nice choice, by the way."

"I guess there are a few perks to private air travel." He smiled.

"But the watchers aren't able to find us using their power?"

"That would typically be the case."

"Why not in this instance?"

"Magic." He grinned.

"I have so much to learn."

"Look," he said, pointing toward the window.

The city of London lay beneath us, the charming blend of old and modern architecture stretching as far as the eye could see. I'd visited the city before, but there was something about it that always took me by surprise.

"I know exactly where we're having dinner," I asserted excitedly.

Fitz gently grazed my face with his fingertips.

"When you're happy, excited… God, you're beautiful."

"How's my energy now?"

He lifted his arm, directing my attention to the goose bumps rippling across his skin, a result of our contact. "Electric," he answered, a smirk pulling at his lips.

CHAPTER TEN

T he following evening, we dined at Ye Olde Cheshire Cheese, taking in the history, good beer, and discussion on European politics, which I found intriguing.

"Are you actually arguing for Scottish secession?"

"I'm not arguing one way or the other... necessarily. I'm just stating facts."

"So, let's review the facts."

"Right, well," Fitz began, a studious look blanketing his features. "Scotland is its own nation, whether the British claim it as theirs or not. It always has been, and we've never welcomed English rule with open arms."

"But the English do rule."

"Aye. After hundreds of years of shocking and gruesome persecution, torture, and murder."

"I was waiting for that one."

He winked. "Facts."

"And the economy could sustain itself I suppose?"

"Hey, just curious. Do you ever stop analyzing anything long enough to *feel*?"

"Sure, but feelings make me kind of uncomfortable."

"You're joking."

"Yeah, sure."

"You're impossible."

"Don't act like you didn't already know that about me."

"Well, to answer your question, I think it could. The culture is overflowing with doers, Hads. We're a nation proud of our heritage and our future. Hard work and perseverance thrive there."

Banter aside, Fitz's love for his country was touching. It became increasingly obvious that in his eyes, no separation existed between himself and previous generations. Though his parents moved the family to the States, his bloodline was purely Scottish, and that same pride and love of country lay within his breast.

After exhausting the subject of Scottish secession, I could no longer turn my thoughts from the looming appointment the following morning.

"I'm a little nervous about meeting with The British Museum tomorrow."

"I understand, but you shouldn't be. They'll love you."

"What if they don't?"

"Well, at least if they don't, you'll know, and without them even saying a word."

"You know, you're kind of an ass sometimes."

"But a charming one."

"Most of the time," I teased.

Having filled myself with steak and ale pie, and a fair amount of ale in general, I paused to appreciate the establishment. A pub since 1538, it was rebuilt shortly after the Great Fire of 1666. We sat underground in the lowest level of the structure, our meal set to dim lighting, a roaring fire, and wooden tables set on cold stone flooring. Literary legends like Charles Dickens and Sir Arthur Conan Doyle enjoyed the food, drink, and company of this very establishment, and I felt happy to do the same. Fitz and I were clearly drawn to eateries filled with local food and history, and it felt surreal that many of our conversations occurred in establishments where fascinating conversations had taken place for hundreds of years.

Between the faint glow of the lights, the steady fire, and our full bellies, we were lulled into a bit of a trance, and we eventually surrendered to the night, emerging from underground into the cold air of the evening, our bodies jolting back to life. Fitz instinctively reached for my hand as we wandered through the crowds in the courtyard, seemingly packed no matter the weather.

Our hotel wasn't a short walk, but we preferred the distance on foot. I didn't mind prolonging our time together; the end of the evening was my least favorite part of the day. Whatever energy flowed between us during our time together, it hibernated while we were apart, leaving us drained and alone. I was surprised at how quickly I readjusted to the connection, and without it, I felt incomplete.

Upon reaching my room, Fitz placed both of his hands on the door, resting them on either side of my shoulders, and placed his forehead on mine. We stood there motionless, eyes closed as we enjoyed the moment.

"I don't like leaving you," he said, his accent thickening with his drowsiness.

"You don't have to."

I opened my eyes, and he tilted his head to meet me in a gentle but thorough kiss. My blood boiled with desire, as a rapidly growing energy hummed through my body.

"We're not going to move into dangerous territory, Hadley. I'm going to do right by you, I swear it."

I stood on my toes to kiss him again, and the shock returned, our energy flowing freely between us – witch to witch – until releasing one another into the restless night.

*   *   *

I traipsed my way out of the crowded ground floor of the modern high rise, the bustling streets of London alive in their greeting. There's no city in the world quite like London, with its unique mix of palaces, tube stations, teahouses, and pubs. Finding the least trafficked area along the front steps of the building, I sat amongst the office dwellers, most of which sought to eat their lunches in the late September sunlight. As a native Seattleite, I understood their desire to soak up the last of the warm rays before the cold, rainy season set in. After checking my phone to ensure I hadn't missed a call from Fitz, I leaned against the nearest wall, allowing my thoughts to roll over in my mind.

The interview that concluded only moments before was the last scheduled on my London list. The appointment went well, but after meeting with the museum earlier in the week, I realized working outside of a firm sounded like the right move for my career… and my sanity. My career developed at private firms, and I was continually pulled onto various projects, always consulting with multiple clients. Although the variety of the fast-moving environment taught me a great deal, the thought of a steady partnership within an institution sounded like a fresh challenge and a desirable change of pace. The museum seemed like a perfect fit for both parties, and they shared that the professional retiring from the position was more than willing to wrap up early – meaning I could start in less than a month.

I wouldn't make a decision just yet, not without exploring one last option on a list of its own. I added it to the docket belatedly, just the night before I left the States. When I called the main line, they patched me through directly to the hiring manager, who informed me they had an immediate opening. The PR manager ran into a health problem and decided to move back to Inverness to be near family. The position wasn't yet filled, and they were very interested in my visit. I hadn't told Fitz about that one yet. I wasn't sure how to tell him this last-minute whim would take me to Edinburgh.

CHAPTER ELEVEN

"No, come on, Hadley. Not like that!"

Apparently, I was off to a rough start unlocking my magic. My current task was to meditate – for whom or what was unclear. When I squinted, Fitz knew I wasn't exactly following his guidelines.

"You need to still your mind. Your powers will never immerse your mind with all of those frickin' thoughts buzzing around in there. It's a wonder you get anything done at all. And I told you when you do this I can't concentrate either."

"Geez. I'm sorry. Tell me what to do again."

"This is a first."

"I'm going to punch you again."

"Fine," he replied tartly, though a slight tug at the corner of his mouth threatened to break his demeanor into a full smile. "Quiet your mind. Stop thinking."

"I can't stop thinking. How on earth am I supposed to just

make it all stop?"

"You are actually overthinking the process of not thinking, aren't you?"

"Yes, hi. I'm Hadley. Have we met?" I quipped, arm extended.

"You can control your mind, Hadley. Your mind is one of the most powerful things in the universe, and you can control it. You want magic? Power? This is the key to unlocking an entirely new world."

"I still don't understand how to do this."

"I can't tell you how. Only you know the answer to this."

"Fantastic. I don't see how this is helping."

"You know how it's helping. Remember what I told you," he demanded, a stern look blanketing his features.

Fitz had explained why witches born into human families don't fully acquire their powers until adulthood. One of the main difficulties we faced was having no guidance early on, and no knowledge of what we were or how to come into our power.

"You don't suddenly float objects through thin air. When children first show some otherworldly sense of understanding, that's when parents or mentors begin power training."

"What exactly constitutes otherworldly?"

"Seeing into others' futures or pasts as if you've lived them, opening others' minds to hear their thoughts, speaking with spirits of the departed – the list goes on."

"Speaking with spirits? Seriously?"

"Mm-hmm."

"Then what happens?"

"The student is first taught to meditate. If there's too much distraction, your mind and power are like oil and vinegar – they can't combine. But when you give them room to breathe, they fully infiltrate one another. It's only then you can claim your power, and be taught to control it."

"The council has known for years about my powers. Why didn't I start this process sooner?"

"Your power materialized slowly due to human DNA obstructing its path. When I first met you, you knew things about others because you were essentially pulling information from their minds, but you weren't yet hearing their thoughts. There are even humans, though rare, who have this ability."

"How?"

"They have magic somewhere in their lineage. After a family mixes with humans, the power weakens with each generation, until there's not much chance a descendant could fully match their power. Every so often, that former magic shows back up in DNA. Sometimes, these people are like you and their mind and power can combine. For others, they'll possess some ability, but they'll always remain more human than witch. Until we knew that you could access your power, we were supposed to wait… or to be specific, they demanded I wait."

"There are people out there like me, with these abilities, but they never become a witch. They just live with their oddities and think there's something wrong with them, like I did."

"Maybe it's better they not know the truth... that so much lies just outside their grasp. But I always knew you'd match."

"Do you know why my magic is matching with me? Like, my witch ancestor isn't too far back or...?"

"We'll work on your ancestry and find out. My suspicion is you have recent magical ancestry on each side of your lineage. It would explain why none of your living relatives have abilities. It might just be the combination of your mom and your dad's lineages."

"I guess it's just chance I'm the only one in my family to have power?"

"Right. It works the same way as all DNA. Not all siblings have the same eye or hair color. You just have the right combination."

"That'll be interesting to see, especially since Gram has this superstitious nature. She's not too far removed from having some sort of power. Her intuition is uncanny."

"We'll tackle that mystery in the next few weeks, and then you'll finally have some answers. But for now, let's get you matched to your magic."

After years of countless questions, I was thrilled I would finally have my overdue answers. And the sooner I matched with my magic, the sooner I'd have them. So, there I sat in the deafening quiet of the beautiful penthouse sitting room attempting to navigate out of my self-described purgatory.

After a fair amount of debate, Fitz and I reached an

agreement – it would be easiest to share a two-bedroom suite, allowing almost constant focus on my development. We canceled the remainder of our separate reservations and upgraded at a nearby hotel, where Fitz said it would be quieter for my training.

I feared our attraction to one another would challenge the success of the project, but I was wrong. As strong as my desire was for Fitz, my desire for magic was stronger. My desire to finally understand myself won over almost anything else. In turn, I was certain of Fitz's desires, but when it came to training, he had laser focus. His mission was to guide and assist me in becoming a successful, functioning witch, and he was hell-bent on that mission.

Between my determination, Fitz's coaching, and the knowledge of everything at stake, I hadn't stirred from our room for hours, and I wasn't going anywhere until some sort of breakthrough occurred. My focus shifted outside, searching for anything that would quiet my raging mind. Shangri-La held an incredible view of London, and gazing through the large panes, my eyes traced the path of the River Thames, rolling ceaselessly through the city. I took notice of the vessels floating brightly against the murky water and the buildings that shot up on either bank until the blinking glow of the London Eye captured my attention. I focused on the wheel, studying its bright lights and steady, circular motion, and by following the slow, rhythmic spinning, my mind stopped.

For a split second, I panicked at the loss of vision. Fitz warned me not to fear the onset of the blackness, and with the recollection that my condition was normal, I adjusted – though slowly. The darkness took my mind, leaving a complete absence of everything else. Then, after some indeterminable amount of time, a large eye materialized, the color of fir trees in a deep forest, lush and verdant, an enlarged pupil at its center. The eye's gaze darted about, as though it sought something in the abyss. Something stirred behind the eye, and I squinted, curious what might lie beyond the pupil, before everything evaporated like smoke winding its way into the night sky.

I gasped, and Fitz ran to my side.

"What is it? What happened?"

"I found the darkness," was all I could manage, as my eyes scanned the room, registering that my sight was restored.

"That's good. What else?"

"There was an eye."

"Where was it?"

"I don't know, just in the darkness. It was huge – the only thing I could see."

My answer made him smile, though my own thoughts remained puzzled.

"What on earth was it?"

"You did good, Hadley," he began, reaching toward me before quickly pulling his hand back to his lap. "You saw your mind's eye."

"What exactly does that mean?"

"Your mind's eye is your third eye – your witch's eye. It couples with your magic to show you the things you can't see with your own two baby blues."

"I saw something else, too. It was past the pupil of the eye. I could only see movement. When I tried to see past the eye, the vision dissipated."

"You saw your magic."

My head snapped up, meeting his gaze. Butterflies danced in my belly, fluttering about violently. "Why did it disappear?"

"Why do you think it disappeared?"

I thought for only a moment before the disappointing answer surfaced. "Because I started thinking about what it was."

"You have to still your mind long enough for the interaction to occur between mind and power. You've only been meditating a few hours. Keep trying. It will happen."

I broke out into what must've been the goofiest grin of my life.

Fitz shot a questioning glance.

"I saw my powers."

"Pretty damn cool, isn't it? I'm so proud of you."

"I'm a witch."

The outline of my witch's eye danced freshly in my mind, my skin prickling at the nearness of my power. I swung my legs toward the window and closed my eyes, eager to answer my magic's beckoning call.

"Let's get some food before you start again."

"But I need to try again," I whined.

"What you *need* is nourishment to help sustain you...

especially before you get hangry." He eyed me dubiously. "Then, you need to try again."

He was right, but the call of the witch's eye consumed me. Finally, Fitz and his practicality won, as I considered meditation was indeed much harder on an empty stomach. We decided to walk to the pub around the corner, and Fitz extended his hand. My jacket floated from a chair near the door to where I stood, hovering until I extended my arm.

"I need to do that!"

"Just think, magic could be at your disposal very soon."

"You're *insufferable* right now."

He smiled deviously.

CHAPTER TWELVE

Green and gold trimmings decorated the walls of the small room, eventually leading to the half-filled liquor bottles that embellished the mirror hanging above the bar. Laughter broke loudly from a table across the room, and groups of couples, friends, and even newly formed acquaintances adorned the tables and bar stools strewn across the old wooden floors. I found myself relaxing at the change of scenery, which allowed me to free my thoughts from the last few hours. I ran a finger around the rim of my glass, watching the dark beer swirl in tandem with it. The liquid ceased its movement only after my finger did the same. Stunned, I looked up to find a smirk on Fitz's face.

"When did that start?"

"I guess right now?"

"You're close, Hads. Your power is *so* close."

I smiled, returning my attention to the glass. A small jolt of electricity pulsed through me, and as my finger resumed its previous path around the rim, the beer again answered the call of my magic. Fitz explained the mechanics behind the mix of power and chemistry, and we lost ourselves in the subject momentarily, before I decided it was time to steer the conversation in a different direction.

"There's another interview I haven't told you about yet."

"Let's hear it."

"When I researched openings over here, another option came up, but I didn't make a firm plan to visit. I decided to experience London and then see how I felt before reaching out... but right before I left for Paris, I changed my mind and booked an interview."

"This last option isn't in London?"

"No."

"Where then?"

"Edinburgh, at the castle."

I expected the words to elicit some sort of response from Fitz. Instead, he sat there quietly, eyes transfixed on his drink. Finally, I broke the silence.

"What are you thinking?"

"I'm thinking about what to say."

"I don't have to look into the castle if you prefer I don't come to Edinburgh."

"No, that's not it at all – I promise," he said, reaching his hand across to mine. "It would honestly be great to have you in Edinburgh. Besides the fact that we could continue our work on your powers, I want to have you near; you know how I feel about you."

"Tell me what it is, then."

Picking at the peeling, plastic edges of the menu with his free hand, he slowly led into his explanation. "It's that I don't want to influence your decision in any way. Of course, I want you in Edinburgh, but that isn't fair. I don't want you to feel pressure about coming to Edinburgh if it doesn't feel right."

"I think it would make the most sense for your mentorship to continue. I have so much to learn, and your style of teaching works for me, Professor MacGregor." I laughed before adding, "And you know how I feel about you, too."

"It feels good to hear you say that."

"I'll go to the interview, and we'll take it a step at a time. I do want to make sure it's a good career move, so we'll have to sort it out from there. But it's a start."

"It'll be tricky going back to Edinburgh with you."

"I'll be matched to my powers by then – a full-on witch. Won't that make a difference?"

"Yes, of course. The council won't pose any difficulty with our relationship moving forward. I just don't know how they'll react to what's already passed."

"Do you think it'll be bad?"

"I have no way of knowing yet, but Dad will have more of an idea soon. We'll consult with him before we leave for Edinburgh. We'll figure it all out."

"At least if they find us at this point, I shouldn't have a tragic accident or mysteriously disappear… right?"

Fitz smiled humorously. "Right."

"Well, it's either face the consequences or run."

Fitz squeezed my hand, triggering an unrelated question that lingered in the back of my mind.

"So... random question," I began.

"Hmm?"

"Earlier, after I came back to this reality...?"

Fitz chuckled at my response. "When you returned from the depths of your mind."

"Right. You reached for me, but then you pulled back. Why?"

"Oh, that. My instinct was to reach for you – to make sure you were okay. Then my mind caught up, and I worried about the mix of our energy after your encounter with your mind's eye. It might have hurt you more than it comforted you."

"Makes sense."

"You thought... what? I didn't want to touch you after all?"

"Well, of course, I went straight to the worst-case scenario!" I exclaimed, pulling a laugh from Fitz.

"It's going to take a long time for you to understand that I never wanted us apart. We'll never be forced from one another again."

"A long time, or a lot of you spoiling me?"

"Both," he smiled, leaning across the table to kiss my forehead.

*   *   *

I settled into my former meditative state and began the

process of quieting my mind. When I observed Fitz's daily meditation, it seemed so natural for him – so necessary, and I was uncertain I could integrate it so effortlessly into my life. Fitz was quick to remind me he'd been meditating since childhood, and once I matched with my powers, I would feel its draw and its promise to ease my mind's burden.

Even if I wasn't certain about that, I did feel more confident in myself after seeing my third eye – and more focused. I knew what I was working toward, and my mind stilled with considerably less effort. Focusing again on the large wheel and its bright circular motion, the rest of the world slowly faded into black. I softly nudged myself to remain blank when my mind's eye reemerged, before slipping into the abyss.

Darkness took hold, along with a twinge of panic. Recalling panic would pull me from the state where I found my magic, I breathed deeply, drawing in the positive, and exhaling the negative. Peace wiggled inside, slipping from the pit of my stomach through the rest of my body, as though a healing power swept through my bloodstream.

On the coattails of the calmness came a heightened sense of awareness, and a dim shape wavered in the darkness. A large, transparent eye stared back at me, and I waited patiently as it regained its strength. It was rather like a painting coming to fruition, each brushstroke breathing life into the unblinking object as the colors intensified.

Simply observe. Let the moment be.

The eyelid closed, slowly and deliberately, before lifting to reveal the full intensity of the deep, forest-colored iris. A movement behind the eye shifted my gaze, and my power grew more distinct than before, drifting in an untamable cloud, all the while intensifying into the same mesmerizing color as the eye. It gathered itself together just as smoke billows from a chimney and slowly slinked through the pupil of the eye. Rolling tentatively through the air, the cloud whirled closer, and its edges shimmered, dancing to some imperceptible tune. The hair on my body prickled, standing on end at the nearness of such a presence.

Is it electric? I almost wondered.

My magic halted mid-air, threatening to disappear altogether, but I recovered quickly, dropping my mind into thoughtless observance. Encouraged by the air's stillness, the cloud continued its forward movement. My mind and body both grew serene, increasingly at peace as the gap between us and my power diminished, shrinking the distance between me and something I needed as much as the air filling my lungs. My arm instinctively greeted the cloud, closing the final space between us.

My fingers burned at the initial contact, before a surge of energy slowly pulsed through my fingers, consuming my hands, arms, chest, and eventually my entire body. The crippling ache lingered until I was fully aware of the power coursing through me, adjusting to its newfound home. I fell to the ground, my legs unable to support the weight of my body, as my limbs contorted in pain. Air-filled shrieks escaped my lungs, my feeble attempt to relieve the pain building inside of me.

A throbbing sensation replaced the pain – much like the dull beating pulse following a physical injury. Weightlessness followed, spreading from my fingertips until gradually radiating throughout my entire body, leaving behind no trace of the former discomfort. I perceived the air in a completely new way, freshly aware of its interconnectedness, understanding its relationship to the electricity snapping inside of me. The weightless sensation grew stronger, and the air lifted me from the ground, suspending me mid-air. My body lay limp and weightless for only a moment, before twitching began in my limbs, causing them to flail about violently, my entire body spinning and sputtering in the darkness. Once the twisting subsided, I floated back to the ground in utter exhaustion.

A heavy weight settled in my chest, and I focused on inhaling and exhaling until breathing became involuntary once again, finding comfort in the familiar rise and fall of my chest. I mustered the energy to sit up and looked in the direction of my mind's eye, seeking its steady gaze upon me. The ever-present eye stared, expressionless, and I crawled timidly in its direction, proceeding slowly until I was mere inches away, consulting my power for my next move.

I understood the pupil was a doorway from whence my magic came, and I needed to cross through it. I hadn't fully appreciated its breadth. It stood at least fifteen feet tall, and the pupil was so large I could step right through it. As I studied the intricate detail of the iris, my proximity awakened its power, and the entire eye began to shimmer. I looked down at my Converse-covered feet, slowly raising my right foot to step through the pupil and into the other side, but of what, I knew not.

As my foot made contact with the ground, the detonation of a forceful explosion flung me violently across the empty space. I turned in the midst of the blast and inexplicably floated my feet to the ground. Though my landing was magically graceful, the ringing in my ears proved the explosion was real. I turned to my witch's eye but found only darkness. The final infusion had occurred, and both my magic and mind's eye rested comfortably inside my body, each in harmony with one another.

With my task completed, I woke from my reverie.

Fitz's usual carefree expression was replaced with creased brows and worried eyes. "Say something."

"Like what?" I asked grumpily.

"There you are. How do you feel?"

"Like a train toppled over me."

"Here, take these – they'll help with the headache," he said, offering medicine and a glass of water. He was prepared for this. Even if I felt like I'd been run over, at least the feeling was expected.

I looked around the room hoping to orient myself, waking from my dazed stupor. I was still sitting on the floor of our hotel room. The river and the grey skyline still lay beyond the window panes. And the London Eye still flashed brightly, though it wasn't quite so easy to gaze upon with the pounding in my head.

Fitz knelt before me and pressed a cold, damp washcloth against my forehead. I placed my hand at the base of his skull, twisting my fingers into his hair. I tugged until he moved his body closer to mine, our faces only a few inches apart. Instinct took over, and I closed my eyes, drinking in his deep scent, which was heightened after receiving my powers. His presence was tangible all around me, and I could feel everything about him — his heartbeat, his energy, and his power. He was far more powerful than he ever let on. No wonder he was chosen to guide me.

I allowed the connection to navigate where it willed and found a small stream of energy forming between the two of us. I couldn't fully comprehend it, resembling the brilliant glow of vintage light bulb wires in a dark room. Our connection I thought to be imaginary turned out to be real. Even when magic was merely fantastical to me, I had begun to understand it, innate as it truly was. I followed the length of the stream and found Fitz. It was only then I noticed a second stream of light from Fitz back to myself. I opened my eyes to Fitz, who was still bent forward with his eyes closed, a peaceful smile forming across his lips.

"You let me in."

"What do you mean?" I asked, clarifying that we were, in fact, launching into a very odd conversation.

"The streams. You saw them?"

I nodded.

"You found a stream that led to me — a path I created for you. I've waited a long time for you to find it. The other stream just formed between us… it came from you. You created a path for me to find you as well."

"How did I do that? I mean, I don't understand what's happening."

Fitz crossed his legs and scooted closer until our knees touched. He gently took my hands in his. "I know this is all fresh and a bit scary, but this is normal for us. Okay?"

I nodded.

"I'll explain everything. Why don't you tell me what you want to know most, and we'll work our way around until you're clear."

"Thank you," I returned with feeling. "What are these streams exactly?"

"Our energies formed a connection between the two of us."

"Can this happen with just anyone – between witches, I mean?"

"No. They form between those who… have certain feelings for one another," he continued slowly, choosing his words carefully.

Apprehension radiated from his body, but it was my turn to ease his nerves. What existed between us was the least of my concerns. We started out as friends with an easy connection; love soon followed, and a remarkable openness always existed between the two of us. Our relationship felt more natural than anything else ever had.

"What actually prompts the streams? You said yours has existed for a while, and mine just formed. Can you explain that?"

"They form as feelings and trust for someone develops. Once you decided you trusted me, the connection formed. With the assistance of your magic, you created a path for me to find you."

"What's the purpose of the stream?"

"It carries vital information between us. It grants heightened awareness of the mood, feelings, and safety of one another. You'll know immediately, and with certainty, if I'm upset. I'll know with the same certainty if you're ever in danger."

"I've felt that already."

"Aye. I think that's partly due to mine forming so early on."

"Fitz, mine would have formed a lot sooner if I had my powers. I think part of it already existed from my side. It just couldn't fully form until now."

His fingertips brushed the side of my face gently until my cheek rested in his palm. "This connection is formidable, Hadley. These streams are life and vitality flowing between us. You have a direct line to my soul, and I to yours."

His words struck me with full force, leaving me momentarily short of breath. I became fearful for the first time, knowing he'd have a front-row seat to the Hadley show. What would happen once he *really* saw inside?

Fitz's brows furrowed, his eyes tightly shut. "Never worry again that I'll leave you."

"You feel that?"

"God only knows why you feel that way."

"All of the ugly parts inside me."

"I already know you, Hads. I know you better than anyone else. I want you – the good and the flaws. All of it. It isn't our nature to run away from the tough bits."

I nodded slowly, registering what he was telling me.

"I can't bear the charge your fear animates in me. Your distress is excruciating. I'm consumed with how to rid you of it."

I caused Fitz pain, and I didn't yet know how to remedy that. Closing my eyes, I succumbed to instinct, allowing it to guide my actions. I closed the gap between us, pressing my lips firmly to his. The intensity that once caught me off guard only propelled me forward – I anticipated the charge of the kiss. Unlike his slow, deliberate movements before, Fitz was consumed with need. One of his hands laced tightly to mine, and he cupped my face with the other. I responded by placing my free hand behind his back, pulling him closer.

We lost ourselves to the intoxication of one another, until I pulled back, searching his face for any signs of its former distress.

Fitz grinned as he stretched out on the cool floor, dragging in the deep breath his body sought. "You'll be the death of me," he mumbled, pulling a hearty laugh from me.

"Well, I don't have to touch you again."

"Oh, like hell you don't. You might kill me, but I suspect I'll enjoy every bit of it," he responded, leaning onto his elbows. "But for now, how about a little change of pace?"

"What do you have in mind?"

"Power training?"

I was on my feet before he could blink, my headache nearly forgotten. "What are you waiting for? Get up!"

It was Fitz's turn to laugh as he rolled to his feet. His hands slid around my waist, pulling me back to him. "Yes, ma'am," he drawled, kissing me quickly, a happy gleam in his eyes.

CHAPTER THIRTEEN

As we strolled along the River Thames, hand in hand, I realized that much like Paris, some of our best moments were spent wandering softly lit streets. The city cast a dim glow onto the river, and I picked out the blinking brilliance of the London Eye, which we officially dubbed the patron saint of my magic, much to our own amusement. I tugged my scarf tighter around my neck, as the gentle, but cold wind rustled the colorful leaves, the branches swaying ever so slightly above us.

Fresh air was in order after an afternoon full of power training. I was surprised at how easily I summoned my magic from the depths of my mind and how natural it felt to have power at my disposal. Even with this new wonder, there was still something else fighting within me for my attention. Fitz's explanation of relationships and streams made me wonder just how quickly relationships between witches formed and how unbreakable they were. I found the question on my lips as we approached a bench overlooking the river.

"Honestly, we don't do the whole human dating bit – we're programmed differently, as you well know. Once we find our missing half, we lose little time in starting our lives together."

"So, desire is just different for us."

"Oh aye. Because we do have desire, but the impulse to find our mate is always just under the surface – always palpable – and we don't typically quell the loneliness by just hooking up randomly."

"But it happens sometimes?"

"There's an exception to every rule. There might be an occasional schoolgirl crush, as I like to call it, but it's almost always one-sided and of short duration. I don't know if I've heard of one of those becoming very physical either," he added, his face thoughtful. "When there's such a strong urge to find your other half, anyone else just feels like a distraction – like someone that could throw you off course."

"You feel this way about me?"

"You know exactly how I feel about you. You've known since the first day I met you – when you wandered into our living room, laughing uncontrollably with Izzy – at God only knows what."

"I felt the same way. I couldn't explain it or rationalize my feelings. I had no idea what I truly was, and for someone who thought they were human, it felt pretty odd."

"I've beaten myself up over that. I came so close to telling you everything on that last day, but I worried about putting you at more risk. I thought letting you leave was going to kill me."

"Yeah, it sucked. But I can't imagine what it was like for you either. I can only just now appreciate what that would have been like, and all the while knowing I was so angry with you when I just couldn't understand."

A strange look crossed Fitz's features.

"What is it?"

"There's nothing wrong." He paused momentarily. "I love you."

"I love you, too. I never stopped."

He couldn't keep the broad grin from his face, though I think he tried. His hand rested at the base of my skull, his thumb gently gliding back and forth, chills rising behind the warmth of his touch.

"Do most couples marry?"

"Yeah, or at least everyone I know married after finding their mate. Pretty quickly."

"Do people divorce in the witch world?"

"Not that I know of... it's just not in our nature to find the... person in this world who was made for us, only to give up when things get tough. We mess up, we get angry, we have problems, but we fight for the love we've been given."

"Why the pause on *person*?"

"Sometimes I forget how little escapes your notice. We aren't people; we're not human. But I'm not sure if throwing around the word *creature* is going to freak you out at this stage."

"Don't tiptoe around me. It won't become normal any faster if you do."

"Okay, then. Nothing but witchy norms from here on out."

"A witchy norm sounds like a good norm."

PART TWO:

ALTERNATIVE PLANS

CHAPTER ONE

Forfar, Scotland
January 1662

Esther

I peered through the hazy windowpane, observing the snow drifting lazily to blanket the earth in white. It was an exceptionally cold day, even for January, but I loved the way snow transformed the world into something new. As a wee bairn, the excitement was almost unbearable when I woke to the brightly covered hills, and even as an adult, the sense of nostalgia was strong. Hamish wasn't quite so fond of snow, which reminded me that Millie should toss another log on the fire. Hamish left for town in the wee morning hours and had not yet returned; my thoughts further at war with one another the longer his absence stretched.

The fresh wood crackled as the fire roared, two figures materializing in the flames. Hamish had worried about the visions, but it took little time to discover who they were. I stared into the eyes of my many times great-grandson, as confused by his appearance as ever. Though I was gifted with strong foresight and grew accustomed to frequent visions, this one vexed me.

My foresight manifested in the elements – water, fire, earth, and air, as my power mixed with the spirit of the land. Oftentimes I recognized those I saw – family, neighbors, friends, and even acquaintances, as I watched their futures, intent on their stories and how they would unfold; however, my witch's eye occasionally watched the future for me, revealing crucial events. I'd seen the melancholy battle of Culloden Moor, the colonization of the New World as it headed west, and the invention of some sort of horseless buggy you ride inside of – a car, I believe. With my mind so often preoccupied in times that had not yet passed, I had to be mindful of my speech – Hamish often said I spoke in strange ways. Perhaps I'd not been mindful of that lately.

The flames grew restless, and I lost Fitz and Hadley in the all-consuming blaze. Their appearances set my nerves on end, as frequent manifestations often meant I had a connection with creatures' futures, and I felt Fitz and Hadley were in trouble. Their bodies floated through the in-between, seemingly set on a trajectory that would bring them to my time. Traveling centuries into the past would be a tricky passage, and even with Fitz's power, I prayed they wouldn't attempt it without a pressing reason. Perhaps I was wrong. *Or, perhaps this was the reason they caught my witch's eye*, I reminded myself yet again. It was possible I was summoned to guide them through their journey in the olden times.

The light in the room brightened, and Hamish's figure filled the doorway.

"Well, then. Did ye succeed?"

Hamish eyed me dubiously, as he shook the fresh powder from his overcoat.

"The truth, Hamish."

"I pleaded with every witch in the area."

"No one will help us, then."

Hamish cut his eyes sharply – he was searching for the right words, but he wouldn't find any. There was nothing left to be done. I reached out my hand, summoning Hamish to my side.

"Damn them all to hell."

"Aye, and what would that do for ye?"

"I canna understand, Esther. The council will do the same to their families if it comes to it, and yet, none will stand now and fight."

"Come to me, *mo ghaol.*"

Hamish obeyed, my rising nerves undoubtedly registering in his body.

"Ye've done well, my darling. I could ask no more of ye."

Tears welled in his eyes, as he pulled me closer to him. I rested my head on his chest, watching the flurry of activity on the other side of the panes. Icy flakes floated upon an invisible force, making their slow, winding descent to the ground, where they burst into flames. A chill ran down my spine. Fate beckoned, and it wouldn't be long until I was forced to answer.

CHAPTER TWO

Edinburgh, Scotland
October 2018

Hadley

Scotland took the breath right out of my body. As my eyes surveyed what lay beyond the train window, I'd already fallen in love with the hauntingly beautiful land. The playful hills stretched as far as I could see, greeting the rolling fog joyfully, as old friends do. I imagined anything might happen there. Its beauty and historical tragedy created the perfect backdrop for fairy tales, legends, and the accounts of heroes. I wondered what my story might become in such a place. Perhaps it wasn't quite the substance of legend, but I was easily lost in my own fairy tale. How many adults discovered one morning that their childhood fantasy was fulfilled? I possessed the power to live as fully as my magical DNA always intended – able to not only protect myself, but also those whom I loved. Even though

Fitz and I would soon face the council, I had to believe everything would turn out all right.

I felt the warmth of Fitz's hand on mine and turned to a man formed of this land. His strong figure was crafted to survive the harsh environment, but the magic about him was palpable. And that magic transformed him into a creature straight from the stories this characteristically superstitious culture passed from generation to generation. Though, the more I learned of this witchy life, the less superstitious I found those who heeded the warnings and tales of the past – and the more intelligent.

"We coexist much more easily with the humans now that they're, as a culture, more enthralled with science," Fitz explained. "They need to make sense of life and the mysterious, and many humans are turning to what they consider a more reasonable explanation of why they're here. They certainly live less magical lives than their ancestors. But to be honest, I think it's nice no one is trying to burn us at the stake. Let them have their science."

"What about the cultures who still believe in magic?"

"Most of those cultures respect the practice and art. They're open to guidance. In equal respect and thankfulness for their… discretion, our species rewards them with favor."

"Reward them how?"

"Some of these cultures live in hard times, so perhaps a neighboring witch summons a rainstorm for a drought to cease. Maybe they cure tribal members of disease. We can't overtly do too much or it would draw notice from other cultures, and we can't provide any level of help that would tip the balance, but we help when appropriate."

"We keep this balance because…"

"We aren't God. And we need to leave the balance of the universe intact. The advances and setbacks of the human race must remain mostly unaltered. Anything that significantly alters humanity must be left to Fate. There are consequences for pissing off Fate. She's a tricky mistress," he answered, smiling.

The conversation hung freshly in my mind as we neared Edinburgh.

"How superstitious are people around here?"

"It's a modern city with modern people, but you'll come into contact with historians, English professors, archaeologists, and the like. These highly intelligent humans are close to the past. They're researchers, observers of humanity. Superstitious, no. Perceptive, yes."

The train pulled to a stop, and Fitz smiled, the buzz of my energy swirling all around us. As we exited the bustling Waverly Station, the fresh air felt unusual – animated somehow, as its tiny movements danced wildly across my skin. My feet greeted the earth of Scotland and were immediately met by a burst of energy, which climbed rapidly, humming throughout my body. My energy, my blood, *everything* within me responded to an invisible force quivering through the elements. I hesitated, looking at Fitz through a questioning glance.

"Magic grows stronger in certain areas of the world. When we physically die, our spirits hang around our homeland. You feel that concentration of power, and your own powers will strengthen because of it." He grinned, bursts of his euphoria hitting me in waves. "Your body is feeding on the collection of energy and spirit. Edinburgh has a rich, magical history. Paris and London have strong footholds as well – you're becoming more in tune with yourself since you perceive the magic here."

The feeling of power pulsing through my body was sensation enough, but this knowledge was exhilarating. Standing in the midst of the historic city, my brothers and sisters across countless generations were granting me vitality. Humans passed us blindly, consumed with their daily lives, completely unaware of the life transforming before their eyes. The energy of my magical family strengthened my own, and for the first time, I felt like I belonged to something on a grand scale, greater than my dreams ever envisioned. After years of tumbling through life, searching in vain for others like me, feeling ill at ease in my own body… I was no longer alone.

*   *   *

Fitz paced the room, his cell glued to his ear. We had immediately checked into a hotel and avoided Fitz's flat at all costs. His father finally called with more information, and my foot tapped nervously, awaiting the update. As he punched the button to end his call, my stomach flipped.

"Dad says things are fine."

"*Fine?*"

"He said he received a visit this morning. He told them he

heard from me and that you acquired your powers. After some back and forth, the council member left. He received a call this afternoon telling him the case would be dropped, though they want proof that you're a fully functioning witch now."

"Do you buy that – that they're going to drop the case?"

"Here's the thing… well, first of all, no. I don't think they're going to drop anything. The council works in strange ways. If they let this go, there's a reason."

"Well, that sounds ominous."

"It could be… they might need us for something in particular."

"I don't understand."

"They might want to leverage a particular skill set for something. Or maybe my dad's pull with them was enough. All's well that ends well."

"I doubt that. It feels suspicious."

"I agree. But for now, I think we should play along. We'll provide proof that you have your power. And most importantly, we'll remain on our guard. Trust me, if they need something from us, we won't wait in suspense too long. If that's all okay with you?"

"I don't think we have much choice unless we decide to run. But what are the odds they wouldn't eventually find us anyway?"

"Slim."

"We don't want to live that way – not unless it's a last resort. Let's stay and face this."

"I'll call and schedule the meeting."

CHAPTER THREE

E dinburgh. It exceeded my expectations, idyllic and dramatic as it was. Throughout Old Town, the remarkable architecture, cobblestone streets, small pubs, and charming tourist shops donning tartans and Scottish trinkets all culminated into a uniquely Scottish experience. And if that was somehow insufficient, the expansive and ever-present Edinburgh Castle sat atop Old Town, granting a glimpse into the ingenuity and realities of medieval times. In the castle's 1,100-year history, researchers believed it was besieged twenty-six times. Its history boasted ties to the likes of Robert the Bruce and even Bonnie Prince Charlie and his '45 uprising. The massive structure previously housed everything from royalty to prisoners, but its seemingly final role was preserving history, educating and entertaining tourists, and adding jobs to the Edinburgh economy.

I strolled down the esplanade near the castle entrance, only to pause, my attention captured by the impressive structure. The gray stonework rose high above my head, and many plans must have been thwarted over the years upon facing this monster. The thick, impenetrable walls held two large, wooden doors in place, which opened to a courtyard filled with tourists. I hopped into the lengthening ticket line and unnecessarily paid for admittance among the many families and friends, laughing and chattering on carelessly. My chest swelled as I considered joining the ranks of castle employees, contributing to others' happiness in such a way, preserving history and architecture for generations to come.

An hour later, I had lost myself to the castle, which was grander than I expected. The views were breathtaking from any of the outer walls, granting unparalleled views of Arthur's Seat, St. Giles, and along the Royal Mile. My eyes scanned from New Town over to the Firth of Forth rolling toward the North Sea, and I wondered if this magical city was the place I would soon call home. I wandered the grounds in awe, and so engrossed in the history as I was, a small jolt of panic hit the pit of my stomach upon realizing only a few moments separated me from my impending interview with Mr. Murray. I rushed through the doors of the Great Hall, and navigated around the throngs of tourists scattered about the sunny courtyard, though I think I received some assistance from the supernatural in reaching his office on time.

*   *   *

Mr. Murray was a distinguished older gentleman in his early sixties if my appraisal was correct. A white button-down, charcoal waistcoat and slacks, and expensive leather shoes accompanied his tartan inspired jacket. As he drew closer, I took stock of his handsome features and the twinkle in his blue eyes, shining brightly above a fluffy, gray beard. I found it odd when he didn't shake my hand, lightly nudging my elbow instead, guiding me toward his office. Something protective resounded through the gesture – almost fatherly, which was an interesting way to begin an interview. As I settled into the leather chair opposite the desk from him, I looked around the office.

"Not too shabby, aye?" he smirked, a thick Highlander accent rolling off his tongue.

Although not large, the space was comfortable, decorated in a traditionally masculine style. Two leather chairs nestled into a corner next to a small table donning two glasses with a bottle of scotch cozied between them.

"My assistant wants to throttle me half the time," he added, his hand sweeping over the stacks of books, magazines, and loose papers adorning the mahogany desk. I rather doubted that. Mr. Murray had a lot going on, but he was equally organized if the appearance of his desk bore any true reflection of his character – and in my years in the workforce, I found it usually did. Each stack appeared neat and orderly, clearly an organized system in play. The window near his desk opened to the center courtyard, his office perfectly positioned to observe the happenings of the castle. Not too shabby, indeed.

"Perhaps I should have led in with this, but what has you interested in leaving the States to pursue a career in Edinburgh?"

Roughly forty-five minutes into the interview, I was enthralled with the details of castle business when Mr. Murray posed the question. And at this precise moment, I felt a tingle working up my spine. It was fleeting, but the signal was clear – this man was no human.

Out of all of the opportunities, I was banking on the one where I'd report to another witch. My mind raced, wondering if he realized I was also a witch, but of course, odds favored that he did. I was a rare case, after all. Most witches would've been comfortable with their powers from an early age. Sure, he knew – I suddenly understood why he didn't shake my hand at the beginning of the interview.

I responded as calmly as I could.

"I'm ready for a new challenge and very interested in expanding my horizons in another country. Scotland has such a rich culture and wonderful outdoor community. I think it's the perfect place for me."

"Oh, you're into the outdoors then?" he asked, stroking his neatly trimmed beard.

"Hiking and canoeing are both avid interests of mine."

"You're sure to have endless adventures here, especially through the Highlands."

I smiled, hoping to hide my growing apprehension.

"Well, if you don't have additional questions, I'll let you get on with your day, Ms. Weston. I plan to call your references this afternoon."

"That sounds perfect. I really appreciate your time."

"It's been a pleasure. I look forward to speaking again soon."

I extended my hand, my eyes intently awaiting his reaction. When our skin made contact, a small tremor moved through my hand. Fitz was right – I certainly sensed contact with another witch. But unlike the intensity I felt with him, a dull energy pulsed just under the surface at Mr. Murray's touch. Even so, it provided all the knowledge I sought. Mr. Murray was definitely a witch, and a powerful one at that.

Walking down the corridor, I wondered if others of our kind worked within the castle. Could they determine I was a witch from afar, just as Mr. Murray had? I mentally filed this question away to discuss with Fitz and stepped into the courtyard to find the creature in question.

"You know, if it weren't for your modern clothing, you'd fit right into this medieval place, you bloody Scot."

"You're a real charmer, you know that?" Fitz leaned over, planting a kiss on the top of my head. "Finally. I thought you were going to stay in there forever," he murmured, tugging me closer to him.

His warmth was rather inviting against the lingering nip of fall. I slipped my hand in his and recalled my question.

"Aye, as your skills develop, you'll be able to determine if another witch is close. You'll sense their energy. Every witch's abilities are slightly different. They have varying levels of power. You'll learn to pick up on their energy and perceive those slight differences. It'll be even stronger between the two of us, though – I know you're not far by simply feeling your energy or catching your scent on the breeze."

"What do I feel like? How far away can you feel me?"

"When I walked through the castle gates, I knew you were still inside. A respectable distance, I suppose. Your energy feels like sunlight dancing on my skin at such a distance. Similar to standing beneath the canopy of a tree on a day like today. The wind moves through the leaves, and I catch glimpses of your light and warmth. As the gap between us closes, it begins to feel warmer, more pleasant."

My grip instinctively tightened on his hand. "And my scent?"

"Your scent is caramel," he returned, after a slight inhale. "Your scent is sweet, your warmth is palpable, and you're miraculously standing in front of me with your hand linked through mine. Who forgot to tell you that you deserve the whole world?"

I shook my head lightly, smiling.

"It's come on gradually, but I know your scent and feel as well."

"Like you're downwind from a farm?"

"Way to ruin the moment!" I laughed, pausing briefly to collect my thoughts. "You smell of oak… of a whisky with hints of fruit and spice. I noticed it when you hugged me that first moment in Paris. I assumed it was the scent of drink and cologne, but now I know it's you. It's comforting… you make me feel at ease."

That elicited a shy grin from Fitz.

"And the feeling your energy gives me. Well, I'd liken it to your description. That feels just right."

Fitz opened his mouth to respond, but the hair on our necks suddenly bristled, shutting down his response before he could even begin. Though his expression remained blank, the shift in his energy buzzed in tandem with mine. We were being watched.

"Don't look around," his voice whispered in my mind. "Something doesn't feel right."

It seemed my exploration of the castle would have to wait for another day. We simultaneously turned toward the large, wooden doors, needing nothing but our internal communication to signal it was time to depart.

CHAPTER FOUR

The next morning was gloriously filled to the brim with magic, my spirit effervescent as Fitz covered the creation of fire. I first thought it would be risky in the hotel room fireplace, but it occurred to me that he could likely extinguish a fire before it did any damage. It was incredible watching Fitz call up fire, and he did so with such little effort, the result of years of practice. His ease with the craft motivated me to practice harder and become comfortable with it. After studying his command of the elements, we settled on the couch before a blazing fire to work on my communion with them.

Fitz and I both worked elemental magic. Moments would arise where we'd have need of spells, but for our type, spells were only necessary for particular circumstances. Instead of relying on spells to connect us to the elements, our power linked with them directly. Elemental witches were more powerful than casters, but we also carried a heavier burden – which was why Fitz placed so much emphasis on meditation, and I already identified its necessity to ease my mind and release my excess energy.

"Why have you used magic around me so little?"

"Well, you're not quite comfortable with your magic yet, and I didn't want to seem like a show-off."

"I like watching your magic at work. It kind of fascinates me and motivates me to work harder."

"Noted."

Fitz's finger circled the smooth surface of the moonstone in my ring.

"I think it's time you learn the rest of the details surrounding my family's ring."

I leaned forward instinctually, craving the rest of the story.

"I told you my grandmother was murdered in the witch trials. She wore the ring until the end of her life. My grandfather was supposed to retrieve the ring immediately after her death, but he was so consumed with grief… Our family thought after strangulation, the captors would burn her remains at the stake. When collecting the ashes, he would also collect the ring," he trailed off momentarily.

"But they didn't?"

"They decided to burn the bodies in barrels of hot tar."

"Holy hell. I mean, I know it's all horrible, but how does that feel even more barbaric? I mean, it honestly just feels weirder somehow."

"Aye, it was."

"So, he didn't have any remains to collect."

"Right. Then he wasn't sure about the ring, whether or not it was still in the tar or if it was taken from her hand before that. So, he and another witch combined forces and discovered someone removed it right after she was strangled."

My stomach turned as I considered how horrible an end these poor creatures and humans endured, and my heart sank thinking of his grandmother. I couldn't even fathom the heartache his poor grandfather endured.

"What were their names?" Though I couldn't alter the past, I could at least ensure they weren't forgotten.

"Esther and Hamish MacGregor. They assumed the last name of Lockie for a time, but were just then using their true clan name again."

"Why? To protect Esther?"

"Oh no. I'll give you a history lesson later," he offered with a wink, "They were using the alias for protection because the MacGregors were outlawed by the king."

"So, you come from a distinguished line of outlaws?"

"Aye, just like me." He smiled.

"They were already hiding who they were as witches, but then they were outlawed because of their bloodline."

"Right. Hamish had already been through a lot before he actually lost Esther."

"Poor Hamish. I can't imagine."

"We found his journal in the attic at my great-grandparents' house when we were organizing a few years ago. Hamish never forgave himself for not solving the mystery of the ring. He felt like he dishonored Esther by not carrying out her final wish."

"He did his best, I'm sure."

"He searched tirelessly for the ring. He turned the town upside down, used locator spells, but the ring was gone. Another witch must've taken it; a human couldn't have concealed it from Hamish."

"Fitz, there were a lot of innocent souls lost to the trials, and most of them weren't even creatures. But Esther was a witch. Why didn't she resist or flee?"

"She had a good reason. The most powerful witch in Scotland sat on the witch-hunting committee."

An audible gasp escaped my lips.

"He infiltrated the committee to prevent as many deaths as possible, but he needed to remain inconspicuous – meaning he couldn't be overzealous."

"This witch couldn't save Esther?"

"No, and he wouldn't allow Esther to resist by utilizing magic. She was quite powerful, but not powerful enough to stand against him. And she had three children to consider."

"He would've leveraged those children against her in a heartbeat."

"You bet."

"Did she possess the power of transport?"

"We think so."

"Even so, she couldn't transport herself, her husband, and three children," I guessed. "Anyone left behind would've fallen to the committee, and more than likely, they would've eventually found her anyway."

"She had no choice but to acquiesce to Fate. So, she didn't resist arrest, endured torture, and was brutally murdered."

"How was she compromised?"

"Dad and I discovered a woman named Helen Guthrie was at the heart of the Forfar witch trials. She was accused and arrested along with her thirteen-year-old daughter. Helen realized that as long as she remained useful to her captors, she would also remain alive and able to protect her daughter."

"It would be easy to hate her if it weren't for the fact that she was a mother protecting her daughter – no matter the cost."

"Harsh times, harsh measures I suppose. Helen told all she knew and all she could imagine. She implicated several women: some witches, some humans. Helen exaggerated Esther's ability of foresight and claimed she used it to alter the future in evil ways, doing the bidding of the devil. Esther didn't stand a chance."

I was so engrossed in Esther's story that I jumped at the sound of my ringing phone.

"Answer it!" Fitz exclaimed, anticipating Mr. Murray on the other end of the line. He stood, kissed my forehead, and walked out of the room.

The call was pleasant but brief. As soon as I hung up the phone, Fitz appeared in the doorway.

"Well?"

"Don't you already know?"

"I tried to close the connection to give you some privacy, but you seem excited."

"They made a generous offer – higher than they originally intended because they don't want me to pursue another offer."

"I knew they'd want you."

"I accepted the offer. I'm moving to Edinburgh."

Fitz pulled me from the couch and into his embrace. "I couldn't ask you to stay for me," he mumbled, his face momentarily lost in my mess of hair.

"Oh, Fitz…" I smiled. "If you're here, where else would I be?"

His grip loosened, allowing his fingers to lightly travel the distance of my cheek. He planted a gentle kiss on my forehead before drawing me in tightly.

How long had we stood there clinging to one another, I later wondered. We eventually landed back on the couch, staring through the window at an unobstructed view of my future workplace.

The fact that Fitz upgraded my room to a castle view suite was something we were still fighting over. He wouldn't allow me to spend a dime… or, well, pence, as long as he was around. The hotel was beautifully appointed, and the bathroom bigger than mine at home. Besides one interesting experience in their restaurant, which we were still laughing over days later, the stay had been perfect.

"When do I get to meet Henry?"

"Soon. We'll go practice at his place this week – I just want to wait until after the appointment with the council."

"When do I get to see your place?"

"Aren't you full of questions?" he smiled. "You want to come over?"

"Yeah. Why, is that weird? You come over to my room."

"No, not at all. I just didn't know how to ask you over, I guess. It sounds so suggestive. There's no proper way for a guy to say, 'Hey, want to take this back to my place?'"

"You definitely don't ask like that." I giggled.

"I think it's fine for us to be at my place at this point. I mean, the council isn't trying to track us down any longer. We have the meeting scheduled. Come over tonight for dinner."

"You'll cook?"

"Of course, I will. I love it. My dad does most of the cooking back home, and he taught me a lot growing up. It's soothing after a long day. The methodical chopping, the sizzle of the pan, the smell of the food."

"Well, when you put it like that…" I smiled. "I actually enjoy it myself."

"Something else in common, then."

"Do you use magic to cook?"

"Not to actually cook, but to prep sometimes, sure."

"Tell me more."

"Well, for instance, I hate chopping onions… the burning, watery eyes and all that. If I were ever captured, there's no need for waterboarding, just give me one hundred onions to dice. Nasty business, so I ask the knife to chop them for me."

"Oh. My. God."

"You'll get there, Hadley. Patience."

"One of my strong suits."

He smirked. "I better get going then. I need to stop by the store."

"Where's your place? Can you just jot down the address?"

"I'll arrange for a car to pick you up."

"Fitz."

"Why do you always fight me when I try to take care of you?"

"Not always, just sometimes. I can manage this one on my own."

"Fine, but don't walk. Please. I'm a bit worried after being watched at the castle."

CHAPTER FIVE

Despite it being my idea, I was nervous as I walked over to Fitz's home. We spent a lot of time together over the past few weeks and reaffirmed our love, but things were different now. This was his home in the city that would soon be mine, as well. This was real – in a new way. And what were we exactly? Though I knew creature relationships escalated quickly, we hadn't labeled ourselves as anything definite either. I shook my head and checked the directions on my phone again. Fitz would be angry if he found out I walked over alone, but my desire to stretch my legs and admire the city at night was acute.

Realizing I was about halfway to my destination, I picked up the pace, a shiver running the length of my spine. I almost paused before instinct smothered my curiosity. Although the night air was crisp with the chill of autumn, it wasn't the culprit of the sudden cold in my bones or the pinpricks of a witch's glare assaulting my skin. I was being watched, and not by someone with mild curiosity either.

I glanced around confidently, remembering the advice I was given over the years: when alone at night, appear confident and alert. I hoped that advice was applicable to creatures, as I pressed onward, my heart beating wildly against my chest. My sense of time was distorted, and it seemingly ticked away slowly. Thoughts danced through my mind. Had our Parisian stalkers returned? Was this the council? *Was I in danger?*

The pinpricks grew stronger, and I feared the creature would overtake me before I reached the street's next intersection, though the Royal Mile was already in view. I reminded myself to breathe, releasing a deep sigh of relief upon rounding the corner into Old Town's bustling main drag. The witch's stare faded along with the darkness of the street I left behind, and I focused on propelling myself closer to Fitz. Deciding I was safer amongst the crowd of people, my pulse slowed, and I checked the map a final time.

If I was reading the map correctly, Fitz's humble flat lay within one of the most impressive addresses in Old Town. Ramsay Garden towered over the city and only drew shadows from its western neighbor, Edinburgh Castle. I walked right past his home as I strolled down the esplanade to my interview. The majestic Scots Baronial style building was beautifully adorned with a red ashlar and white harled exterior. I studied the entrance dubiously and placed my hand on the buzzer.

"What's wrong?" Fitz asked as he threw open the door.

"Nothing."

"I was just about to call you."

"Okay…"

"Hadley."

"Fitz."

He eyed me warily, and I reached for him instinctively, knowing his touch would quiet my agitated energy. "Don't worry about it. I'm just happy to be with you."

He kissed me, pulling me through the doorway. My mouth watered as I entered his flat, surprised to find that dinner was crab ravioli.

"What, did you go out and catch crab this afternoon?"

"Yeah, right after I milked the cow and churned butter," he returned, allowing the change in conversation, although concern still simmered underneath his humor.

"Oh, please tell me you're the proud owner of a cow."

"I'm sorry. I'm going to have to let you down on that one. For now."

Fitz's flat was stunning. The wood floors were walnut in color, complementing the stormy gray walls of the living room. Large bay windows adorned the west-facing wall, allowing for ample light during the day, but were just then flaunting their view of the castle, all lit up for the evening. His furniture held deep, rich colors in the woods and warm brown leather, rustic like a beautifully worn saddle. Books, new and old alike, were randomly stacked on most surfaces, and a half-empty decanter held a golden liquid, sure to be single malt scotch.

He led me into the kitchen, and I sat at the breakfast table, tucked into a small nook, while he completed his final flourishes to our meal. My eyes flickered around the kitchen, surprised by the comfortable size of it. I expected a smaller space, with his flat housed in an older European building.

"I decided on this flat solely for the kitchen space. It was the largest I saw – the former owner was a chef and expanded it. You should've seen the rest of the place, though. It was pretty tragic but completely worth the work for this setup."

"This place suits you."

The kitchen cabinets were mahogany and the counters a gray concrete. Copper and stainless steel completed the look. Warm and comfortable, just like him. I grinned as he set our plates on the table, the thought of passing many an evening in this manner flitting across my mind.

*   *   *

"How's Izzy?" I asked, taking another appreciative sip of wine. Dinner went off without a hitch, and I almost forgot I was anxious at the beginning of the evening. Curled up under a blanket on the couch, I was relaxed and happy.

"You like this one, don't you?"

"You have good taste in women *and* wine," I countered, pulling a deep laugh from Fitz.

"Aye, that I do."

His fingers skimmed the length of my thigh, taking their time in meandering back to my knee, where he rested his hand before recalling my question.

"Izzy's good. She was in her last year at the UW when you moved?"

"Yep."

"She accepted a job in grant writing with Seattle Children's."

"That sounds perfect for her."

"Yeah, she's always had a big heart, and this allows her to put her skills to good use."

"I'd like to see her."

"She's anxious to see you again. I think it's about time to arrange that."

"Really? That would be amazing!"

"I'll call her tomorrow and ask about her time off. She'll hop a plane in a heartbeat."

"I can't believe you kept poor Izzy away."

"I trust her more than anyone else to be around you, and to help you… I didn't want to pull her further into this mess while you and I were breaking the rules."

"You were right to do that."

"There's no harm in it now. You have her number. Call her any time, if you'd like."

"I'd love that! It's funny to think about the difference between who I was when I met Izzy and who I am now. I had no idea who I was then, and I was wildly suspicious of her when we first met."

"I've often wondered what you thought when you first met us."

"Izzy is kind of... eccentric, you know – in the best way. Although, when I met her, I only knew she was different. I tried to throw suspicion out of my mind, but I just couldn't. Oh, and I always had this uneasy feeling like your dad was watching me."

"Yeah, because he was watching you."

"I know, which I can understand now, but at the time..."

"Old man must've creeped you out a little."

"There was a constant internal struggle between two trains of thought: either I was crazy or you guys were."

He laughed. "Maybe both."

"Maybe. But I'm okay with that."

Fitz insisted on walking with me back to the hotel, although I didn't need any convincing. As we crossed the hotel lobby, anxiety rolled through my body. I hadn't yet mentioned my earlier encounter. Fitz would overreact, but the thought of being alone haunted my mind.

Fitz's internal battle raged, and his warring energy washed over me. We were feeding each other's negative energy, leading one another down a rocky path. He knew something was wrong before I even arrived at his home, and that knowledge simmered just under the surface the entire evening. I would've felt the same way had the roles been reversed. As the elevator propelled us toward my floor, my internal struggle came to a halt. It was time to end our game.

"Someone was watching me again tonight."

"Excuse me," he returned, his eyes immediately wild.

"Don't overreact."

"I'm not overreacting."

"Really?"

"First of all – *really*. You know I can't help it. And this sort of thing just isn't done. You don't watch other creatures."

"Okay, fine."

"So, what's going on?"

"When I walked over to your place, someone was watching me."

"I told you not to walk over," he growled.

"I told you not to boss me around."

He met my eyes sternly.

"Look, I can't explain how, but I know it was the same witch from the courtyard. They never made contact or anything, and trailed off right before your place."

"They knew I'd sense them. Which means they know who we both are and that we're together." He instinctively grabbed my hand.

"Together," I repeated.

"What is it?"

"I know how we feel, but we've never defined anything."

Fitz's face scrunched in confusion.

"What would you say we are?"

"You already know the answer. You have all of these human ideas floating around in your head. We're not human, Hads. We've already formed our connection to one another. You know I love you."

Fitz pulled me through the door, throwing a glance at the

lock before it secured itself.

"I know; I do," I murmured, a bit distracted by his display. "But this is the first time we're having a conversation to actually define what we are."

Fitz glanced across the room, and the curtains suddenly obstructed our view of the outside world.

"When we're apart I feel like a vital piece is missing from me."

My confession pulled his attention from securing the room, his expression softening. "Our souls don't understand we're only apart for brief intervals of time – that the separation is temporary. They only recognize the absence of one another and aren't satisfied until reunited."

"I feel the truth in that."

"So, to answer your question, I consider us bound together. Forever. Don't you agree?"

"Yes."

Finally. A longstanding tightness released from my chest.

"I'd like to stay here tonight."

"And to think, only a few hours ago you were worried about asking me to dinner at your place."

He returned a smile, though distractedly.

"Sounds good to me. You could probably call the front desk for a toothbrush. Unless…"

"Unless what?"

"Can you just produce that sort of thing with a snap of your fingers or something?"

"I'll call the front desk," he said, reaching into the air. Without warning, the phone flew across the room and into his impatient grasp.

"Oh, God. Please teach me how to do that."

"All in good time. You're doing great. You'll be calling up objects in no time."

Getting ready for bed was infinitely more fun as I considered all of the objects I could call into my reach, wondering if I could brush my teeth without using my hands. Upon entering the bedroom, I initially reached for my leggings, but after some debate, I settled on my pajamas. They outranked my leggings on the cute scale, much of the top a transparent lace. It wasn't an attempt to seduce Fitz necessarily, but I thought he might shoot down the request I was about to make – and I needed all of the ammunition I could muster. I marched into the living room to find Fitz lying on the couch.

"Well, don't you look adorable?"

"Are you coming in here or what?"

"Hadley!"

"What? Please, don't be a prude tonight. Besides, you're able to offer more reliable protection at a closer range."

"You are something else."

"Come to bed, Fitz."

I expected resistance, but he crossed the room, standing just in front of me. My eyes searched his, hoping for an opening into his thoughts, but to no avail; he remained carefully impassable. He physically turned my body around, leading me into the bedroom. We held each other's gaze as we climbed onto the bed.

"What are you afraid of, Fitz?"

"I'm afraid of screwing this up."

"What do you mean?"

"I know I haven't handled everything well in our past, and I want to do better. I'm not a prude. If you read my mind, it would make you blush."

My heart quickened, and Fitz let out an irritated groan, rolling onto his back.

"What now?"

"The last thing I need right now is your body responding to my confession."

I laughed lightly, taking hold of Fitz's arm and tugging him to face me again. "Okay. I'm calm."

His eyebrows rose at my response.

"Just… continue. Please."

"Look, it's important we do everything we can to actually cultivate our relationship. I don't want to rush things and then realize we should have taken more time to let other aspects of our relationship develop first."

"I get that. There's so much going on between us, but also just with me. With my powers, my mind, my body. I agree."

"I just don't want you flying into everything head first, and then regretting it later."

"I don't think that would happen, but I also appreciate that we're trying to take things at a reasonable pace. There's a balance, though, and we're currently tipping the scale."

"Okay… are you comfortable with me staying over?"

"This feels better already – more comfortable than being without you. If you still need some space, that's fine, but don't stay away on my account."

"Have you gone mad, then? I had to talk myself down last night, so I wouldn't come over here and sleep outside your door."

"That worried?"

"You have no idea."

"No more of that."

"Deal."

I slid my body closer to his and rested my head against his chest. We shimmied ourselves until we fit snugly to one another, clinging tightly to our newfound territory. Peaceful energy radiated through me, and I closed my eyes, allowing foggy calmness to take hold. In this safe and happy place, I fell into the waiting arms of peaceful sleep.

CHAPTER SIX

For whatever reason, I painted the council as the type of organization to office in old, dilapidated buildings with buzzing, flickering fluorescent bulbs and employees who smelled like old food. I couldn't have been more wrong. As the attractive brunette's heels clicked down the hardwood hallway, leading us past large, black pane windows, I was distracted by both the grandeur and the tastefulness of the offices. Everyone smiled and nodded as we met them in the hallway and seemed genuinely pleasant. Several creatures spoke to Jeanette, our guide, who was full of banter and laughter, and she knew everyone by name.

Jeanette left us in a small room surrounded by brick walls and a large picture window, massive trees full of red and yellow leaves swaying gently on the other side of the panes. The table was sturdy, of good quality, and topped with a large Mac monitor. I tapped my fingers nervously on the wooden desk, and Fitz slid his hand onto mine.

His dad assured us that we had nothing to fear. The council would verify my power, and we'd be free to go, though unease still rested in the back of my mind. What if they decided on a different course of action? What if they wanted us to do something in return for their dismissal of our rule breaking – something we found unethical or dangerous?

A petite woman with gray hair and Prada framed glasses entered the room, gliding effortlessly toward the desk.

"Hadley. Fitz. Such a pleasure to meet you both." She shook our hands, and her eyes widened. "Oh my. Such power you *both* have!"

I shifted in my seat, and Fitz once again reached for my hand.

"Mrs. Cameron. It's nice to meet you."

"This will go quite quickly. Hadley, I'll just place my palm on your forehead, and then I'll feel the palm of your right hand. Will that be all right?"

"I don't have much choice, do I?"

Mrs. Cameron smirked.

"She's happy to oblige," Fitz intervened.

"No need to be nervous, Fitz. I imagine I'd have the same response if I was in Hadley's position."

Mrs. Cameron was, indeed, quick. She closed her eyes, muttering unintelligibly under her breath. Her palm rested gently on my forehead, before she then took my hand, palm up, in hers, as she grazed and circled my open palm. After a few minutes, she opened her eyes and smiled.

She returned to the opposite side of the table, typing rapidly before hitting the enter key with force and meeting my gaze. "You certainly have matched with your power. There's no doubt about that. The power you each possess is extraordinary. Fitz, you were right about Hadley from the beginning, and we should have trusted your judgment, but you both understand our concern?"

"I'm afraid I don't," I returned, meeting her eyes unabashedly.

"Hadley."

"No, Fitz. I don't understand, and I won't sit here and pretend I do. I am a witch. Truthfully, I always have been. Fitz was able to see that. If y'all are so wise and use such discernment ruling over us, how could you miss that?"

Fitz shifted uncomfortably in his seat.

"It's not that simple, I'm afraid."

"Oh, but it is. Things either are, or they aren't. I *am* a witch. The council forcing us apart *was* wrong. You made the wrong call."

"We made the best call we could, and we did it to keep everyone safe. I know this must have been a difficult season for you."

"Do you? Tell me something: can you really understand what I've been through?"

Mrs. Cameron quietly held my gaze, and if I weren't so angry, perhaps her intensity would have made me uncomfortable. "No. I guess I don't," she acknowledged, sighing. "But here we all are. You have come into your powers. There are no rules being broken. You are free to move forward with your relationship without any further involvement from us."

"Great," Fitz returned, shooting a pointed glance in my direction. "One question, though."

Mrs. Cameron nodded for him to continue.

"Someone is watching us in Edinburgh. Is it the council?"

"No, we haven't had anyone watching since you've been back – we didn't even know of your whereabouts. We trusted you to come forward and meet with us, as you and your father said you would, so we stopped trying to find you, truthfully."

"You're certain?"

"Quite. Is someone bothering you?"

"We've had a couple visits from someone watching in the shadows."

"I'll look into it. We'll find out who it is and ensure your safety."

"Thank you."

"Thank you both for coming in and taking care of this bit of business. You're valuable members of witchkind, and we'll do all we can to keep you safe."

*   *   *

"Aren't you a feisty one today?" Fitz quipped.

"I just got super angry sitting in there."

"Do the words *captain obvious* mean anything to you?"

I smirked.

"You know, we were there to be exonerated from our 'crimes' basically. You could have landed us back in the hot seat."

"For expressing my frustration? Are we ruled by some sort of communistic government that can't be criticized?"

"I'm not saying that. I'm just saying you could've been a little more… diplomatic."

"So, despite all of that – do you think we're done now?"

"No."

"Oh, great."

"We're done with this chapter, but we'll hear from them again. Did you see her reaction to our power? Her surprise wasn't genuine. I think she already knew what she'd find. They want something from us."

CHAPTER SEVEN

"Are you kidding me?" Fitz yelled from behind a small fir tree. His closest friend, Henry, offered his estate outside of Edinburgh for us to focus on my fire skills. As excited as I was about fire, meeting Fitz's best mate, as he called him, was also an exciting prospect.

"Obviously not."

"I ought to fire one back so you know how it feels."

"I can take it."

"Seriously, please don't set me on fire. It would ruin the afternoon."

I snickered, pulling a smile from him as well.

Mastering the skill of fire creation was a huge step in training. Once I understood how to commune with the elements, asking them for what I sought was easier and more intuitive than I anticipated, for which I was grateful. It made me feel like a real, certified witch, and that was a true confidence booster this early in training.

The next step was creating fire with my body and then using that fire to protect myself. I never imagined there were so many ways to command fire. I could throw it like a baseball, wield it through a bow and arrow, shoot it from my fingertips, and radiate it from my entire body. I was basically a dragon, I observed to Fitz, who rolled his eyes playfully.

Throwing it took little practice. Fitz noted it was one of my most natural skills, with an appreciative nod. The bow and arrow worked out quite nicely, as well. My father hunted by bow until he grew too sick. He said he preferred a clean kill under an open sky to uncertain animal welfare conditions for those raised by humans. As such, he taught me to wield a bow and arrow long ago, and apparently, that was skill enough. Radiating fire from my entire body? Evidently, I wasn't half bad at that either. I gasped as the air ignited all around me, absolutely in awe at the way the flames responded to my request.

However, using my fingers as a gun to shoot fire was the issue at hand. I almost set Fitz ablaze with a misfire. Twice. Though he was trying to maintain his humor, someone almost lighting you on fire is a harrowing experience. He walked over to demonstrate again how my form should appear.

"One more time. Legs here. Back straight. Arms tight and slightly bent."

"Do I really need both arms out?"

"Your ability is still materializing, but you'll have twice the strength with both hands. My best guess is it'll fully develop in the next week."

"Best news I've heard all day."

"Arms just a little lower. It's a slightly different form from shooting a firearm. Yep, perfect."

I adjusted per his instructions and shot.

"Now, that's better."

"I was a lot closer on that one."

"Try it again. Remember, focus on what you want."

I took a deep breath, mindful of my form, and reveled in my desire to set the target ablaze, envisioning how flames would lick the air. I closed my eyes for a brief moment, asking my magic to guide my efforts.

"Fire," I breathed, and took my shot. Flames leapt from my fingertips, brilliant against the waning daylight. "Oh my God," I whispered, mesmerized by the target afire in magical desire made real.

"That was perfect!" Fitz beamed, lifting me from the ground. My lips found his, both of us alight with excitement. "Let's see that again."

As the minutes ticked on, they saw an increase in my confidence. Firing off shots, one by one, I hit my mark, my energy bursting at the seams. Finally, I paused, a sudden urge for Fitz taking hold.

"Damn," he breathed. "Your eyes."

My head tilted in curiosity.

"They're on fire, Hads," he explained, his hand resting at the base of my skull.

"I don't understand."

"They're red, orange, yellow… the same as the fire you're expelling."

"Is that… normal?"

"Yeah, I think it is for you." His heart rate doubled, as he met me in a kiss, fiery in its own right. "Let's head inside – you need to rest, and if I know Henry, he's pouring drinks as we speak."

Henry's estate was straight out of a fairytale. A lengthy driveway wound across the rolling hills of the countryside, crossing property so extensive that no neighbors were visible, even with the lack of foliage. The Palladian-style home was grand, sitting atop a hill in the center of his acreage, constructed in the late 17ᵗʰ century by Henry's wealthy ancestors. The home remained in his family for hundreds of years and was recently left to Henry after his parents moved to Greece. His dad's health issues weren't compatible with the cool Scottish climate, which led to retirement abroad.

We stepped through the French doors from the patio and into a large sitting room, where Henry awaited our arrival, extending wine glasses in our direction.

"Hadley, I hear this is a favorite of yours, so I ordered a few bottles for the bar," Henry announced, his large, hazel eyes twinkling mischievously. My mouth gaped as I sniffed the dark liquid.

"This is the Chateau de Ferrand we had in Paris."

I looked to Fitz, who nodded for affirmation.

"Henry! Thank you."

"Of course. Fitz tells me you're joining our wee circle in Edinburgh. Between that and your fire coming in, we have cause to celebrate."

"I can't tell you how appreciative I am of all this, and not only the wine. Thank you for allowing me to practice here."

"You're welcome here any time." Henry raised his glass, and we followed suit. "*Slàinte mhath!*"

I took pause to study this dear, old friend of Fitz's. Those mischievous eyes were set below a strong brow and hair the color of champagne. Combed into a deep side part, I found it reminiscent of old Hollywood, in the style of Cary Grant. Henry appeared young, maybe younger than his actual age, and his thin figure was draped in an expensive and well-tailored suit. Though he appeared a bit aristocratic, something in his countenance was deeply warm and inviting, and I gave myself permission to like him straight away.

We sank into large, leather chairs near the fireplace.

"Hadley, perhaps you'd better do the honors," Henry prompted.

I smiled, inhaling deeply, and envisioned the neatly stacked wood alight in flames... and suddenly it was.

"Nicely done," Fitz offered, a proud gleam in his eyes.

"Brilliant," Henry concurred.

The rest of the evening fell into the rhythm of becoming better acquainted. Henry told me of his family's history in Scotland, leaving me envious that he knew so much about his family and who he was.

"I wish I knew more about my family."

"Your case is pretty special; not all of us are born to human parents, defying all odds and challenging our societal norms."

"It makes me all the more curious."

"Sure it does. We have the resources, and we'll get it sorted."

Soon. I would finally know where I came from. But until then, I contented myself with stories of Henry and Fitz's families and was delighted when Henry shared his own story of coming into the craft.

"You caused an *earthquake*," I marveled.

"Aye. It was a minor occurrence, but an earthquake nonetheless."

"What on earth were you doing to cause an earthquake?"

"Oh, that's the best part, isn't it, mate? He was planting a garden for his mother," Fitz answered, howling with laughter.

A book flew from a nearby table, its trajectory set for the back of Fitz's head. Just as I thought it would make contact, Fitz's caught the book in flight, and with minimal effort.

"Fitz is annoyingly good – almost impossible to catch off guard," Henry offered, rolling his eyes.

"He's quick, too. You should've seen him *move* when I almost lit him up with my fire pistols."

It was Henry's turn to laugh. "Maybe I should join your training after all."

"I'll inevitably entertain you with my witchy antics."

"Of that, you may be certain," Fitz added, a boyish grin

spreading across his lips.

A quick intake of air accompanied a change in Henry's countenance. His brow furrowed, as he tilted his head, eyes darting toward Fitz before settling on me.

"Henry? What is it, mate?"

"You two... you're mated?"

"I wondered how long it would take you to sort that out. You're losing your touch."

If looks could kill crossed my mind, as I considered Henry's countenance.

"Were you planning on sharing this information with me or no?" Henry demanded, his accent growing husky.

"You know I was."

"Hmph," Henry returned, though his features softened. "Your energies. It's impossible to perceive where one ends and the other begins. It's all tangled up, and I can't sort it."

"Aye."

"When?"

Fitz's gaze landed on mine, as he considered the question. "Two and a half weeks ago?"

I nodded in affirmation.

"And already so lost in one another. It makes sense, I reckon. You've only lacked Hadley's full power to lock things into place. Still... that's intense."

Henry's eyes met mine. "Are you good, then?"

"What do you mean?"

"The connection you two have. It's strong, intense. Even I can feel it. How are you doing with it all?"

"A piece of me has been missing – for years there's been a sense of anxiety hanging over my head because of it. That's finally gone."

"I think she's known subconsciously since we met. A part of this formed long ago."

Henry let out a long, audible sigh. "Damn, guys. As long as you're good, then so am I."

"Thanks, buddy."

"Yeah, mate. As long as you both know I'm here if you need to talk. Hadley – you, too, not only Fitz."

I thanked him before we fell back into a lighter topic, but our conversations unlocked a new door. Open friendship. I desired such moments for longer than I could even recall. With these guys, I could be myself, and I didn't have to conceal the person I'd become. They were aware I expelled fire from my body, read minds, and made my desires real. And most importantly, they could do the same. I was perfectly normal in this house. We passed several hours by the fire trading stories of our magical experiences and laughing like old friends.

*   *   *

As we drove back to town, I quizzed Fitz about Henry's father.

"I didn't want to pry too much on this subject with Henry, but he mentioned his dad has health concerns. Are our health risks the same as humans?"

"Essentially. The biggies like heart attack or stroke are exceedingly rare until we're quite old. Cancer is almost non-existent in our world. The minor concerns like hurting joints, arthritis, etc. are pretty rare until we're very old."

"How old is Henry's dad?"

Fitz hesitated for a moment before answering. "One hundred twenty-three."

"How is that possible?" The oldest person in the world was what — one hundred fifteen? They certainly weren't in any condition to move off to Greece. "He would've been eighty-five when Henry was born? What am I missing?"

"Most witches choose to have children earlier than Henry's parents to stay on a more human timeline, but there are a lot of creatures who don't choose a traditional lifestyle. Hads, if you saw Henry's dad you'd think he was in his late sixties now."

"People often think I'm a lot younger than I am. Is that typical with us?"

"Aye. But not just because our bodies reflect age slowly. We have longer life spans than humans. Our bodies age slower."

With his careful approach to the subject, I knew he was hesitant to share something. My curiosity got the better of me before I could halt my mind, and my eyes must've been the size of saucers.

"Hadley?"

"Oh my God. I'm really sorry."

"You're inside my mind, aren't you?"

"I promise I didn't mean to. I just… lost control."

He exhaled slowly, requiring a moment to check his feelings. Even his good nature had limits, and I waited patiently until he was ready.

"It's okay. You're new at this, and honestly, you won't develop proper control until I track down someone to help you with that power."

"Thank you for understanding."

"Of course."

"Do we really live to two hundred? Because I can't even wrap my mind around the conversation we're about to have."

"Aye, somewhere between two hundred and two-twenty-five usually. Our magical energy slows aging. It prevents major diseases from taking root. As our bodies finally age out, they become more susceptible to illness, but it takes longer."

"Wait, so how old *are you?*"

"Thirty-three. Don't worry, you're not with an old man."

"Thank God. That would have been awkward."

Fitz laughed, amused with my concern.

"Okay, so Henry's dad is ill much earlier than he should be?"

"Oh aye, and when Henry's ready, he'll relate his dad's tale to you. He was active in the First World War. He was involved in one of the biggest battles in our history. Because of the damage, his body invited illness early. Luckily, what ails him now isn't life-threatening, but moving to a villa overlooking the ocean in Greece is his method of coping."

I'd stumbled into a world far greater than commanding items to fly across the room and hiding my abilities from humans. Reality now involved my body producing flames, slow aging and prolonged life, and a world where silent battles were fought and would never make it onto the pages of human history books. Fitz was first to break the silence.

"You take all of this much better than I expected for someone discovering this world as an adult. Mankind and creatures alike can be pretty hardened by the time we reach adulthood. To discover magic exists and process the details so easily is amazing to me."

"I was born for this life."

CHAPTER EIGHT

W e passed the following morning quietly at Fitz's flat, lazily munching on breakfast, post-meditation. After a taxing day of training, and leaving Henry's late in the evening, rest was in order, and I vowed I wasn't changing out of my pajamas until at least noon, much to Fitz's amusement. With a leisurely morning in, and a brief respite from training, I pushed him for the rest of the story regarding his family's ring, curious about its significance for Esther.

Fitz topped off his coffee and settled onto the couch beside me. "The ring held a lot of power – power that was forbidden. One of our laws states that you aren't allowed to host or harbor a witch's power in an object."

"The reason for that being?"

"Two reasons: taking power from another witch is a heinous act, and it would also make anyone too powerful if they controlled the power of multiple witches. You see how your strength grows in certain areas, and that's only from our energy reacting with one another's. Can you imagine controlling the power of five witches?"

"You'd be unstoppable, which would be especially horrible in the wrong hands."

"Exactly. Esther saw her fate as a young woman, and it haunted her family until their last days. Her parents, aunts, and uncles all channeled their powers into the ring right before their death. Before Esther's capture, her only surviving aunt brought the ring to her. There was nothing Esther could do. All of the parties except one had died, and this woman was left with a big secret and a big responsibility."

"This was their attempt to save her life," I guessed.

"Aye, but the witch on the hunting committee held the power to stunt the release of power from the ring. The risk ended up outweighing the reward for Esther."

"Esther carried the burden of seeing her own death. She sacrificed herself for the benefit of her husband and children, and she faced Fate with dignity," I offered.

"I'd like to honor her by finding that ring."

"What has you worried?"

"You feel that, huh?"

"Of course I do."

"The ring could fall into the wrong hands. Maybe it already has… I think of the evil our kind has battled over the years and wonder if my family's power is being used by the wrong team."

"Yeah, I get that concern. I'd like to help you with your search."

"I'd be grateful, but don't feel obligated."

"I don't feel obligated. You're important to me. Commencing a mission to potentially stop evil and maintain peace amongst witchkind isn't such a bad mission either."

"It does sound rather important, doesn't it?"

"I know you have meetings to prep for, but show me your research later?"

"Sure." He smiled. "Speaking of important things…"

"I'm not going to like what you have to say."

"You ignored Jordan's call again."

"Fitz…"

"I know this is complicated, and I'm not trying to tell you what to do. You wouldn't listen, anyway." He laughed. "You should talk to her. I know you miss her."

"I will. I'm just not ready yet. I don't know how to explain all this."

"Okay. But Hads, she's your best friend. Don't put it off too long."

*   *   *

With Fitz's afternoon schedule full of meetings at the UE, I used the time to pack the last of my belongings neglected in my hotel room. We hadn't spent a night apart since the evening the witch followed me, and well, with us professing our love for one another, it seemed like staying at his place was a natural progression.

I walked halfway through the room before realizing my suitcase was propped open near the window – not where I left it. The maid might have moved it, I reasoned, though I'd declined housekeeping for days. I tiptoed the final distance, holding my breath as I peeked into the bathroom. Unused towels were strewn about the floor and vanity. Not the work of housekeeping, I realized. I assessed the remainder of the room, prepared to shriek and run for the door should I find someone lurking under the bed, or in the closet – I watched one too many horror movies in my youth. I came up empty-handed, and fell onto the bed in relief, allowing my heart rate to steady.

Realizing I forgot my cell on Fitz's coffee table, my eyes scanned each of the misplaced items, committing them to memory. I then tossed my belongings into the suitcase, tugged at the zipper, and made a mad dash for the lobby, a strong wave of anxiety slithering through my body. I rushed through checkout, as the prickle of another witch hung heavily in the air, a warning that I was under watch. Unlike the previous occasions, no witch's glance chilled my back, but though the creature attempted to mask their stare, my third eye still perceived their presence. I paused at the front door, allowing the bellman to load my belongings into the cab. Standing in the cool afternoon light, I sensed an energy shift, and slowly, but surely, an icy chill ran up my spine.

"Very good, here you go."

The bellman opened the cab door, and I slid into the backseat of the taxi, taking the opportunity to follow the trail of energy. A creature stood in the doorway, unmistakably witch, and the chill grew stronger as I met his icy blue eyes. The slamming of the car door did little to dispel my growing anxiety, though I held the witch's gaze firmly, refusing to release him as the cab drove away.

CHAPTER NINE

"Again?" Fitz yelled.

I briefly pondered concealing the incident but recalled there were the pesky little energy streams to consider. Fitz was waiting at home when I arrived. He felt my nerves and was wearing holes in the hardwood as I entered the living room.

"Calm down."

"Really, Hadley?"

"You don't have to yell. You're such a brute when you're pissed."

"That's what this witch is about to find out."

"Oh God," I shot back, the sarcasm dripping heavily below my rolling eyes.

The look he sent in my direction could have killed someone, but he took a deep breath and exhaled slowly, as I stared unfazed in his direction.

"I don't know what the hell they want, and it worries me."

"He."

"What?"

"You don't know what the hell *he* wants."

"You saw him?"

"Yeah, or I saw someone. I can't say for sure it was the same witch all three times, but I definitely think so."

"What did he look like?"

"Tall – maybe mid-thirties? Light brown skin. And blue eyes," I shuddered. "They were this icy, transparent blue. When our eyes met, I felt cold."

"I don't know anyone who fits that description. I'll call my dad and see if he might know him. You and I both felt the truth in Mrs. Cameron when she said it wasn't the council. If this isn't them, then I have no idea who it is."

"Talking with your dad is a good start. We need to figure this out."

"We'll handle it, but for now, maybe you shouldn't be alone unless necessary."

"You think he'd approach me?"

"Maybe. He wouldn't cause a scene in public. If he caught you off guard with no one around, though…" he trailed off, his knuckles white from clenching.

"He was pretty brazen, like he wanted me to see him, but if he had any intention of approaching me, he had his chance."

"Hadley. What are you not telling me?"

I paused, taken aback by the venom in his voice.

"Please," he whispered, squeezing his eyes shut. "Just tell me."

"Someone has been in my hotel room."

Fitz's eyes flew open, though he remained silent.

"I thought maybe it was housekeeping at first. But it wasn't. Someone moved my stuff, threw towels around – I guess to see if I hid anything? And there was a... strange energy in the room."

"So this bastard came into your room."

"It seems that way."

"Seems that way?"

"Well, I don't have hard evidence it was him. It just seems highly likely considering he was watching me."

"I'll kill him."

"You'll do no such thing!"

"Don't you dare defend this creature," he returned, teeth gritted.

"Defending someone is a hell of a lot different than what I just said."

"If we run across him... I can't keep myself from attacking. My instinct will be too strong."

"You'll control yourself. I know you can be smart about this."

"Maybe."

"If he wanted to attack me, he had his chance. I don't know what he's looking for or why he's watching me. But he could've easily confronted me in my room if that's what he wanted."

"You might be right, but if it's all the same to you, I think I'll just be your shadow for a while." He slid his arm around me absentmindedly, pulling me tightly against his chest.

"Fitz," I whispered, warm adrenaline pulsing just under the surface, though the thought of my supernatural stalker was far away.

He answered my call, his lips finding mine, and for the next portion of the afternoon, Fitz demonstrated an ability to make me long for something so badly it hurt. Self-control was morphing into a hard-fought battle for the two of us. After all, we were in love. There would be no irreconcilable differences, no giving up on one another.

And as our species wasn't the waiting around type, I guessed that our relationship would continue to develop quickly, and not only because Fitz needed me physically, although I guess there was that, too, considering we were lying on the ground panting for air. His hand lay firmly on my stomach, riding the rise and fall of my irregular breath.

"You know, we're usually pretty well in control of ourselves, but I honestly don't think I'll survive that again. Remind me why we're trying to take it slow?"

"Oh, some crock about making sure we don't screw this up or something."

"My sentiments exactly."

CHAPTER TEN

hat do you want?”

“Food.”

Henry laughed. We spent the evening in deep discussion around mental transport, as I began my understanding of this ability. Henry wasn't gifted with mental transport but knew a great deal about it. After a fair amount of discussion on the subject, Henry promised Fitz he'd provide training to the best of his ability. He understood Fitz's reluctance to involve another witch in my training, and couldn't help but to acquiesce to the earnest request of his best friend. And so, this chain of events led to us sprawled out in front of a fire in Henry's sitting room, branching into the mechanics of my newfound skill, while I teetered on the verge of so much possibility.

“A girl after my own heart, but I don't think that's going to help us here.”

“Right.” I thought hard. “I want to see Gram.”

“See her right now, or in years past?”

"That's an option?"

"Aye. You can see her now, or you can see her at any point in her past. You have the power for it."

"You have the power for it. I like the sound of that."

"Do you have anything of hers on you?"

"These earrings – my granddad gave them to her when they first married." I tugged at the back and slipped the first earring from my ear.

"Just one is sufficient. Hold it in your hand where you can see it."

"Like this?"

"Perfect. You won't always need an object, but it's helpful when you have it, especially until you're proficient in the craft. Take a few deep breaths and relax."

I followed his instruction and fell into the steady rhythm of breathing.

"You're beginning to relax, but your mind is still tied up in the excitement. Forget everything. Just breathe and listen to my voice."

I closed my eyes and focused intently on my breath, pushing everything else from my mind. This was no different than my regular meditation, I reminded myself. My magic was instinctive, fueled by both need and strong desire. It had no use for frivolous thoughts.

"Good, now open your eyes. Connect with the earring, and tell me what you feel."

"I feel its strength… the ridges from how it's cut. The gold that holds the diamond into place."

"Close your eyes again and ask your witch's eye about the person who created it."

Nothing.

"Let everything else go," Henry prompted, sensing my difficulty.

The darkness faded as I focused, my curiosity taking root, revealing a dim, windowless room, where a jeweler peered through a microscope. A cut jewel lay on the opposite side, ready to be set. My eyes popped open, pulling a smirk from Henry.

"I saw the jeweler. He was looking at the diamond."

"Well done, you!"

Henry requested I navigate to the same vision once more before we moved to my next task. I did so dutifully, my sights set on mastery of another skill.

"Now you'll repeat the process, but I want you to find the day they were sold to your grandfather. Once you're in that vision, ask it to navigate to the time the earrings were given as a gift to your grandmother."

"Got it."

"Don't lose focus. Ask your vision what you want to know — breathe. You have full control over where time takes you. It answers to *you*."

Time revealed a salesman standing behind a jewelry counter filled with rows of gold, silver, and precious stones on an emerald bed of velvet, all of the style my generation called antique. The salesman placed cash into the register while speaking with a handsome man in a navy suit. I knew my young grandfather instantly, having seen his likeness hanging in a frame by Gram's desk for as long as I could recall. He then handed a box topped with a big white bow over to Granddad, who ran his hand nervously through his short, chestnut hair before accepting it.

As he disappeared through the doorway, I asked time for a glimpse of Granddad gifting the earrings to Gram. The edges of my vision blurred, and the darkness grew until it was once again all I could see. I waited quietly, attempting to maintain focus, hoping I hadn't failed. I tore my interest away from the thought, returning to the peaceful nothingness.

Light dawned, and Granddad walked into a room where a woman sat in a satin dress the color of pearls. Her long, auburn hair was curled about her face, which was carefully painted for the festive occasion, her blue eyes bright against her porcelain skin. Gram was beautiful, and I was grateful to catch a glimpse of an event I couldn't imagine if I tried, their wedding photos having been tragically destroyed by fire years ago.

Sure enough, Granddad handed the box to Gram, who opened it slowly, as though she already knew of the precious treasure that lay inside. Once opened, a single tear ran the length of her cheek, and she embraced Granddad tightly. When Gram gifted the set to me, she shared that Granddad was living on a small wage at the time and went without quite a few comforts in order to afford the gift.

I slowly navigated to the present and opened my eyes to

Henry's smiling face.

"How was it?"

"I don't have words... amazing."

"Think you're up for one more tonight?"

"Yes, of course!"

"I don't want to overtax you."

"Henry, you two made me rest for a whole day," I accused, pointing in Fitz's general direction in the adjoining room. "An entire day without magic! I'm going to explode magical energy everywhere if you don't let me do this."

"Fine," he returned, as his hands rose in surrender. "You were telling us earlier about the first time you met Izzy. What if you traveled to that day? You should pick a scene from your own past."

"That's going to be strange."

"To say the least. But you need a recent destination after the last journey. Fitz has the watch Izzy gave him that summer."

He held the item in his open palm, a mischievous grin on his face.

"You sneak."

He passed the watch to me, and I sat motionless for a moment, preparing for another venture in time.

"Focus on what you want. Ask time to take you there."

I clutched the watch tightly and listened for the ripples of time, more aware of the experience than before. After a short span of darkness, I opened my eyes to a summer day in June. Everything was spectacularly clear – giant spruce trees, swaying ferns, the sparkling lake. I took a deep breath, trying not to lose my nerve. Izzy appeared in the distance. And then, my former self. I heard the rise and fall of our voices in conversation as we chattered about school and internships.

I closed my eyes again and asked time to move forward. I stood in my parent's kitchen with Gram. She was setting jam supplies on the counter, clearly anticipating my return. I missed her more than I realized. She narrowed her big, blue eyes in concentration and reached for another mason jar. She was every bit a Southern woman: drawled, charming, and feisty. For as long as I could remember, she wore her hair cropped above her shoulders, warm auburn with sun-kissed strands, a testament to the amount of time she spent in her garden. It amazed me how she never colored her hair, and I hoped to have the same luck at 80.

"How did it go?" Gram asked, as my former self walked through the back door.

"Good. I met one of our new neighbors on the creek. She scared me to death – I heard her splashing around before I saw her."

"Izzy?"

"Yes, ma'am."

"Nice girl, nice family."

"She *was* nice. There was something about her though, that just didn't…"

"Didn't what, honey?" Gram questioned, a coy look on her face.

"This is going to sound stupid, but there's something about

her that just didn't seem quite human. She's too pretty, too graceful – beyond what's humanly possible."

Gram chuckled at my response, but an odd note rested in her laughter.

"What is it, Gram?"

"Oh, nothing. It's a silly thought, but I do know what you mean about them."

"You met the rest of her family?"

"Sure did."

"Did they seem – I don't know – like her?"

"Yes. Both kids were handsome, and how did you put it? Graceful beyond what's humanly possible, and plenty smart, too." With Gram that usually meant they had a quick sense of humor, one of the traits she admired most in a person.

"What about her parents?"

"Smart, funny, both seem pretty successful."

"I wonder what's up with them."

"Maybe nothing, maybe something," she remarked, a twinkle in her eye.

Gram was as superstitious as anyone I'd ever met. There was rarely an old wives' tale or nontraditional remedy she didn't heed and pass along for future reference. As a child, I found it fascinating about her, and as an adult, I found it quirky and endearing.

"I'm going to shower off," I said, pulling my hands through my matted hair. It was a wonder I hadn't been the one to scare Izzy with that tangled mess. "Tanner and I are going into town to meet some friends."

"Sounds good, priss."

I made a break for the stairwell, turning at the last moment.

"Gram… did you mention my name to Izzy?"

"I don't think so. Why?"

"No reason. Oh, I'm riding bikes with Izzy tomorrow."

"That's great, honey."

A man's voice filtered through the front door, and I froze in recognition. Daddy. My thoughts raced around haphazardly, but I knew I wasn't ready to see him – not yet. Tears welled as I asked time to release me back to my rightful place. And as my eyes opened, I was greeted by a face as familiar to me as any other. Fitz wiped away my tears and stood.

"I'll be in the living room while you two finish up."

"Henry?"

"Yes, ma'am?"

"You said you don't have this power. How do you know so much about it?"

He sighed and reached for the nearest bottle of scotch. "Fancy a glass?"

"I'm fine, thank you."

He poured a healthy serving, taking a sip of the amber liquid, and I waited patiently for him to begin. I came to the idea that perhaps I shouldn't pry, and was just about to voice that opinion when he began.

"I haven't talked about this much, but it'll be good to tell you.

My mate, Emily, possessed your ability. I was with her during her training – that's why I know so much about it."

"I haven't heard you mention Emily before," I observed, leaning forward curiously. Neither Henry nor Fitz ever talked about Henry's mate.

"It's not a story with a happy ending. I'll tell you nonetheless if you'd like."

I nodded sheepishly.

"I was thirteen when I met Emily. It's pretty rare, you know? Even for creatures, to find their mate so young, but we were lucky. Emily was beautiful and smart, with a quick, dry wit." He laughed, though without humor. "I was hopelessly in love with her. Our parents let us secretly wed at sixteen. Our family and witch friends celebrated with us, but the humans wouldn't understand, not with our age."

He paused, pulling slowly from the glass.

"We did everything together. Studying, school, traveling. She *loved* to travel, and after we completed secondary school, we took a few years off, traveling and working around the world. We decided to come back to Scotland for uni. Don't get me wrong; things weren't perfect, but we were happy. Then a business trip to Inverness changed everything.

"We made a short holiday of her work trip. We drove up the Friday before and enjoyed the weekend. We were driving home – just outside the city. We were so close." He hung his head quietly, breathing deeply.

I placed my hand on his free one, and he held it firmly for some time, before pressing on.

"A drunk driver hit us. Nasty, drunk pig. Our bodies can withstand a great deal, Hadley. We can push past a lot of human limits, but Emily couldn't do it. He was flying eighty miles an hour down the old lane. He slammed into us, pinning our car between his and a nearby building. Emily and I were both crushed, but she had too much trauma to her head. She died instantly."

"Henry... I am *so* sorry," I whispered. "I am so sorry this happened to you."

"I've been over it time and time again, punishing myself. Convinced there was something I could've done differently. I wish every day I died instead of her. I'll never understand why it had to be her," he paused, a tear rolling slowly toward his jaw.

I could have told him he lived for a reason. How grateful Fitz and I were to have him in our lives, or how Fate gave him a second chance, but none of it would change the fact that Emily was gone. Instead, I wrapped my arms around him, locking us quietly in an embrace, until he found what he wanted to say next.

"I'm sorry."

"What on earth are you apologizing for?" I asked, releasing him.

"You didn't ask me for all that."

"I'm sorry if bringing it up was too much..."

"No, I need to think about it sometimes. It ultimately helps, I think. I need to remember all of it – even the worst part of our story."

"Thank you for telling me about Emily. I'm glad you felt like you could."

"I was a real mess after that. Almost died myself. Broke most of the bones in my body, went into cardiac arrest, was in a coma for two days. I had a long road to recovery, and that was only physically. Mentally was far worse, and I didn't give a shit about anyone for a long time."

"You clearly do now."

"Aye. I was twenty-eight when Emily died. After about a year, I met Fitz. Best thing that could've happened to me. He helped me turn things around, go on to pursue my master's degree, and honestly helped me become the man I wanted to be for Emily."

I smiled. That sounded like Fitz all right.

"I had fifteen years with her. It was too short, but I'll never forget what it's like to love someone with everything in me."

"That's a gift for sure. And to have experienced so much life with her. A lot of beings never have that."

"But you do – and will. There's so much more to come."

"I'm a lucky girl."

"Aye, and Fitz is one lucky bastard. He knows it, too."

It was good to hear Henry laugh again.

Right on cue, Fitz entered the room, embracing Henry in an overly dramatic hug, pulling laughter from us all. We stayed at Henry's late into the evening, talking and laughing in a way that's only possible once you've opened yourself up to each other. I couldn't begin to imagine what a loss like Henry's felt like, but my admiration for him grew. Creatures like him were special – the ones who loved, lost, and found the will to live again after tremendous tragedy, and when we left for the evening, I held Fitz tighter and dearer to me than before.

CHAPTER ELEVEN

"**I** think I found something," Fitz yelled across the room. We practically, or perhaps not so practically, tore apart Henry's attic over the span of three days. I started my new job the following Monday, and we wanted to make some real progress on Fitz's family project before my attention was divided. Between spending most of our time at Fitz's place or over at Henry's, and with Fitz indeed acting as my shadow, we hadn't seen nor felt the snooping witch. As we turned most of our attention to the MacGregor family mystery, Fitz's dad investigated the problematic witch's identity. Divide and conquer, as they said.

With Fitz delving further into his research, his dad sent over all the family records, journals, grimoires, enchanted objects, and the like. And by sent over, I mean that I stood in Henry's attic one afternoon with Fitz and Henry, while the items suddenly materialized in the space. The attic was extensive, and Henry offered right away to house the collection. The three of them felt the collection would be more difficult to locate in Henry's home, should someone come snooping for information on the ring. I expressed concern over such a treasure lying in someone's attic, but Fitz was quick to point out how heavily protected it was.

"There's no reason to worry. This protection spell Dad and I worked up is intricate. It would take someone a considerable amount of time and effort – enough that we'd perceive it. And with the alarm spell, if they ever did crack the code, we'd know immediately."

"Sounds like you've thought of everything."

"Almost."

We worked our way into the middle of a large, wooden chest and discovered Annabel's grimoire and the corresponding 1661 journal wrapped neatly in linen, the fabric alone betraying their age, its color further resembling that of the leather-bound books with each passing year. Esther's aunt, Annabel, was the last living relative in the family pact and gifted the ring directly to her. If Annabel left any details surrounding the protection or summoning spells for the ring, we'd find them in either of the two books.

The oversized leather couch in the sitting room was to be our stage for further investigation of the books, and I bounded down the stairs, happy to leave the drafty attic behind. The sitting room was a bit cool itself, and I extended my arm, tossing flames toward the neatly stacked logs in the fireplace. They burst into a roaring fire, and I sank into the couch wearing a satisfied grin, convinced I'd never tire of fire bursting to life at my fingertips. Though Henry assisted us in tearing through the attic earlier in the day, he drove to town for the evening, giving his housekeeper the night off – meaning Fitz and I would be able to examine the materials undisturbed by Olga, who was sweet but intrusive. As an afterthought, Fitz nodded his head and a bottle of Glenfiddich and two glasses landed on the table in front of us.

"Henry keeps a few bottles around for me. He prefers Bunnahabhain 25 Year, but I find I'm just not that extravagant."

I smiled thinking of Henry's innate taste for the finer things and floated Annabel's grimoire to Fitz's side. In return, a crystal glass landed in my open palm, a thistle pattern distinct against the generous amber pour, and we settled down to the task of solving a mystery. Hours passed, finding us increasingly engrossed in Annabel's writings. She left very specific incantations for her type of magic in the grimoire, and her journal held a fascinating account of life in 17th century Scotland. Although the objective might have been searching for specific spells, we relayed various spells and passages back and forth to one another, feeling no necessity of a deadline.

The fire crackled through the evening, a soft soundtrack to the slow sipping of scotch and the happy conversation of two history buffs combing through 17th-century artifacts. I was reading aloud, as we enjoyed a particularly humorous account of Annabel's conversation with the local butcher, when the next passage caught my attention. It was there I discovered a summary of her experience with passing the magical ring to Esther. The passage was written cryptically, and knowledge of the events was required for the reader to understand the significance.

Took the wee item to E today while H and the bairns were away.

Exceedingly surprised and angry at first, claiming we broke our word and
wronged our brothers and sisters. She refused. I advysed hir of the great sacrifices
we experienced to pass this to hir. Said she would be unable to use this item to hir
benefit at any account. Eventually relented. Showed her P and S.

"P and S... do you think she's referring to the spells?"

"Let's comb through the grimoire, and see what we find," Fitz suggested.

We located Annabel's protection and summoning spells. Each witch has a unique method for casting their own incantations, which can range in complexity and strength. Though magic wasn't always worked through spells, Annabel certainly cast a spell on this occasion. She taught Esther her own spells, in the hopes that only she would be able to access, use, and summon the ring – Esther, and her bloodline. Fitz read the summoning spell aloud.

That which was lost
Soon shall be found
Desire in your heart
Show us here and now.

Flames leapt in the fireplace, and the hair on my neck stood on end. Although no ring appeared in our midst, it was clear the elements understood Fitz's request.

"The elements are responding."

"Aye, it looks like the spell and the elements recognize my blood, but I think something was omitted. Something I need in order to fully access her spell."

"You think Annabel left something out on purpose?"

"I do. She would've been guarded about this — it should have occurred to us sooner that she would make it a little more difficult to find the key."

"May I?"

Fitz placed the grimoire carefully in my open palms, a curious expression on his face. This was intricate and required focus and strength, but my lessons with Henry were going well, and I felt confident. This was the purpose of my magic, after all.

I placed the book on the worn, wooden planks in front of my crossed legs, as Fitz sat quietly on the couch, sensing my need for space. I simply stared at the pages, which were softly illuminated by the nearness of the fire. I felt life within the grimoire, and I drew closer, taking an experimental sniff. I was met by the scent of aged paper and long-dried ink, as I searched for details of the woman who put ink to paper. The scent grew stronger still, and I rode the waves until I found the path I sought. My fingers traced the text, seeking the subtle changes of the page.

The air grew musty and damp, and heavy with smoke, along with the nostalgia of a distant memory. Everything was fuzzy, like I was peering through foggy glass, and I closed my eyes briefly as my sight cleared.

I found myself in a rustic cottage. The walls and flooring were simple wood planks and stone, with visibly rough craftsmanship, though the walls were in good shape. The counters were heavily marked from the wear of sharp knives, the result of repetitive motion over the span of many years. No fridge, no dishwasher, no electricity... I was searching for any sign of modern convenience when a woman emerged from an open doorway. I jumped at her sudden appearance, but my presence didn't register with her.

"I'll be with ye soon enough, Alannah," she barked out over her shoulder. "The mistress will be none the happier for it, either!"

Alannah's companion was a plain, middle-aged woman draped in a simple period dress. Her chestnut hair was adorned with gray, and a severe expression hardened her worn face. As she cleared dishes from the counter into a large wooden bucket, I thought how pleasant her features might be, should she allow even a hint of a smile. But times would be difficult for many people, especially those in her line of work.

"Murdina!" a voice rang through the doorway.

My newfound companion turned quickly on her heel, clamoring out that she would be a moment more. Murdina's eyes then landed in my direction, and as her quick footsteps brought her closer, I held my breath. To my great delight, she walked right through me.

"I actually did it," I exclaimed under my breath. Recalling the events Annabel recorded in her journal, I gazed through the open window at the early morning light. Annabel would prepare for the day in a less trafficked area of the house.

Though simple, the house was larger than I expected, and I wound through several rooms and one lengthy hallway before perceiving hushed voices on the other side of an upstairs door. I proceeded timidly, calculating the odds that I could transport myself through the door. I touched the door softly and asked my magic to deposit me on the other side.

A small but tidy bedroom was brightly lit, the morning sun pouring through the east-facing windows. A large, four-poster bed stood boldly in the middle of the room, covered in thick, wool blankets. My eyes scanned over the few items crammed beside the bed and landed on an oak desk in the far corner of the room. Annabel sat at the desk, deep in discussion with a man I discovered was her husband.

What, is he human? I marveled, my mind immediately ticking through the difficulties involved in a creature-human relationship.

He jumped from his seat, and his brows furrowed angrily, as he stalked out of the room, slamming the door behind him. Annabel's left hand extended toward the ceiling, her journal materializing into her open palm. She set the book gently on the old, wooden surface, and the pages flew open to a blank sheet. Her hair fell loosely past her shoulders, the gray strands not yet smoothed back for the day. I moved closer to peer over her shoulder when my vision dissipated like smoke on the wind, and I was left staring at Fitz.

"No! I was so close."

"You just lost concentration, that's all."

"How long was I gone?"

"Maybe ten minutes."

"Ugh."

"I don't want to break your concentration, but I can hardly wait to know what you've seen."

Miraculously, I returned to where I left off, peering over Annabel's left shoulder. The passage was a few days prior to her encounter of passing the ring to Esther. I was close, but not quite close enough. I closed my eyes, asking my third eye to work with time to guide me forward.

I was sucked into a wind tunnel, billowing around with total loss of control. I once endured a tornado with Gram. We weren't far from her home when the large, swirling funnel appeared on the horizon. We had little time to react, running frantically toward a ditch behind other carloads of people, clinging to the hope that they knew what was best. I'd never forget those few horrifying moments when the elements betrayed us, and large objects flew impossibly through the air. That experience was the closest to which I could akin this moment, but even that didn't feel quite sufficient.

When the wind died down, my sight was restored, and I watched Annabel gather her belongings. Excitement coursed through my veins, as I followed her into the streets of Forfar, Scotland – circa 1661.

CHAPTER TWELVE

Annabel made her way down the dirty path, which was lined with horse dung and the contents of chamber pots, one of the less appealing attributes of the time. Annabel's narrow lane was soon behind us, and we strolled down the main thoroughfare of town, greeted by the sounds of a marketplace in full swing. Though she spoke to very few, Annabel was watched by all she encountered – merchants, housewives, children, and even other witches regarded her path through the busy street, and while some made eye contact, many observed her progress only after she passed them. Fitz's family was well known by the small town's human population and even watched by other witches, who undoubtedly knew the witch-hunt was coming for Esther. The sight provoked a fresh wave of gratitude for the lack of human observance in modern times.

Annabel, though simply dressed, was vibrant against the crowd, and held that of a stately appearance – the woman demanded respect. Her gray hair was pulled firmly into what must have been the style of the time, and she held that towering mass high, meeting the gazes of others unabashedly. Annabel turned down a wide lane lined with trees, and eventually made her final steps toward what I hoped was Esther's home. A lengthy, two-story building lay ahead. It could've been a string of townhomes found in modern times, albeit a little rustic for our era. But they appeared sturdier and cleaner than the area around Annabel's home, everything recommending this row as a more affluent area away from the main street of town.

A thick, arched wooden door swung open to reveal a large foyer, and the young servant girl stood aside allowing Annabel to pass into the grand, open space. The girl didn't speak, though her doe eyes flitted timidly back and forth to observe Annabel as she closed the door. She then signaled for Annabel to follow her, allowing me the opportunity to view Esther's home. The height of the space was the span of two floors, and a balcony emerged from the stairwell, stretching the length of all four corners of the room, revealing several doorways – almost as many as the ground floor. The room was mainly comprised of wood and stone, and though each had the rustic appearance of a medieval time, the masonry and carpentry work were of good quality, the materials of the space all working together seamlessly and in harmony.

A sizable tapestry suspended from the second floor's vaulted ceiling, laying flat against the far wall, the soft, faded colors indicating a family crest, sure to have served as a symbol of family loyalty for many generations. I wondered if the tapestry was recently added to the decor, or had it hung openly in defiance of the king's orders against the MacGregors for some measure of time? Stag antlers further decorated the solid, wooden half-wall of the balcony, and tables and chests alike were strewn against the backdrop of stone walls, made from the same deep wood that constructed the stairwell and balcony. Esther's home was well-kept, and I wondered how many generations of Fitz's family called these walls home before Hamish and Esther came to know them.

A lady's maid walked Annabel into the sitting room without hesitation, where she received a warm greeting from Esther. Esther was beautiful, and I discerned both expressions and features I recognized from Izzy's fair skin, emerald eyes, and auburn hair. She was too ethereal to be human, and I was sure many a plain housewife in the small community found resentment in it.

"Dearest Aunt, I feared ye would never return."

"Och aye. Same as I, truth be told."

"Well, it's a joyous day now that ye've returned."

"It is always a pleasure to return home."

"Do take a seat."

Annabel looked down at her hands, an uneasy countenance washing over her. "Ye ken, my business that took me away, it was of a delicate nature."

"Oh, aye?" Esther asked as she poured a dram of whisky, handing it over to Annabel.

"Aye, and I must speak to ye about it."

Esther nodded slightly, her eyes narrowing in curiosity.

"As ye are aware, your parents and the family have endured

torturous thoughts and visions, finding no rest even in sleep, even in death…"

"Aunt."

"Hear what I have to say, Esther."

"We struck an accord, or have ye forgotten? We are never to speak of these things."

"I remember well, child. Do not think because my body ages that my memory ages in turn."

"Why do ye trouble me then?"

"I have good reason, and ye must hear it."

"Make it brief. Hamish will return soon. I'll not trouble his mind today."

"With your parents conceiving ye at such advanced ages, they believed they would surely die before your vision came to fruition, and as such, they entrusted a grave task to me," Annabel fumbled along.

Esther shifted in her seat, taking a deep breath, but allowed Annabel to continue uninterrupted.

"Child, I do not speak of the past to harm ye, but to tell of our burden and our cause."

Esther nodded wordlessly.

"Before their deaths, your parents called each of the living family forth and held council to consult on what could be done to prevent your early death. Each side of your family was heavily represented, as ye must ken that we each wanted to protect ye, my dear."

"I had no knowledge of this council."

"Oh, certainly not. It was arranged with great secrecy and maintained in such."

"When did this pass?"

"Some fifty years ago."

"Who still living knows of this?"

"Only I and your Uncle John."

"What came of this council?"

"We convened for days upon days. We considered any and every course of action. Somewhere in the deep of night, an idea emerged."

Annabel fidgeted slightly. This was it.

"This idea… this is why ye've come."

"Aye."

"I won't like it."

"Ye won't, but there's no helping it. What's done is done."

Annabel leaned forward slightly, looking Esther in the eye, before proceeding. "Your own excellent parents wrestled with the idea, but in the end, there was nothing else to be done, and each of us would risk more than this to save ye."

"Aunt, what have ye done?" Esther asked, her voice barely audible.

Annabel reached into her pocket and removed an object neither of us could yet see. "Open your hand."

Esther obeyed, though slowly, just as a small, shiny object caught the sunlight and fell into her waiting grasp.

I instinctively ran my fingers over the moonstone on my own hand, considering the items were practically identical. My mind raced. How did Fitz procure my ring? With the similarities, it couldn't be a coincidence. Tearing my focus from my own finger, I gazed upon the horrified face of Esther.

She looked from the ring that lay in her grasp to her aunt, before dropping the item to the floor. "Ye have brought great shame to this family!" Esther yelled, making no attempt to conceal her anger.

"Esther, my child."

"No, do not attempt to justify these perverse actions."

"Ye are too harsh. Hear what I have to say."

"This is a crime! I won't let my husband and bairns take part in the blame for this. They have endured enough."

"They don't have to endure any more suffering."

"What are you saying, Aunt?" Esther questioned as she paced the room, walking off her violent energy.

"Hear what I have to say," Annabel responded softly, pointing toward Esther's seat.

After a moment's hesitation, Esther followed her instruction.

"Ye say this is a crime, and though that may be true, the law does not always dictate what is right. These humans have done a great evil to our kind. They fear the unfamiliar, but fear does not justify killing the innocent. Ye have done no wrong, no evil to them. Ye, who are blameless, do not deserve to be put to the death, child. As such, your aunts, uncles, and your own parents have placed their powers into this object."

"Surely not yours, as well?"

"No, I have not yet done so. My death before your capture wasn't foretold, but I'll forfeit my power to this ring before ye are taken."

"Ye will do no such thing."

Annabel stooped to pick the ring up from the floor.

"Dearest niece, what is foretold is wrong, but we have provided a path to fight this evil. We will alter the future; we will make it right."

"We could yet suffer dire consequences changing the future in such a way."

"Perhaps. What would ye have us do? Would ye not do the same for your own bairns?"

Though their arguments continued, Esther finally accepted the ring, promising to keep it safe – though she never committed to utilizing its power. When Annabel argued that it was the dying wish of Esther's parents, Esther broke, unable to reject the ring or her parents' energy. Fighting the humans' bloodlust was a worthy cause, and Esther eventually admitted the truth in that. Although Esther would ultimately refuse to utilize the enchanted object, I wondered if her family's power gave some measure of comfort to Esther in her final weeks.

As the initial shock passed, Annabel continued her mission, giving instruction to Esther on utilizing the ring. I wasn't sure I heard correctly at first, but Esther repeated the words back to Annabel.

That which was lost
Shall soon be found
Desire in your heart
Ignite with the moon
Bring the ring
Here and now.

"I only need to alter the word moon?"

"Aye, my child. As ye ken, my powers draw strength from the moon. Yours, from the earth. Alter only this word, and the right to summon is yours. Let's have a try, shall we?"

Annabel tapped the ring, muttering unintelligible words under her breath, resulting in its sudden disappearance. "Proceed."

Esther held up her palms and Annabel's incantation escaped her lips, just as Fitz had done over 350 years later, and about an hour into *my* past – whether it was mental or physical, time travel was a strange concept.

Without ceremony, the ring materialized in Esther's open palm.

I could've easily lost myself for hours with these women, but it was time to return to the future… or the present, as it were. With my research complete, I envisioned Henry's sitting room. I thought of Fitz's anxious face and my desire to be with him once again.

The heat of a nearby fire warmed my face, and the familiar scent of scotch welcomed me back to the present.

"I know what to do," I whispered.

CHAPTER THIRTEEN

We sat by Annabel's grimoire, and Fitz's hunger for knowledge was palpable, but there was one question I needed to clear up first.

"Esther's ring looks just like the one I wear."

"It's a replica."

"How do you know what the ring looks like?"

"I don't know firsthand, but had it made based on a vision of my aunt's. Her mind's eye saw the ring, and she sketched it for us. That sketch is somewhere up in the attic actually."

"Why did you give this to me?"

"Because I knew you were my mate when I met you."

"What does that have to do with Esther's ring?"

"Hads, I'd risk everything to keep you safe, just like Esther's family did for her. It seemed a proper gift, especially in light of our circumstances at the time."

I squeezed his hand and focused on my recently acquired

knowledge, ready to relay everything. Fitz's powers were fueled by the earth, just as Esther's. He repeated the modified incantation, and as the last word escaped his lips, the fire again roared. This time the ground rumbled, and the lights flickered, though yet again, no ring appeared.

Fitz worked the spell several times, the fire flaring higher, the ground shaking harder, and the lights flickering longer with every attempt. Although the elements yielded a greater response, the ring remained to be seen. Fitz sighed, turning to me.

"Are you sure you saw this correctly?"

"Of course, I'm sure."

"Don't be snippy. It was only a question."

"Only a question. Your tone speaks volumes."

"What tone?" he quipped, the tone in question still lingering in his voice.

I arched my eyebrow but remained silent.

"I don't mean to sound frustrated with you. I'm disappointed this isn't working."

I slid my arms around his waist. "We're going to figure this out. It's not you. Your words are exactly as Annabel taught Esther."

Fitz nodded, his face pensive.

"Would I be able to use the spell, even though I'm a different bloodline?"

"The spell might work; it's less likely outside our bloodline, but possible. Although, the spell might recognize you since we're mates."

"How about I try? It'll at least help us narrow down what's going on."

"Good idea."

I repeated the words just as Fitz and Esther before me, substituting air, the element from which I draw my magical strength. As the last word escaped my lips, an expensively furnished room materialized. Apparently, I wasn't able to call forth the ring, but perhaps the ring summoned me instead.

I searched for any sign I'd been there before, but the room was unfamiliar. Dark gray walls spanned the space, and several large paintings popped brightly against the deep color. I crossed the worn hardwood floors, curious about the maps hanging from the opposite wall, hoping they would lend some clue on my location. The largest map was a rendering of Europe dated 1648, along with a smaller map of 1600 Scotland and a 1650 version of Forfar and its surrounding area. Wondering if I remained in Scotland, I turned seeking other clues.

Two oversized, mahogany chairs and a matching table were positioned in a corner of the room. Letters were strewn on the surface of the table, all addressed to Dr. Belmonte. I sifted through the items, not even certain what I was seeking, but as I lifted the final letter, an audible gasp escaped my lips. Esther MacGregor's magical ring lay at the center of the surface, glimmering in an effort to be discovered. My hand reached for it hungrily, but I was met by an invisible force, sending a small shock through my fingertips.

The ring was enchanted and by someone's magic outside of

Fitz's family. Though I tried, nothing would grant me access to the magical item, and there was precious little I could do about that. There was little I could do with the ring without my physical presence anyway, but if I wasn't able to secure the ring, I could at least continue my search around the room.

I was unable to open either door in the room, nor was I able to transport myself to the other side, and I was confident that whoever Dr. Belmonte was, they understood the treasure in their possession. The thought stopped me in my tracks, wondering if a witch so powerful would detect I had been in the room. If only I could see outside or into the hallway, maybe I could learn a little more about where I was. I scanned the room yet again, hoping I missed something in my initial search. I considered it odd that the room had no window, but no sooner did the thought cross my mind, then a window appeared. I tossed open the curtains to find a mountain range just beyond a small valley. The range was impressive, answering my earlier question. I might be gazing upon the Alps, but surely not Edinburgh.

Turning from the spectacular view, another map caught my eye. Rather than having overlooked it the first time, instinct whispered that the enchanted room chose what to reveal, and when. To my great surprise, a map of the Olympic National Park in Washington State hung from the wall and was covered in red ink. By studying the markings, I understood which area Dr. Belmonte was most interested in – a large, red "x" marked the High Divide Trail, which wasn't far from my mom's home. There was no indication of what might be found along the trail, and having spent a considerable amount of time there, I was at a loss. I committed the details to memory and combed over the room one last time, before asking my powers to deposit me in Henry's home.

I first saw Henry, who was waiting alongside Fitz for my spirit to return to my body. In my excited state, I practically choked on my words while relaying the details of my adventure, describing the room and the great power holding the ring in place.

"You actually saw the ring?" Fitz questioned. The light in his eyes was enough to draw a wide smile across my lips. He committed a lot of time to finding the item, with the knowledge that he might never discover what he sought. Here was his answer after years of research – and I could feel bursts of his excitement in my own breast. "I can't believe we finally have a lead on its whereabouts."

"It was exciting. I just hope this name leads us somewhere. I could find my way back to the room, but if I can't open the desk drawers or exit the room, I think we're at a standstill."

"Most of the maps were of Scotland, you said?" Henry asked.

"One of Europe, one of Scotland, and one of Forfar. All were dated from the 17th century and at least looked like original drawings. The good doctor is clearly interested in the time period when the ring was created."

"And Forfar," Fitz added. "That's where the ring was certainly forged, but I just can't make sense of it – surely they wouldn't have extracted it from the 17th century."

"We have to consider that possibility," Henry returned. "Just because it shouldn't be done, doesn't mean that they didn't do it, mate. We don't know what type of creature this is."

"I think we need to keep in mind that there was an Olympic National Park map, too. The others were a bigger focus, but something about it is tugging at me."

"You know the area well, aye?" Henry asked.

"I can't even count the number of long weekends and summer camping trips I took with my parents in the area when I was growing up. My mom lives by a lake in the park."

I almost said *my parents*. Would it ever get any easier?

Fitz slipped a hand onto my shoulder. "Henry, it's close to where Hadley and I first met."

"Your parents have the lake house there?"

"Right."

"Have either of you been to the trail?"

"Yes, of course, but I don't remember anything out of the ordinary," I began, trying to recall any useful details. "The trail is pretty long. I think eighteen miles or something like that —diverse terrain."

"I think it's worth our notice," added Fitz. "Hads, try to think on it further and see if anything odd comes to mind."

"Fitz, show me the spell you've been using."

Fitz performed the summoning spell, the elements answering in the same frustrated manner as before.

"Well, it's apparent the elements are irritated. Someone definitely has the wee thing under a potent protection spell, just as

Hadley speculated."

"That means they've been waiting on someone to call the ring. Do you think this person knows who we are?" Fitz wondered.

"Not necessarily. But they realize this power can be called forth by someone, and are either using the ring for their own purposes or buying time until they figure out how to tap into its power. The incantations Annabel used are strong; not just any old bloke could hack into that power."

"Okay, so let's start researching this creature, cross-reference Scotland, Forfar, and Washington State, and see what we can come up with," I added.

"Aye," Henry agreed. "Great work, Hadley. You'll make one powerful witch yet."

"Be careful what you wish for."

CHAPTER FOURTEEN

Between preparing for my move and researching Dr. Belmonte, the days passed quickly. I was lucky on the move front. My mom volunteered to oversee the process in the States, and I only needed to collect my belongings on the east side of the pond. My mom always loved a project, but after Daddy died, they became somewhat of a saving grace for her – something she could pour all her attention into. With that business settled, my next task was finding a place to live in Edinburgh. Fitz casually mentioned his adjoining neighbor was moving out, having accepted a new job in Glasgow.

"I could contact the realtor about renting… or purchasing."

"Fitz, I can't afford a place in your building."

"Of course you can. We need to get your banking information to the council for deposits, plus the government will help you sort out wherever you want to live."

"Excuse me?"

"So, you don't live in the world you think you do. Your entire human life has been a lie. Yaddy yada yada."

"Be serious!"

"Humans, as a whole, don't know about us, but the leaders of their countries sure do. They understand secrecy is imperative, meaning there's a specific branch of their administration that carries out business with witchkind. Only their highest levels of leadership are aware of our existence."

"What ensures their secrecy?"

"The knowledge that almost every country in the world has an agreement with us, so they don't need to make enemies. We could take down an entire nation if we so choose. If they blow our secret, our Cardinal Court – the highest court in our government – could have it ordered to take them out. It's a pretty compelling reason to be discreet."

"My God. I guess I really don't live in the world I thought I did. But how does this affect my bank account?"

"Each country funnels money into secret accounts that fund the supernatural within its borders. So, you'll essentially be funded by lovely Great Britain." He paused briefly. "I told you Henry's father was involved in the First World War. And I mentioned how I think the council wants something from us – we're occasionally asked to support our country and our government with our talents. It's rare in times of peace for regular citizens to be called into any major action, but every once in a while it's warranted."

I was astonished.

"Countries vary in the amount they funnel, depending on their economic state and how many witches live within their borders. You'd be amazed at what else your tax dollars fund, but we won't even broach that subject today."

"My head is already bursting with information."

"Right. So, the money is basically keeping you on retainer. But if we're ever needed, they won't hesitate to ask."

"That seems kind of… scary?"

"Aye. It's one of the reasons I'm worried about Cameron's reaction to us. I've thought a lot about it since our meeting. I think she already knew about my power. Yours took her by surprise, a bit. But that gleam in her eye…"

"I can't wrap my head around this."

"It'll take some time to feel normal, but eventually, it will – even the scary parts."

"What is it?" I questioned, his nerves present in the pit of my stomach.

"So, how do you feel regarding an inquiry on my building?"

"Sounds great."

Fitz looked surprised by my enthusiasm.

"Look, first of all, after all the council put us through, I'll take that money and find myself a nice place to live. No qualms there. And secondly, why wouldn't I want a place by yours?"

Fitz smiled, shaking his head softly.

"Are you ever going to stop being surprised I want to be near you?"

"Absolutely not. I'm beginning to think someone bewitched you. How else can I explain it?"

"Explain what?"

"You're intelligent, powerful, stunning, and funny," he rattled off, a mischievous twinkle in his eyes. "What are you doing with me unless it's bewitchment? Oh, God… or pity. I'd like to think it's bewitchment myself. At least it makes for a more romantic story."

I pulled him closer to me. "Hmmm… And besides the fact that you have the body of a Norse legend, intellect, *and* humor. Let's also not forget for some unbeknownst reason you failed to mention the power you possess is beyond reasonable."

Fitz shot me a questioning glance.

"Yeah," I responded roughly. "I didn't need Cameron to tell me you're powerful, and she doesn't even know the half. You better believe I can feel your power. You've been holding back around me… a lot."

"Rule number one: never fully expose yourself when dealing with a vixen."

"A vixen, am I?"

I asked the air to close the final gap between us, and it silently responded, pressing Fitz's body against mine.

"*Very* nice, Hadley."

"Shhh…" I placed my finger across his lips. He proceeded to kiss my finger slowly, before brushing his lips along my arm. As he reached the tender skin between my neck and shoulder, I released a satisfied sigh. In the past several weeks, I discovered a completely new world full of wonderment, but at that moment, the only marvel on my mind was calling Fitz undisputedly mine.

* * *

Later that afternoon, Fitz made a coffee run while I returned to the mysterious room where the ring lay just outside my grasp. Since I was summoned by the ring, I was uncertain if I'd traveled in time or the present, meaning I would rely solely on instinct, trusting the ring and my magic to guide me back. We moved Annabel's grimoire and journal to Fitz's flat, as it became increasingly difficult for me to be apart from them. Henry said he'd seen it before with Emily – items used as a catalyst by spirit travelers would become a part of them. It often meant the individual would have need of the item again, so I kept the books nearby, anticipating that moment.

I set the grimoire on the table and began Annabel's summoning spell. A large map of Europe materialized… and then a room with dark gray walls. I crossed the room quickly, anxious to discover if the ring still lay on the table. My sigh of relief disturbed the deafening quiet, though I still couldn't grasp the enchanted object.

After practicing my opening skills – or break-in skills as I called them – over the previous couple of days, I was ready to unlock Dr. Belmonte's sealed desk drawers. I sank into the rolling chair and placed my hands on the desk. Mental transport was such a strange experience. Though my body wasn't physically in the room, my hands felt as though they truly touched the desk, and my feet perceived the imperfections of the wooden planks on the floor. I ran my fingers across the cold surface of the desk, lingering along the coarse grains of the wood, allowing my mind to connect deeper with the elements.

Its life began in a lush, green forest with innumerable trees, alive with untouched vitality, and I watched as men cut the trees and hauled them to a mill. The tree became lumber, and the lumber was then worked into furniture, before a young woman stained and sealed the desk, crafting it into a finished product. And finally, a staggeringly handsome man bought the desk and brought it home. His olive skin and dark eyes were perhaps Italian, and though his physique was lithe, it was also chiseled and strong. This would be Dr. Belmonte, I reasoned.

Though Dr. Belmonte was handsome, something ominous rested in his features, and the longer I watched him, the more uncomfortable I became. Adrenaline coursed wildly through my system, and anxiety rested in the pit of my stomach. I momentarily rested my mind, contemplating my next move, before closing my eyes once more. I waited patiently, borrowing knowledge from the elements, asking them for the intelligence of what passed in this room.

Dr. Belmonte spent countless hours writing in code, making indecipherable calculations, and hiding his work within the desk. His voice sounded in my ear, imparting words that would open the drawers. I took a mental record of the spell, allowing the vision of Dr. Belmonte to dissipate, and promptly recited my new prize. To my delight and *amazement,* four soft clicks fractured the silence, each of the locks unbolting themselves, and I tugged at the top drawer.

But before I could look through the drawer, I froze. The click of another lock disturbed my progress. I returned the desk to its former state, and jumped from the chair, just as the door swung open to reveal the man I'd begun investigating. He locked the door and tried the handle, ensuring no one else could access the room. Dr. Belmonte crossed the space decidedly, though looking distractedly around him, before taking a seat in the chair I vacated only seconds before. He called for the locks to open and pulled at the bottom drawer. I was blanketed in a false sense of security, believing I'd escaped his notice, but suddenly, Belmonte slowly cocked his head in my direction, a slight smile rolling across his parted lips.

"I can feel you, spirit traveler. I know you're here," he stated plainly, as if he were offering to pick up the check for coffee. "I may not know why you're here or who you are, but I will find out. No one enters my home without my permission, not even someone who smells as lovely as you. Make no mistake, I'll know you when we cross paths again."

CHAPTER FIFTEEN

B elmonte leaned back in his chair and placed his arms behind his head, waiting for my next move. After a moment's internal debate, I returned home.

"Hadley!"

"What is it?" I mumbled, struggling to regain consciousness.

"Thank God. Are you okay?"

"Of course I'm okay. What's your problem?"

"My problem is I left to pick up coffee and returned to find your limp body uninhabited, white as a ghost, and perspiration on your forehead. You scared the hell out of me."

"Crap, I'm sorry. I didn't mean to do that. It's just that when I found the room again, I was finally on to something…"

"It's okay, take your time."

"I figured out how to open the desk drawers, which was exciting, but then I was interrupted by Dr. Belmonte. Fitz, he couldn't see me, but he knew I was in the room. I mean, he didn't know it was *me*, but he knew someone was there."

Fitz held me, listening quietly until I related the chain of events.

"He said he could *smell* me. How is that even possible?"

"That's odd. It was only your spirit there. Maybe he just wanted to freak you out by saying something creepy like that."

"Well, it worked."

"Hey, you don't have any reason to fear him. You know why?"

I shook my head.

"Because I'll never let anyone hurt you. And more importantly, you're a fiery, strong, mesmerizing witch. No one can mess with you unless you let them."

I sensed the truth in his words... he believed in me, which counted for something. "Well, let's get that coffee in our system. I want you to help me run through a few things this afternoon."

"There's my girl."

*   *   *

I sat on the edge of the bed that evening while Fitz showered, reflecting on the many changes that occurred over the past couple of years. I tried not to think of the past too often – following my therapist's advice that it was healthy to process grief – but it wasn't healthy to dwell on loss. With all that occurred since Paris, it became difficult not to think about the summer I met Fitz, and in doing so, I realized there were a lot of memories I repressed in the deep recesses of my mind.

For roughly nine months, I felt like I lost everything. I lost my dad. I basically lost Fitz. I gained a career, but at times, I felt I paid the ultimate price for it. I wanted to feel wholeheartedly that my experiences made me stronger, that they shaped the witch I became for the better, and there had been no right or wrong decision to make. I made my dad happy in his last couple of years. And Fitz came back to me. As my head sank onto the soft pillow, I allowed my mind to return to a day I tried to forget for a long time. I closed my eyes, allowing the onrush of pain… but also the happiness of seeing Daddy's face again.

*   *   *

November 22, a date I'll never forget. My dad fell in the hallway, unable to stand, and we helped him to the bedroom. The chemo dragged on for months, the promise of it extricating the cancer turning to ash in our mouths. After each treatment, Dad felt increasingly weak for the following few days, my own mental strength withering with him, though I couldn't give up – my hope wasn't yet gone. After all, my dad was a pretty tough guy, and growing up with him was a splendid adventure. We spent countless days on the trails, chasing the mystique of the mountains. He always split our own firewood and could fix anything that broke around the house. As a child, I was convinced he could do anything, and I'm not so sure I don't still believe that.

But on November 22, I acknowledged for the first time how completely helpless I felt. I noticed the change of expression on his face, how his features seemed less bright and his skin no longer vibrant. I hadn't really appreciated the hollowness of his face, the loss of his beautiful, dirty blond hair, and how his thick, athletic figure was wasting away. His structured jawline and gray eyes were the only familiar features I recognized in this foreign face.

Once we settled him into bed, he was too weak to get up on his own, the previous treatment claiming too much life from him. His joints ached, he couldn't keep any food down, and my entire world was crashing all around me. Mom, Gram, and I rotated sitting with him, helping him out of bed as needed, and procuring anything that might make him more comfortable.

"I need you to make a promise to me."

"Anything."

"You can't tell Tessa and Aden how sick I am today."

"Dad..."

"I'm serious. They're so busy right now, and Tessa just got that new promotion. It's hard enough watching you worry, but you're here. They can't be here right now, and I don't want them feeling guilty for that." He leaned over in pain, even the act of conversation taking its toll on his energy, but I knew better than to tell him to rest. The man had always done just as he damn well pleased.

"Dad, you always put yourself last, but now isn't the time for that. Their managers would understand."

"I know you can't understand this now, but everything your mom and I have done from the moment we knew we were expecting the first one of you kiddos has been for you. Every decision with our home, our careers, our lifestyle... it's all been for you. Y'all are my life's work. Having any of you put your lives on hold for me would be the opposite of what I've wanted for y'all for the past thirty-one years."

I was debating heavily on career decisions for post-grad school, but while kneeling beside my dad that afternoon, I knew if I stayed in Washington rather than take the job offer in Boston, I'd not only let my father down, but I'd actually take away from any happiness he had while battling this monster. It was with renewed purpose that evening that I faced the soft glow of my laptop, replying to the offer that changed the course of my life.

After discussing the offer with him, he told me I needed to take it. I'd never seen him more proud of me, and he told me it would give him something to work toward.

"I'm going to get better, and this gives me something to look forward to, Pumpkin. I'm going to come see you in Boston. We'll have a blast."

In the next couple of months, he rallied, and we all felt real hope again. He somehow convinced my mother to drive him across the country in their camper, along with my sister, Tessa. The doctors advised against it. My mom fretted the entire trip. I nearly had a stroke over it. It took them two weeks because my mom worried about him being on the road. But Dad was extraordinarily happy, sitting in my living room, a wide mischievous grin highlighting his features.

His miraculous turn continued for a couple of months but declined quickly last December. And that was that. He never healed. I never actually showed him Boston. We mourned beside his casket last January. But he made it to Boston because he was my dad, and he intended to be a man of his word.

CHAPTER SIXTEEN

"Your affinity for fruit-infused water is unlike anything I've ever seen," Fitz observed one evening after work. I grabbed my cucumber water and met him on the couch.

"I like to hydrate. Lay off."

"You seem like you're really in your element lately."

"I feel good, and although I owe a huge portion of that to my magic, being back at work is definitely a factor, too."

"You love what you do."

"Yeah, my career has been a bit of a lifeline over the past couple of years. It felt like something constant and reliable when I wasn't finding much of that elsewhere."

"Losing your dad was traumatic for you. I know how close you two were."

"We had so much in common. I think he understood all of my strangeness in a way that few people could."

"That's a pretty special thing."

"You know, I resented my career right after his death because I felt like I missed too much in the end. I felt conflicted about the decisions I made because, my dad... he…" I paused, searching for the right words. I had only said the words aloud a few times, and it still felt like I was talking about someone else's life.

"He passed away, and then you felt robbed by your career."

"Yeah, but then I remembered how much joy it gave him to see me advancing in life. It would have broken his heart if I gave that up, and then my career became one way to honor him. Spending time on the trails was another way to do that. When I'm out on the trails, I remember all the time we spent hiking together. It helps me feel closer to him again."

"Hadley, I'm so sorry."

"Thank you."

"I wasn't quite honest with you back in Paris when you mentioned your dad's passing. I didn't stay away. I came to the funeral home."

"You what?"

"I did. I needed to see you, to do what I could to help you. But I never made it inside." He laughed without humor. "I was stopped, literally reaching for the door handle. I even saw you in there," he paused, clearing his throat. "I'm sorry I couldn't be there."

I scooted closer and placed my hand on his.

He held onto it tightly, a flurry of sadness and regret floating through our connection.

"I know it's not your fault. What happened?"

"A few of my father's colleagues showed up. They'd foreseen my decision and were waiting to see if I would actually go in or if I'd change my mind. When I reached for the handle, one of them called my name."

"I still don't understand all of this."

"Right, cause it's bullshit."

"What did they say?"

"That it was better for you if I kept out of your life until we knew for sure your powers would fully develop. They said unless there's a damn good reason, humans shouldn't know about us, so we can't get close to anyone who might develop any sort of attachment to us."

"I don't like that the council tries to dictate who we love. Just look at our situation – it was pointless. They were dead wrong about us. Why do they do this?"

"As long as it isn't a human, they don't care. They're terrified about our secret getting out." His expression darkened.

"Do you think they're right about that?"

"Honestly… I understand a part of their worry. And at the same time, I don't. Humans are unpredictable. I understand the council's fear of them, but you can't control other creatures and who they love. They were wrong about us – that's a fact."

"I don't understand why they were worried enough about the two of us that they showed up at my dad's funeral? Or why they expended so much time and energy on us. I just don't understand why one relationship bothered them so much."

"They *really* want me to follow in my father's footsteps. I need to be the kind of creature who adheres to the rules for that to happen. Which is why our situation thoroughly pissed them off. I think it's also why they're letting things go so easily."

"But that isn't what you want."

"Doesn't matter. They haven't forced anything yet, but I've had a feeling for a long time that it'll all come to a head one day. Now I'm sure of it."

I squeezed his hand. "Well, if it happens, we'll handle it. We're in this together – no matter what."

Fitz kissed my forehead, his eyes tightly shut. The council made him nervous, but together we could face anything. We'd already faced so much.

"Okay, so back to the funeral."

"Aye. So, according to them, I let things go a little too far at the lake."

"They figured out it was a relationship between us."

"They wanted me to leave and allow Dad and Izzy to finish the observation after I felt our connection. The council expected I'd try to see you again if you went through a major trial, either before your powers developed or even if they didn't."

"Well, they were right about one thing, then."

"They knew I couldn't help it, the bastards."

"They knew we'd eventually do what we've done."

"Yeah, they suspected we'd get ourselves in trouble."

"So, what happened at the funeral? You realized you couldn't come in?"

"I was worried about making a scene, and that couldn't happen – certainly not at your dad's wake. They reiterated the reasons to keep my distance and told me to be patient, to let things run their course. It was harder to walk away from the funeral home than it was to let you walk out of my house for Boston, and I thought that was going to kill me."

"Thank you."

"For?"

"For trying to be there. For being honest with me about how you felt and what happened."

"It feels good to talk about it. Plus, it felt like something you should know."

"January is *not* our month. I had my struggles. Maybe you already know that."

"I was careful with you. I wouldn't have seen any of your intimate struggles… if anything seemed too invasive, I let Izzy take over. She wouldn't share anything with me I didn't need to know."

"Thank you for respecting me."

He smiled.

"I couldn't understand our connection, having no idea things like this even existed, but I did know there was something abnormal between us. At first, I thought I was going crazy… the connection was too strong to deny it. That day in the barn…"

"When we shocked one another."

"Yep. I mean, things didn't seem normal before, but after

that day, I knew something was going on between us."

"You're *really* observant. I knew you realized something was going on."

"It only fueled my curiosity. Along with the fact that I fell for you so quickly. I felt like my feelings were too strong. I knew there was some sort of connection beyond what I could even understand."

"I wanted to tell you everything. You know we're not made to keep secrets from one another. When we find that person we have this connection with, there's no holding back."

"I can see that and understand it now." I paused, finding the courage to tell him the one thing that no one else knew about me.

"The moment I left the lake, I began to feel uneasy. Like something was missing, like my gut was telling me something was wrong. By the time I reached Boston, I felt a bit of hysteria over it, and I can vividly remember sitting on the plane on the tarmac, waiting to exit, and feeling like my stomach was flipping.

"I wondered if I was just nervous to move so far from home and leave my parents on the other side of the country, especially with my dad being so ill, and I know there was some level of that. But I couldn't get you out of my head. I kept seeing your face, and I felt like I was missing something only you gave."

Fitz's heartbeat raced through our streams.

"The first night in my new apartment, I was brushing my teeth when I was seized with hysterics. I basically fell on the bathroom floor and couldn't catch my breath. It was absolute panic and fear, which was only multiplied when I couldn't figure out why it was happening. Everything felt wrong. I was so worried about you."

"I'm so sorry." Fitz's face was downcast, but it wasn't my intention to make him feel bad about the past. I knew he struggled, too.

"Fitz, this is not your fault. I'm not telling you this to make you feel bad – I just feel like I have to share it. Everything is okay now."

"No wonder Izzy clammed up when I asked how you were sometimes. I would have this anxious feeling take hold, and I'd ask her to check on you. She always said you were fine – stressed about some big decision – but she never told me any of this. She knew I'd take the next flight out."

"I can see that this timeline was right. Izzy did the right thing."

"She's a pretty good sister," he added, smiling. He was trying to lighten the mood, but I already felt a burden lifted. I'd hidden those moments… harbored them for far too long.

"Can we calm others from a distance?"

"Any witch can craft a calming spell, but it takes a powerful and exceptionally intuitive witch to craft the spell and then send it across the country."

"I thought as much."

"Izzy cares for you like a sister."

"Sometimes, I'd be in the middle of an attack and then inexplicably feel fine – it was something I couldn't explain – until now."

"It was Izzy. I'm sure of it."

"Thank God for her."

Fitz smiled.

"I guess the one thing in all of this I don't understand, is why you told me the council didn't know about my abilities."

Fitz sighed. "I'm sorry I wasn't completely truthful with you. Honestly, I was figuring things out as I went along. I didn't know what knowledge might put you in more danger. I didn't know what would make you more anxious, or even fearful." He paused, pursing his lips while deep in thought. "I can't say that I'd do everything the same way again – of course, I wouldn't – but what's done is done."

"Forgiven. I know it was a big burden to carry. But don't do it again. We're partners, and we carry burdens together."

"You have my word."

I wasn't pleased with all of Fitz's decisions, but we'd been placed in a ridiculous circumstance. Which choices would I have made if our roles were reversed, I wondered. Truthfully, I couldn't say. But we were already learning from our past, and these lessons would make us stronger – in our relationship and as individuals – and that was really all I could desire in that moment.

CHAPTER SEVENTEEN

Weeks passed uneventfully at the castle, until a strange breakthrough with Mr. Murray occurred one afternoon. I crossed the castle's Great Hall as footsteps echoed behind me. For a moment I froze, worried my supernatural stalker had returned, but almost as quickly, I recognized the energy.

"Mr. Murray, to what do I owe this pleasure?" I asked, not bothering to look behind me.

"Good afternoon, Ms. Weston. I'm surprised you're no longer ignoring our identities."

"Do you find yourself surprised often?"

"But rarely."

"Well, we both know what we are. There's no reason to pretend any longer."

"Might I ask what you're working on this fine afternoon?"

"I'm gathering material for a pamphlet marketing and I are pulling together – for donors attending next year's function. The new year will be here before we know it."

"I'm glad you're hitting the ground running."

"Is there another way?" I smiled. "I reviewed the previous documents we handed out, and they lack a real emphasis on how vital donations are for preservation. It would be good to show actual project completion that's been funded by our donors."

"Brilliant. I can't wait to see what you pull together."

Mr. Murray lingered, his expression betraying there was more to his visit than curiosity.

"Well, I'd better get on with it, if there's nothing else. We're under a time crunch to get everything turned in time."

I kneeled to photograph a recently repaired wall, eager for Mr. Murray's departure.

"Be careful, Ms. Weston."

I stood slowly, facing him with an expression that I'm sure was one to kill.

"I'm a seer," he stated with some resignation. "I admit I was looking into you more than necessary. I apologize for that, but this position is important to the success of the castle and our restoration project. I care about this place immensely."

"What did you see?"

"I saw you in that room. Hadley, Lorenzo Belmonte is dangerous. He *will* find out who you are, just as he told you. Lorenzo has a nearly impenetrable protection spell he cloaks himself in, which complicates things. I know you haven't calculated your next move, but I'm concerned."

A group of tourists shifted their gaze from the military weaponry on display to observe us suspiciously, curious about our heated whispers. Realizing I must have looked upset, I carefully checked my expression.

"Mr. Murray, do you think we could finish this meeting elsewhere?" I asked, sending him a silent message we were being studied by the humans.

"Of course. I believe we'd be more comfortable in my office. This way, please."

*   *   *

"I can't believe you were watching me."

"I apologize – truly. Hear me out?"

I nodded.

"You are a new witch coming into your powers, and I needed to ensure you're being properly coached so problems won't arise around here. And truthfully… I didn't have time to await information from the lower councils – not if we were going to make you an offer quickly – so I've just checked in here and there. I stopped after I saw you in Lorenzo's office, but I had to warn you. I would have done it sooner, but I just received approval to discuss it."

"Approval?"

"From the upper council."

"This isn't just about me being a green witch, is it? You know about me and Fitz."

"Aye," he returned through pursed lips.

"Did you know our story when you hired me?"

"Aye. I thought you two were quite brave."

"Thank you," I nodded. "Do you know if anyone else has been watching me?"

"I did not know about him until today."

"This creep has watched me several times, lurking around in the shadows. Just last week there was another incident. This has been going on for weeks."

"I'm sorry if he caused you any alarm. Jess is enthusiastic about new witches in the territory."

"Someone went through my hotel room."

"Oh! I'm so sorry that happened to you. But, it couldn't have been Jess. He wouldn't go that far."

"I'm not so sure about that."

"Truly, it must have been someone else. I'll look into it. My sincerest apologies if he's worried you."

"Yes, well he did cause some alarm, and I'm afraid Fitz is none too pleased."

"Oh dear, yes. I'll have a talk with Jess. Please apologize to Fitz."

I didn't much like his answer, but I needed to focus on the larger issue first.

"What do you know about Lorenzo?"

"A fair amount I suppose. I sit on the council for the Scottish National Coven – I assume you've grown familiar with the witchkind government structure?"

I shook my head and made a mental note to ask Fitz for

more information. "I'm actually not all that clear on government structure. I'm still learning the ins and outs."

"There's a group of us elected to our national coven council, held twice monthly in Edinburgh. We send one representative to the European Coven Council, which happens monthly in Vienna. Then two representatives from each continental coven council are sent to the United Covens Affairs quarterly on the Island of Little Cumbrae."

"Is that here in Scotland?"

"Aye, a wee island west of Glasgow. The location has been inconspicuous for years, and with the owners belonging to the Scottish National Coven, we have complete secrecy there."

"That's a lot to take in. We're an organized bunch, huh?"

"That's putting it mildly."

"So, is Dr. Belmonte involved in the council with you?"

"He no longer deserves the title *doctor*. He violated his oath to do no harm many years ago."

"So, that's a no, then." I smiled.

Mr. Murray sighed. "Lorenzo went rogue many years ago, claiming our government prevented witches from reaching our full potential. He believes we should rule over the humans rather than coexist. He caused quite a stir – almost exposed us to humankind. It's all rubbish, of course, and we were able to stomp out his wee movement before it escalated beyond repair."

"And then?"

"We called him to trial; then he disappeared. It's taken us

years to locate him, but we've recently pinpointed his location."

"Is he in Scotland?"

"No, he's in a place called Opimae." After noting my look of confusion, he added, "The name is Latin for luxurious or lush, and the land on which this city stands is certainly that, you know? You suspected him still in Scotland because of the maps?"

"Well, the landscape outside the windows in that room solidified he was elsewhere, but I wondered about the affiliation with Scotland because of his study of the area."

"The maps are there because he sought an object of great value. I'm sure you noticed the map of your homeland?"

I nodded.

"Lorenzo acquired that map while on the run and plotted the perfect escape. The area he sought refuge in is located in the Olympic National Park."

"Why there?"

"There was a particular area there he needed to find."

"I saw markings along the High Divide Trail. Why would he go there? Easier to lose the council?"

"There's a portal located off the trail."

"A portal? I don't… wait, so where does it lead?"

Mr. Murray leveled his gaze. "To another world. The portal leads to another universe."

Though I paced the room restlessly during our discussion, my legs suddenly lost the will to stand, and I sought refuge in a nearby chair. I put up with a lot over the past couple of months, but this was too much.

"Another universe? How is that possible?"

"It's magic," he quipped, smiling.

"What's it like?"

"It's unlike anything you can imagine, a place where you can practice magic freely."

"Tell me everything."

"How do I know I can trust you?"

Throughout our conversation, Mr. Murray silently contemplated the same skepticism of me that I had of him. Something in my gut told me I could trust him, but there was only so much I could share.

"Why have you trusted me so far?"

"Because my instinct says I can, but the rest of the story is... well, it's classified."

"I understand. To tell you the truth, this isn't simple curiosity. Of course, I want to know about another universe where witches are able to transport back and forth. But it's more than that."

He nodded reassuringly.

"It's not my tale to tell."

"Aye, and so where does that leave us?"

"Would you be willing to meet up later? How much we disclose is up to Fitz, but I think we can reach some sort of mutual disclosure. I think we can help one another."

"I'm as interested in Lorenzo as you are. We'd love to bring him to justice for what he's done, but we're in desperate need of additional resources."

"Tonight at seven?"

"Sure, let's meet at Whiski? The owner is a friend, and he'll give us a private table to discuss."

"Sounds great. See you tonight."

CHAPTER EIGHTEEN

F itz was quick to approve of the meeting at Whiski.

"He said Lorenzo was seeking an object of great value."

"Do you think he knows about the ring, then?"

"I didn't ask, and he didn't offer any more information. I thought it best to wait for you, but just be aware of that."

Fitz nodded, though his eyes indicated he was already lost elsewhere.

"Hey, I know we discussed James Murray, but you didn't mention how powerful he is."

"Right. I don't actually know him. I only know what I shared before – that he sits on the Scottish Coven Council, and that my dad respects him."

"I wish I knew more about him. We should have asked for more info."

"I still don't perceive any harm from your daily interactions. He's a good guy. My dad thinks the world of him."

"He's still a part of the council."

"Yes, but he had nothing to do with our separation. We need to give him a fair shake."

"I know. I am – I promise. I'm just a bit wary."

"I understand. This is big, though. Hads, this could be the break we've been searching for."

"It seems strange he agreed to talk so quickly."

"It sounds like Lorenzo created a big problem for them. Maybe they're just worried about his next move. Or… maybe this situation right here is why the council let us off easy before."

"You're onto something there."

"Oh, and don't forget because Murray has a seat on the council, he knows a great deal more than you can imagine. As soon as a green witch of human lineage who, along with her mate, defied council orders and then crossed this border, you can bet the Scottish Council did everything in their power to find details on us."

"Has anyone in this witchy world heard of privacy? Honestly!"

Fitz smirked.

"That's an eerie thought. Just when I thought things were settling down."

"Being a witch is different from being a human in so many ways, and this is just another example. With the connection we all have to one another, it's much harder to keep secrets. It's just our nature."

"Speaking of which…"

"What is it?"

"I found out who's been watching me."

"Murray knew?"

"Apparently, his name is Jess. We can ask more about it later – I was mostly focused on getting answers about Lorenzo – but Murray made it sound like he was a curious witch and said he wouldn't have been the one snooping in my room."

"You can't be serious. A curious witch?"

"Yep."

"First off, that's not exactly smiled upon – a random witch snooping around in the shadows. Secondly, that just doesn't happen, so I'm not buying it. I'm going to kick his ass."

"Oh, yes. Please do," I returned, my voice dripping with sarcasm.

"Look, you're my mate, and like it or not, I will kick anyone's ass up and down the Mile if I see fit. No one will so much as think about watching you again."

I slipped my arms around his waist. "You're a little overboard sometimes."

"This is not overboard," he returned, his hands resting on my shoulders. "Don't underestimate these creatures and what they might want from us, and don't underestimate our connection. I can't turn off my protective instinct – it's innate."

"Hmph."

"Let me ask you this. If someone hurt me, what would you do?"

"I'd make them pay," I said matter-of-factly.

Fitz raised an eyebrow, a rather smug look on his face.

"Okay, point taken."

"I'm serious. Don't underestimate other creatures. This is a different world."

*   *   *

When we entered the pub that evening, it took little effort to follow Mr. Murray's energy trail to a back room, where he sat nursing a dark beer, scanning the crowd through its doorway.

"Looks like his friend came through on the privacy front," I whispered to Fitz. Though the front of the restaurant was cramped, empty tables surrounded Mr. Murray's booth.

"Can you feel that?"

I closed my eyes briefly, awaiting the onrush of whatever Fitz perceived.

"Oh. The privacy spell."

"At least we won't have to worry about keeping our voices down."

"Hadley. Fitz. I'm so glad you both made it."

"Of course. It's a pleasure to meet you, Mr. Murray."

"The pleasure is all mine. Please take a seat, and you both can call me James."

The pub was small and as quaint as Scotland itself. Tables were randomly strewn about the front room; a lovely bar was decorated with countless bottles and a busy bartender, one who took pride in his work. The front door bordered a wall of windows, and I could see the charm of sitting amongst the window tables, watching tourists explore the Royal Mile. A traditional Scottish band sat in the front corner, their melodic stories tumbling out in Scots Gaelic, along with the captivating sounds pouring from the instruments in hand. I was momentarily entranced, before Fitz's voice sounded through the music. Apparently, I had lost myself for a few moments, and pleasantries were over.

"Yeah, Hadley filled me in on your discussion. What I'd like to understand is why you're entrusting us with this information, and what you hope to gain from it."

"We believe Lorenzo is preparing another uprising, which means more fighting. Hadley wandered her way into his *home* – do you understand that no one on the UCA has been able to do that? The councils have searched for years for a creature who could do what Hadley has done. I know you seek him for a reason of your own – something of immense value to you. I hope I can count on you both to join us."

Fitz nodded to me, confirming he felt truth in James.

"So, when you say join us… is this working behind the scenes, or are we talking fieldwork?"

Fitz warned me that the council wouldn't disclose details like these to creatures unless they intended on recruiting them. I knew the conversation would lean in this direction, but I wasn't sure I was prepared for what followed.

"It would be both, and I'm afraid the fieldwork has a real level of danger. It's one of the reasons we've spent years searching for the proper individuals to fill these positions."

"What exactly do you mean by fieldwork?" I questioned.

"You'd both play major roles in the mission against Lorenzo," he began, clearing his throat. "With that being said, you'd be essential in the planning phase, and during this time you'd undergo extensive training. Once completed, you would travel to Opimae with a council member and be key players in enacting our strategy to prevent Lorenzo's plans. You would actively participate in preventing war."

"You believe we can do that?"

"Hadley, look at what the two of you were able to do on your own. The council tried but couldn't prove you two were even in contact, even with the most skilled seers available. When you decided to slip off the radar, you did. And you weren't located until you allowed yourselves to be found. You believed in something, and you accomplished it. If you can do that alone, imagine what you'll accomplish with the council's resources."

"Well, when you put it that way."

James chuckled. "And that's in addition to your power, intuitiveness, and your innate sense of good – of right and wrong. You're the type of witches other creatures will trust, which is immensely important."

"Can you see the future of this crusade?"

"No, I can't, but I've done extensive research and formulated which skill sets I believe are essential for defeating him. You and Fitz have exactly what we're looking for in our crusade leaders. It surprised me when I discovered you two are mated. I hadn't anticipated that, but it works nonetheless."

"That does seem strange, doesn't it?" Fitz asked.

"Aye. And beyond that, you two are more powerful than most witches I've known. Your powers exceed normal standards alone, but together... well, it's extraordinary."

"Speaking of extraordinary," Fitz began. "I've heard rumors of another universe inhabited by creatures, but until now, I discredited those accounts."

"The UCA gained knowledge of a portal around two hundred B.C. The portal was adjusted to Washington, and it was a secret shared with no one outside witchkind, not even the leaders of the day." He smiled. "As you can imagine, it seemed a safe location at the time, and it has remained one of the most discreet locations in the world. Shortly after its creation, we began to patrol the portal to ensure no one entered or exited who shouldn't. It would be quite a mess if dragons suddenly roamed Earth freely. The humans would have some questions about that, don't you reckon?"

We snickered at the thought of other creatures making their way into our world, but we knew it would be tragic.

"They'd never stand a chance here. They'd be captured, poked, and prodded until humans pulled every bit of information possible from them. Then humans would know of the portal, and our way of life would end," I said soberly.

"Precisely. This is one of many reasons it's imperative we maintain control of entrances and departures. Any creatures, apart from witches, are not allowed to cross the portal into Earth. It's simply too dangerous at this time."

"But witches may cross openly?"

"Any well-intentioned witch is allowed to enter Opimae and free to return, but our governments wish to maintain records of passage. Think of it like your passport that gains you access to foreign countries on Earth."

"How did Lorenzo ever make it through?" Fitz wondered.

"We had a newer agent on the job the night Lorenzo passed through, which was undoubtedly planned. Lorenzo wore a disguising spell, and unfortunately, the new agent didn't notice. Another agent reviewed the film the next morning as she archived the recordings and realized something was amiss. It was a rookie mistake that cost him his career, and us a villain."

"Where is this universe located? What do you know about it?" I asked.

"Roughly three universes from our own. The planet is much like Earth, rotating its sun. Magic is practiced freely and openly without fear or repercussion. Their convention is similar to our structure, and much of our knowledge and communication is through them. We've maintained a peaceful relationship over the centuries. Unlike Earth, their world is made up of many creatures – witches, elves, dragons, and even water witches, or mermaids, as we call them here."

Fitz and I caught one another's gaze, marveling at the new intelligence.

"How is it possible? That so many mythical creatures exist…"

"Well, for one, there aren't humans in Opimae. Other creatures existed here but were run close to extinction. Those left on this side were sent through the portal for protection. Another reason the portal has fallen to myth, even in witchkind."

"Fear anything that's different: the human motto," Fitz stated plainly.

"Unfortunate, but true. We saved those we could."

"We need to see this place," I began.

"And Lorenzo needs to be stopped. Will you join forces?"

Fitz and I exchanged a glance.

"Hadley, should we take some time to discuss this?"

"James, would you mind if we take just a few minutes to talk?"

"Absolutely not. This is a lot to process. I need to make a call anyway."

James exited the room, his phone in hand, granting us privacy to discuss our future.

"Came to dinner with my boss. Might join a crusade to fight evil on a foreign planet."

Fitz laughed. "Aye, just another day."

"Look, I know this is going to seem odd," I began, as soon as James was out of sight. "But I think joining might be the right decision. And I cannot believe I just said that."

"I can't believe it either."

"There is *definitely* a part of me that wants to be spiteful and tell the council where to stick it." A devious smile spread across my lips.

"But?"

"This is bigger than us. We have to think about things on a larger scale."

"I agree. But I have to admit the thought of you doing this scares the hell out of me."

"Man, your faith in me is steadfast, isn't it?"

"Come on, Hads. It's not that I don't think you're capable. You're unbelievably intuitive in your magic, but you have to understand my position."

"I'm as protective of you, as you are of me. We're both going to have to curb our protective instincts – at least a little."

"What if I can't?"

"Then you'll put us both at risk."

Fitz swirled his drink, the scotch trickling back down the length of the glass. It was a sign I knew well – he was about to share something he found no pleasure in.

"You know we don't have a choice?"

"About joining?"

"Yeah."

"This is one of those moments where we're called, and have to answer."

"Right." He nodded. "I think this is it. They played nice when we returned to Scotland because they were already considering us for this."

"Shit."

"Aye… shit."

"So James probably had his eyes on us from the beginning, and then I paid a visit to Lorenzo's home…"

"Right. Your break-in sealed the deal."

"And here I thought I wowed him with my PR skills."

"Of course, you did. But that wasn't the only thing about you that wowed him."

"I don't trust the council."

"How could you?" he agreed, shrugging his shoulders. "I think we take it a day at a time. James wasn't responsible for what happened to us. He's a good guy. That's as far as I can see right now."

"That's a good way to look at it. We take things a step at a time and assess as we go."

"Exactly."

"Regardless of any of the rest of this crap, you need your family's power back. Lorenzo can't have it. We have to fight this."

"I want that ring back more than I don't want to help the council."

"Why are you looking at me like that?" I questioned.

"Oh…" His smile widened. "Honestly, I'm just in awe of you sometimes."

"What? Why?"

"You're so sure. Brave."

"No. I'm scared, Fitz."

"Me, too. But we're facing this head-on, my brave lass."

Our conversation drifted back and forth, as the minutes ticked by, but we knew what we had to do. I gripped Fitz's hand tightly. Fitz waived to James, who was waiting patiently near the front door, pretending to be otherwise engaged.

"Well then? You've reached a decision?"

"Aye, we'll join you."

"Oh brilliant! I can't tell you how pleased I am to have you with us," James returned, clasping his hands together happily. "Come to the council meeting at the castle on Saturday. We'll brief you on everything."

"You seem confident in us, but I have doubts."

"That's a normal feeling, Hadley. Don't let it overtake you. You are more capable than you realize, and you will receive every possible attention from our trainers."

This helped steady my racing mind, which suddenly found every doubt I had in myself. I came to dinner with my manager from work and somehow agreed to travel to a magical land in another universe to fight a warmongering sociopath. Was I crazy? No, I knew I wasn't. I wasn't human; I was a witch. With my power and intuition, I knew we were right to trust James, and we needed to honor Fitz's family.

"There's only one condition," Fitz said.

"Anything," James replied sincerely.

"He – Lorenzo – has something that belongs to my family. I want it back."

"Ah, I was hoping you'd bring that up. I suppose you're wanting your wee ring?"

"You knew?"

"We've known about the ring for a long time. Thank God for council records." He smiled. "You see, we were the ones who first took the ring after your grandmother's death. The local coven knew what she possessed but believed she wouldn't fight her way free. The leaders decided there was no danger in leaving it in her possession until her death – unless her decision changed. They hoped it would grant some comfort as she suffered in her last days. Upon her death, your grandfather was to collect the ring immediately and release the power. I'm sure you know this."

Fitz nodded slowly.

"The council leaders sent representatives to collect the ring with the intention of locking it away until your grandfather was composed enough to release the powers. They thought it would give him closure. But the ring mysteriously vanished one night under careful watch. The guards were incapacitated and all the spells meant to protect the ring were disarmed."

"Oh my God," I whispered.

"Exactly right, Hadley." James nodded. "It requires vast aptitude and force to undo the work of so many other powerful witches. When the guards awoke, they described a man that our current leaders confirmed as Lucio Belmonte, Lorenzo's father."

"How did they realize it was Lucio?"

"Careful information gathering, then utilizing those clues to look back and observe the removal of the ring. Lucio was cautious and thorough, and I feel fortunate they were able to even discern that much."

I reached for Fitz's hand, trying to imagine how he felt.

"He gained knowledge of the ring in his own time, studying history much like yourself, Fitz, and then transported through time to bring the item back to his present."

"To bring forward an object like... what an immense amount of power."

"Oh, quite."

"What did Lucio want with the ring?" I asked.

"His own selfish desires – he passed along his animus for our laws to Lorenzo. He trained Lorenzo from a young age to carry forward his ill will in the world."

"And Lorenzo's mother?"

"Ah, Adelina. She was quite powerful herself, but cared not for how her husband treated Lorenzo, as long as it meant more power for them."

"What a sad life," Fitz lamented.

"It is an unfortunate tale to be sure. But as an adult, Lorenzo chose to carry forward that malice rather than overcome it, and now he is beyond the reach of any goodness. He must be stopped."

"Why would he go through so much trouble to retrieve this ring?"

"Not many creatures are even able to perform a power transfer – especially these days. It's so rare. Perhaps Lucio even held knowledge that one day you would stand against Lorenzo. It's difficult to say."

"Do you know if he's tapped into the power of the ring?" Fitz asked.

"No, we aren't certain. Our identification of Lucio was recent, so we're early in this part of our investigation. We hope to learn more soon. Lorenzo hid while building his army, and now the Opimae government is unable to arrest him without disaster. We've been unable to penetrate the perimeter of his home – that is until Hadley broke in. You casually discovered something we've been unable to do for years, my dear."

"I didn't do anything special. I talked to the elements the way I always do."

"It seems Hadley disarms others' spells. When I couldn't utilize Annabel's summoning spell, Hadley immediately transported to the ring. She couldn't call the ring to her either, but the ring somehow summoned her. Her powers seem to find the loopholes and latch on. It's incredible actually."

"Extraordinary! Since you've agreed to help us, you will soon have the UCA's network at your disposal. We'll find the perfect trainers to assist you in fine-tuning your powers, Hadley. And Fitz, we'll place you in skilled combat training as well. Your instinct to protect Hadley will make it impossible for you two to train together at first, so we'll begin your training separately, and then we'll finish together. Hadley is strong – powerful – and she'll have no problem defending herself, but you'll make yourself vulnerable if you don't learn that."

"When do we start training?" he asked, his hand finding a firmer grip on mine.

"We'll discuss the game plan on Saturday and begin training immediately after. Hadley, take tomorrow off and rest."

James insisted on picking up the check, citing council business.

"We'll see you in a couple of days then. After the briefing, please ask any additional questions or raise concerns – that's reasonable throughout the entire training, and into the crusade. We're keen to know your thoughts."

"Sounds great," I confirmed.

"The ring will be released back to you, Fitz, once we free the power from it. Consider it as a part of your reward for helping us."

"Is that something he'll be able to help with? The actual releasing of power, I mean."

"Of course."

James took his leave, turning on his heel before pausing.

"Oh, and Fitz…" he called back, over his shoulder. "Hadley has reveled in her newfound power long enough. It's time to show her what you can do."

CHAPTER NINETEEN

The following afternoon, we stood in Henry's backyard, my baby blue rain boots bright against the moody Scottish landscape. The wind nipped at my bare fingers, and I regretted leaving my gloves at our flat almost as much as I longed for the heat of the sitting-room hearth.

"So…" Fitz began cautiously. "You understand that you and I possess elemental magic, and our magic is stronger than the average witch's."

I nodded.

"And that like you, I read people's truths and lies, having a strong instinct that way."

I nodded once more.

"There are a few other things I haven't told you about."

"Show me."

"Are you sure?"

"You're treating me with kid gloves again."

"I believe your first words after dinner were 'what in the actual hell just happened?'"

"Well?"

"We just took in a tremendous amount of information in the last twenty-four hours. I know your head is spinning; mine sure is."

"It's a bit overwhelming, but I told you I feel peace about this decision, which is insane, but there it is."

"I feel it, too. We're either mad or brilliant."

"Probably both. I can handle this. So, please, without further adieu…" I waved my hands impatiently.

I was ready to further my complaint when Fitz turned his head curiously. I followed his gaze, finding a familiar face staring back at me.

"Mom?" I questioned, thoroughly confused. She couldn't be here, could she?

My mother walked toward me. "Hello, honey."

I tentatively moved closer, not realizing until that moment just how much I missed her. As I touched her arm, she dissipated right before my eyes.

"What happened?" I questioned before the truth dawned on me. "She wasn't there, was she?"

"No."

"She was an apparition." I stared blankly where my mother disappeared.

"I apologize for my choice in apparition. When you asked me to show you, I just pulled out the first person I could find in your memories."

"I thought you couldn't read minds."

"I can't. Not everyday thoughts as they run through people's minds, but I can latch onto memories. I sense those you care about and tap into that emotional part of your brain that helps me recreate those you love. Or a place you love. I connect with memories."

"Show me a place in my mind."

"Are you sure?"

"Yes," I responded, uncertain if I truly was.

He took my hand, as he searched my eyes, prying into the far reaches of my mind. Slowly, his expression changed, and he nodded in the opposite direction. What I saw almost took my breath away. A large field with deep green ryegrass stretched across the distance. I turned my head, anticipating the quaint, two-story farmhouse, where I spent so many summers. Fitz and I walked closer to the house, and I studied every last detail as if I'd somehow forgotten – this was produced from my mind, after all. The white paint, large windows framed in maroon shutters, and a wrap-around porch were forever burnt into my mind.

"All I need is a glass of Gram's sweet tea."

"I don't think I can help you with that one."

"Oh, don't even try. I'm pretty sure Gram could reach across the Atlantic and slap you for messing with her tea."

"Trust me, I know where you get your sass."

I laughed heartily, soaking up those few borrowed moments.

"You are damn beautiful, you know that?"

I smiled in return.

"I can feel how happy you are here."

"Some of my happiest memories are from this place. I miss Gram."

Knowing it was time to say goodbye, I closed my eyes briefly, savoring the feeling of Gram's kingdom, and opened them again to the landscape of Scotland. "I've experienced a lot of new things recently, but that was unbelievable! What an extraordinary talent. Thank you for showing me… and for taking me to Gram's."

"Oh, aye. There's nothing much to it."

"Wait, are you blushing?"

"Don't look at me," he countered playfully, walking off to the kitchen. Though his remarks were lighthearted, it was difficult for Fitz to be praised. I thought he would be used to it considering the vast amount of power he possessed, but Fitz was humble, and for that, I was inordinately grateful.

"I have one last thing to show you," Fitz announced upon returning from Henry's kitchen with tall glasses of water.

"Bring it on."

"Pick a place."

"What?"

"Just pick a place. Name somewhere that fascinates you. Anywhere."

"The Virgin Islands."

"*Nice*, Hadley," he smirked. "Okay, chug that water."

I obeyed, curiosity taking root.

"Now come here."

With one arm secured around my waist, he used the other to remove my boots and then my socks, the cold, damp ground striking the soles of my feet. He pulled me snugly against his body, and I held him instinctively.

"Hold on tightly," he whispered, his breath warm on my ear.

The world spun, sliding away from the light, and weightlessness consumed our bodies. Ever so slowly, stars came into focus, their illumination momentarily blinding after the absolute darkness. Mesmerized, I extended an arm, before Fitz reminded me to hold on tightly. The stars spun away, replaced by many indiscernible objects, each swimming around us. Color returned, bringing shades of blue and green into our vision, along with the nearly oppressive weight of gravity.

The spinning ceased, and I discerned ocean, sun, and land. I gasped when my toes met the smooth, warm sand. Unlike the beaches I'd visited in my short lifetime, the lush tree line mingled with the sand, the palm trees providing a welcome refuge from the bright rays of the sun.

"Is this real?"

"This is no mind trick. Welcome to St. John."

Stunned, I grasped his hand tighter and walked toward the crystal clear water, mesmerized as it sparkled like hundreds of diamonds in the afternoon sun.

"How long can we stay?"

"We don't have to be at training until tomorrow morning."

We journeyed over to Cruz Bay, securing essentials for an afternoon by the sea, and staked our claim on a deserted stretch of sand. As I sank into a beach chair, Fitz floated a Corona in my direction, and I fired off my first question.

"Does it always happen like that?"

"Like what exactly?"

"The darkness, the stars, the weightlessness, the spinning..."

"Oh, aye. It's always been like that. We're navigating through the elements and time in order to find another place."

"How difficult is that for you?"

"*Difficult*. It takes a lot of practice and concentration. It's my most difficult power to control."

"Can you go *anywhere*?"

"Anywhere on Earth. Any further and you begin to deal with gravity in a different way. The distance alone is pretty troubling."

"You say you're navigating through time. Can you visit the future or the past?"

"I can visit the past, not the future. Though witches can see the future, it isn't a certain track. We're not God; we're not omniscient, so we only see the future in a limited way."

"What do you mean?"

"There are unknowns. People and creatures change their minds. When we make a decision, we alter the future. When we change our mind, we alter the future again. Then there's Fate... and God."

"You talk about Fate as though it were an animate being."

"She is. Trust me, you'll see that. She can't really be explained or even fully comprehended, but she's there."

"And God?"

"Well, God can do as he pleases, and he can change the rules any time he sees fit. And the game, come to think of it."

"Do most witches believe in a higher being?"

"In some form. We're obviously from different countries and religions, just as humans, but with the power to see the world so clearly, it's hard to reason a higher being doesn't exist."

"So many humans act like we're all evil. Like, we're devil worshippers," I said, pulling laughter from Fitz.

"Isn't that the most ignorant thing you've ever heard?"

"What? I hear hell is nice this time of year."

"To be honest, I can't lay all the blame on the humans. We've had witches egging on that narrative out of indignation. But yeah, humans have posed as witches over the years, causing harm to our reputation."

"Even those persecuted haven't all been witches. They were humans, and some of them did aggravate their captors with wild stories."

"Devil's advocate, though. Some of them were just doing what they could to end things," Fitz countered.

"Because of the torture?"

"Days of sleep deprivation, the absence of food and light, and being held in freezing conditions would cause almost anyone to confess, just to put an end to the torture. And that's only the beginning of what those poor men and women endured. Death seemed better than living."

"It honestly makes me sick to my stomach. And there are still people today who want to cast a negative portrayal of the craft. The overzealous witch-hunters might be dead, but the stigma lives on."

"It's frustrating when humans don't even want to understand the truth. There are far more creatures trying to do good than not. It's the same for humans. I have a hard time trusting them as a species, but most of them do try."

"Did you grow up in church?" I asked, circling back on our earlier conversation.

"Aye – Protestant, to be exact. And I've seen some things."

"I thought I had seen some things."

"And you ain't seen nothing yet."

"I grew up in church, too, although you probably already knew that."

"Yes." He grimaced. "Sorry if that still feels strange to you, me knowing so much."

"It's okay."

"Does it give you peace with your father?"

I cocked my head.

"To believe he's in a better place."

"Yeah, definitely." I paused, collecting my thoughts. "His last days were horrific. I still try to picture him healthy. That's what he would've wanted, for us to remember the good times. I believe he's in a better place, and that he's whole again."

Fitz nodded slowly, reassuringly.

"Okay, enough of that."

"Fine. Tell me what else you're curious about."

"Let's revisit this time-traveling situation."

"Let's," he returned, grinning.

"So, with varying levels of power mixing with God and Fate, witches have limited future vision…"

"Right. You might set out to travel to one particular part of the future, but with the threads of time and humanity changing, you could land in some type of non-reality, basically trapped in time."

"That sounds like my worst nightmare."

"It would be anyone's worst nightmare."

"So, the future is an ever-changing beast, best left alone."

"It isn't stable enough for someone to be able to physically transport themselves, especially with how quickly it changes."

"This is so fascinating!"

"You're able to travel anywhere mentally, present or past. It's essentially the same."

"Yet, it's not *quite* the same," I said, picking up my feet, allowing the sand to sift through my toes. "Plus, I can't take you with me. Do you often travel this way?"

"No. It's tiring, especially when I bring someone along. Of course, that depends on the distance or how far into the past I'm traveling. But sometimes I take off on a whim."

"What about the past? Have you visited it much?"

"Some. I only stay for a short period of time. I don't want to accidentally alter the past. It's tricky and tiring, but the experience is truly incredible. We'll pick a year and go when we have more time."

The sun descended, announcing the approaching evening, and I envied its calm path, sinking into the arms of the night. It was a stark contrast to the thoughts pinging around my mind. My mate could transport us anywhere in the world, and to any time, past or present. I could mentally do the same. We were witches. I'd fallen for him at twenty-seven, nearly lost him under mysterious circumstances, and found him once more in Paris. The past swirled all around my mind.

"I miss Midnight."

"Your emotional connection tells me you aren't referring to the witching hour."

"No." I laughed. "She was my cat when I was growing up."

"Please tell me you had a black cat."

"I was entirely consumed with the idea of witches as a child. My parents first thought it was a phase, a passing fancy from Halloween. But they came to realize the intrigue ran much deeper, and trying to sway me was useless. It felt real sometimes," I recalled sadly, remembering the child I once was. "As I grew older, my thoughts turned from adoration to fascination. I stopped with all the costumes and spells and kindled more of a sisterhood with our kind. That's when I begged for my first black cat."

"You knew who you were, Hads. You and your power sought one another for years. Your magic was awakening you."

"Awakening me?"

"From an ordinary life. You were never meant to be normal."

I climbed out of my chair and waded knee-deep into the gentle water of the Caribbean. I questioned who was nearby, awakening my third eye. A boat lay far off the coast, loaded with wealthy college students on school break. Around the corner, separated from us by large, slippery rocks, were newlyweds caught up in learning one another. Outside these few people, Fitz and I were alone on this tiny portion of the island, for which I was grateful.

I felt Fitz's presence behind me, a perk of our strong connection. His hands found my waist as his face nestled into the crook of my shoulder, planting a sensual kiss on the sensitive skin. A low sigh escaped my lips, encouraging him further, as he slid his hand across my abdomen, leaving a trail of goose bumps in the wake of his fingers. Magic brought his desire to life, as it twirled my body around slowly to face him. He searched my eyes, his fingers tracing the length of my cheek before planting a slow, long-expected kiss on my parted lips. Secure and happy, we lowered ourselves in the calm, shallow water of the Caribbean, holding tightly to the beauty of pink sunsets, warm breezes, and the most devoted of hearts.

PART THREE:

A CRUSADE COMMISSIONED

CHAPTER ONE

The following morning dawned on Edinburgh, bringing with it the butterflies of a new chapter. We approached the castle with a considerable amount of nervous excitement. Though we were eager to learn more about Opimae, we were also painfully aware we'd train under a microscope, one with many powerful witches at the other end – and we had reached our threshold for being watched.

Fitz's voice broke through the still, morning air. "Don't be nervous. They're here to help us."

"Then why are you nervous?"

"Get out of my head!"

"I'm not in your head. I can just feel your energy, and it's making me more nervous."

"Damn. I'm sorry. They *are* here to help."

"Yes, I know. We're all one big team, and we'll forget the past and roast marshmallows and sing 'Kumbaya.'"

"You're cute when you're feisty."

He planted a kiss on my forehead. I rolled my eyes, though a smile touched my lips, in spite of myself.

"Truthfully, I'm nervous because I don't like being the center of attention. I've never liked it, and after years of blending with the humans, it's difficult to be the focus, even if it's only our kind."

"But you're a college professor. You lecture in front of large groups of students."

"That's different. Most of my students are dedicated to their work, being that my classes are upper level. I'm not the focus, the material is. And my students only see my human facade. But this isn't about my profession. *This*," he continued, pointing in the general direction of the castle, "is solely about us, our relationship, our training, our personalities... *we* are the subject matter now."

"That's true. But that ship sailed the moment we fell in love. They already know so much about us. So, really their current focus is preparing us for our journey."

"You're right," he agreed. "What makes you most nervous?"

"That I won't be able to learn fast enough. And I keep thinking I'll wake up and realize I've made a mistake."

"Aye, I understand. But we've already established we have no choice. If you said you don't want to do this, I would beg and plead and demand they find someone else. Though in the end, none of that would matter. When the council calls, you answer."

"And they've called us."

"Time to answer."

James's greeting was warm, though brief, as he excitedly

ushered us into the meeting room where our day would truly commence. My skin felt the full assault of careful observation, as the eyes of the court danced wildly upon us. I hastily took stock, my eyes darting from creature to creature – all eleven of them. It was my understanding the council was composed of twelve members, meaning someone was missing.

"There's a lot of experience in this room," I mentally conveyed to Fitz, who was likewise focused on the council, registering the faces and potential ages of the members.

"Welcome to our Cardinal Court," James exclaimed, slightly overzealous. "Composed of the top twelve governing officials from all over the world, this council has been elected by witchkind and sworn in after approval and appointment by the United Covens Affairs. They're called to intervene in the most pressing matters – issues where the lower levels of government are unable to reach a decision, or in situations that are crucial to our worldwide community."

"Like the current predicament with Lorenzo and our passage into Opimae," I surmised.

"Precisely. Allow me to introduce you to our governing officials. You might have noticed we are missing one member. Not to worry; she will join us tomorrow."

Home was Brazil for Mariana, one of the most beautiful creatures I'd ever beheld. Her full figure and deep golden locks were intimidating enough, but when she laid her hazel eyes on you, you'd forfeit your soul if she were to request it. Her smile was infectious, and she was incredibly kind; however, something in her energy warned she was ruthless when provoked. She was the first to welcome us to the council meeting and expressed her gratitude for our willingness to join the fight against Lorenzo.

Liam hailed from New Orleans and did indeed wear a Southern charm about him. His countenance was calm, easy – the result of years in power. He was one of the older members of the council, and my mind marveled, curious about his actual age. His full head of hair and neatly trimmed beard were both white as snow, and his simple, well-tailored gray suit worked with his smart demeanor.

Another U.S. representative accompanied Liam. Mia was originally from Maine but spent most of her formative years in Seattle, and I initially thought we'd connect over growing up in the Pacific Northwest. But the fact that Liam and Mia were both from the States was about where their similarities ended. Mia possessed a passive-aggressive skepticism that loomed about her, attacking the air between us. She interrogated us with questions to which we were sure she already knew the answers. I had the distinct feeling that she wasn't a fan of our track record. Her bright blue eyes were a stark contrast to her raven hair, and strong waves of energy fired off her pale skin. I wondered how she could ever pass as an ordinary human, striking as she was.

* * *

The morning passed quickly, ravenous as we were for details concerning our new mission, and the arrival of lunch seemed almost impossible. Mariana walked us through the finer points of government structure to provide a true understanding of those with whom we would work. Even though Fitz seemed pretty knowledgeable about government details, he was able to garner some new information, and I was glad the morning wasn't a total waste for him. But when Liam spoke about the portal, Fitz's energy shifted, buzzing hungrily for details.

It was difficult to break from the session, even with our longing for sustenance, but this too was an opportunity to continue our learning. We talked further with Mariana, who worked with uncontacted tribes in the Amazon. Though several of these tribes were considered uncontacted by the humans, witchkind found an opportunity to help. Mariana and her team assisted in ways that wouldn't directly alter the overall fate of the tribes but provided tools to help them stand against humans who stole their land and murdered their tribal members. I was amazed by the work of witchkind, and how most humans would never know of our contributions to their society. I often worried about embracing my future with witchkind and finding the will to process my lingering anger with our government, but as Fitz kept reminding me – these officials took no part in our separation. Learning about their contributions to society and their desire to do good certainly helped my willingness to forgive.

Additional chairs in the meeting room caught our notice after lunch. Fitz and I locked eyes, curious what this meant for the afternoon session. We hadn't much time to speculate, as Albina nearly floated across the room, a smirk light on her lips. There was little about her that didn't highlight she wasn't human. Long, honey locks framed a flawless face, highlighted by a striking pair of green eyes. She was so alight in magic that her milky skin nearly glowed.

"Hadley, what a pleasure to have you here. We have so much in common!"

"It's wonderful to meet you, Albina." I smiled, curiosity setting in. It was difficult to imagine what I might share in common with the Russian beauty.

"We are the sole two individuals in this castle who acquired their powers beyond childhood. That's a handy piece of information now, isn't it?"

"Albina… would you be willing to share your story with me?"

"I know you're curious, but first we should probably discuss the addition of chairs here. Oh, wait. Chai! Come officially meet Hadley."

Chai was petite and carried herself with dignity. Her jet-black hair was cropped, gathered in a clip at the crown of her head, and adorned with chunky streaks of gray, hinting at an age of at least a hundred years.

"Ni hao, Hadley. It is an honor to have you with us."

"The honor is all mine, Chai. Thank you for the warm welcome."

"Oh yes," Albina chimed back in. "The chairs."

"We weren't expecting anyone else?"

"You didn't think we'd let you cross into another world to

fight a powerful, narcissistic maniac without a little help did you?"

"Well, when you put it that way."

Fitz meandered over from his conversation with Felix and Damian. Felix was every bit as charming as anyone might expect of a Brit, with a thick, aristocratic accent and donning a navy suit. His dirty blond hair was groomed into a pompadour style, suiting his business meets suave personality.

A human's guess would have placed Damián in his late seventies, and I couldn't help but notice his suppressed energy – sadness stifled the air around him. His hair was thick, and fully gray, set above eyes the color of the sea, a war waging within them as tumultuous as the body of water they resembled.

"Damián lost his wife a few months ago after one hundred and sixty-two years of marriage. He looks young for his age – can you believe he's two hundred and one? Anyway, heart attack. Tragic. Half of Argentina is in mourning for her, I swear. She was very influential." Albina's words crossed our minds as though she spoke aloud. I was stunned by the commitment they made to one another, a bond that lasted over 160 years. A heart attack seemed too human an end for such an inhuman creature.

A large wooden door swung open, bringing with it a gust of wind and a figure I recognized instantly. Fitz's father, Ian, crossed the room, stationing himself directly in front of his astonished son.

"Hello, son."

"Dad!" Fitz exclaimed, pulling his father into an embrace.

Ian's gaze shifted to me. "Hadley. It's wonderful to see you again."

"Mr. MacGregor, it's been forever. So good to see you."

"Don't you dare – it's Ian."

Ian possessed a warmness about him that invited others to feel welcomed and accepted, undoubtedly where Fitz inherited the trait.

"Dad, I'm happy to see you, but why are you here?"

"I'm here to help you. And so is everyone else," he replied, pointing toward the others who entered the room during our reunion with Ian.

My eyes scanned across Henry, a couple of witches I didn't recognize, and one special human. "Jordan," I gasped.

CHAPTER TWO

I wasted no time in embracing my best friend. "What on earth are you doing here?" I asked skeptically. Jordan couldn't be allowed in such a place. She was human, after all.

"We're here to help you and Fitz."

"Jordan, do you… I mean are you aware we're…"

"That you're a witch?"

"Oh."

"Mr. MacGregor brought me up to speed," she replied, taking my hand in hers. "Honestly, this is some *weird ish*, but we've always known you're gifted, right? It makes sense."

"I think I'm in shock. I guess if anyone can be calm under weird circumstances, it's you. I don't know how you're here, but I'm thrilled."

Jordan. She always understood me on some level – she knew I was odd by human standards, but never once made me feel different from her. I studied the woman in front of me – she was tall, with deep brown skin and tight curls the color of coal spiraling to her elbows. She didn't give her brown eyes enough credit – they were flecked with amber, almost the color of Henry's favorite whisky, with irises framed in black. She might be human, but there was nothing ordinary about Jordan.

"Hi, Henry," I blurted happily. Henry had become family, and I kept no secrets from him. Whatever the reason for his presence, I hoped he could stick around. I observed him inching closer throughout my conversation with Jordan, clearly anxious to speak with me, but unwilling to interrupt our reunion, as well-mannered as he was.

"What's with the anxiety?"

"Well, I gave my word yesterday that I'd accompany you to Opimae, and I know I'll get a proper ear-bashing from Fitz over the whole thing."

"So, you want me to help calm him."

"Aye."

"I'm assuming you don't have much choice, and Fitz doesn't have the authority to stop you?"

"Right, but it would be nice if he didn't have a hissy."

"Done."

"Yeah?"

"Yeah. You two are thick as thieves, and he needs you to have his back while we're in Opimae."

"The council can fix this," Fitz's voice chimed in authoritatively.

"Fitz…"

"Hadley, he's my best friend, and this is a dangerous situation. I'm already up to my eyeballs in anxiety with you, and I won't have your back like I normally would, Henry. I'll be too focused on protecting Hadley, and instinctually she'll be my focus."

"I can handle myself, mate. Besides, you need me in Opimae to help protect Hadley, keep her power hidden from Lorenzo," he nearly whispered. "Yeah, we're each summoned to this crusade, and we'll all be in some level of danger. But Hadley… none of us are able to locate the loopholes like she can, and Lorenzo will sort that out. I'll do my part to protect her."

"You've thought this through? Is it only pressure from the council, or do you truly want a part in this?"

"You know my father is a decorated war hero, as is his father before him. I hail from a long line of warriors, and though I have seen little battle, their valor rests in my veins. I'll do what I was born to do."

Fitz exhaled slowly.

"Hadley needs me, too. She's family now, and even *you* won't prevent me from protecting our family."

Fitz placed his right hand on Henry's shoulder. "I'm proud to have you fight with me, brother."

Henry smiled, and I turned to Jordan.

"Why do you look so smug?" I inquired.

"Your turn," Fitz offered, nodding to Jordan.

"No."

"I have four people close to me who joined our fight."

"They're all witches. The council can't force anything on Jordan."

"You're right, but you and I know too well that the council doesn't expose our kind to humans. If she's here, there's a damn good reason."

"Don't be reckless, Fitz." Not awaiting his response, I turned to Jordan. "I need you to consider what a human body is capable of withstanding. There's more magic in this world than you can even begin to comprehend, and you'll have no defense."

"That's not actually true," Henry interjected. "When we get to Opimae, she'll develop some sort of power."

I looked for James in the thickening crowd surrounding us.

"Is this true?"

James knew more about Opimae than anyone, and he'd be the least biased.

"Aye, it's true. There's no knowing what type of power she'll develop, but a few humans have passed into Opimae on council business, and each developed power."

"Like what?"

"Well, I wouldn't expect her to develop a witch's gamut of powers, but she might, for instance, develop superhuman strength and speed."

"How is that possible?"

"We believe it has to do with human body chemistry and how it interacts with the elements of a foreign planet. Their bodies are adapted to Earth, but if you remove them from their home planet, their bodies will acclimate to that new environment. It's rapid evolution, so to speak, and not so far fetched for a planet charged with magic. Your powers will intensify as well. Something to look forward to," he said dreamily.

"Jordan has a sense of otherworldliness," Ian began. "It's one of the reasons I asked the council to consider her for her role. You need her as much as she needs to be there with you... and a part of this crusade."

"You don't need to do this."

"I would do this if it gave *you* a better chance of success alone, but it's more than that. This is about my future, too; it's about all of our futures. Witches aren't the only ones who will be affected if this disagreement ends in war. I won't sit on the sidelines."

"You're on the sidelines right now because you're human! Don't you understand that? You have no self-defense against a witch."

"I'll develop a skill that will help. I'm not a liability because I'm human – I'm an asset. I have a role to play, too. I need to do this."

"Hadley, we don't know what the council will do if Jordan refuses this mission. Our secret has already been shared with her," Fitz sounded in my mind.

I simply nodded in response. The thought was sobering, but perhaps we could still sort things out later on.

"Now, with that settled, I'd like to introduce Isaac," Fitz

chimed in.

My eyes settled on Fitz's Italian friend – olive skin, chocolate-colored strands styled much the same as Felix's, and dark eyes with endless depth. He was tall like Fitz and Henry and had the lithe, muscular build of an athlete. Isaac and I shook hands, and his connection to Fitz resounded through my witch's eye. I wanted to know everything about their history, but I stifled my third eye from revealing details. It was Fitz's tale to share, and we needed to return our focus to the council, now that we were all on the same page, more or less.

"I'm sure you're wondering about Molly," said Prisha, the Indian representative to the council, her hand raised in the general direction of the door. The final addition to our party was propped lazily against the doorframe.

"Molly, do come over and meet everyone."

Molly dragged her combat boots across the space. She sported shoulder-length hair, dusky in color, except for the few blonde streaks jolting through it. With milky skin and wide, umber eyes, she was as striking a creature as any in the room.

"Hi, everyone," she muttered. Rude wasn't the proper descriptor for Molly, but a casual, almost disinterested atmosphere hung about her, which piqued my interest. It seemed odd that she could stand next to Cardinal Court members, who were introducing her to a host of new witches with whom she would soon travel to a new universe, and remain so relaxed. She almost seemed bored.

"Molly is from Calgary, and we've selected her as your final travel companion. Well, aside from James," Prisha continued in her husky, Hindi accent.

Lost in her hypnotic voice, my head snapped over to James as her words sank in. "You're coming!"

"Aye! Albina told me just today. I'm thrilled."

"So are we. You're a great addition to the group."

"Thank you, Fitz. I'm honored to be a part of this."

Henry shook his hand as James added, "And Molly is going to be fantastic."

"We selected Molly based on rigorous criteria. There, of course, will be others to help you in Opimae, but we built a strong team coming from this side," Ella's soft voice explained in perfect English, though her German dialect was heavy.

Ella remained in the background for much of the morning, and I realized she was an observer. Paying close attention to the scenes and conversations around her, she soaked up information, meaning when she did step forward, the woman knew what she was talking about. Ella was quiet, but not shy. She was observant, but not a wallflower. She smiled, her pale blue eyes focusing on Fitz and me.

"Hadley, Fitz… you two are perfect for this crusade, and it is such a coincidence that you are together. None of us anticipated that. Fitz, your father, Ian, is a longstanding and honorable employee of the council, and his skill set makes sense for him to accompany you. Like you, he harbors great power, and possesses a discernment I've learned not to question."

Fitz didn't object to his father joining our group, but the

council used Ian in a high capacity, and accompanying us wasn't a choice for him. It was duty. Like Ella, Fitz wouldn't question his father's discernment, and certainly not regarding council business.

"Henry and Isaac, though they are your friends, were proper matches for this expedition because of their skill sets and power. This is something else I wouldn't have anticipated, that two of your best mates would also best fit these roles, a warrior and a reader – although we do work with Isaac regularly."

I then understood why Fitz didn't raise an argument about Isaac joining us. After sensing their close connection, I was surprised Fitz let that one go. Ella was filling in the blanks for me.

"Lorenzo possesses great power, plus he could utilize the power of the ring if he hasn't already. Because of this, finding a group of powerful witches was first and foremost, but we needed certain abilities to complement each other. You each hold special power," Albina added.

"Now we come to James and Molly," Prisha began. "This crusade has been years in the making, and James headed research and data collection from this project's inception. We've always known Lorenzo would rise again in protest; we just didn't know when. We waited patiently for each of you, you see. Because of James's knowledge of the situation, his gifts, and his commitment to this project, he is the perfect council representative to accompany you. I also believe he is a good fit for the group morale," she explained, turning to Ella.

"Molly hails from a long line of prestigious witches in North

America. Her ancestors have been a bit nomadic since escaping the Salem Witch Trials. She and her parents were no different, living in the Yukon while conducting a research project until we recruited them for a special project in Calgary. Molly harbors the power of transport, just like Fitz. She doesn't rattle easily, nor fold under pressure. She'll be your chameleon and a quick thinker. Having no prior connection to you, she'll be key for unbiased opinions and decisions and will assist in maintaining group stability."

"Welcome, Molly. We're excited to have you with us," I said.

A mix of welcoming voices followed suit.

"And Jordan," Albina said kindly, turning to Prisha.

"She has a great capacity for understanding and kindness. She's always known about your abilities?" Prisha questioned.

"Yes."

"And she accepted you without question. Jordan exercises an understanding and discretion almost beyond human. She is analytical and calculated but can accept information that can't be technically understood, at least not by humans. We wanted one crusade member who was not a witch, but that person needed Jordan's characteristics. She and Molly will essentially act together in many ways to help calculate and think through plans. Opimae intelligence also wants to utilize her skill set, and Jordan also maintains a fresh, un-witchlike perspective."

"As we searched for the proper group for the crusade," Ella added, "we realized the very group for which we searched, lay right in front of us. If we could pull the right individuals and talents from a group already connected to one another and who trusted one another, why wouldn't we? And many of you already have ties to the council."

"You each have the corresponding qualities to comprise the necessary team, and so you have been summoned to fulfill this mission on behalf of witchkind. You were each born for this. It seems Fate found a way to bring you all together." Albina nodded.

"Fate," James echoed.

CHAPTER THREE

After a long day of overwhelming information, new faces, and old friends, we retired to Fitz's flat to relax and enjoy dinner. Fitz and I invited our small, core group over that evening for everyone to become better acquainted.

Steak and ale pie was our selection, a very British meal indeed. Fitz prepared the beef, while Jordan and I chopped vegetables. Isaac and Henry whipped up sticky toffee pudding, and Ian set the table and tidied behind us. As a dinner plate soared past my head, I looked around the flat at each of us employed in helping the collective, and I smiled reflecting on how well we already worked together. It gave me hope.

"When did you arrive?" I asked Jordan.

"We made it last night. Mr. MacGregor showed me around the city this morning while we waited for the council meeting. I'm already inclined to be quite in love with it."

"Jordan!"

"Dang! I'm sorry, Ian."

"It's amazing." I smiled. "How are you able to take off work for this?" I asked. Jordan worked as an intelligence analyst for the FBI, and time off was never simple for her.

"Apparently, someone very high up contacted my manager and said I was being reassigned," she said, her eyebrows rising.

"What the senior councils want, the senior councils get."

"So I'm learning. The next day Ian showed up and asked me to pack my bags."

"Let's not even pretend like this isn't a better opportunity. The assignment they had you buried in was beneath you."

"Oh, I'm definitely not complaining."

"Isaac, what about you? What's your nine to five? Where do you live?"

"London. I've just made partner at my firm, so I plan to stay there a while, much to Fitz and Henry's dismay." He grinned broadly.

"Traitor," Ian teased.

"That's a mouthful coming from a Scottish American," Isaac shot back, pulling laughter from everyone, and roaring applause from Henry.

"Lawyer?" I asked.

"Correct."

"Partner is a big deal," Jordan said.

Isaac smiled. "It feels good."

"You must love London to stay there and brave being

branded a traitor."

"Don't let him fool you. It's not London so much as the boyfriend," Henry interjected.

"Now I need details."

"Well, there isn't anyone yet. A seer told me a few months ago that I'll meet my mate in London and gave me a description. I'm keeping my eyes open."

"Hopeless romantic, that one." Henry winked.

"What if I don't know he's 'the one?'"

"*You'll know*," Fitz and Henry responded in unison.

"Either way, that's *not* keeping me in London – Fate will take care of things one way or the other. I know her that well," Isaac added drily, eyeing Henry meaningfully.

"That was a joke, mate."

Isaac punched Henry playfully.

"Come on, guys. We're in civilized company," Fitz interrupted, smiling.

"Isaac is humble, so he won't tell you that his firm is prestigious and he's a legal genius, but I have no issue telling you that," Henry offered.

"One of the many reasons the council just can't seem to leave him alone," Fitz added, nodding.

"You're one to talk," Isaac returned. "You've just found a way to evade their big projects until now."

"Look at all the skills and acumen in this room," Ian added. "Amazing how they sniff us out."

"Speaking of acumen," Jordan began, "what is it that you do, Henry?"

"Nothing exciting – investing."

"And *he* won't tell you how much time he spends mentoring businesses he invests in, but he dedicates a considerable amount of time to helping them reach their full potential," Fitz added.

"Stop talking me up, mate. I have a reputation to uphold."

"You two. How do you know each other?" Isaac quizzed, looking at Jordan and me.

"Lordy!" Jordan smiled. "We go way back!"

"Junior high, I guess?"

"Yep. You were at Gram's that summer. It had to be seventh grade."

"I used to spend all of my summers with my grandmother in Mississippi," I explained. "Jordan and her family had just moved to town that summer."

"What took you to Mississippi?" Isaac questioned.

"My dad's a professor and was offered a job at Mississippi State. My mom's an ER doctor and was able to get a job with the hospital there. So, we packed up and moved."

"Where were you moving from?" Isaac asked.

"D.C." She sighed. "And I was a city girl. *But* the experience did give me Hadley, so it wasn't all bad."

"These two are family," Fitz added.

"And you know Jordan from before?" Henry asked.

"I met her at the lake the summer I met Hadley."

"I accepted an internship with the National Park Service that summer. So instead of spending the summer with Gram in Mississippi, she came to stay with us in Washington State. And so did Jordan – she was at Amherst at the time."

"That was an interesting summer," Jordan mused, taking a sip of Merlot. Her eyes cut to mine, and I nodded, signaling I was okay. I'd say she worried too much, but she had her reasons. She miraculously found a way to take two weeks off work after Daddy died to stay with me. And I was a wreck.

"I'm glad you're here," Isaac said. "I've heard about your intel skills. And I can sense how close you and Hadley are."

"We're sisters," I said, matter-of-factly. During my formative years, I felt most myself when I was with Jordan. When you find women who make you feel more yourself when you're with them than apart, you've found your other sisters – the ones the world forgot were yours all along.

Fitz smiled broadly.

"What?"

"You two make me happy."

"Yeah, you're all right yourself, Fitz," Jordan shot back, raising her glass.

"Oh! Before I forget – Hadley, show Henry what you learned with the veggies."

"Right! Henry, watch."

I resumed chopping the carrots and channeled my energy into the knife, slowly releasing it from my grasp. The knife sliced through the vegetables, even after my hands pulled away. Jordan's jaw dropped in amazement, and everyone applauded. I maintained my focus on the instrument, and it slowly traveled through the air back into my waiting grasp.

"Brilliant. Well done!" Henry encouraged.

"She's been practicing non-stop, a very diligent student."

"Okay, *now* this is all real," Jordan muttered, her eyes wide.

Conversation soon fell into a steady rhythm. I added the last of the veggies to the sizzling pan and crossed the room to Fitz. I placed my hand on his nearest shoulder, and he cocked his head in my direction, wearing the goofy grin I loved so much.

"I love you," I whispered for only him to hear.

After dinner, Fitz prompted me to show off my new property. Negotiations moved quickly with my inquiry into the next-door apartment, and I closed on it only two days before. Our crew wandered around the space, while I explained our plans to have a door added between the two flats.

"Yeah, I agree," said Ian, floating his hand near the wall, searching for studs. "Just there would do for the door. You two will have a great space. Fitz has the best view, with the castle being just there, but Hadley has a better master suite – and the more private side of the building."

"It's perfect," added Jordan. "It suits you two."

After an evening filled with family, friends, food, and views, Fitz and I had much to reflect on as we lay tangled in bed. Relaxed in his arms, I could no longer keep my curiosity at bay. I needed to know about Isaac.

"Oh, right. I'm not surprised you picked up on our connection. Henry and I first met Isaac near campus, and when we stumbled into him, a few human tourists were harassing him outside a pub that night."

I shook my head. "So, what happened?"

"You saw Isaac – he's tough. He was holding his own, but he was outnumbered. So, Henry and I jumped in."

"Right place, right time."

He smiled. "The three of us had a few drinks after the brawl, and we've been close ever since. You weren't able to perceive connections when you first met Henry, or you would have noticed that one as well. Now you know our relationship so well you don't pay any mind to it."

"I see what you mean. I've always known you and Henry were kind of a package deal. Now I see Isaac is, too. What did I do so right? I mean, three for the price of one!"

I could almost feel his smirk.

"Aye, we're brothers, us three."

A soft smile settled on my lips, and I closed my eyes, reflecting on our beautiful little family coming together.

CHAPTER FOUR

T he following afternoon began with lunch before we split into individual training sessions. Fitz pointed to empty seats beside Omar and Solomon, the African representatives on the council, and we joined them in an effort to learn more about their backgrounds. Though the naked eye would have placed them somewhere around forty years of age, ninety and ninety-six, respectively, were the true tallies.

Omar grew up in his native Morocco, traveling much of Europe after attending college in Britain, and eventually returned home to join his local council, serving witchkind faithfully ever since. He dressed in traditional Moroccan garb, and the bright colors of his djellaba were cheerful against the winter weather that recently set in. His dark eyes were lively and set above a face with bone structure any model would envy. Something about him was regal, even with his lighthearted disposition, and sitting next to Solomon, they looked like true African royalty.

Solomon's gabi was a simple off-white, but bright green, orange, and pink decorated the end of the sleeves and the bottom of the garment. The stark contrast between the white robe and his umber skin was stunning, and his smile immediately put me at ease. His eyes were ever-changing, alive like the Northern Lights. Solomon told us that he carried the spirit of Ethiopia and its people with him and that their very spirit reflected to the world through his eyes. Though he traveled the world on council business, he proudly declared his Ethiopian heritage kept him grounded and true.

Omar and Solomon carried a quick wit about them, and we laughed our way through much of the lunch hour. We perceived their close study of us, their easy mannerisms inviting honesty and trust.

"They must learn a lot from people," Fitz's voice sounded in my mind. "Can't help but trust them."

"Disarming, intelligent, and easy to talk to," I agreed.

Solomon was assigned as Fitz's lead coach, and once lunch concluded, Fitz kissed the top of my head and followed Solomon down a long corridor to begin training. Prisha then accompanied me to my room. She wore a bright smile, her slim face complemented by long black hair and a muscular build. Something about her countenance was warm and friendly, which eased the nerves growing in my belly.

As we entered the power training room, two new faces greeted us, and I had the distinct feeling it would be another day of overwhelming information. Prisha introduced Chloe – the final Cardinal Court member. Chloe was selected as my lead coach, meaning she was responsible for appointing and overseeing my magic tutor, as well as overseeing my combat coaches and training.

"Chloe joins us from Australia."

There were few places in the world that made as much sense as Australia did for this woman. She looked young, but her cunning blue eyes held wisdom and experience. Wavy, blonde hair hung to her lower back, bleached by the sun, much in the same way her golden skin had been kissed by it. Her build was that of an athlete, and I wondered if perhaps she owed years of surfing for her sculpted, lean muscle.

"Right on. I'm so happy to meet you, Hadley."

"Same to you. I'm sorry I missed you yesterday."

"Oh, the fault was mine. I had some urgent business back home, but all is well now."

"Australian witchkind was on the brink of civil war roughly a year ago, and Chloe has been instrumental in bringing the two parties together. Really amazing work."

"Thanks, Prisha. It hasn't been easy, but we're finally in a good place – settling down and moving forward. Of course, that doesn't mean we don't have the occasional hiccup," she offered, winking.

"The things humans don't know… that I didn't know until recently."

"You know, Hadley. I wanted to mention something before we get started. I can feel in your energy that you're still a bit skeptical of us."

"Chloe –"

"No, it's okay. I just want you to know I understand. I would feel the same way."

"I appreciate that. It hasn't been easy."

"I've launched an investigation into the lower councils, and I hope that will help."

"An investigation?"

"From what I've heard, I don't believe things were handled well, so there will be an investigation. I want you to know that I'm sorry for what you and Fitz went through, and I'm here to help you every step of the way through this crusade, all right?"

"Oh, Chloe," I nearly whispered. "Thank you."

Chloe smiled. "Well, let's get started, shall we? This is Hope, or Maka, as her tribal friends call her."

Chloe chose Hope from the Sioux Tribe of the American Dakotas to improve my understanding of my abilities and to assist me in controlling them. Hope was short and slender, with bronzed skin and raven hair. Her dark eyes seemed to perceive everything, and I was struck by their intensity. Her physical being was almost otherworldly, and the lighthearted energy of a free spirit wafted casually around her. She was deeply rooted in the elements and tradition, but it was easy to see that she embraced today's world with all its possibilities.

Hope began by learning more about my struggles. I related my difficulty with mind reading, and how I progressed slightly in controlling it. "I have so little control of that power. I've started before I even know I've begun. I really have to get a handle on it."

"I hate to tell you this, Hadley, but controlling your mind is a matter of practice. You're making progress as you continue to focus on controlling it, and you'll find yourself progressing more with time."

"I've tried to be especially cognizant around others, but it's difficult to maintain that focus in a crowd of people."

"At some point, it'll become second nature to you. When you first learned to ride a bike, you had to focus on your balance, peddling, and where you wanted to go, but at some point balance and peddling became innate for you. This talent will be the same. Keep focusing on what you want, and together, we'll get there."

"Perfect. Sometimes the reception is a little fuzzy or in and out," I lamented with a smile.

"Oh, I know exactly how you feel. I've been there, too."

"It's encouraging to talk to someone who's been through this."

"It must seem overwhelming right now, but you haven't had the benefit of training through childhood. You've only had months to discover the world we've experienced since childhood. I know without a doubt, you can master everything in the time we have – you harbor such strong and unique magic inside you."

"Thank you, Hope... or Maka? Which do you prefer?"

"I don't mind much either way. I'm called by both."

"Maka is beautiful. It's tribal?"

"It essentially means earth. In our Lakota mythology, it's

related to our earth spirit. When my mom was pregnant with me, she knew my abilities would be strong. Since she could feel my power so clearly, she named me Hope. But because they didn't know definitively what we were, many members of my tribe only sensed my strong connection with our earth. I come from a long line of healers. The nickname just stuck," she related with a smile, shrugging her shoulders.

"I'll call you Maka if that's okay. It's lovely, and I think you're an earth goddess after all."

Over the next few weeks, I trained relentlessly with Maka, building on the skills I mastered through my training with Fitz and Henry, and working hand in hand with them to advance new skills. During weekdays, Maka and I met over my lunch break, and James insisted I leave early each afternoon to devote more time to my craft. On weekends, I spent my mornings with Maka and my evenings working with Fitz or Henry, constantly in a state of learning, mastering, and progressing toward my goals. Once the council agreed that I mastered the basics, we moved on to my specialized powers, focusing first on mind reading.

Maka exposed me to many different circumstances where I needed to control my mind, either to stay out of others' minds or to find a particular train of thought. We used meditation to strengthen my control and patience. Each day was challenging, but rewarding, and for the first time, I could control my gift – and even think of it as such.

* * *

After the fifth day of focused mind training, our crew

wandered over to Whiski, which quickly became our regular haunt. A woman's hand invited my notice, its aggressive motion catching my eye. She was angry, of that I was certain, but what did the nervous man across the table do to deserve all this? My eyes lingered long enough to attract an onlooker of my own.

"Would you look at those two," Henry observed.

"I wonder what's going on?"

"Don't you know?" Jordan asked.

I looked up, smirking proudly.

"No, I don't believe she does," said Ian, his tone that of a proud father.

"Hadley, did you stay out of their minds?" Fitz asked.

"It required very little effort."

"Okay, now can you focus and tell us what's going on?" Isaac demanded.

Fitz's reproachful look did little good, as curiosity took root amongst our companions.

Henry shrugged. "I'm with Isaac on this one. Inquiring minds need to know."

"It would be a nice test," added James, a mischievous twinkle in his eye.

I listened briefly, intent on hearing only enough to quell the curiosity at the table and no more. "The poor idiot cheated on her."

"*Poor?*" Jordan questioned, her eyebrows raised.

"Oh yeah. You should see the damage she left to his flat *and* his car."

Our table erupted in sympathetic noises, which turned abruptly to laughter.

"And not only is she intelligent and beautiful, but you'd have to be pretty dense to not realize she would turn volatile."

The woman's voice rose, and the poor idiot, as we later officially dubbed him, jumped from his seat and nearly ran through the door. The beautiful girl was left alone, both hands pressed firmly around her beer, tears pouring down her rosy cheeks and spilling onto the table.

"So... should we do something or leave her alone?" Jordan asked. All eyes pointed in my direction, as I focused on the answer.

"She's embarrassed by the scene. She lost control when arguing with him and never meant for all that to happen. The other woman sent her a message with more info right before he entered the pub. She doesn't want to be noticed, but then again she wouldn't refuse the kindness of a stranger, I don't think."

"I'll walk over then," Jordan volunteered. "And assess from there."

After Jordan helped her into a cab, we adjourned for the evening, as the following morning would bring another long day of training for everyone.

"Well, if Hadley's proficiency in her other skills comes as quickly as this one, she'll be kicking our asses in no time."

"Does that concern you, Henry?" Fitz teased.

"Of course it does," he responded, much to everyone's amusement, and we all parted ways into the full moonlight.

CHAPTER FIVE

By the time the first light shone weakly through the low-hanging clouds, I was tucked away in my office, finalizing the donor pamphlet I was intent on creating the very afternoon of our crusade's inception. I was proud of myself for seeing it through, even with the demands of power training. I laid the freshly printed pamphlet on my desk, smiling in anticipation of James's delighted response to the finished product. Maybe there was something comforting in my familiar work, offsetting all of the new information, faces, and training. As control over my magic became increasingly innate, the council ruled it was time to cover spell creation combat training. The thought of combat still struck fear into my heart, but less and less with every milestone, I found.

Realizing it was time to meet Maka, my jacket met me at the office door, and I rushed to the esplanade, finding the morning rain had moved out. Cool, wintry sunlight filled the streets, and even with its cold, blustery counterpart, it was a welcome sight after a lengthy streak of dreary clouds and rain – which tested even my love for moody weather. Maka and I walked the few blocks to our favorite coffee shop in companionable chatter, anticipating the warm food and strong tea that would soon fuel our afternoon.

While awaiting our Earl Grey, Maka issued a challenge – I needed to find a particular train of thought in the busy space, and then ignore the babble of the crowd altogether. The small shop was crammed with young professionals and tourists, and the noise was almost deafening, even without the extra clamor of their thoughts buzzing through the air. Scanning the crowd, I slowly shut out anything that didn't benefit my objective, obeying Maka's orders dutifully.

"You are a true proficient."

"I have a wonderful tutor. I'll give you her number."

As it turned out, Maka was a blessing in more ways than one. Magnetic energy channeled between the two of us, strengthening what would have certainly been an already natural friendship, and that made the long training days far more enjoyable than they would've been otherwise. A soft, but palpable, anxiety buzzed underneath the surface of the group – the uncertainty of our future and the certainty of Lorenzo's growing power lay heavily on our shoulders. Though, with a strong community of wise creatures like Maka, we could envision a real chance of success.

As we reached the esplanade, Maka's face tilted expectantly toward the sun, and we paused briefly, enjoying our last few moments outdoors. Chloe met us by the gate, excited to attend our afternoon training session. I originally thought it would be awkward to have an audience while I worked with Maka, especially from a Cardinal Court member, but I was wrong. Chloe was supportive – my cheerleader of sorts, and it helped me grasp how dedicated she was to my success. Some of my most valuable sessions were the result of Maka and Chloe's joint teaching.

"Power and physical combat training go hand in hand," Chloe explained. "As a witch preparing for a fight of this magnitude, one without the other just isn't helpful to you."

"Just hearing that is unnerving."

"Honestly, that's good. It means you understand the gravity of the situation. However, you'll feel more comfortable and more – let's see what I want to communicate here – this will all feel natural to you eventually. It will feel like second nature before we ever let you leave Earth, so don't dwell on it."

"Okay," I returned simply, managing a smile.

"Have you been meditating?"

"Yes," I answered truthfully. Fitz meditated daily, and we fell into a routine together.

"And yoga?"

I grimaced.

"It's all right; I won't scold you," Chloe returned, laughing. "But I will encourage you to make room for it. Hadley, with your mental abilities, you carry a massive amount of anxiety in you. You harbor other creatures' negative thoughts and energy without even realizing it. Regular yoga practice is just as important as meditation for you. They work together to remove the bad stuff – not just from your body, but from your thoughts and your spirit, as well."

"I know. That's horrible, isn't it? I know it'll help me, and I still haven't made room for it… I'm just having trouble balancing everything. I want to do better."

"Hadley," Maka began. "Oh, Hadley. You have so much going on right now. You discovered you're a witch only a few months ago, and you're mentally wading through those changes and what they mean. You moved to a new country. You're in a relationship that, yes, began several years ago, but is different now in many ways. You started a new job. And finally, you are training to meet an adversary in a foreign world."

I laughed softly, nodding my head.

"No one would find their balance quickly, and you shouldn't blame yourself for not getting there with the snap of your fingers."

"Thank you."

"You're exhausted," Chloe stated. It wasn't a question, but I answered anyway.

"Yes."

Maka took my hand gently. "Chloe is right about yoga. For someone who possesses your talents, it's imperative. Once you get into a routine, you'll feel the anxiety peeling off – layer by layer, you'll feel closer to your balance. Don't deprive yourself of inner peace."

These two women felt my exhaustion, my weariness… the load I carried over the past couple of months. I dutifully promised to adjust my routine, knowing I wanted better for myself.

"Not to change the subject…"

"Oh, I think we've exhausted this one anyway."

"How does this all work? My power channeling into combat?"

"I'm glad you asked. Though there is certainly physical combat, witches also fight by crafting spells or utilizing skills that either act in place of brute force, or enhance it."

"Brute force?"

"Yep. I know we have you guys exercising currently, but you're about to go through an intense program to build on that."

I nodded slowly.

"Over the next few months, you and the team will train heavily with three instructors. Each instructor will focus on a particular area crucial for your success in Opimae."

"We'll all train together?"

"Individually and together – about half and half. So, would you like to learn about your new trainers?"

"Absolutely."

"Good. They've been waiting so patiently out in the hallway."

I closed my eyes briefly, sensing the energy on the other side of the door. One of the energies was guarded, shifting around wildly. The second felt almost nervous.

"The first trainer will focus on physical fitness. Luckily, most of you are already pretty fit and have done well in your mandated regimens, but we need to deepen your stamina and agility."

"Do you think there will be a fair amount of physical exertion?"

"We honestly don't know what to expect. It's likely you'll have to fight your way through difficult terrain, and it's possible you'll engage on a battlefield. There's also the possibility of another witch temporarily stunting your magic. If that occurs, you need to be a badass physically."

She smirked, but the words sent a cold shock through my body. Someone could take my life in mere seconds, and we all needed to prepare for that.

"With that in mind, I'd like to introduce our physical fitness trainer."

A tall, muscular frame filled the doorway, and though I recognized his face instantly, I wasn't prepared for the charge of energy that accompanied him.

"Holy shit. You're a witch."

"Nice to see you, too, Hads."

Tanner ran a hand through his dirty blond hair and crossed the room, lifting my rigid body off the ground and into a warm embrace. Tanner and I met in a history class at the University of Washington and bonded instantly. He grew up on Lake Crescent, only a few houses down the gravel road from my parents' cabin. He and I were inseparable for years. After he met Jordan, the three of us shared a friendship few could comprehend. We were the three musketeers, and I thought I knew everything about him... though I obviously missed one very important detail.

"You've got to be kidding."

"Didn't you ever wonder about us? Everyone else did; how we could be so close, spend all that time together, but nothing was happening in the romance department."

"Everyone found our relationship odd, except for us."

"We were kindred spirits – the same species surrounded by a lot of humans. We were familiar to one another, and you unconsciously clung to me because of that."

"Jordan…"

"Jordan was used to your oddities years before I ever entered the picture. I probably make about as much sense to her as you do, but it works somehow."

"Well, I declare."

"You sound just like Gram!"

"You do know how to compliment a girl," I said, beaming ear to ear. My grandmother was my favorite human, as Tanner well knew.

He was right – we were magnets, but there was never any sort of romantic chemistry. We bonded over hiking and life on the Olympic Peninsula, and as our friendship developed, we carpooled out of the city on weekends. We were hiking buddies, camping fiends who lived on trails and mountaintops summer after summer.

Staring at my companion of many years, the urge to give him a nice smack to the back of the head overwhelmed me, and I acted unceremoniously on that desire.

"What was that for?"

"For keeping a secret from me."

"Because I had a choice?"

I gave him an amused look.

"What now?"

"Looks like combat has already begun," Chloe interjected.

"She's a feisty one, all right."

"So, Tanner will be your fitness coach. He will increase your physical ability and endurance."

"Right. We'll toughen you up as much as possible through some basic training. Running, swimming, trail running, climbing, strength training. We'll get you strong enough to outperform and outlast your opponent. That's the ultimate goal."

"Not really looking forward to it, but sounds all right."

"And here's your second coach," Chloe said, extending her arm toward another familiar face. I noticed the witch slink in, and although we'd never spoken, I didn't need an introduction to him either.

"You watched me," I stated coldly.

"I apologize."

"That doesn't seem awfully sincere."

"I didn't mean to alarm you. The council shared their interest in you, and I knew I'd assist in your training, should you agree to this. I wanted to observe the new prospect in her natural hab–"

"Jess is overzealous," Chloe interrupted, leveling her eyes toward him in an icy glare. I wasn't the only creature to sense Chloe's tense energy. Tanner's eyes flickered between her and Jess warily.

Things were getting interesting.

"However, he is an excellent coach."

"I'm sure he is. It just doesn't sit well with me."

Everything within me was burning. Jess's entrance ignited the flame of my fire magic, and his continued presence only stoked the flame higher. I closed my eyes momentarily, willing my body to cool down.

"I'm sorry," Jess returned, a grim expression resting on his features.

"Jess, why don't you share with Hadley how you're going to help her?"

His frosty gaze settled on my skin. The sting of a witch's gaze usually settled with time. The longer you knew someone, the lesser the reaction, and the longer you were in contact with another creature, the more the sting dulled into comfortable familiarity. Yet the pricks of Jess's gaze offered no sign of abatement.

"We're going to have a lot of fun. You'll learn task execution with me. We'll focus on hand to hand combat, martial arts, and the like."

"Sounds demanding. If I'm going to be ready for all that, I think Tanner has his work cut out for him."

"Bring it." Tanner smiled, though I still felt the mounting tension in his energy.

My two coaches couldn't have been any more different. Where Jess was eerily observant and cold, Tanner was enthusiastic and warm. I intended to persuade Tanner to stick with me through

Jess's training – the thought of being alone with Jess sent a chill down my spine.

"So, who's lucky number three?" I quizzed.

"You're looking at her," Tanner answered.

"What? Chloe?"

"You and I are going to tackle power enhancement training together."

"It sounds complicated. I'm glad you're the one training me on that."

"I'm thrilled because it's the special part."

"Tell me more."

"Tanner will strengthen your body. Jess will strengthen your self-defense and strategy. Power enhancement is the added boost that will take each of those abilities to the next level. We'll cover combat that includes levitating yourself and other objects, fire, crafting spells, and generally leveraging magic for added strength. Then we'll strengthen your instinct."

"Wow."

"I know it's a lot to take in. We're going to make you invincible."

"I like the sound of that."

Tanner's hand met mine in a high five, his excited energy mingling with Chloe's and my own. The moment would have been perfect had I not met Jess's gaze from across the room, my instinct pleading with me to run.

CHAPTER SIX

"And that's when I learned women are easily twice as smart as men."

Laughter erupted as I walked into Henry's living room. "I don't think I've ever walked into a room with you in it, and not walked into roaring laughter."

Tanner shrugged his shoulders and drained the last of his beer. "What can I say? I just tell it like it is, and I guess people think it's funny."

"Tell it like it is? *Oh my*."

He winked at Jordan and Chloe, who laughed in turn.

"You shouldn't encourage him like this." I smiled, rolling my eyes playfully at Jordan, who simply shrugged.

Tanner's gaze shifted suddenly to Chloe, and I knew him well enough to feel concerned over the change in his energy. But as quickly as I took notice, it was over, and Tanner immediately changed the topic of conversation.

"Can you believe this? The three musketeers joining the fight to save all that's good in the world."

"It does seem pretty unbelievable, doesn't it? Although if we have to camp in Opimae, we're pros."

"Or have to eat nasty ass dried food."

"Or use whisky to disinfect wounds," Jordan offered.

"And disinfect our bellies while we're at it," Tanner added seriously before we broke into laughter.

I wiggled myself a little tighter against Fitz and found the courage to ask the question – the one that came to mind immediately following my reunion with Tanner. I stalled all afternoon, unsure if I actually wanted to know the answer.

"Is our friendship organic?"

"What do you mean?"

"She's wondering if your friendship was planned. By the council," Fitz clarified. We hadn't discussed it, but of course, he knew.

"This might be difficult to believe, but no, it wasn't. Our friendship was totally organic. I had no idea I'd train you guys one day."

"You knew I was a witch coming into my powers, right?"

"Yeah, absolutely. I figured that out pretty fast. I wanted to be careful around you, but we just bonded, you know? I didn't think our friendship would be a problem, but I did have the MacGregors' blessing."

"Really?" I turned toward Fitz.

"Dad told him to be careful around you, but he didn't perceive any harm in it."

"That seems pretty perceptive – you realizing what I was."

"Nah, not really. Even though it's rare, we all know about the witch born to human parents scenario. The signs are pretty hard to miss."

"Okay, wait… follow up question."

"Yes, detective?"

"You were always athletic, but you started training hard right before I left the lake."

"Yeah. The council hired a buddy of mine – you remember Slingshot?"

"How could I forget," I returned, drily. He'd never been a good influence on Tanner.

"Yeah, so they hired him as a trainer around that time, and he knew another position was going to open up. These positions are the kind you work your ass off to get a shot at, and I decided to go for it."

"You've been with the council all this time. And here Hads and I were thinking you were a personal trainer for regular ole humans like me," Jordan interjected.

"Yeah, sorry about that. But come on, J. I couldn't exactly share that with you two."

"When did the council hire you?"

"I trained about a year before they announced the opening. At my first interview, they said I had an innate gift and was exactly

- 292 -

what they were looking for. They canceled the rest of the candidate interviews and hired me on the spot. Pretty strange actually."

"Could this be any weirder? Seriously, does anyone else find this odd? The three of us becoming friends, Fitz's family being assigned to me, this group having so many connections and friendships, and yet miraculously we all fit what the council needs?"

"This group has turned everything on its head," Chloe began. "I can't believe in coincidence any longer – not after the interconnectedness of this group."

"I can't wrap my mind around it. We each made decision after decision, unknowingly bringing ourselves closer to one another, and closer to this crusade. Just look at my last-minute whim on Edinburgh. Any way you slice it, it's strange."

"It does muddle up your brain, doesn't it?" Fitz added thoughtfully.

"We talk about Fate as though she's had a hand in all this…" I began.

"So, maybe Fate wanted your paths to cross, even before the crusade," Solomon finished, nodding.

"You're onto something… I mean, you're special. All of you. You were ordained by Fate. Maybe it seems weird to us, but you were born to be who you are, and I think you were all destined to find one another," Chloe stated.

"So were you, Chloe," James added. Our conversation now attracted the attention of the entire room.

"That's true," Jordan said. "We wouldn't be here without

you. You've given us a reason to fight."

"We've often said we'd have no hope if it weren't for this team, but I guess there would be no team without the council."

"I know our relationship with the council is complicated at times, but look around – most of us have either been raised with family employed by the council or have been employed by it ourselves. Regardless of whether we sometimes agree or disagree, we do know what you've sacrificed to serve," Isaac offered. "You've worked hard for this, too."

"I've heard about the riots in your country. It's difficult to see the damage they've caused to our progress, but word of your efforts to disband the inciters is getting around. Creatures are recalling why we need you all over again," Fitz added.

"What's their argument?"

"That the council demands too much of witchkind."

"It's interesting, isn't it? When the council calls, our duty isn't optional, and I have as complicated of a relationship with the council as anyone. I've broken your rules, and I've resented you," Fitz admitted, his gaze shifting from his father to me to Chloe. Solomon's hand rested supportively on Fitz's shoulder. "But overall, most creatures live a comfortable life. How many actually decline the extra money?"

"Not many."

"They want the money, but with zero expectation in return," Solomon added.

"I know we haven't done everything right, but God, have we

tried. And I do understand your position, Fitz. The more I'm learning through this investigation, the more I think the lower councils made a mistake. Besides, no one could sit in the same room with you and Hadley and think they can keep you apart," said Chloe, her gaze resting on me. Isaac wasn't the only hopeless romantic amongst our group.

"We have new blood rising in the ranks," Solomon began. "I think this new life will help the council evolve – and for the better."

"Things are better than they've ever been. The councils are learning and growing. Some people just want to stir up trouble," James insisted. "These protestors certainly aren't the first, and they won't be the last."

"Do you think they've been incited by Lorenzo?" Fitz quizzed.

"It's something we've considered," Chloe returned. "The organizers themselves have nothing to lament. We've asked for their cause – they give us nothing of substance. General statements, no real examples… nothing we can solve. They want more money and less government, but they can't actually tell us why."

"It's a good thought, Fitz. Money from Lorenzo and the promise of future glory would be cause enough for some to riot, regardless of the damage. It would be a good strategy on Lorenzo's part to divide the council's attention," Henry pondered.

"These are troubling times to be sure," James began. "But that is exactly why we must focus on this mission. You're going to restore more than you realize."

"You, too, James," Jordan smiled, her hand lightly squeezing his.

A short pause in conversation was replaced by the rhythmic reverberation of song in the air, as Ian began a traditional Gaelic tale. Fitz and Henry were quick to join in, soon followed by James. As Fitz pulled me closer to him, I felt the rise and fall of his chest, then the vibrations traveling across the air. The vibrant air swirled and enveloped me, and I closed my eyes, reveling in the new experience. My magic was shifting, changing, growing, and granting new awareness to me. I opened my eyes to the smiles and subtle sways of my companions, and I smiled along with them. Many things flowed through the air alongside the elements – vitality, happiness, love, hope… and magic.

*   *   *

As headlights led us away from Henry's, my thoughts rolled around ceaselessly. The council wasn't perfect, as I well knew, but most of the members I'd come to know desired what was best for our kind. We lived in a cocoon within the human world, one where we received monetary funds as a birthright. And if any creature forfeited the money, the council would never call upon them. But certain creatures desired the perks without expending any effort. For others, the thought of unreserved power was too appealing, brewing resentment against those in power.

I wasn't naive – officials abusing power and position within our government must have been a reality. It was inevitable. So were mistakes. But my own experiences demonstrated that the negative aspects wouldn't overshadow all that had been won… all that had been righted. This was my first glimpse at the real volatility amongst our kind.

A bright light suddenly assaulted my eyes, as our headlights met a metal sign reading *Lady Stairs Close*, the courtyard entrance that led our friends to their temporary home. Council guests resided in the flats across from the Writer's Museum for the duration of their council business, to include those in Fitz's Land Rover – Chloe, Jordan, and Tanner. The fact that their flats were located on the third floor was of little consequence, considering the windowless turret concealed luggage floating lazily around the spiral stairs, and groceries… and creatures.

As Fitz rolled the car to a stop, Chloe and Jordan ran through the archway, escaping the bone-chilling night air.

"Tanner?" I called before he shut the car door. "Before you go, I have a question."

"Shoot."

"When Chloe was introducing Jess earlier…"

"And gave him that ice-cold stare."

"Yes!"

"What?" Fitz asked curiously.

"When Chloe was introducing Jess to Hadley, she said he was overzealous and gave him a glare that would have burned the soul of a lesser creature."

"That's one way to put it. I wonder what that was about?"

"No idea, but I'm going to keep my eyes open."

"Same. You know… he gives me the creeps," I admitted.

"Probably because the asshole was stalking you," Fitz added, strangling the steering wheel.

"Yeah, Hadley almost lit his soul on fire, too."

"You brought it up?"

"Yeah, but she didn't have to say much. There was actual fire in her eyes – I mean, I didn't even know that could happen."

I looked over at Fitz, batting my eyes playfully.

"Good girl."

"I didn't realize my eyes were blazing. Do you think Chloe noticed?"

"I think even the paint noticed. It's all good, though."

"Okay, well get out of the cold. I just wanted to ask."

"See you two tomorrow."

CHAPTER SEVEN

The following weeks fell away quickly, each day yielding more hope and increased strength. After weeks of training individually with Tanner based on our personalized needs, one particularly frigid morning dawned on the second phase of his course. Frost sparkled across the rooftops of Edinburgh, and our witchy senses detected the possibility of snow, a tingling sensation resting within our breasts – the sign of a storm brewing. Tanner was in an especially good mood over the past week, and he decided to go easy on us, allowing the course to be conducted indoors. Our smaller, individual training rooms were tugged open, resulting in one sprawling obstacle course. Well-worn monkey bars, towering walls strung with ropes, a dirt pit intended for crawling, and various other obstacles lay about the space.

Chloe's smile was especially bright as we filed into the room, and as her arms reached for the ceiling, Christmas lights suddenly illuminated the dark room, met with joyful shouts and laughter.

Having remained so focused on our gains, and with our schedules impossibly full, we had little time to enjoy the wondrous season. Chloe shared that a few festivities were arranged over the next couple of weeks, because even while training for battle, Christmas would not be forgotten, and as such, hot chocolate and mulled wine awaited us at the course's finish line.

Even without the holiday cheer, training with Tanner was surprisingly enjoyable. Originally, I worried about fitness training, but apparently, gaining new strength was addictive. Sure, I loved hiking and climbing, but when it came to pull-ups and endurance building runs, I was usually the first to opt out. Tanner achieved the impossible – he made those monotonous tasks not so monotonous, and the results were undeniable.

And on that Tuesday morning, while claiming my place beside Fitz in the glow of holiday lights, breathing deeply and awaiting the wave of the flag, the air belonged to me. I was in communion with the elements: my continued meditation, yoga, and fitness challenges spurred my entire being to adapt – and to thrive. With the pop of a flag against still air, our tennis shoe-clad feet slammed against the concrete, propelling us toward softer ground.

Fitz initially claimed first place, surprising no one, as he turned out to be the fastest runner in the group, but when he hesitated briefly, his eyes scanning the room for me, he allowed Isaac to pass him and take the lead. Though it was still early in training, he needed to worry about me less – or we'd find ourselves in trouble in the field.

I leapt toward the bars, my fingers grasping the cold metal without pause. Even with several bodies in between us, I caught glimpses of Isaac's bulging arms during our side-to-side sways across the bars. He really was a beast. Molly fell behind during the initial run but passed me as we approached the wall, and I feared I might land in last place, using that energy to propel myself forward. I pulled past Molly and Ian on the wall, which would have been unlikely, even a few weeks ago. My arms were undoubtedly the weakest part of my body, but through extensive work alongside Tanner, my progress was discernible.

Between the wall and crawl space, Fitz once again overtook Isaac, though his lead was slight. As our bodies emerged from the crawl, Ian regained his position ahead of me, threatening the heels of the younger guys. Though Ian and James were much older than the rest of us, their bodies responded well to exercise. I considered we each accelerated quickly, given the transformative power within us, but I also couldn't deny the fact that the male bodies seemed to respond twice as fast, which I found infuriating. And I was determined to work twice as hard.

We were greeted at the finish line with high fives from Chloe and loud praise from Tanner and Solomon. Breathing heavily, I reached for my water bottle before indulging in Chloe's treats, utilizing the opportunity to sit with Molly.

It would be unfair to claim Molly wasn't pleasant, but she was equally reserved. She was undisputedly the wallflower of the team, though I couldn't wonder why. Having been recruited by the council as the sole team member lacking a previous connection to the rest of the group, I'm sure she found it difficult initially to find her place socially. Though James fell into the same category, he was a guiding force from the council and possessed a warm and social personality to recommend him effortlessly.

Though she was consistently polite, Molly remained distant, and although this pattern held without sign of abatement, it didn't prevent me from reaching out when opportunity presented itself. I considered her purpose in the group – serving as a non-biased opinion – could lead to this behavior, though my third eye knew better. It wasn't that simple. But I still hadn't waved the white flag.

"Tanner said our times were good today," I reported.

"Yeah, it felt pretty good. Your arms are getting stronger. I saw that on the bars."

"I can feel my body changing. I like it."

"I can't believe I actually like this stuff, but it's kind of fun," she returned before draining her cup of hot chocolate.

"I think Tanner has a gift for making the mundane more fun."

"For sure. How long have you known him – Tanner?"

"Since college."

"It's interesting how everyone came together. I mean, I have zero connection to anyone on the team, so I still don't know all the threads."

Finally, we were addressing the elephant in the room.

"Does that bother you?"

"No, I needed to be an outsider for my role. But I wonder why I was selected by the council – a lot."

"I'm glad you're here with us. You make us stronger. You have a big purpose in all this."

She nodded her head ever so slowly. Even though I lived in a constant state of curiosity when it came to Molly, I refused to infiltrate her mind. At times, her energy felt sad, yet something still tugged at my third eye, telling me I had it all wrong.

Fitz floated packets of energizing powder next to Molly's water bottle. None of us exactly understood what was in the secret powder, but it was some sort of magical concoction of Tanner's that he swore by.

I grinned in Fitz's direction, and he winked in return.

"You two are *absurdly* cute, you know that?"

"Why is it that I have no idea if you just complimented or attacked me?"

Molly laughed. "One of my many talents."

Mia's voice interrupted our exchange, her tone harsh.

"You need to stop worrying about Hadley. You're going to cost us this mission if you can't get past it."

"I'm working on it, Mia."

"Could've fooled me," she called tartly over her shoulder, already halfway across the room.

"His instinct is strong. It can't be controlled overnight. These things take time," I said.

"Yeah, I get how things work, but thanks for your input,

Hadley," she answered coldly. "I get that I'm not mated, but I'm not ignorant."

"I implied nothing of the sort. You came up with that all on your own."

Mia paused, her eyes wide. She was unaccustomed to being challenged.

"Is there something you'd like to share with the class, Mia?" Molly chimed in.

"Excuse me?"

"Maybe you could start with why you're so defensive?"

"I'm not defensive. I'm pointing out an issue that needs to be addressed quickly."

"It can't be addressed quickly. That's not how this works, and you know it," I challenged.

"Okay, let's all calm down," Fitz began. "I'm working on the issue, Mia. I'll need a little more time, but I'm doing my best."

"Apparently, your best isn't good enough for Mia. But that seems to be the norm around here."

Mia crossed her arms, her eyes piercing my skin.

"Could you offer encouragement rather than criticism just once?" Molly questioned. "Would that kill you?"

"We're training for something serious — we all get that. We're doing our level best. A little support from you would be nice," I agreed.

"All right, everyone," Chloe began calmly. "We've been going really hard this week, and I know we're all on edge. Let's get back to celebrating our wins *and* the beautiful season. We'll finish this conversation another day."

Chloe gently ushered Mia through the door, but not before I made out the rise and fall of Chloe's voice. "You know, you get farther with people by supporting them. We are pushing this team as hard as physically and mentally possible and it would be helpful – "

Fitz gave me a weak smile, and though the energy of the room felt tense, we slowly slipped back into idle chatter. Chloe soon re-emerged, nodding to Fitz, then in Molly's direction and mine. Her smile looked forced, and I hoped we hadn't created an issue for her.

Molly and I fell into silence, and my eyes trailed Chloe across the room, her conversation with Tanner attracting my focus. Molly wasn't the only subject in the room who ignited my curiosity. I couldn't quite decide what was happening between Tanner and Chloe. They weren't together – they certainly weren't mated, yet the bond between them was more than friendship. The way they held each other's gaze was enough to arouse suspicion, but they gravitated toward one another, trusted one another; their energy reacted excitedly to one another… I wasn't going to intrude on Molly, and I made the same promise to myself regarding Tanner, even though I wanted to break that promise so badly.

"You've noticed it, too."

My focus snapped to Molly, unsure of how to respond. "Noticed what?"

"Really? I know you're watching them."

"You mean Tanner and Chloe?"

She cut her eyes toward me, one eyebrow raised – her nonverbal signal to cut the crap.

"What do you think is going on?"

"No idea, but something is off. You know Tanner better than I do, but I would swear he's into Chloe. And it seems like she's just drawn to him or something."

"And yet, they aren't mated."

"Maybe there's another connection we don't know about, but it's not right. They're more than friends."

"I might just ask him about it. I mean, I'll at least know if he's lying. If there's something happening within the group, I'd like to know."

"More than that – you *need* to know. We can't afford anything pulling focus from the mission. Too much is at stake."

Tanner called us into action.

"If I notice anything else I'll tell you," she said, reaching for my hand, and we pulled one another from the floor. "You and Fitz are our leads anyway. But keep me posted, will you? It's my job to help you with things like this."

"Yeah, you got it."

It was an interesting start to our alliance, but I jumped at her offer just the same. After all, part of Molly's purpose was to confer over strategy – to help maintain accord within the group regarding major issues and offer an unbiased perspective. Our team couldn't afford for this situation to evolve into an issue, though I already knew it would. Molly and I were about to embark on our first task to maintain group stability, and I could only hope we were ready for it.

*　　*　　*

I rolled over, my eyes aching as they met the green numbers of the alarm clock, which were shining brightly against the darkness of the room. *5:30.* Almost an hour earlier than my alarm, and even then, it was often difficult for this night owl to rouse myself from sleep. But training claimed a large portion of my afternoon schedule, and I shifted my office hours to begin by 7:30. It was necessary to make headway both at work and in training, and I was slowly progressing toward a better balance of the two. Even so, the previous few weeks passed so quickly, I hardly knew if my memories were real or those of dreams. I was exhausted – we all were.

Task execution training began at the end of the week, and nerves surfaced as the thought of Jess loomed in the back of my mind. He joined our fitness sessions regularly, his eyes always pressed hard and cold upon me. His relative obsession didn't feel romantic, but rather like he sought to understand the way my body moved. I convinced myself it was his attempt to assess the way I would fight. But if that were the case, why didn't he study the others? Why did Chloe seem so skeptical of him if she was the very one who selected him as our trainer?

I rolled over to Fitz, resolving to push the questions from my mind, at least for another hour. I lay motionless, focusing on the respite of sleep, lulling myself back into a state of tranquility. I watched the low-hanging clouds' slow movements and their reflection of the warm illumination of the city until I drifted back to sleep.

Where did reality stop and the dream begin? Bright morning sun poured through an open window, along with a slight breeze. Summer in Scotland was magic in its own right. The sun cast golden rays across everything it found, warming the worn floor and the top of a curly-headed beauty seated at the breakfast table. I floated across the room, seeking a better view of the paper in front of Chloe, finding a list of baby names scribbled across it. Was this a dream or another time? Though I wasn't a seer – the future wasn't mine to ponder – I wondered if my magic found a loophole after expending so much energy on the puzzle of Tanner and Chloe.

Heavy footsteps sounded in the hallway, and Tanner soon emerged, barefoot, a pair of jeans the sole obstruction of his sculpted physique. He peered over Chloe's head, resting his hands gently on her shoulders.

"I know what they mean by glowing," he whispered sweetly, leaning over to plant a quick kiss on her parted lips.

The vision dissipated as the alarm clock sounded violently in my ear. What on earth did I just see? I couldn't be sure of much, but of one thing I was absolutely certain: Tanner and I needed to talk – and soon.

CHAPTER EIGHT

I glanced over at Molly, who would soon outpace me if I couldn't maintain focus. Tanner combined our remaining classes in the hopes we'd each push each other, and we were falling into a steady rhythm of progress. Molly and I were ultimately becoming more than classmates – we were accountability partners, inspiring each other to work harder. As we swung from the bars that afternoon, I considered that even though most of Tanner's classes were pretty enjoyable, arm days did truly benefit from having Molly in the room. Does anyone actually *enjoy* pull-ups?

I stole another glance at my partner, realizing her pace was slowing. Following her gaze, I found Tanner and Chloe huddled in the opposite corner of the room, seemingly lost in discussion. I elbowed Molly gently in her left arm, simultaneously maintaining a grip on the bar, my own arm straining in protest. She turned to me, her coffee-colored eyes wide with wonder, and her forehead creased in surprise. Before I could pry, we attracted Tanner's notice. He broke away from Chloe, marching over to the bars.

"What's with you two today? An off day in the field could be your last one. Come on!"

"Ease up," I muttered under my breath. Tanner shot a reproachful look in my direction, almost daring me to speak again, but after an admittedly dramatic intake of air, I shifted my focus back to the bars. I propelled myself upward, as bolts of energy spun from my fingertips, wrapping haphazardly around the bars. Perhaps we could've done without the theatrics, but my sudden burst of energy satisfied Tanner.

Molly's expression piqued my curiosity – and I wouldn't be able to let it go. By the time Tanner released us for the evening, I could barely control my buzzing energy, which was threatening to burst again from my body.

"What was that look for?" I asked as soon as we were out of Tanner's earshot.

"I think I know what's going on." Her expression darkened, the left corner of her mouth lifting slightly, but there was no humor in it.

"Let's get dinner?"

She hesitated briefly, before nodding in agreement.

Jordan and I had plans to dine that evening at Whiski, and Molly and I scurried over behind schedule. We waved at the manager, who was well acquainted with the lot of us, and found Jordan at one of our usual tables in the back.

"Oh, hey!" she exclaimed, beaming at the sight of Molly.

Jordan shared my concern over Molly's lack of connection to the group. I knew she'd be pleased when we arrived together.

Though I'd spoken with both Jordan and Molly about the Tanner situation, this was our first discussion as a team. After running through the information we'd acquired, I directed us toward Molly's new information.

"You two are close enough to just ask him about this," Molly remarked. I didn't miss the hint of annoyance in her voice.

"I just have a hunch that when I ask, it'll go poorly."

"Probably, but I think it's about time to rip off the bandage. I mean, if the three of us noticed it, I bet everyone else has, too," Molly countered. "At least to some extent."

"Which leads us to why we're all here tonight. Molly maybe had a breakthrough," I explained to Jordan.

"Let's hear it, then."

"It's mostly an instinct, an intuition I felt today during pull-ups, but I also heard Chloe say something that put the thought into my head. Then I thought about your dream, Hadley."

"What did Chloe say?"

"She told Tanner she thinks she's under an enchantment. It's funny because I couldn't hear anything else during their entire conversation. Then I heard that clearly – it was almost like the elements were throwing those words in my direction."

"That's so odd."

"Do you think he's trying to help her figure out if she's enchanted?" Jordan questioned.

Molly took a deep breath, her gaze shifting downward.

I placed my hand over hers briefly. "Molly. You're not going to be judged over anything you say here tonight, even if it's bizarre, or if you think you'll upset us. Just spit it out."

Molly's head tilted back slowly, eyes turned toward the ceiling. She nodded before continuing. "I think he's the one who placed her under an enchantment."

The waitress set a tray of drinks on our table, startling us from the spell we were under. "You ready to order, then?" she asked, her voice overly enthusiastic.

"I think we'll need just another moment," I answered, a smile springing to my face, though I heard the distance in my voice.

"Don't be angry."

"Hold on, no... I'm not. I'm just processing. What makes you think that?"

"A couple of things." She paused, looking from me to Jordan, gauging our expressions. "Okay, so they're close. Weirdly close for two witches who aren't mated. Their body language is all wrong. Then she said she's under an enchantment. And I know you understand this, Hadley – I just have this feeling he enchanted her. My gut tells me that."

"Okay, yeah. I understand that. All of it, honestly," I acknowledged.

Jordan nodded. "I'm with you so far."

"Okay, so get this. Recently someone was telling me about a friend of hers. This friend was a seer, and she foresaw her own death.

She also foresaw meeting her mate, which would happen only six months before her death. So, she enchanted him. She placed him under a spell where he wouldn't recognize her as his mate."

"Why would she do that?" I wondered, my mind spinning.

"Because she didn't want him to grieve her. She didn't want him to meet her, fall in love, and then mourn the loss of her six months later."

"Is that... allowed?"

"God, no. You'd be in some deep shit if anyone found out. I think the only reason she shared it was just to get it off her chest before... you know... she died. Clear conscience and all that."

"So, you think Tanner and Chloe are mates, and he enchanted her so she won't realize that?"

"Yeah."

"Tanner isn't a seer, though."

"I know. Look, I might be wrong. I just don't think I am."

"This doesn't sound like Tanner," Jordan countered. "What would make him do something like that?" she continued, before turning to me, a horrified expression crossing her features.

"Whoa. Hold on," Molly interjected hurriedly. "I'm not saying I think he's going to die in six months. I mean, I hope not. I'm just saying, I think he's guarding her heart for a reason – and there could be a few different reasons for that."

"Okay," I returned, shaking the worst-case scenario from my mind. "So, if Chloe is under an enchantment, then she's still drawn to Tanner, which is what we're seeing play out now?"

"Right. There would still be a connection. Complicated feelings. The whole thing… they just wouldn't feel that final click."

"That must be confusing for Chloe."

"Oh yeah. Think about having these complicated feelings for someone, and then you can't sort out why."

"Damn," Jordan said, forcefully. "That is *screwed* up."

"You know what's even more screwed up?"

"What?"

"I think Molly's right."

CHAPTER NINE

"**I** don't understand," Fitz's voice sounded through the open door. "You're going to waltz into training and ask Tanner if he enchanted Chloe to prevent the two of them from mating?"

"Oh yes, that's definitely my strategy." I rolled my eyes, laughing. "You're such a dork."

"Aye, but a lovable one."

"You bet."

I bounded into the bedroom, having killed the lights in the rest of the flat. I climbed onto Fitz's lap, and he pulled the covers around us. "No, I'm going to get him alone *after* training, and then attack."

Fitz wore his most horrified expression, which provoked a presentation of the TV remote as an award for best actor from me, followed by laughter from both of us. "There's really something wrong with the two of us." Fitz laughed, as I floated the remote back to the bedside table.

"Focus!" I said playfully, my hands resting on either side of his beautiful face. Our eyes locked for a second too long, and energy burst wildly in the space between us. I closed my eyes, shaking off the intensity of the connection. Fitz pulled me close, tucking his head under my chin.

"I do need to get him away from the castle, I think. Go for a walk or something and then casually mention I've noticed something odd between him and Chloe. Then decide my next course of action based on how he reacts."

"I hope you know there won't be anything *casual* about this conversation."

"Aye," I returned, emulating Fitz.

His lips twitched, hinting at a smile. "And if he's angry?"

"Then he can be angry, which will probably be the case, and then it'll turn into a fight. But you can't go around placing Cardinal Court members under an enchantment."

"Now, *that* is true."

"What would happen if a council member found out?"

"He'd be in a hell of a lot of trouble – immediately suspended from his job; therefore, ending his career."

"Great."

"Talk to him, and we'll go from there. He trusts you more than anyone else on the team."

"Would you do this to me?"

"Enchant you? Absolutely not."

"Good, but I'm a little surprised."

"Why?"

"You're so protective of me."

"I can appreciate where someone is coming from. Trying to save their mate from pain, but that's also robbing them of the greatest joy. I wouldn't take this away from you for anything, and I would be pissed if you did that to me. I'd be livid if I found out anyone stole the knowledge of my mate, for any reason."

"It isn't fair to Chloe. I can't imagine not knowing you."

"For years I wondered about you – where you were, what your laugh sounded like, what your opinion would be about this and that." He rubbed his thumb across my cheek, followed by his lips. "Grief is the price we pay for love," he quoted.

"You've watched Henry go through hell. You've seen the price."

"Aye, and he would give someone a proper ass whooping for meddling with his memories of Emily, or for preventing his years of happiness with her. He's told me time and time again how lucky he was to have known her, to have experienced the world with her. He says she still influences him and his decisions even after being gone."

Fitz was right, as was Henry. Everyone deserved a choice in the matter, a chance to know the creature meant for them. I'd pay any price for Fitz, and if we were right about all this, Chloe deserved the same, no matter what Tanner thought the future held. I fell asleep some hours later, wrapped in Fitz's arms, my head resting on his chest, finally exhausted from contemplating the intricate web being spun.

*   *   *

After consulting Molly, Jordan, and Fitz, we all came to a conclusion: if evidence continued to support our theory over the next few days, I was to pull Tanner aside one evening after training. A week passed since my impromptu meeting with Molly and Jordan, and a conversation with Tanner was well overdue. We each had the ability to perceive the magic Tanner would use for an enchantment, especially when in Chloe's presence. I didn't want to feel its power; I really didn't, but with every passing day, I sensed the magic more clearly.

CHAPTER TEN

We began our training with Jess, though Tanner and Chloe attended all of my classes – Tanner to continue working on our physical strength, and Chloe to prepare for power enhancement. Tanner and Chloe's attendance gave me the perfect opportunity to observe them, but I was grateful for their daily proximity for more reasons than one. I still couldn't trust Jess. He wasn't necessarily harmful – or not overtly. But he made me uncomfortable, and odd energy loomed in the elements when he was present. We mainly trained individually with Jess, especially during the first few weeks of his course, but we did sporadically participate in group sessions. Though it was comforting to have the team with me, group sessions also caused a fair amount of trouble.

One stormy evening, following a particularly tense group session, Fitz and I had our own clash over Jess. We were early into task execution training, and I was hanging stockings over the fireplace when I mentioned I still felt uncomfortable around Jess.

Fitz offered to attend my solo sessions. I didn't dislike the idea, but I expressed concern that Fitz would lose his patience, which would only perpetuate the issue. Apparently, that was all it took for suppressed feelings to surface.

"You just said you were uncomfortable with him, and I've had the desire to pop his head right off his body from the moment I found out he was watching you."

"Okay, maybe you shouldn't join my sessions. I'm sure Jordan can hang out."

"Now you don't want me to come?"

"Let's not get dramatic about this."

"Seriously?"

"Why are you mad?"

"I don't like the way his eyes linger on your body, and he doesn't even try to hide it when I'm with you."

"I don't understand why it bothers you *that* much. You know I'm yours."

"It's a complete disregard for our relationship. Why doesn't it bother you?" he questioned heatedly.

"It does bother me. That's obviously what I just said. Exactly *what* is it you're implying right now, Fitz?"

"I've implied nothing. If he's bothering you, why won't you let me handle it?"

"I'm used to ignoring men's stares. It's not like Jess is the only man or creature that looks at me. It's just uncomfortable because I have to be around him every day."

"Wow, Hadley."

"What now?"

"You are *not* helping. You know how protective I feel."

"I don't think you need to protect me from every creature's eyes. You're overreacting. Are you worried about something?" I growled, as the light bulb above my head shattered to pieces.

"I just find you to be a bit naïve about the whole thing," Fitz spat, though he observed the glass shards distractedly. "This isn't just about Jess staring at you, or that he stalked you, which was a heinous act; he has thoughts of taking you from me. I can sense them. He's not harmless, Hadley. You'd do well to be mindful of that. I'd hate for him to catch you off guard one day – don't forget he rifled through your hotel room."

"James said it wasn't Jess."

"James is senile if he believes that."

"That is *so* unfair."

Fitz's demeanor grew wilder by the second.

"I thought witches didn't have stray feelings for someone other than their mate, anyway."

"Aye, and I told you there are exceptions. He doesn't have a mate. Maybe he has an obsession with this sort of thing. He's clearly demented."

"I doubt he's daydreaming of stealing my affections. I think you're just pissed about him following me, and I get it. It pisses me off, too. I don't like being around him every day. But we don't have an option."

"That only adds to my concern here, and of course I'm still pissed. Why wouldn't I be?"

"This is ridiculous. Look, he creeps me out, and you're not helping. Why would you talk about him catching me off guard? God Almighty, Fitz."

Fitz sighed, though he didn't argue.

"I think he's a weirdo," I continued. "I don't like him. I don't want to be around him. He makes me really uncomfortable. I just don't think he's trying to play games."

"You're right. My intuition is typically *way* off base. Keep it up then."

"You don't have to be a jerk about it."

"Neither do you. You're acting like I'm completely unreasonable."

"What do you want from me, Fitz?" I yelled.

"What do I want?" he said, his voice rising. "What I want is to corner Jess in a dark alley and cause him enough pain that I feel he's atoned for every thought of you that has *ever* crossed his mind. What I want is for him to never lay eyes on you again, for him to never experience what it feels like to be close to you."

My breath grew ragged. I'd never seen Fitz so angry. His eyes were wild – nearly primal – and his energy buzzed through the room, making it difficult for me to focus. My hair stood on end at the nearness of his electricity.

"What do I want, Hadley? I want every single part of you. I want to pull every thought of you from Jess's mind. And I want you to hear me because I don't want to explain this again." He paused, registering my energy – feeling my nerves, feeling my flurry of emotions. He closed the distance between us, placing his hand tenderly against my cheek. As he pulled away, both my hair and his sweatshirt I'd stolen, released a flurry of broken glass, which traveled toward the trash can.

Then – "No one could replace what you are to me. You might think I'm delusional, but I'll always protect you, even from the creatures or things you might not see the danger in. Because I don't much care if you think I'm mental, as long as you're safe."

And just like that, my resolve crumbled. "I know, Fitz. I love you."

"You have all of me."

His lips found mine, as we clung to one another, and for the remainder of the stormy evening, our bodies slowly, and intentionally, sorted out our differences.

*　　*　　*

The following morning, I prepared for a full day of training, recalling the previous night's argument with Fitz. Perhaps I did think him a bit neurotic, but after a good night's rest, I was calm enough to consider Fitz's position. I couldn't doubt his perceptions – Fitz read other creatures nearly as well as Isaac, who was very talented as a reader. I resolved to observe Jess as inconspicuously, though as thoroughly, as possible. I laughed recalling my reaction to Fitz's concerns. I shared that Jess made me uncomfortable and proceeded to shrug off every concern of Fitz's. My pride wounded my judgment. Yes, Fitz lost his temper, but why was I so defensive?

I entered the training room, finding Jess, Tanner, and Chloe seated at a far table lost in discussion, and I nearly groaned. There sat all three creatures occupying far too much of my brainpower. *When did things get so complicated?* I wondered, rubbing my temples slowly.

"You're early today, but that's good. Let's get started."

Jess planted so much distrust between the two of us, and Fitz and I weren't the only ones who felt the effects of his poison. Even the simplest things he said left me uncomfortable – there was always more behind his words than what he actually said.

Thankfully, Tanner attended the all-day session, interjecting regularly and making edits to my strength training regimen to support the various stances and maneuvers Jess taught. After lunch, we focused heavily on proper posture to support my back safely through combat, and Jess adjusted my stance, his hands lingering on my hips. Tanner's eyes narrowed, his gaze firm on Jess's hands and his jaw set tightly. Tanner vowed to keep an eye on Jess, and his promise was in truth, but I needed more. I had resolved to stay out of the minds of those around me, but that was a resolution I decided to break.

While we took a short recess, Tanner talked strategy with Jess, and I took the opportunity to discover what was truly on Jess's mind. I breathed deeply, willing my focus to shift to the elements. I found the air, and followed its path to Jess, awaiting the typical onslaught of thoughts, feelings, emotions, and soon heard... nothing. Absolutely nothing.

Unfortunately for Jess, Maka taught me about this in training.

Witches could place protection spells around their minds, but it was extraordinarily rare. Not only did these types of spells require great strength, but they also required continuous effort. They consumed too much energy to be used casually. As such, witches guarded their minds only in dire times – times when they couldn't trust those around them. So, what exactly was Jess worried about?

CHAPTER ELEVEN

"**I**'m telling you, that little shit is up to something," Henry bellowed.

After discovering Jess's mind protections, Fitz and I conferred with Henry and Isaac, seeking other opinions on the subject. The four of us were gathered at Henry's estate, sorting out the facts. Henry and Isaac were well aware of our history with Jess, and both had even attended several of my sessions to ensure I'd never be alone with him.

"No doubt," Fitz agreed. "Isaac doesn't even have a lead."

"I've consulted my best resources in the business. Ran background – nothing. Traced accounts – nothing. Looked into any and all documentation we could find – nothing. He's a ghost prior to two years ago."

"If *you* can't find a lead, we have a problem," Henry groaned.

"Jess is good; I'll give him that. Whoever he is, he's no

amateur at covering his tracks."

"The worst part is that we're supposed to be learning from him, and I don't know if I even trust his teaching," I added.

"Do you think he was planted in the mission?" Henry asked. It was the question we'd all undoubtedly considered, but this was the first time it was brought to the table.

Isaac let out a long, slow whistle.

"You mean by Lorenzo?" I clarified.

"Damn, mate. Do you understand how bad that would be?"

"It'd be a deadly mistake on the council's part, and that's a heavy accusation, I know. I'm just thinking out loud."

"It's not unreasonable, not by a long stretch," Fitz returned.

"I don't think any one creature could cover his tracks like this – not alone," Isaac added.

"Someone's vouching for him. He couldn't land a role like this without major backing, as strange and untrustworthy as he is. Especially considering Chloe appointed him, and she clearly dislikes him."

"I agree, Henry. I think she was pushed into the decision, and I'm going to talk to her."

My skin prickled as three sets of eyes landed warily upon me. I knew what they were thinking, but I could no longer risk everything, pretending Jess wasn't the liability we all knew he was.

"I don't know, Hadley," Fitz began.

"Look, Chloe and I have a certain bond. She won't be offended if I ask. I'll do this tactfully, but it needs to be done. I'm asking for support – from all of you."

Fitz gave it a moment's thought before nodding his head in agreement.

"You have our support. Be cautious," Henry ordered.

"This is your most delicate task yet," Isaac agreed. "But you've got this."

I nodded gravely, already lost in preparation for a conversation I had hoped to avoid.

CHAPTER TWELVE

C hristmas came and went, as quickly as Santa's sleigh. Fitz and I spent Christmas Day with our team, with the exception of Ian, who was granted leave to join the rest of Fitz's family in Seattle. With a few days' rest, I mentally prepared myself for January. There was Jess to consider. And Lorenzo. Though the upcoming year would bring its fair share of trouble, I believed it would also bring victory. Training resumed the week after New Year's, and the thought both sobered and focused my mind.

Soon after training resumed, a little luck was finally on my side. Instead of lingering after the session, as he tended to do, Jess seemed to have a commitment that evening. I packed my backpack and found Tanner and Chloe, their hushed whispers silencing at my approach. Chloe accepted my invitation to happy hour, and we were soon on our way to Whiski.

As we popped into our usual haunt, I felt butterflies wrestling in my stomach. This was delicate. I needed to ask a Cardinal Court member if she was forced to appoint a creep whom she distrusted as one of our trainers for the most important and potentially deadly crusade of our era. There was no easy way to go about it, but once we were seated, I decided the most direct way was usually the best.

"I wasn't exactly sure how to bring this up."

"I can feel your butterflies. You shouldn't be nervous with me. Say what you came here to say."

"It's about Jess."

"You don't trust him."

"Not at all. And, Chloe, I'm not the only one."

"I probably shouldn't discuss this with you… but I trust you. So, I think I'm going to anyway."

I waited patiently, sipping golden Glenfiddich until Chloe decided what to share.

"I need you to swear your secrecy on this. I know you can't conceal this from Fitz, but you can't share beyond that."

"You have my word."

She hesitated briefly but soon enough began. "I don't trust him either – or not fully. When he applied for this position, I rejected his application. Something told me he was a bad choice. That afternoon, Ella called and said I needed to reconsider Jess for the position."

"Ella? Why on earth would she vouch for Jess?"

"Evidently, he has stronger ties within the organization than I realized, and she was concerned I'd ruffle a lot of feathers."

"So, it didn't matter that you found him ill-qualified."

"I thanked her for the advice, but I was willing to take the risk. This crusade is too important. Later that afternoon, I received a call from Damian, who told me the same thing."

"Wow."

"Don't get me wrong, I don't think they have ties to Jess. I think they had my best interest at heart, and I realized I needed to consider what they asked of me. The next morning, Mia and Prisha called."

"Let me guess, more of the same."

"Jess is highly respected among many in the European governments because of his work with them, and that sentiment trickled through the U.S., Argentina… you get the idea. They told me if I rejected him, there would be major fallout from the lower councils, and we didn't need that kind of discord in the midst of everything else."

"So, you hired him."

"And I've second-guessed that decision every step of the way, although part of my aversion to him isn't fair. It isn't his fault so many people advised me against selecting another candidate."

"What about the rest of your aversion?"

"Honestly, I just don't trust him. There's something about the guy that creeps me the hell out."

"Exactly how I feel. Did you know Jess watched me before James approached us about the mission? Fitz and I worried for weeks about the witch in the shadows."

"See, this is what I worried about. His behavior isn't normal."

"It isn't. Have you seen the way he touches me? I don't trust him, Chloe, and that makes it difficult for me to focus in training."

"Too right it does. But please, *please* don't let this get in the way of your training, because it's so important. I think he's doing an all right job teaching you all. He surprised me. He's creepy, but I think that's the extent of it."

"Maybe. It's just difficult for me to understand why the council would put us in this situation. Or how the other members of the Cardinal Court put pressure on you to hire this type of creature. Honestly, my feelings toward the council aren't quite healed, and now this..."

"I'm so sorry. I can't believe I'm sitting here woman to woman telling you I can't do a damn thing about a guy who makes you uncomfortable. But I can't. We're too far in now, and the court won't support a change."

"It's okay," I lied. "I know you can't change this."

"I wish I knew what to say to help your trust in the council."

"No one could *say* anything to help with that. God knows this situation doesn't help, though."

"If you're going to be mad, be mad at me. Yes, I had a lot of pressure to make the choice I did, but at the end of the day... it's on me. I didn't stand up in the beginning, and now I can't."

"That's not fair to you. I know the decision wasn't easy. I don't envy you or the position you were placed in. I can't stand Jess. And I'm pissed at the people who pushed for him. Maybe I *should* be mad at you, Chloe. But I'm not."

"Oh, Hadley." Chloe smiled.

"It's a real mess, isn't it?"

"You know, if it helps you feel better at all… I don't think he's dangerous. Seriously. You know I'm at every practice, and I promise you'll never be alone with him. I won't leave him alone with any of you girls, and I'll do a better job of stepping in. I need you to remain focused and work hard, okay?"

I knew I couldn't promise that, not in truth. I'd attend every practice and still work my ass off, but I wouldn't trust anything Jess taught me. Fitz and I would arrange alternate plans.

"Deal," I agreed, the sound of my false promise ringing in my ears.

CHAPTER THIRTEEN

W ithout betraying any of my newly acquired details, Fitz informed Henry and Isaac that we attained additional evidence Jess wasn't to be trusted. The three of them were close enough to trust each other at that. And so, the four of us discussed and devised our own strategy.

Our first course of action was to enlighten Jordan and Ian. Though we remained careful in our conversations, we were certain of their discretion and loyalty, and they had each expressed their own concerns over Jess. Plans for a second training camp were secretly formed and would soon be established on Henry's estate. I felt a certain sense of guilt at the exclusion of the rest of the group, but it was too early to approach them. We couldn't yet trust Molly's complete secrecy, and Tanner's odd relationship with Chloe complicated things. I made my concerns about Jess known to James, whose quick dismissal of the subject confirmed our instinct – we wouldn't include him in the new pact.

We brought each of Jess's new teachings to our secret sessions, altering the moves, or exchanging the approach entirely. None of us dwelled on the theory that Jess was a mole, but we were compelled to take the possibility seriously, the threat weighing heavily upon Fitz and me, as crusade leaders.

Around the same time, Fitz and I received mysterious signs in the elements. We left Henry's just before supper one evening, opting to dine at home, rather than staying out late with the rest of the crew. Fitz pulled dry wood from our storage locker and started a roaring fire, as I heated leftover stew from the freezer. A quiet night with one another was just what we needed, and after dinner, Fitz opened his most recent notes on a research project, while I set my sights on tea and yoga. Suddenly, a humming noise rose from the fire, and the flames danced vividly. It was the third time that week.

"What do you think it's trying to tell us?" I wondered, handing him a freshly brewed cup of tea.

"Hell if I know, but it's making me slightly mad."

I looked at him, eyebrows raised.

"You know, mad, bonkers, off…"

"Your head," we finished in unison. As the edge of his lips curled, I ventured on.

"Have you seen this before?"

"No. I've heard of this sort of thing certainly. Witches have transported messages through the elements as long as we've existed."

"You really think someone is sending us a message?"

"Aye, I do. Don't you feel the magic?"

"Of course. I don't understand what this all means, though."

Fitz nodded, his gaze still hard upon the flames. "It's difficult to say."

"Why use fire?"

"Sending messages through elements is untraceable. Unlike the trail left by modern technology or even paper, no one can store or trace these."

"That's a good reason."

"I think this message is being carried a long way. It would explain why the sender is having difficulty getting the message to us."

"As in..."

"This message could've originated on another planet, like Opimae. Or in another time."

"Another time... Like, the past?"

"Or the future. Although if it were the future, they'd have an easier time sending the message backward," Fitz mused, his pen tapping the papers in his lap distractedly. "Plus, they'd risk changing the past."

My mind was spinning. As flames leapt erratically in the fireplace, I had to consider they could be a direct link to another time, which was unnerving, to say the least.

"No, the future doesn't seem right. I think it's certainly another planet or the past, but God, that doesn't quite narrow it down, does it?"

I shook my head, lost in thought. Were the flames a sign of solidarity or peace from someone on our side? Or were they bad tidings… a warning perhaps?

"It could be a warning of sorts. After all, we are embarking on a dangerous journey," Fitz replied.

"It could be about Jess."

"Possibly. I guess we'll have to wait and see."

I chewed my bottom lip, a sure sign of mounting nerves. I was really, incredibly horrid when it came to waiting. "I'm going to do a little yoga."

Fitz ran his fingers lovingly across my neck and shoulder, down the center of my chest, and finally rested his hand on my thigh." Good idea. Your body isn't the only thing that's tense – your energy is *tight*."

I stood slowly, half lost in reverie, half lost in the feel of Fitz's touch, and wound lazily across the distance of the room.

"Hadley?"

"Yep?"

"Don't let this nag at you. Whoever it is, if they're trying to communicate across such a distance, they must believe it's important to reach us. They're not going to give up easily."

"You're right."

"And Hads."

"Yeah?"

"If I haven't told you enough lately, you're my world."

CHAPTER FOURTEEN

Turning the page of my book, I rested my eyes on Fitz, waiting on him to do the same. Finally, the moment came, and I took my chance. "Something occurred to me today."

"What's that?"

"If you're able to travel into the past, why haven't you gone back and prevented the ring from being picked up by Lucio?"

"You remember the conversation we had a while back about not altering the past?"

"Even to save so much trouble and potentially save all that's good in creation?"

"Right."

"And not even to maybe warn the council or Hamish?"

"That's still altering fate. I'd alter the course of action by others. I told you about Fate. Something like that would alter too many threads of history and present. It could potentially jumble up everything."

"Lucio did."

"Aye, and there might yet be consequences from his actions. To jumble things around a second time…" he trailed off, his face apologetic.

"It just *sucks* that you have the power to potentially prevent all this, and yet, you can't."

"It's a tough pill to swallow, no doubt."

"I get it. It's just – there are too many people involved in this disaster, and I worry sometimes. I believe in my best moments we can do this, but in my worst moments, I'm afraid of the outcome."

"Are you afraid we won't make it?"

"I'm not afraid of dying. I see it like this: we've already died in a way. We've chosen it, at the very least."

He looked at me, perplexed.

"Our former selves have died – the people we might have been. We sacrificed our lives for this cause, and we make that sacrifice every morning when we wake up and choose to continue this mission. I've known from the beginning that death is the most likely end to this venture."

"And you signed up willingly."

"And I signed up willingly. So did you. And Henry, and Jordan, and all the others standing with us. Not one of us was coaxed or forced into this. The day I decided to stand against Lorenzo, I knew there was no turning back. No, I'm not afraid of death."

"You never cease to amaze me."

My mouth twisted into the awkward, lopsided grin I always

seem to wear when I don't know what to say.

"Don't you dare."

"Don't I dare, what?"

"You were just thinking of how to deflect my praise, and I won't stand for it," he responded mischievously.

"I'm just being a little awkward. Move along, nothing to see here."

"Nothing to see, my ass."

"You know," I added on a more serious note, "we make each other better."

"We make each other stronger – braver. That's the way it should be."

"Are you afraid?"

"Only of losing you. I could bear anything else."

"Have a little faith."

"It's not that at all, and you know it. You're fierce. Your power is strong. Our training is intense. And nothing will ever happen to you, not as long as I'm around. Or Henry, or Isaac."

"I don't know why y'all act like I need three protectors."

"It's not like that, exactly. They think of you as family. And they'd save you before me."

"I doubt that."

"Oh, you shouldn't. They know very well if they helped me, while leaving you in danger, I'd be hell to deal with."

"I hadn't considered that."

"Well, now you have."

"I've gone from being a girl who couldn't really relate to anyone to a woman surrounded by the most incredible family. I've never felt more known or loved."

"There's nothing like it."

"Witchkind for the win."

*   *   *

Fitz surprised me the following morning over breakfast, sharing we'd dine somewhere nice that evening, a night to celebrate being young, happy, and alive. We hadn't taken time to enjoy life as a young couple in love since the morning we transported back from St. John. My mind was full of Chloe and Tanner, Jess, our alternate training camp, whether we should tell Molly about the second camp, Mia's contemptuous attitude, and what type of message was trying to manifest in the elements. Yes, a night out would do some good.

I felt bold as I dressed for the evening. A red, floor-length dress was my selection for the occasion, donning capped sleeves, a plunging neckline, and a silhouette that hugged tightly to my torso before loosening on its descent to the floor. I carefully applied makeup, covering a bruise on my cheek from training, and coiled my hair at the nape of my neck. I felt better than I had in weeks by the time I shimmied into the living room.

Fitz stood by the fire, draped in a tux, complete with a white button-up and black bowtie, a glass of scotch in hand.

"Holy hell," he mumbled as I walked through the door.

"Okay?"

"You're beautiful," he whispered, his hand sliding around my waist, pulling my body toward his. He kissed my neck, carefully avoiding my freshly painted lips.

After assisting with my coat, Fitz held out his arm and led me into the cold, damp evening streets of Edinburgh. He was tight-lipped about where we'd dine, but as we turned deeper into Old Town, I narrowed down the options. We avoided the steady trickle of water rolling down the street, and I turned my eyes toward the sky, finding that the clouds had cleared, a welcome break from the heavy rain of the day.

Reaching the Royal Mile, Fitz turned toward the esplanade of the castle, rather than the many restaurants of Old Town. As we approached the gates, I looked at him curiously. There was a teahouse inside, but the castle was closed for the evening. He smiled, and a rap from his free hand resulted in the large wooden door swinging open.

"James?"

"Good evening, my lady. Sir." He nodded at Fitz, who was struggling to keep his composure.

"Right this way."

We followed James to an upper courtyard, set with a table draped in white linen. Surrounding the table was a beautiful array of plants and flowers, and strands of lights spanned the distance of the ancient, stone walls. The courtyard was open, exposing us to the cool night air, though roaring chimeneas were placed strategically around the space, all alight in their promise of warmth. The soft illumination of the castle's medieval architecture resulted in a magical backdrop.

James took my coat, replacing it with a soft, fuzzy wrap, and seated us properly before disappearing under a dark archway.

"Okay, what the hell is going on?"

"Patience, Hads. Just enjoy the night," Fitz answered, smiling coyly.

Soft music floated in the breeze, as a waiter arrived with Chateau de Ferrand to begin our meal.

I smiled. "This always reminds me of Paris."

The waiter took pride in our dinner, explaining that the chef selected and prepared the meal as a direct complement to Fitz's wine selection. The meal was, indeed, flawless, and my dinner partner, smug.

As dinner was cleared from the table, I leaned forward. "Oh, is this all?" I teased.

Fitz reached for my hand, and his brow creased. I perceived his mounting nerves through the main course, though my suspense was short-lived.

"Actually, there's something I'd like to talk to you about."

"You know you can tell me anything."

"Hads... You know I've loved you since the first day I met you. You're my best friend... the only person I need by my side. I'll love and protect you. Forever."

I inhaled sharply, anticipating what came next.

He knelt before me, and I raggedly exhaled, my heart pounding in my chest.

"I don't want to travel into the next world without this ring on your finger. Please say you'll be my wife."

I dropped from my chair and into his arms. With my lungs unable to grant me the air to respond, I pressed my lips longingly against his, and his fingers wound through my hair. I pulled away, laughing nervously, and took a napkin from the table to wipe my lipstick from his face.

"Of course I'll marry you, Fitz."

His hand stroked my cheek gently before presenting the ring. I extended my left hand, inviting him to slip the beautiful ring onto my finger. Platinum metal bands held the infinity diamonds into place and were molded together to form an "X" at the front and again at the back of the ring.

We embraced once more, a silent request for strength, clinging to each other as we rose from the stones. So engrossed in the moment as I was, I didn't notice the figures emerging from the shadows until they were standing beside the table.

"Finally, Fitz!" Henry pulled me into a warm hug. "Congratulations, Hadley. I'm so happy to have you as a sister – well, officially."

Alight with excitement, he then embraced Fitz, as the others surrounded us with smiles and laughter. Jordan, Isaac, Ian, James, Molly, Tanner, Chloe, and Solomon; they were all present and ready with congratulations.

"Hads! Get into these loving arms," Isaac exclaimed, beaming.

"Isaac! Oh my God!" I laughed, holding him tightly.

"I know, baby girl. Now, let me see those diamonds."

Another flash of a camera reminded me that Jordan was on the scene. She wiggled her way into a group hug with Isaac and me, only to be followed by Tanner.

Fitz had invited the crew to join us for drinks and dessert, and it couldn't have been more perfect. Jordan touched up my lipstick, before capturing the rest of the celebration through photos. Sitting atop Edinburgh, one fiancé and eight friends made one woman feel as though she were sitting on top of the whole world.

CHAPTER FIFTEEN

I veered to the right, trying to escape the impending blow, but in my rush, I left my core unprotected. Jess's fist met its mark, and I tumbled to the floor. Pain exploded through my abdomen, but not before my hand met Jess's jaw. The cold mat took my weight, along with my breath, momentarily. Jess rolled to the ground, his fall much more graceful than my own. As my breath returned, a wave of nausea rolled through my stomach, and I shifted to my side.

Jess extended his hand in my direction, but I slapped it away in protest.

"We're on the same team, Hadley."

"Could've fooled me," I muttered, pulling myself from the floor.

"You all right, Hads?" Tanner called from across the room.

"Yeah, I'm good."

Training with Jess was exciting in more ways than one, though I wish I could say any of them felt like the good type of excitement. His training was tough, and we all earned cuts and bruises. I endured a bit of an interrogation one day from a castle coworker, who seemed concerned for my safety. James assisted me in assuaging her fear, telling her we'd joined a local martial arts class. He returned to work more weathered than normal the following day, and I could only shake my head at his commitment to the mission.

"Okay, what went wrong there?" Jess questioned.

"I lost focus. I left myself unprotected."

"I know it's a lot to remember, especially in the moment, but the more focused you are, the less I'll hurt you. And I really hate hurting you."

I scoffed.

"Hadley," Jess began sternly. "I do *not* like this part. But I'll rough you guys up as much as I need to right now. It'll save your life in the field."

I nodded curtly.

"Again, from the top."

I shifted my body into position.

"Not like that." He sighed. "Here, let me show you."

Jess's hands grazed my sides, finding their mark just above my hips. He shifted my body into position, and a violent mix of emotions flurried through me. I was relieved an afternoon meeting prevented Fitz from joining the session, knowing Jess's actions would have resulted in a fight. Embarrassment washed over me, inexplicable as it was. I had done nothing wrong, but Jess's behavior often left me humiliated and anxious. I couldn't refuse to work with him – I just wanted training to be over.

The sound of Tanner's heavy footsteps echoed loudly through the open space, and Jess's hands dropped at his approach.

"I think she's got it, Jess."

"Her stance was off. I think I can handle my own training."

"Enough," Chloe's authoritative voice silenced them both.

Tanner wouldn't release Jess from his gaze for a moment longer, but he eventually relented, stalking back to Chloe's side.

"Your friends don't like me."

"You're not exactly a likable guy."

"Still irritated with me, I see."

"Just keep your hands off me, and stop antagonizing the creatures who care about me."

"I care about you."

I sneered.

"I do. I care that you're trained properly, so you have a better chance of survival in the field." He shot a glance at Tanner, clearly irritated at his interference.

"Tanner cares about me more than you do… I'm not saying you don't care about all this… hell, I don't know," I paused. "I'm just saying he cares about me a lot. And Fitz most of all."

The look on Jess's face was impassible, and I wanted to know more than ever what hid behind his cool countenance. Approaching footsteps broke our gaze, but to my surprise, it wasn't Tanner.

"Surely we're not done for the day," Chloe bristled.

"Oh no, we were just about to pick up where we left off,

before the interruption."

"I don't know if you need to pick up exactly where you left off, but yeah, it's time to get back to work."

Jess and I resumed, the remainder of training suffering from the things that were said – and done. When the awkward afternoon session ended, Tanner was quickly by my side. His fingers gripped my chin, pulling my face to the side, and swore.

"Come here," he coaxed.

Tanner pulled out a fresh butterfly bandage and replaced the current one above my eye.

"I know this part sucks. But you're making so many gains."

"It's okay. Honestly, I'd rather get a little beat up here than God knows what over in Opimae."

"Getting knocked around in training is one thing. But getting knocked around by that guy..." Tanner shook his head. "Let's get out of here. I'm walking you home."

CHAPTER SIXTEEN

"Dude's an asshole," Tanner offered unceremoniously, as we exited the castle.

"No doubt."

"Did he make you too uncomfortable?"

"No more than usual. Thanks for stepping in, though."

"He better not touch you like that again. Fitz isn't the only one losing his patience."

"What are you not telling me?"

Tanner's mouth twitched slightly. "I threatened to kick Jess's ass weeks ago. Chloe smoothed things over – told me I'd get kicked off this assignment, and then I wouldn't be able to help at all."

"Tanner!" I laughed. "Oh my God. Well, thanks…"

"Yeah, don't mention it."

"He's getting more blatant."

"It's weird. I thought he would back off – you are a force to be reckoned with."

I laughed.

"Nah, Hads, don't do that."

"Do what?"

"You know you are. Maybe call up your fire magic again. That seems to scare the hell out of him."

"I haven't exactly been a delicate flower."

"You've snapped on him a few times, and it always has a bigger impact than when I get pissed, or Fitz, or Chloe."

"When Chloe gets pissed, it seems like it just eggs him on."

"I've noticed that, too."

"Of course, he acts perfectly in front of Mia. Which is a nice reprieve, but…"

"Pick your poison? It's either creeper Jess or the ice queen?"

"Exactly."

"I hadn't thought about it before, but yeah, you're right. He does act normal when Mia's around."

"What do you think he's doing? We have so many theories floating around, but I honestly don't think he wants me… not like that."

"Damn, Hads. I don't even know at this point."

"Whatever his endgame, he's definitely trying to piss you guys off."

"It's working."

Tanner and I made it back to the flat, dropping onto the sofa, and I waited for him to break the quiet.

"Honestly, I'm at a loss."

"He knows he can't come between you and Fitz. I don't think he's one of those guys who gets off on causing trouble between mates."

"That's the trouble with Jess. His actions don't make sense — my witch's eye can't seem to understand any of it."

"Yeah, I feel the same way. You would think one thing based on his actions, but then your intuition just tells you you're way off."

"When he watched me before, it didn't feel romantic. And when he touches me, it doesn't actually feel sexual — he's almost always glancing away like he's curious about who's watching. It's almost like… yeah, he's trying to stir up trouble, but it's not specifically with me and Fitz."

"I keep asking myself why. What does he gain from this?"

"What if he was planted by Lorenzo?" I questioned.

"Shit. That's a heavy accusation."

"Do you think it's an unreasonable one?"

"No."

Silence followed, as I found the words I needed to ask him. "Hey, I need to ask you something. It's completely off subject."

"Okay, shoot."

"I've noticed something going on with you and Chloe."

"I have no idea what you mean."

"I wouldn't mention it, except it's become pretty obvious. I can see you aren't mated, but this isn't friendship. Sorry for being so direct. I wouldn't press, but it's important."

"There's nothing going on with us. I mean, we're working

closely to make sure you guys are ready for what's coming. That's all."

"That's not what your body language says."

"You said yourself we aren't mated. I understand things are pretty uncertain right now. There's a lot of speculation with Jess and all that, but you're letting your imagination run wild."

"Don't do that, Tanner."

"What?"

"Don't act like I'm an idiot. I can see plainly there's more to it. If you don't want to tell me about it, then just say that."

"I'm not acting like you're an idiot."

"I know what I see."

Tanner scoffed.

"I'm not the only one who sees what's happening."

"So, what? You're all spying and forming stupid opinions about us?"

"Why the hell are you so defensive?"

"What the hell are you trying to imply?"

"Did you enchant Chloe?"

Tanner jumped from the couch, staring at me like I had grown another head. "Are you kidding me? This is bullshit, Hadley," he yelled, stalking across the room.

"Don't talk to me that way, and don't you dare walk out of here."

"Do you realize what you just said to me?" he asked, pausing in front of the door.

"Yes, and I want the truth from you."

His body was rigid, his hand firm on the doorknob. I held his gaze unyielding; refusing to look away, though the storm in his eyes was as palpable as if lighting bolts actually flashed within them. I thought he might change his mind, but after another moment of silence, he walked out, slamming the door behind him.

CHAPTER SEVENTEEN

I brushed my fingers lightly over Fitz's forearm, tracing a sizable bruise. Though I knew it was courtesy of Jess's training, the sight of Fitz's injuries always provoked my protective instinct. It was impossible for me to see his bruises and not want to destroy Jess – or whichever creature it came from – in return. We could ultimately control our instinct, but it was a constant battle.

"We could just elope," I offered casually, forcing my focus back to my conversation with Fitz. We were debating when we should wed. With our days full of work and training, it seemed like the right opportunity might not arrive before our departure to Opimae. It's not that I wasn't ready to say my vows, but I didn't want to create additional stress by pulling together a wedding at such a crucial time. We were preparing for battle, and no one's attention needed to be pulled away from survival training. I cared little about a formal ceremony anyway; the courthouse was fine by me. Either way, I'd be wed to Fitz, and I didn't much care how it happened, as long as it did.

"I don't care for the thought of the courthouse," Fitz responded, sliding his hand down my arm. "I'm not completely against it. It would be nice to have our close family and friends there, though."

"That would be nice, but if you want it to happen before Opimae, we don't have many options..."

"You're distracted."

"I'm sorry."

"Tanner?"

"Yeah, it's bothering me – he hasn't said more than two words to me since our fight."

"Hads, it's been two days."

"Exactly! He's one of my best friends. I can't stand this."

"Give him time."

"Again… patience. Not my strong point."

Fitz chuckled. "Well, we can't all be wrong about this, and you and I have a duty to lead this team. You're doing the right thing."

"He's mad because we're right. He won't talk to Jordan either."

"I'll say it again. Give him time. He'll talk when he's ready."

"I hope you're right. Between Tanner being pissed at me, Jess's asinine behavior, and Chloe's complete lack of manners around Jess, training is *not* much fun."

"At least Jess's training is about to be over."

"Thank God for that! But the main thing is I want Tanner at our wedding… *and* not pissed off at me."

"This is teaching you patience, Hads."

"You're always telling me to have patience."

"*Well?*"

I sighed, and Fitz pulled me into his lap. "Stop with the nerves. Tonight will be nice. We haven't seen the whole crew this week."

"I can't help it," I whined, covering my face.

He pulled my hands away, holding both wrists in one hand, the fire in his eyes setting my heart alight. "I bet I can do something about that," he replied mischievously. He pulled my face to his, kissing me thoroughly.

"Good thing we don't have to be at Henry's for a while," I added rather breathlessly.

Fitz turned his full attention to the business of helping me forget all about my nerves.

* * *

"Here you go." Molly set another slice of pizza on my plate and plopped onto the couch beside me. Pizza was a rare treat for us, our meals being meticulously preselected by Tanner, even when we dined out. We were savoring every last bite.

"Who invited the ice queen?" Molly grimaced.

"Solomon." I smiled. "Why is he so nice?"

Molly laughed. "Mia watches you like a hawk."

"I genuinely don't know what Fitz and I did to make it on her naughty list."

"She's had her eye on you guys from the beginning."

"Lucky us."

"It could be your track record before the crusade. I mean, your defiance of the council was pretty big news. Or maybe she's just harder on you two because you're our leads."

"Probably both, honestly."

"It's all good. I've made her list, too. I'm just an honorable mention, but still."

"Well, you and I haven't exactly been easy on her."

"Someone has to call her out. That woman is *mean*."

"Look at her scowling at Isaac. What on earth did Isaac do to deserve a look like that?"

Molly and I fell into laughter, which attracted Mia's gaze. We waved enthusiastically, which received a half attempt in return.

Jordan shot a big grin in our direction, shaking her head lightly.

"Hey, has Tanner talked to you tonight?" Molly asked.

"No."

"Have you given him an opportunity?"

I smiled.

"You need to give him a chance to talk to you."

"He doesn't want to talk to me. He's pissed."

"You're wrong," Molly returned decidedly.

"You don't mince words, do you?"

She grinned. "Maybe not, but I'm right about this."

"Explain it to me, then."

"You're missing the subtle clues in his energy. Yes, it's agitated – all muddled up. I feel doubt, fear, confusion, but not anger.

When we hold secrets like Tanner's, we actually want to get them off our chest, and to someone who cares about us."

I paused momentarily, trying to pick out what Molly found in Tanner's emotions. The woman read feelings like a wine connoisseur smelled all of the complexities in a glass of Malbec, and I found her gift astonishing.

"You think he's ready for that?"

"The shock has worn off — he needs to share his burden."

I nodded.

"You know, no one is in the kitchen right now, and I'd love another beer."

"You're devious," I responded.

"You should probably ask Fitz if he needs anything."

I followed her eyes to Henry's favorite leather couch, which currently held Fitz, Solomon, and Tanner.

"Fitz, you need anything from the kitchen?" I offered, hoping I didn't sound too rehearsed.

"I'm good, love. Thanks."

I caught Tanner's glance from the corner of my eye and strolled into the kitchen. Trying to grant Tanner enough time, I found no shortage of tasks to be completed in the kitchen. I moved stacks of plates into the dishwasher while floating empty pizza boxes into the old stone fireplace, which was roaring with life, warming the old space as it had for hundreds of years. I grabbed two beers from the fridge and turned to find Tanner across the kitchen island.

"Oh, hey."

"Hey."

I stood awkwardly, holding our beers.

"Double fisting it, huh?"

I laughed, feeling better instantly.

"I'm sorry about the other day. I shouldn't have stormed out like that."

"It's okay. I'm sorry, too. I could've been more tactful."

"No, don't apologize." He paused, tapping his finger on the smooth granite surface. "Especially when you're right."

I set our beer on the counter and opened mine quickly.

Tanner's left eyebrow rose.

"Sorry, I just think I'm going to need this to get through the conversation we're about to have."

"Me, too, honestly."

I slid Molly's beer into Tanner's grasp and waited for him to begin.

"A friend of mine from school is a seer. No one you've met, but I've known her since we were kids. We don't talk much anymore, but she asked to meet up right before I left the States to come here. I thought it was strange, but I met her in Seattle." He paused, draining a good portion from the bottle. "She said she'd seen something about my future, and debated about whether or not to tell me, but ultimately thought it would save my life."

He took another sip, his nerves radiating through the space. "She said she'd foreseen my request to join this crusade, and the council would approve it, allowing me to travel with you guys to

Opimae. She saw my death – she said Lorenzo would kill me."

"Okay, so you decided against asking to travel with us, right?"

"Hadley."

"Oh my God, Tanner."

"Let me finish."

It took a minute, but I nodded for him to proceed.

"I know it's the right thing to do. I might die. I might not. Any number of things could change before then, but I know I'm supposed to be a part of this. I submitted my request about a week ago."

"Have you heard back?"

"Yeah. Yesterday, they accepted."

"For God's sake, Tanner. You don't need to do this."

"Yeah, I do. I'm destined as much as anyone else on this team. We both know there will be more than one casualty by the time this is all over." He paused, shutting his eyes tightly. "And that's okay. This is important, and I think a lot of innocent people are going to die if we don't get the job done."

"How did your friend see that? There aren't many loopholes when it comes to Lorenzo's protection spell."

"I have no idea, but she did. She hasn't seen anything else, though – I checked."

I chewed my lip, my mind racing. I knew Tanner well enough to understand how he operated. He'd made up his mind, and I'd never convince him to opt out of the crusade. Instead, I focused my effort on an area where I could make some headway – at least initially.

"Your belief that you might not come back alive... that's what's going on with Chloe?"

"The same friend saw my mate – Chloe. I wrestled with it a long time before doing this, but once I was scheduled to meet her in person, I kind of panicked."

"You enchanted her."

"Yeah."

"Why?"

"Because I might not come back, and I want to protect Chloe from that. She'll spend these few months with me, and then what? She receives news that we'll never get married; we'll never have a life together? Nah, it's not fair to her."

"Do you understand what will happen if the council figures out you've enchanted her?"

"I'll be dead before they figure it out."

"What the hell, Tanner? Don't say things like that. You just said something still might change."

"I'm just operating right now like it won't. We both know it isn't likely."

"You think you'll die, then you think you won't. You say things might change so you asked to join us and then you say they likely won't... you're all over the place."

"Honestly, my opinion changes by the hour."

"I guess mine would, too. But I think you should tell Chloe."

"That's not the plan."

"This isn't fair to her, Tanner."

"You don't know that. You don't know her as well as you think you do. I know her pretty damn well, and I'm carrying the grief for both of us right now."

I leaned across the counter, taking Tanner's hand in mine. "You know I care about you. Honestly, I'm pissed right now, and that's because I care. I want you to live, and I want you to have a good life as long as you're with us."

"I know."

"You can do as you please, and I know you will." I paused, laughing. "Please just think about telling Chloe. Yes, it'll be a disaster if it comes out, but I'm a woman in love. I might not know her as well as you do, but I know she'd want this time with you. She'd want the chance to love you and be loved. Please, just think about it."

"Shit, Hads. How did things get so complicated? Remember when we were just living on mountains with no cell reception?"

"Life is messy, and it definitely won't get easier from here."

"That's the truth."

"Tanner."

"Hadley," he returned, his eyes reducing to slits.

"I need you to think about what I've said."

"I promise I'll think about it... for you. Just don't get your hopes up. And please keep quiet about all this."

"When are you going to tell the others you're coming with us?"

"I guess now?"

CHAPTER EIGHTEEN

Saturday mornings accompanied by the steady patter of rain against a windowsill were forever my favorite, and best complemented by a large cup of tea. From Seattle to Edinburgh, I had a thing for moody weather, though the weather was the only thing that was inclement on this particular day. Wrapped in a blanket underneath the bulk of my fiancé, we permitted the morning hours to slip away in eager study of one another. At some late morning hour, Fitz's eyelids drooped, and he fell to peaceful sleep, wrapped in my arms. My head buried itself in a pillow as I retreated into my mind, contemplating the crusade's current status.

Jess's training was complete, and although he occasionally attended sessions, I moved into the power enhancement phase, meaning Chloe now conducted my daily training. Chloe was encouraging, the effects of her training immediately taking root, proof that power, trust, and companionship propelled my skills further than Jess's antics ever could. I *excelled* in power enhancement, even more quickly than my teammates, and Chloe believed it was fresh confirmation I was born to harbor great power.

Tanner and I returned to our norm, our natural friendship ultimately prevailing over his anger and fear, which removed the weight of one burden from my shoulders. We continued our dialogue regarding Chloe's enchantment, our regular conversation easing his mind, and though we made progress, he hadn't yet conceded to come clean with her.

Molly was feeling rather superior over her proper diagnosis of the enchantment, and after much deliberation, our secret team invited her to our private training camp at Henry's, a verdict that brought with it a sense of peace. Though Molly remained reserved – and arguably distant – with most of the team, she did consistently participate in our social gatherings and never missed an alternate training session. And our relationship continued to develop, bordering on friendship. I'd broken into her confidence, leaving damage to a wall she couldn't repair, and she let me in.

Fitz and I hadn't settled any details regarding our wedding, as our crusade continued to absorb our full attention. And if Fitz wasn't willing to settle on the courthouse, we'd wait longer still – yet, the time since our engagement wove an even closer bond between us than before. In the midst of working, training, and spending time with our friends and teammates, it was difficult for us to establish a real routine, but we found stability in one another. It was a priority for us to decompress together, to spend time discussing our day and our lessons – the good and the frustrating. Even considering the uncertainty of our future, I was learning to live in the moment and to truly appreciate it. And I was happy. Really happy.

*　　*　　*

I couldn't concentrate, not on a single thing. I glanced over my shoulder, my senses vividly aware of the rays shining through the windowpane, and I slowly wiggled my weight backward until cool, winter sunlight touched my skin.

"I'm sorry this isn't something we can do outside. We should've gone to Henry's today to get out of the city," Chloe offered regretfully.

"It's okay. This isn't so bad – it's not all that warm outside."

"Still… it would have been nice."

"Maybe, but I don't think it would help me focus."

"I can feel your trouble today. Are you just distracted?" She frowned.

If you only knew, sister, I thought to myself. "Slightly," came out instead.

"Ground yourself back to the earth, to the elements. Meditate with them for a few moments, and then find your path back into the air."

I nodded, closing my eyes cheerfully. Communing with the elements was one of my most relished practices. They were teeming with wild contradictions. The entire world rested within them, and then again – nothing at all. But they *were* everything, and I often woke from these meditations in a state of enlightenment, though admittedly with an accompanying sense of bewilderment.

My mind connected with the unseen: the elements were

excited, zipping around happily, though elusively. I first found light as it shined upon me, noting its distant warmth. Afternoon light was often difficult to catch. Its characteristics altered quickly – always changing, always fleeting. I concentrated on the golden rays until I anchored to them, following their path into the air.

Beyond the door, a figure moved through the hallway, and the subtle click of their shoes meeting the stone floor permeated the elements, a soft swoosh of air resulting from the disturbance. A tiny, but palpable, shock shuddered through me. I snapped into hypervigilance, entranced by the air, recognizing each of the tiny molecules surrounding my body – the invisible force traveled through me, granting vitality to my lungs. I asked the air for what I sought, and it answered. Its characteristics shifted and changed, permitting weightlessness to overtake me. The ground no longer supported my body, and I cautiously opened my eyes. Though the ground was somewhere below, the air cradled me – granting life, granting freedom from gravity. I couldn't risk a glance at Chloe, not then, my ability too experimental to survive the distraction.

After committing the atmosphere and the correct path to memory, I requested the air deposit me safely to the ground, and immediately sought Chloe's glowing face. She embraced me warmly, her excited energy mingling with mine. A hefty amount of practice was required if I was to accustom myself to such a delicate skill, but mastering it was an irrefutable necessity. The thought of combat sent a searing nerve through the pit of my stomach, but the longer we trained, the more confident I grew. Though nothing could fully prepare us for the fight ahead, we were completing the best training available. And soon, we'd appreciate its worth.

CHAPTER NINETEEN

The crew was gathered at Henry's when Tanner finally embarked into the next phase of his life. It was a Friday night, and supernatural energy permeated the elements. I wasn't the only witch who experienced a remarkable week of training – we were each celebrating breakthroughs of our own. James noted it was the time for such things, that one triumphant progress would build into another, and then yet again. The promise of transformation resulted in a good mood all around. In the midst of food, whisky, and excellent company, I left the demons at bay. I lost all thoughts of Lorenzo and war the moment Tanner leaned over and whispered in Chloe's ear. She nodded in response, and they disappeared into a dim hallway, leaving us for a lengthy stretch of time.

James was apparently the sole creature unaware of their odd relationship, questioning several times where they'd gone, wondering if anyone had seen them. Henry rolled his eyes dramatically at James's insistence, and it was nothing short of a miracle that we persuaded him a search party wasn't necessary.

"They're in deliberation of something I'm sure," Fitz said finally. "Or have just gone for a walk."

"In this damp evening?" James gasped.

"Aye, who knows? They're fine, though, I'll bet you that."

"Old man isn't very intuitive, aye?" Henry whispered. Jordan elbowed him, while I shot a reproachful look in his direction – one he knew by heart, though it had no bearing on him, outside of the same smirk it always brought to his lips.

Isaac's arm tucked gently under Henry's chin in a playful chokehold. "Don't be an ass, mate," he whispered through a grin.

"Let go, you eejit," Henry returned drily, as Jordan and I fell to laughter.

Footsteps sounded through the hallway, and the two creatures in question reemerged, Chloe making a beeline for my arms. I glanced over her shoulder at Tanner, who nodded in affirmation.

"Thank you," Chloe whispered, releasing me.

"For what?"

"For helping Tanner realize he needed to tell me the truth."

"You deserve to know. I would want that if I were in your shoes."

I didn't press our conversation further, unaware of how much Tanner shared with her. Was she aware Tanner expected to never return from Opimae? Did she know the depth of his friend's vision?

Chloe rejoined Tanner, gripping his hand in both of hers, as he announced they were officially together. Molly caught my eye, winking, and a loud shout escaped Isaac's lips, thoroughly startling me. Isaac then boomed with laughter.

"Sorry, Hads. I *love* love."

*   *   *

"She doesn't know about my friend's vision," Tanner answered my unspoken question.

The following morning over tea, Tanner shared the important details from his conversation with Chloe, filling in the blanks before my afternoon session with her. Clouds rippled across the sky, tiny slits of light pouring through the cracks. Though the sun was hidden, the temperature was warmer than it had been in months. We ordered our tea to go, not wasting the opportunity to enjoy city views from the esplanade. I tilted my face toward the sky, recalling the many times I watched Maka do the same from the very spot where we stood.

"I think that's a good decision, or at least for now. She just took in a lot."

"Yeah, and I'm not sure if I'll tell her. There are variables; it might not even happen, but I don't want her worrying every day if I'm dead. I want to be honest with her – it just seems like a hell of a lot of worry to dump on her and leave."

Though I pushed Tanner to come clean with Chloe, I understood his hesitation to share everything. It was one thing to tell her they were mates, but to leave her with such a weight did seem gratuitous, especially when she would already worry enough. And I hadn't given up the position that we could be smarter now; we could change things.

"Do you think your energy will even allow you to hide it, though?"

"Definitely. My energy is all over the place. She knows I'm nervous about the mission, and I worry if I've trained you all to the best of my ability."

"So, what exactly did you tell her?"

"That a friend of mine is a seer and she knew I'd join the crusade. I told her I worried about coming back, so I thought maybe it would be best for her if I concealed our relationship. I told her I planned on removing the enchantment if I returned."

"How did she take it?"

"Not well," Tanner answered, grimacing. "She was pretty pissed honestly."

"Shocking."

"I mean, I get it. I would have been, too."

"So, where does that leave you with the enchantment?"

"Once we talked about everything and she calmed down, I asked if she wanted me to remove it, and she said yes. So, I did. And then..." he trailed off.

"I don't think I need the particulars of making up."

He smiled, his shoulder bumping mine playfully.

"What is she going to tell the council?"

"I'm not sure. She told me not to worry, that she'd handle it.

"She's good for you. I can already sense that. I'm happy for you, Tanner."

"Thank you. I feel like I'm finally whole, and you helped

make it happen. I wouldn't have gotten here without you."

"I don't know if this helps, but I believe you're going to come home from Opimae. Not long before I spoke with you about Chloe, I had a dream, but now I don't think it was a dream."

"What do you mean? You think it was some sort of vision?"

"I know it's not one of my gifts, but I think Fate showed me a piece of your future."

"What did you see?"

"You and Chloe. I saw y'all together in what I think is your future apartment. And Tanner… she was pregnant."

He exhaled deeply, taking a moment to find his response. "I hope to God you're right."

"And if I am, do you know what that means?"

He smiled. "Yeah. That I come home."

CHAPTER TWENTY

"Y"ou and Fitz haven't given us any useful information on your stalkers from Paris," said Mia, her tone bordering on accusatory.

"Trust me, we want to know who they are as much as you do."

"Trust you? How am I supposed to know that you want this as much as we do?"

"I don't think anyone involved in this crusade can question mine and Fitz's commitment to its success."

"Of course not, Hadley," Solomon jumped in. "And we know you want answers." He eyed Mia pointedly.

Fitz and I were each called in to discuss details surrounding our experience in Paris, as no progress had been made in identifying our pursuers.

"Good cop, bad cop, I see. A little outdated, don't you think?"

"What are you talking about?" Mia demanded.

"We are all on the same team. We're all working together for the same resolution – we have the same goal here," Solomon interjected, cutting off my impending sarcastic comment. I didn't envy his position – stuck between a stubborn court member whose disdain for me was palpable, and a stubborn crusader who was still skeptical of council representatives like Mia and clearly annoyed with my current circumstance.

"It's easy to say that, Solomon. But Mia's annoyance with Fitz and me has been painfully clear from the beginning. And every time she's involved, conversations become an accusation rather than a collaboration."

"That's fresh coming from you."

"Mia…" Solomon began.

"No, that's all right. Please *do* expand upon your position, Mia."

"You clearly distrust witchkind government and even this court. You act like I'm your enemy when I haven't done anything but help."

My blood boiled. "Help? Are you kidding me? Seriously, where are the cameras? This is too good to be real."

"Okay, Hadley. Let's take a deep breath, shall we?" Solomon said soothingly.

"I'm fine."

"Really? Cause deflecting your fire is *not* on my agenda today," Mia quipped, though her eyes shifted warily from my eyes to my fingers.

Crap. My fire magic. I closed my eyes, following Solomon's instructions, exhaling my anger with each breath.

"Okay, sorry. I didn't mean to get angry."

"This ends now, you two."

"Why don't we start with Mia explaining her problem with me and Fitz?"

"I don't have a problem with you. Stop making everything about you."

"Mia!"

Mia looked toward Solomon and sighed. "Fine. Let's do this. Truthfully, I thought the council made a poor decision selecting you and Fitz. Look, I get it. You two are *powerful*. But you broke rules and caused mass chaos with your relationship. I thought that was too distracting, and I have concerns about what you'll do if you run into a problem with us that you don't like."

"What do you mean?"

"Will you just go rogue like you did before with your relationship issue? Will you put your team at risk like that? And the mission?"

"At least we're finally getting this on the table." I sighed, running my fingers over my face, exhausted. "First of all, we can agree to disagree on that one. Fitz tried every reasonable method to resolve that issue before doing what we did. You know the pull of mates, and he knew from the beginning that I was a full witch – and that I was his mate. Chloe's investigation determined it was an error on the council's part."

"More deflection…"

"Not deflection, truth. You can choose to not accept it, but it's true. It was the wrong call. And we worked with you to resolve things in the end. But all of that is irrelevant."

"How so?" Solomon prompted, eyeing Mia.

"Because the circumstances are different now. This isn't about me and Fitz. Hell, this isn't even about the team. This is about all of witchkind. All of humanity. The fate of good and evil in our world and Opimae. We have one shot to get this right, and we do not take lightly the fact that innocent lives hang in the balance."

Solomon nodded, smiling.

"The past few months have been filled with training, but just as important – it created trust between us and the council. It took everything in me to trust you guys. And I know it has taken effort on the council's part to trust us. But that's where we are. And neither Fitz nor I would do anything to jeopardize this mission."

"Mia, how do you feel about what Hadley said?"

"So, you do trust us, or you don't?"

"I trust Chloe with my life. I'd say the same for Solomon. You, I'm not so sure. I don't feel support from you, and I know you don't like me. So, overall yeah, I guess I do trust the council as a whole – but I view you each individually, so it's not that simple."

"I know it seems like I don't like you. That's not true," she offered, picking at the frayed threads of her ripped jeans. "Regardless of the trust issue – or the concern, I should say – I don't dislike you.

I'm hard on people. Anyone on the council will tell you that. Someone has to be. We can sit around a circle and hold hands, but at the end of the day, you need to know that you're being held accountable for your actions – or that you *will be* if you make bad decisions."

"Okay…"

"And I know I can be harsh. But you're a leader of a crusade, for a mission to protect all that's good in our world and the next. If I hurt your feelings, then God help you with what's coming."

I nodded my head slowly. "It's never been about my feelings, Mia. You can like me, hate me… honestly, it's all the same to me. I have support elsewhere. But I'm a fighter, and if you come *at* me, and especially if you come at my loved ones, we'll have a problem. And if someone tries to hurt the people I love, then God help *them*. It's just how I'm built."

"I understand, actually. I'm the same way."

"This team is vital to our mission. And I'll protect it at all costs."

"That part does make you a good leader."

I nearly choked on my water – a half compliment from Mia was nothing to dismiss.

"So, can we all try to understand one another now? And agree that we're all on the same team?" Solomon questioned.

"Sure," I answered, shrugging.

"Yeah, I'm game," Mia added.

"I think you have more in common than you realize – and it's probably why you bump heads. I'm not saying that you have the same personalities – obviously," Solomon said, laughing. "But you have a great deal in common. I hope you'll see that."

Mia and I both nodded wordlessly. It would be a long road, but it was a start.

Solomon turned to Mia. "Great, now that we've established that, let's finish things up."

"Right. Look, Hadley, thank you for coming back in and walking us through the stalking situation again – seriously."

"Yeah, I'm happy to help." Our conversation felt strained, at best, but we were both trying. That had to count for something.

"The reality is we can't generate a lead in any form. We have no idea who these people are." Mia continued.

"Where does that leave us?"

"Are you absolutely certain you haven't felt anything since coming to Scotland? Not even the slightest hint of something odd?"

"Not outside of Jess. Once we established his… involvement, that took everything in Scotland off the table. We haven't seen or felt anything from the others since Paris."

"We'll keep running searches, and if you think of anything else in the meantime, let us know. Maybe you did lose these creatures, but something seems off. And your safety is vastly important," said Solomon.

"I know. Thank you – truly. The experience was nothing short of violating, and it's always in the back of my mind. Being watched gets under your skin. So you can trust me when I say if I think of anything new, I'll let you know immediately."

"Thank you, Hadley," Mia answered. "We'll do our very best with this."

CHAPTER TWENTY-ONE

"Let me think how I can explain this."

Chloe momentarily dropped Tanner's hand, approaching me in serious thought. Their happiness made me smile. I was relieved I could finally stand in the same room with them without feeling like I was harboring a state secret.

"This requires a ridiculous level of precision. One moment's distraction could be deadly for the wrong person."

Her words sent a shiver down my spine. She was speaking of deflection. If our enemy attacked by fire, we would utilize our magic to deflect it, sending flames back to the person who yielded them. However, one wrong move could pummel it toward someone on my team.

Fire retardant material draped every surface, and I wondered why we weren't wearing anything to protect ourselves.

"You'll be perfectly safe with us, and if Tanner and I aren't able to deflect your fire, then we shouldn't be in this room."

"Okay, Hads, so you'll fire and we'll deflect, but whatever you do, don't move. We won't hit you, but if you move around, well… we can't do much about that."

"I won't move a muscle. Promise."

"Okay, shoot."

I raised my hands, fire igniting at my fingertips, and launched flames – their trajectory set on my trainers. Fire whirled toward Tanner, who stared motionless for a fraction longer than I anticipated, and my heart raced at the thought of *my* fire igniting in Tanner's chest. He raised his hand just as the blood drained from my face. His hand grew foggy, and he batted the fire as though it were a tennis ball, and his hand the racket. The fire bounced across the room, losing its glow somewhere in the tarp.

"Oh my God. That is so cool!"

Tanner smiled. "Again."

I aimed for Chloe, smiling as her hand tapped the fire.

"Don't you dare move," her voice sounded in my head, as the fire raced a couple inches from my face, the warmth spreading across my cheek.

"Oh, you're just showing off now!" Tanner yelled.

Chloe's smile widened, looking into my wild eyes, surely amused at their size. "Hadley, I want you to understand what it feels like when your own fire is blasted back at you. You need to grow accustomed to it before we actually deflect one that's meant to hit you. I don't want you caught off guard when that happens."

"Right… I'm sure we'll get there."

"You will; let's keep going."

We forced ourselves to the point of exhaustion, finding it necessary to push our bodies as far as they'd allow. I fired randomly between Tanner and Chloe, keeping them from anticipating my next move, and they deflected each shot only inches from my body, doing so until I did, indeed, cease to flinch. The thought of my next step was near maddening, wondering how I would fare at deflecting their fire. Self-defense, as Chloe stated, was equally important as the knowledge of when and how to strike. Each day we worked hard, closing the distance between that goal and me.

CHAPTER TWENTY-TWO

Maybe it was Izzy's upcoming visit, or my compulsive longing to understand a strange night from long ago, but whatever the reason, I sat cross-legged on the floor asking time to take me to Izzy. Well, sort of. I asked time to take me to my bedroom at my parents' cabin, where I was lost restlessly in a dream on a cool, summer night. Though I told myself it was a dream, there had always been doubt. I wanted the truth… and I needed to find it on my own. So, I closed my eyes and talked to time, asking for answers from a night long ago.

My former self materialized, sheltered by towering fir and spruce. Bright green moss decorated many of the limbs, and lush ferns blanketed the earth. I wasn't necessarily deep in the forest, with huge trees and abundant plant life present all around the lake, but nothing distinguishing stood out. And there was one troubling question: how did I get there?

Light glimmered from the opposite side of a lofty spruce, my eyes reeling to adjust to the sudden illumination. A tall, slender figure draped with cascading auburn hair took shape in the glow. Izzy. She stood next to a large elk cow, and my past self almost yelled as Izzy reached toward its head. I'd seen countless elk over the years, but none that would allow you near, much less to touch them. The elk, however, seemed perfectly content as Izzy ran her hand down the side of its neck. The animal looked squarely into her eyes, before tilting its head. A small calf limped toward its mother with an injured hind leg.

Izzy proceeded to the calf, taking a seat on the cold ground. She touched her hand to its leg, whispering so lowly I couldn't make out the words. After a few minutes, she stood, and the calf walked over to its mother, *healed*.

"Impossible," I muttered, clasping my hands over my mouth. It was barely a whisper, but it didn't escape Izzy's notice. I watched as I moved from behind the tree.

"Oh, Hadley. What are you doing here?"

"I was just wondering the same thing. I don't know how I got here."

"Don't you?"

"No."

"What's the last thing you remember?"

"Falling asleep in my bed. I don't know how I got here. Why am I here?" I rambled, my voice panicked.

Izzy moved closer, gliding above the ground, the off-white train of her dress floating lazily behind her. I gasped realizing the soft glow of light came from her pale skin, the sight truly ethereal, leaving me momentarily in awe. Every hair on my body stood on end, electric as though I'd taken a shock. Her eyes were as wild as I'd ever seen anyone's.

"Is this a dream?" I asked.

"How should I know? If it were, I'd only be a figment of your imagination."

"I think you know the answer."

She opened her mouth to speak but was cut off by a distant sound. Her eyes widened, and she spoke with urgency. "You need to go. *Now.*"

"Why? What are you talking about?"

"Someone's here. They aren't safe. Go, now!"

"Izzy. What's going on?"

"I don't know. Please, Hadley. Please go."

"I don't see anything. Are you sure someone's there?"

"It's too dangerous. You must go."

A swirl of fog materialized in the distance, yielding a pair of eyes so dark, I could've lost myself in their depths. The sight was ominous – unnatural – and something in my gut told me to run, that I should be terrified, but I couldn't leave Izzy behind.

"Come on, Izzy! Let's go!"

She shook her head and placed her hand on my cheek. "Go home," she whispered gravely, fear resting on her face.

Izzy's words summoned a violent wind, which swirled through the treetops and into a funnel cloud that plummeted to the earth. Taking a chance, I ran toward the cloud, joining my former self, as she was swept away. I remembered the next part vividly – I screamed as the cloud engulfed me. I was instantly robbed of sight, blinded until I woke in my bed, gasping for air. I bolted from the bed, but I was unable to steady my wobbly legs and crashed onto the floor. Confused and exasperated, I curled up on the rug and lay for a few moments, wondering what had happened. Some moments later, my terrified mind finally caught up.

"A dream," I croaked out, still dragging in ragged breaths. "It was only a dream."

*   *   *

My eyes opened to the present, searching for signs I was actually in Fitz's flat. Though the night remained mysterious, I finally made progress, confirming that my body was physically in the woods that night. I had to disagree with my former self – it was no dream, nor was mental transport originally involved. I stretched across the floor, relying on Shavasana to relax, as the event replayed in my mind. I wouldn't find the answers on my own, after all. Izzy would come to Scotland soon, and we would solve the mystery together.

CHAPTER TWENTY-THREE

"Izzy!" I exclaimed, running for the door. I was in session with Chloe when Fitz picked Izzy up at the airport, and I was pacing the living room impatiently by the time they arrived at our flat.

"Oh, Hadley! I've missed you!"

We embraced warmly – a hug that was years in the making. The last time we saw one another, too much couldn't be said aloud, and it was exciting to talk openly with her. We fell into the rhythm of catching up, and Fitz left us to chat while he prepared dinner. I showed her around my new apartment, explaining our future plans regarding the space.

"This will be incredible. You'll have a lot of space, and it could use a woman's touch," she said, winking. "Speaking of which, congratulations again on your engagement. I'm thrilled to have a sister."

"Thank you. I'm absurdly happy."

She grinned broadly, further inspecting the diamonds on my finger.

We settled onto the couch, and she inquired about training, hungry for any details I could share. She, in turn, told me about her job and the life she'd built in Seattle. And sometime after dinner, I asked about the long-ago occurrence I always questioned.

"You're right. That night wasn't a dream," she answered.

"Even the night it happened, I knew deep down it wasn't a dream, but my mind couldn't make sense of it. I thought it couldn't have happened."

"I spend time healing wildlife when I can. I have a connection with nature that way. When you stumbled into the forest with me, I had no idea what to do."

"Why were we in danger? Who was it that showed up?"

"I can't say for sure. At the time, I just knew whoever it was, they didn't have good intentions, and I couldn't risk anything with you. Now that I know everything happening with you guys, I wonder if it was Lorenzo."

"That's a terrifying thought. Izzy! What if he's trying to find me in time?"

"God only knows, Hadley." Izzy's face was distant, lost in reflection. "I wouldn't let it worry you, considering that's the only time it's happened. That *is* the only time, right?"

"Yeah, you're right." I smiled, though the pit of my stomach twisted. "I do feel good knowing the truth of that night."

Izzy smiled. "It feels amazing to have everything out in the open."

We went on to speak of the last few years, words tumbling out, the hours flying by. Somewhere around midnight, Fitz reminded me that I had an important day of training ahead, and we finally parted ways, saving the rest for another day.

* * *

Izzy's visit passed far too quickly. The days were over before I was even conscious of them, and soon enough, it was my last day of training with Chloe. The previous months were full of learning and surprises, though nothing surprised me more than the confidence I felt in myself. I was ready to face Lorenzo, to make him pay for the things he took from me. In my weaker moments, I felt anguish over my loss of the life I would've chosen for myself – working at the castle, joining my fiancé, who would be my husband by now, for dinner with our friends – droning on about nothing much of consequence. I mourned the loss of truly experiencing Scotland, the many weekend trips to the Highlands and exploring the neighboring castles lost in the haze of training for battle.

And in my best moments, I realized all of the lost experiences might yet belong to me. We might win. We might defeat Lorenzo and restore peace to witchkind, a peace that many feared to be lost forever. Lorenzo, in his desire for power, forced a pressure onto our shoulders that created rare diamonds. He pushed our team relationships beyond the bond of friendship, creating a new family. His bloodlust and his need for power created a fighter in me, and a warrior was born.

My body responded to the call of training, pushing it farther than I believed possible. I excelled in the art of fire combat, my best asset, enhanced by the element from which I drew my power – air. I learned to levitate my body and leverage objects to protect myself from those who wished to harm me. I learned to fight – to use my body to protect myself, despite the ominous presence of the creep chosen to train me. No matter Jess's attempts to intimidate and distract me, I won.

Yes, I'd already won far more than I'd lost. And there was still more to be won.

Crafting explosions turned out to be oddly satisfying. I never much cared for that sort of thing, always lamenting the damage done. But speaking an explosion into existence? Fun. I learned there was magic in almost anything. As a witch, I made myself stronger in hand-to-hand combat by speaking my magic into it. I could even use the elements in my favor, which was my newest fascination. The air could turn on me if someone so wished it; pain might be whispered into my body… or I might make it so, in the bodies of my enemies. These were not tools to be taken lightly, and I felt a new appreciation for what I might endure at the hands of others.

No one amongst us didn't find themself lost in worry, at least from time to time. It was easy enough to distract our minds in the banter and friendship of one another, but it was quite another matter when Chloe spoke pain into our bodies, or when she and Mia sent fire raging toward our faces. We couldn't anticipate our timeline, how long it would take to accomplish what we set out to do, and the idea of death, of never returning home, sobered our minds.

Three weeks remained to tie up loose ends. The council handled our sabbaticals from work. Our responsibilities consisted of a few combined training sessions, packing, saying our goodbyes, and preparing for the journey ahead.

"I still haven't decided what to tell my mom," I admitted to Fitz one night as we lay in bed. We spent the day sightseeing with Izzy, who still had a few places in the city to check off her list. She'd visited Fitz a few times, but there truly was so much to see in vibrant, historical Edinburgh. It was nice having the opportunity to play tourist with her since our training schedules had slowed. It felt like I was claiming one of my lost dreams, even if only a little.

"Stick as closely to the truth as possible. The closer to the truth, the better you'll feel, plus it'll be easier to remember your story."

"I don't think she'll buy that I'm tangled up in some mission that won't allow me to communicate for a while. She will flip her lid."

"Look, Hads. I don't know how much your mother already knows…"

"What?" I sat up, my elbow sinking into my pillow.

"I saw your dad before he died. It kind of felt like one of those man to man conversations, and he asked for a good portion of it to stay between us, so I'm not going to share much with you – I'm sorry."

"Fitz. Shit… you tell something like that, and then say you can't tell me much?"

"Aye, this is why I haven't said anything. I know you'll be

pissed at me, but it's a promise I intend to keep, and you'll have to get over it, unfortunately."

"You have a way with words sometimes, you know that?"

"Here's why I brought it up – I told your dad what I am… that I'm a witch."

"How did *that* go?"

Fitz smiled. "The man looked me deadass in the eyes and asked if you were a witch, too – if that's what was going on between us."

I laughed, caught off-guard.

"I told him what you were, and how you didn't know yet. I showed him magic. Hadley, I broke every damn rule in the book. I told the man everything."

"Why?" I drawled out.

"Because I knew he wouldn't make it much longer. You were heartbroken – he knew that. I wanted him to know his little girl would be okay. That one way or the other, you would be fine, and happy. I wanted him to know the council wouldn't keep us apart in the end."

"Oh my God…" I whispered.

"Hads, he died knowing who you are, and with a couple of promises from me… which will stay between him and me."

I nodded, not trusting my voice.

"I tell you this for a reason. He said he wasn't sure if he'd share anything with your mom – a fair amount he promised he wouldn't. But some of it, he might have found a way to share with her cryptically. She might not be surprised by what you tell her."

"So… there are things she might know, others she definitely doesn't."

"Your dad wouldn't have told her you're a witch… but maybe that you're different, and I'm the same kind of different."

"But you wouldn't have known about any of this…"

"No, *but* my dad sensed something strange for years before I met you. He said I'd find someone to equal my power. And my mate and I would embark on something big… something unbelievable. I told your dad I knew we had a big calling in life."

"Why didn't you tell me this before?"

"You were still learning a lot when James approached us with this whole thing… we just hadn't made it there yet, Hads. Plus, I kind of shrugged it off initially. I mean, Dad is pretty intuitive, but that could've meant any number of things really."

"True."

"So, back to your mom. I'd say you have until the day we cross through the portal to talk to her, but the longer you allow this to sit in the back of your mind, the worse you'll feel."

"I'll think about timing. I guess I'll tell her when it feels right."

"You'll get it right," he said, brushing his thumb across my cheek. "And don't worry. You'll come back to her."

"We'll both come back," I countered, more confidently than I felt. I'd have to keep telling myself that until I knew it was true.

CHAPTER TWENTY-FOUR

"Okay, Jess," Chloe directed, her gaze hard on mine. Jess slinked about the room slowly, making a dramatic display with his cautious, calculated movements. His plan was to get inside my head, unsettle me, but it wasn't going to work. In a sudden movement, he leapt forward, arms extended in a posture of battle. My mind's eye opened, and I perceived each detail surrounding his body – the air shifting, splitting, and reforming with his exertion. His heart pounded, amped from the thrill of the fight, and my own heart raced, answering the call.

I jumped from the ground, levitating myself against the ceiling to avoid his pounce. He tucked and rolled smoothly onto the ground. I asked the air to release me and fell on top of Jess before he could regain his balance. We toppled to the floor, rolling and struggling with one another. If we were human, Jess's strength would have given him the advantage, but luckily, *we weren't human*. My power pulsed through every part of my being, granting me physical prowess that otherwise would've been absent.

After a few minutes' struggle, he pinned me to the ground, one hand resting heavily on my throat, and had one of my arms not been free, he might have won. In his rush to end the battle, he made one fatal mistake: he forgot how powerful I was. Power surged through my hands, and I easily broke free from his grasp. Fully charged, I flashed my hands before his face, fire playfully spilling from my fingertips. Jess rolled back on his heels, hands up and a smile on his face. Had this been a real battle, Jess would be covered in flames, and I felt more amused over the win than perhaps I should have.

"Hell yeah!" Tanner shouted, a broad grin on his face.

Excitement buzzed all around Chloe, who I think was just as excited to see Jess put down, as she was proud of my progress.

"Are you kidding? That was so rad!" she shouted.

Jess eyed my hand dubiously before I grinned, extinguishing the flames. He then grasped my hands, pulling me from the floor, and bowed in silent acknowledgment to his opponent.

"Okay," Chloe said, calling us back to order. "Let's see what else you've got. Tanner! You're up."

She leaned against the wall, a satisfied grin setting her face aglow.

*   *   *

Rain blotted the windshield as we drove Izzy to the airport, seemingly appropriate for our last few, pre-crusade moments with her. It was a busy time for her at work, and she couldn't be spared any longer, but that didn't weaken the blow, knowing these might be our last moments together.

I stepped out of the car and pulled her close, while Fitz unloaded her luggage from the trunk.

"I'll text you when I land in Seattle. Please call me when you land in the States. I want to know what's going on, and Fitz will forget."

"I promise."

"I'll miss you."

"No more than I'll miss you."

We stood on the sidewalk, already suffering the coming absence. Rain wet our linked hands, as cars slushed through nearby puddles. She needed to get inside, but there was one thing left to say.

"Izzy, we never got around to it, but I need to say this... thank you," I paused. "Thank you for everything over the past few years. I'm sure I don't even know the half, and I'm so lucky you've always been on my team. I wouldn't be where I am without you."

"It's been the greatest honor of my life, watching you grow into the powerful witch you are." She hugged me once more, whispering, "Now go do what you were born to do. Show him a real fight, love."

She turned to Fitz, tears welling in her eyes, and hugged her brother for the last time, for only God knew how long. She smiled at us both, grabbed her luggage, and left us standing on the curb, wishing like hell it weren't so.

CHAPTER TWENTY-FIVE

C louds parted the following evening, allowing a full moon to shine brightly, blanketing the world in soft, white light. Only one more night separated us from our departure to the States, and subsequently into the unknown of an entirely new world. Chloe was selected as the Cardinal Council member to accompany us to the portal to ensure a safe crossing, and a palpable relief washed over the team when the announcement was made. Chloe was now one of us – a vital part of our team. She was not only an advisor and teacher, but also a friend, and her relationship with Tanner was most certainly to thank for her presence. I had no idea how we would survive Opimae without her.

The council had organized a farewell party. All council members were in attendance, as were our trainers. Maka even traveled from the States to join our evening of celebration. The party was in full swing, everyone lost in laughter and conversation. Prisha gave a touching speech, her words reminding us of the many creatures who stood behind us.

I scanned the room for Fitz, but met Mia's eyes first. I discerned a hint of a smile on her lips, as she nodded in my direction. Though I couldn't say we were friends – or even in a good place just yet – we were amicable. And that was enough for now. I continued my search and found Fitz laughing with Solomon. They'd grown close over the past several months, and I knew he felt the same sadness parting from Solomon as I did with Chloe.

With Fitz preoccupied, I sought refuge for a few moments on the balcony. I'd never loved crowds, with their inherent ability to overload my senses, and I slipped away in anticipation of fresh air before my old friend, anxiety, overtook me.

Edinburgh stretched before me – the city that captivated my heart. The city I chose as my home. I looked to the moon, soaking in the elements that granted strength to my brothers and sisters, wondering at all the moon had seen of witch and mankind alike. I leaned over the castle wall, admiring the lights of the city, when a shadow blocked the moon's glow.

"Jess."

"Good evening, Hadley."

I smiled.

"I'm sorry to interrupt your solitude."

"That's okay. I was about to head back inside anyway."

The thought of Jess tilting me over the stone wall suddenly flitted across my mind, and I took a step forward. Jess caught my arm, and my body stiffened in response.

"I don't mean to startle you," he said, releasing me. "I only wanted to say I'm sorry."

"For what?"

"For being a bit of a wanker. I know we didn't really get on, but I did have your best interest at heart."

I held his icy gaze, hoping he couldn't sense my nerves. Just as I found my response, a third shadow darkened the balcony.

"Hadley, there you are. We were just missing you inside."

Henry held out his arm and escorted me toward the warm glow of the party.

"Thank you, Jess," I whispered. "Enjoy the party."

"Fitz felt your nerves, but he wasn't sure where you'd got off to," he explained. "We split up. He's mad with worry by now, I'm sure."

"I should've expected Jess to follow me."

"You shouldn't have to worry about something like that. And you won't any longer."

I nodded, squeezing Henry's arm a little tighter. Thank God for him.

"Fitz. Here she is, mate."

Fitz's arm slid around my waist, his other grasping Henry's arm gratefully. We spent only a moment in explanation, Henry gently reminding Fitz this was the end — it was all over now. His eyes pleaded what his mouth would not — *don't do something stupid, Fitz.*

Jess rounded the corner, and Fitz's eyes locked onto his.

"Take me somewhere," I demanded.

Fitz shifted his gaze to mine. "What are you talking about?"

"It's our last night in Edinburgh. I don't want to be *here* anymore."

Silence.

"Our last night in our city should be a happy one."

He knew what I was doing, but just when I thought I'd lost, his face grew determined. "Hold on tightly."

*   *   *

The swirl of stars from the in-between faded, revealing the softer glow of our own galaxy far above and the expanse of Edinburgh below. Fitz paced through the grass toward the cliff's edge. He'd brought us to Arthur's Seat.

"A proper goodbye. I'll miss this place," I observed. Fitz and I made the trek to the peak countless times throughout training, but the past week had been busy, and I was resigned to the fact that I wouldn't see this view a final time. I was happy to be wrong.

"Do you remember the first time I brought you here?" he asked. His energy was tense, though his face began to soften.

"My first week in Edinburgh." I nodded, smiling.

"Things couldn't be more different now."

"I can't help but wonder what our lives would be like if we hadn't been recruited for the crusade." I crossed the distance, taking my place next to Fitz. The city lights sparkled endlessly across the horizon.

"Neither can I," he returned. "We found a place to call home together, and then everything changed." He slipped his hand in mine.

"We'll come back."

"We'll be different."

"Aye."

A fleeting sadness crossed his features before he pulled me close. "You're cold."

"The wind doesn't help."

"We can go."

I shook my head, pulling myself free from his grasp. I smiled and reached my hand into the empty air, but as I pulled it back, my favorite gray coat was draped across my arm.

"You're proficient at that these days."

"Once I understood the elements..." I shrugged.

Calling forth objects wasn't as easy as a person might think. Since floating objects were forbidden in public, we had to ask the elements to open themselves and conceal the object until it rested comfortably in our hands. The practice was mind-numbing, but the end result was more than worth the effort.

"I won't apologize, you know."

"For what?" I asked.

"For losing my temper with Jess. He's gone too far – again. I should have put a stop to it long ago."

"You couldn't, and you know that. Tanner was nearly suspended, and don't you dare think I'm unaware of your little tumble with Jess a few weeks ago."

Fitz cocked an eyebrow in my direction.

"Yeah, and see what good you and Tanner both did? You're

just lucky the council wants you on this mission badly enough to pretend they believe you were just... what was it? Oh yes – a bit overzealous in training."

"I never get away with anything with you."

"True, but that won't stop you from trying."

Fitz chuckled.

"It's not like your response is unreasonable. But if you had gone too far... Fitz, there's a breaking point with the council."

"I don't think breaking points exist for you and me any longer – maybe they never did."

"You really believe that?"

"They care about defeating Lorenzo more than anything. If they believe we'll accomplish that for them, then I think they'll put up with a hell of a lot from us."

"Fair point. In their minds, they've already put up with a lot from us. But Jess isn't coming to Opimae, so let's just hope we're leaving all this behind."

Fitz nodded. "You're right, though. This is our last night here, at least for a while. Let's have some fun."

"What did you have in mind?"

Fitz broke into a wide grin and walked to the edge of the cliff. He turned to face me and took a step backward. Instead of tumbling off the cliffside, his body floated high above the ground.

I closed my eyes momentarily, though I already knew what I'd find – there was no one nearby. I asked the elements to support me before stepping off the ground and into the cool night air alongside Fitz. I laughed, albeit a bit nervously, and worked up the courage to look down. The sheer drop was sobering, but I knew the elements well. I reminded myself I had nothing to fear.

"That first night we came here – could you have ever envisioned this?"

"Not in my wildest dreams."

Fitz tugged on my arm, pulling me into his embrace. I ran my fingers the length of his face, before planting my lips firmly against his. He met me in a slow, deliberate kiss as the air cradled us high above our city. And when we finally floated back to the earth, we descended the landmark hand in hand, still hopeful, regardless of the days to come.

PART FOUR:

LOOSE ENDS

CHAPTER ONE

At first sight of the Cedar Creek Inn, a deep breath escaped my lungs, my mind momentarily void of trouble. The three-story farmhouse was positioned to oversee a large field and the great trees covering the mountains to the south, its white paint stark against deep green. Memories bubbled up – my dad walking us down the narrow lane as children in search of elk grazing the fields; my mother lounging on the front porch, a good book in hand.

Fitz parked along the old wooden fence, and we all jumped from the car, eager to stretch our legs. Between the international flight and almost four-hour drive from the airport, we needed space. I saw my mother's cabin from the highway and was glad to distance myself from the car, seeking a distraction from my guilty conscience. I couldn't convince myself to stop; I didn't think I could tell my mother the things I needed to share – not yet. Fitz, Isaac, and Henry sensed my unease, and chattered on ceaselessly for the last thirty minutes of the drive, attempting to distract me. God love them, but the car wasn't the only thing from which I needed distance.

"Wow," Fitz murmured under his breath. "I can see why you love this place."

"This might be the cutest thing I've ever seen," added Isaac. "Why didn't we come here before, Hads?"

"I guess I wasn't ready to share it," I quipped.

"Well, would you look at that, lads?" Henry smiled, prodding Fitz in the ribs. A Scottish flag hung from the front porch, floating gently in the breeze, alongside the flag of my home country.

"When guests visit from other countries, Ben hangs their flag alongside the stars and stripes," I smiled, shaking my head. "I love that he's still doing that."

"It does make a bloke feel welcome."

My eyes scanned the house and surrounding area, registering the subtle changes — a fence repair, a fresh coat of paint on the porch, a new sign. But it was mostly just the same. The creek was still running with the rush of snowmelt, and a soft trickle of water was perceptible in the quiet afternoon. Cows dotted the field, their bodies basking in golden rays, strewn all around an old wooden barn. The structure was popular with tourists, likely one of the most photographed barns in the world. The wood had greyed, faded by the rain, and was contrasted with its blue roof, bright in the afternoon sun.

The front door swung open, revealing a familiar face. His eyes twinkled brightly in recognition behind silver-rimmed glasses, and a crimson Washington State University cap and grey Cedar Creek

Inn polo proudly proclaimed his love of both.

"Hadley!" he exclaimed, his voice warm and inviting. "It sure is great to see you again."

"It's great to see you, too, Ben."

"I thought I heard you, Hadley. Welcome home!" a woman's voice floated on the afternoon breeze.

Ben's wife, Sarah, stepped around the corner, and her arms extended in my direction. She hadn't changed a bit. Her hair was the color of snow, framing blue eyes, and a face defiantly untouched by time.

Ben and Sarah became second parents to me over the years, and occasionally, when college life became too noisy, I found my weekend escape in that very home.

Introductions were made, which included a sly look from Sarah as I introduced Fitz. Room assignments followed, and the bags were unloaded. Ben and Sarah, of course, reserved my favorite room for me. Sarah brightened the room with a fresh coat of paint, but the large, king-sized bed remained the same, with its signature white picket fence headboard and fluffy bedding. The back window held a lovely view of the field and mountains, while the side window gazed over the yard and into town. Fitz's eyes rested on the large Jacuzzi tub in the corner of the room, his eyebrow arched.

"Ha! Of course, that's where your mind immediately wanders."

"You can't fault me when my roommate is as scrumptious as you are," he replied, sliding his hands down my back. A rap at the door halted the moment, and Fitz raised his voice, inviting our intruders inside.

"I'm in love with this place," Isaac declared.

Henry dropped himself on the bed dramatically, surveying our room. "I think their room is cuter than ours, Isaac."

Henry and Isaac's home for the next few days were the two bedrooms up on the third floor. Down the hallway from our room, Ian and Ann claimed their territory. I was thrilled to have Fitz's mother join us, and she exuded a calming presence felt by everyone in the group. In between our rooms, Tanner and Chloe shared a west-facing bedroom, which would soon display the glow of a summer sunset. Jordan settled herself in the room next to ours, and James boarded downstairs in his own suite off the kitchen. Molly made herself comfortable in a more private room at the back of the inn, completing our party. With our need for complete secrecy, we'd bought out the entire inn.

*   *   *

"This is the exact point where we'll exit Earth into Opimae at the other side of the portal. It was confirmed today – Charles is our liaison on the other side."

James paused, savoring a mouthful of eggroll from the takeout we ordered before our meeting convened in the living room. Our maps and documents cluttered the floor, even before we littered it with plates, boxes, several witches, and one human.

"Is that a positive development?" I asked, my curiosity piqued.

"Oh, it's brilliant. Charles is one of the most powerful witches I've ever met, from either side of the portal. He might even give you two a run for your money. He's honest, upfront – he'll give us the real story, no spin."

"James, while I'm thinking about it – Hadley and I discussed something the other night I'd like to ask you about. You said the portal was placed here by other witches?" Fitz questioned.

"Aye. A long time ago."

"Why did they choose this area?"

"Well, at that time, there weren't many people on this continent, only a few native tribes in fact. This area was secluded, and the only method of accessing it was through transport. Obviously, most humans had no idea the continent even existed."

"So, they formed the portal here, thinking it was safe from prying human eyes?" I asked.

"Precisely."

I cut my gaze to Henry, already certain of what I'd find. When James used the word *precisely*, Henry's eye roll was sure to follow. I offered my most reproachful look in Henry's direction and received a goofy grin in return.

"Secrecy was imperative. And truth be told, it's mostly the reason there's a large national park here now."

"To protect the portal?"

"Precisely."

James seriously needed to retire that word before Henry's head exploded.

"The park makes sense in many ways and has been beneficial for human use, as well – it's such a beautiful stretch of land, as you know. But its primary purpose is to protect the portal, and it does a fine job of that."

"I guess it had luck on its side, too, with the west being inhabited later than the rest of the country."

"I wouldn't call it luck," James disclosed with a wink.

"My head is swimming again," Jordan announced.

"It's a lot to take in," Henry agreed.

Footsteps sounded across the dining room, occasioning a brief pause from the team until Ben emerged through the doorway, water pitcher in hand.

"Anybody need a refill?" he asked cheerfully. He made his way around the room, refilling as he progressed, before the maps attracted his attention.

"Those are pretty neat. Is that an old map of Bavaria?"

As he and Ian fell deep into conversation about antique maps and a college trip to Austria, I shifted my gaze to Fitz, who was seemingly lost in reverie, a stern look obscuring his pleasant face.

I looped my arm through his. "It's all going to be all right," I whispered.

He planted a kiss on my cheek. "I know. Take a walk with me?"

Enjoying the last few moments of daylight with Fitz was more than enough to tempt me outside. The marvelously lengthening daylight hours were in full swing, and I wanted to take advantage of that as much as possible.

We meandered the lane in companionable silence, happy to have a few moments alone. The evening was still – peaceful – and the chill of dusk crept into the air. A sense of calm wanted to wiggle in, but Fitz's agitated mood radiated through my body. Excitement and anxiety both muddled themselves among the group, our impending trip through the portal never far from our minds, but I sensed that simmering under the surface for days. This was different. I could no longer manage with the new energy and was just about to share that sentiment when Fitz stopped abruptly, turning to face me.

"Hadley."

"Fitz," I returned playfully.

"I know we've wrestled with a timeline on the wedding, and it would be nice for our families to be a part of it. But I want to be married before we go."

"I do, too."

A new rush of his energy bombarded me. I surprised him.

"We could have a small ceremony, and renew our vows… when we come back. With our families."

The word *if* almost escaped my lips. And *if* I was being honest with myself, I did feel urgency in being wed before we crossed over – in case one of us didn't return, or both. If I was going to die, I wanted to wed Fitz first.

"The more I thought about it the more I wanted it, but I was concerned you'd feel rushed with the short turnaround," he explained.

"No, this is important. We've been on such a tight timeline with all this mess, but we have a couple of days to pull something together – we have time now."

"Let's go share the news with our team?"

As we stepped onto the porch, we peered through the window, observing our loved ones laughing, bantering with one another – our hearts full and our minds set. Fitz reached for the doorknob.

CHAPTER TWO

The room erupted in cheers, everyone sharing their excitement, and though I believed they were each thrilled for us, it also gave the team something to look forward to – something other than the crusade. Something other than Lorenzo. After the initial round of applause and questions, Jordan and Isaac sat down to quiz me about the important particulars of a ceremony.

"Well, we hadn't really considered the details yet. You do think we can pull something together in two days?"

"Are you kidding? Isaac and I already have plans."

"Plans… I… wait, plans in the last fifteen minutes?" I asked disbelievingly.

"Oh, ye of little faith," Isaac said reproachfully. "Is there anything you want in particular?"

"Well, I mean, I've had a little time to reflect on what I want," I answered innocently, a smirk light on my lips.

"Spill, sister!" Jordan exclaimed.

"I want an outdoor ceremony, a gown that's kind of timeless in style, and flowers from Miranda over at the local flower shop. The rest I'll leave in your capable hands."

"Done," they chimed in unison, leaving me with the distinct sense I was in a fair amount of trouble. Fitz smiled broadly from across the room, the happiest I'd ever seen him, devoid of all our troubles in these few, delicious moments.

"Oh, yes. Sit over there amused, you infuriating Scot. Just wait until they get to you."

My words only humored him further. "I finally understand why you're so feisty, Hads."

"Oh please, share with the class."

"You can't help it – it's in your DNA – your family lineage."

"English?" I asked, my voice raising an octave in relative confusion. None of my family ever demonstrated much interest in tracing our ancestry, but I always thought we were English.

"Your mother's side is Irish, and your father's…"

"No way."

"Henry and I have been secretly working on this for weeks, with the best council resources available. Thanks again, James," he tipped his head in James's direction.

"Aye, my pleasure," James returned, winking.

"Gram was a Galloway before marrying your grandfather, the bloodline pure on both her mother and father's sides. Your grandfather – now he bore the name Weston, as do you, but upon tracing back, your people are *not* Westons."

"What do you mean?"

"Remember the story of Esther and Hamish's last name?"

"They changed it because your last name was outlawed by the king."

"Aye. Your grandfather was a Munro. Your ancestor changed his surname from Munro after escaping English troops. He was almost captured after surviving the Battle of Culloden. The Jacobite survivors were branded traitors, and hunted by the English."

"My God," I gasped.

"Your mother's side is Irish – but, it seems they fled to Ireland from a neighboring country during the wars. You, lass, have more than a wee bit of Scottish blood in your fiery veins."

"Henry!" yelled Ian. "Get that bottle of Highland Park. There's more celebrating to be done!"

Henry dutifully retrieved the whisky, as Ben and Jordan trekked to the kitchen for glasses, speaking excitedly with one another. As we sipped and celebrated the day, Fitz pulled the research from his bag, passing around my family lineage, as that lineage was important to more than me. Though our discussion was limited with Ben and Sarah present, we each knew Fitz and Henry uncovered details of a human lineage that produced a witch. James would, of course, want copies for the council, in order to cross-reference additional records for any witches hiding in my family tree.

I snuggled close to Fitz, talking with him and Ben about the lifestyle and characteristics Ben's Scottish ancestors would have shared with ours. Jordan and Isaac were consumed in wedding research, recruiting poor Henry and Molly for dress creation. Ian, Ann, and Sarah chatted enthusiastically and looked on, as the next generation lost ourselves in constructing our future. Little did they know, they'd soon be recruited for construction and baking crews.

*   *   *

Fitz's arm slid along my side, adjusting to support the weight of his head, as his left hand traced circles on my bare stomach, clearly calculating his next move. With Sarah's permission, we raided her wine cellar for a bottle of Malbec to suit our own private celebration of the day, and found glasses unnecessary, as we passed the bottle back and forth.

"We'll be wed by this time in two days," I marveled, thinking of the quick turn of events.

"You're sure it isn't too soon for you?"

"You know I love you, but sometimes I want to shake you. Why do you worry about me so much?"

"I don't want you to feel any pressure. You have enough on your mind already."

"You are well aware I don't feel pressured into anything."

He smirked. "I know we'll plan another ceremony for all the family once we return, but I'm concerned you might not want the real deal to happen this way."

"Fitz." I paused, taking a pull at the bottle, deliberating on the right words. "You and I will be surrounded by people who know who we truly are, people who are traveling directly into danger with us, people who are willing to die beside us protecting our common values. I couldn't imagine being surrounded by a better group of creatures."

"I couldn't agree more," he said, moving his hand up my belly.

"I'm finding it pretty challenging to have this conversation while you're distracting me like this."

"Mmm."

I rolled over, forcing him to support my weight, as I stared into his eyes.

"A few months ago you explained how witchkind falls in love. When we find our mate, it's apparent we're designed for one another. We're physically, chemically, genetically, and soulfully made for one another, right?"

"Right."

"And we don't waste time once we find that person?"

"We do not."

"We don't give up on one another. We are fused together eternally."

He nodded.

"Do you have doubts that we're mates?"

Fitz pulled his weight forward, his expression darkening.

"Stay," I returned, pushing against his bare chest until he sank into the pillows.

"What am I, your dog?"

"No, you're not nearly well behaved enough."

"What? I never pee in the house."

"Thank God for that!" I exclaimed, covering my face with my

free hand. A pair of strong, warm hands pulled my own away from my eyes.

"You know better than to question our connection."

"So do you."

"I didn't say you had doubts about us. I suggested you might feel rushed."

"I know my mind well enough to know what I want," my voice rose.

"You're impossible. Why are you questioning my surety on our relationship?"

"You seem so worried about everything, I thought I should check."

"Most creatures would be happy their mate is concerned for their feelings."

"You know I'm not delicate. I'll speak up if I'm unhappy with the trajectory or the speed of our relationship."

"Fine."

"Don't even pretend to be affronted."

With a roll of my eyes and a curl of my lips, Fitz couldn't withhold his good humor any longer.

"It's difficult to be mad at you when you're sitting on top of me like this and when you look like *that*, even if you are quarrelsome."

His grasp tightened against my hand, and my breath quickened.

"Waiting to begin our marriage isn't going to do us any

favors," I spoke, my voice softening. "Two hundred years isn't nearly long enough, but I'll gladly give you the years I have left."

"I pledge the same to you."

He rose slowly, reaching for my face, his lips meeting mine. We eventually sank into the soft blankets, the glow of the firelight lulling us to sleep, and he held me tightly until the early morning sun called us forth into another day.

CHAPTER THREE

"I need you to focus, Hadley," Jordan ordered. "Molly pulled together two sketches last night we all think would look amazing on you."

I tore myself away from breakfast momentarily to review the papers Jordan laid on the table. I examined each sketch carefully, considering Molly's true talent in design.

The first option was stunning – but once my eyes rested on the second sketch, my decision was made. The soft illusion neckline met the sweetheart bodice to immerse it in lace, which then traveled the full length of both arms, adorning them in small flowers. The skirt was full, and as the lace fell to the floor, it culminated in a thick band, which encircled the base of the dress. It was worthy of any princess, or any witch, as was the case.

"I love the lace on that one," Isaac said dreamily. "The floral features give it such a romantic feel."

"My sentiments exactly. This is the one for me, no question."

"Great. Henry and I will get started then."

"And how does Henry feel about dress duty?" I asked, amused.

"Oh, he's not a big fan, and he has *no* attention to detail," Isaac replied, rolling his eyes. "But he said anything for his new sister."

"That's touching actually."

"He's thrilled to see Fitz so happy. We all are."

My questioning glance pulled the rest from Isaac.

"The past couple of years were difficult on him, courtesy of the council. He was such a beast at one point, I nearly exiled him."

"I know our time apart was a rough patch for him, but I don't know many specifics."

"It was hell on him, but he's happy now. You can understand why he wouldn't want to waste time reflecting on the misery of the past."

"Aw, Haaaads," Jordan drawled out. "How romantic."

"We're discussing how Fitz was miserable, his friends on the verge of exiling him while he fixated on a situation he didn't have the power to change. And of course, you find it romantic."

Jordan smirked. "You're loved by someone entirely, *and* for being exactly who you are. Fitz was tortured by your absence. It sounds like a movie."

With Isaac, Jordan, Molly, Ann, and Henry distracted with my dress, Fitz and Ian passed the morning in the living room, catching up on a few family spells and last-minute training. Tanner and Chloe were who knows where, and I hoped they were making the most of the time they had left. I took advantage of everyone's preoccupation to find Ben and ask him one very important question.

"Of course I'll walk you down the aisle. Gee, what an honor!"

"Thank you, Ben. Tying the knot here is important to us."

Ben and Sarah hadn't pressed where our journey would take us, or what our objective was. It was no longer a question *if* they knew our current situation was odd, but Ben and Sarah already knew I was unusual. They had witnessed my transformation, and unfortunately found themselves subjected to my mind reading now and then. Through the years, they never once questioned the oddities they were sure to have seen, for which I was exceptionally grateful. Whatever they observed, and whatever occurred in this house, our secrets were safe.

With that business handled, I climbed the stairs to check on the progress of the five musketeers. I opened the door to Isaac's impatient voice, his accent growing thick.

"Henry! Slow down – this detail along the bodice needs to be exact."

"You are completely out of control! I'm doing my best. I somehow knew it wouldn't be good enough for you."

"Do you even care about this?"

"Of course I care about this," Henry responded indignantly. "This is for Hadley. Though I want to strangle you *with* this lace."

I crossed the threshold, anxious to discover the type of magic being utilized. Floating between the two of them was a sweetheart bodice enduring its final stitches, and lace appearing out of thin air. With the final stitching of the bodice, it floated alongside Henry's lace, arriving just in front of Molly. With a twist of her wrist, the two pieces hovered lower, and she set to work overlaying the lace onto the bodice. Her nimble fingers moved quickly, and perhaps the unsuspecting human eye wouldn't notice how her fingers never once touched either object. She glanced up briefly, taking notice of my stare.

"One of the greatest gifts of magic is creating something like this without even handling the material. It's good for the lace… and the ivory coloring."

"I don't know if I'll ever find this normal. It's so extraordinary."

"You'll always find this world extraordinary, and that's normal. But sometimes you still look at us like you aren't one of us."

"I guess that's weird, isn't it? I've had strange abilities my entire life, and I've known I'm a witch for I don't know, a while now. I feel like I belong, but every once in a while…"

She smiled, as Ann's hand landed softly on my forearm. Though I felt her calming presence once I crossed the threshold, that sense of peace intensified with her touch. Ann truly had a gift. I smiled, thinking there was no doubt Izzy was her daughter. Ann's auburn hair rested just along her shoulders, framing an ivory face set with piercing, emerald eyes. Ann MacGregor was every bit as charming, self-assured, and attractive as her young daughter. I was incredibly lucky to have such a force as my future mother-in-law.

"Hadley, honey… I don't want to overstep, but I've been wondering – should you call your mom?"

CHAPTER FOUR

My mother perceived the similar peculiarities between Fitz's family and me long ago, and I think that was the only thing saving me from one seriously awkward conversation over my relationship with Fitz. But her perceptiveness only fueled her curiosity. I couldn't tell her what I was, knowing it was forbidden unless directed by the council, and I didn't want to implicate my mother in any way. A hundred unspoken feelings floated in the air, and the elements suffered under the burden of our tension.

I suggested the two of us take a walk, granting Mom the opportunity to ask any questions she might have. As much as I wanted to avoid it, we needed to get that conversation out of the way. Walking along the fence line in the fading sunlight, she began.

"You said you might have a larger ceremony later, so all of your and Fitz's family could attend."

"Right."

"Honey, I just wish I knew about this sooner. I wish Tessa

and Aiden could be here. And Gram."

"Mom, I know. But there's no time now for Tessa to fly in. Izzy is just in Seattle, and she won't be here either. We'll host an event with everyone later."

"It seems rushed."

"It isn't. I wanted to elope, so you can thank Fitz for even getting this much."

"Why do you want to have something like this now and so fast?"

"Mom," I started. I paused, resting my hands on the fence, wondering how to begin. "I'm going to be gone for a little while."

My mother's expression changed slightly, confusion flashing across her features. "What do you mean?"

"Fitz and I have been asked to take care of some business that will have us away for quite some time."

"Just you and Fitz?" she asked warily, her hazel eyes narrowing.

"No. Everyone else here, too, except for Ann and Chloe. They'll go home when we leave. Well, and Ben and Sarah aren't joining us, of course."

"I don't understand. Wherever you're going… we can still talk?"

"I don't think so."

"How long will you be gone?"

"I'm not sure. It depends on how quickly we finish."

"Hadley, you've got to give me something here. This sounds

crazy."

"I know."

"This can't deal with your work."

"It deals with another type of work, but I can't talk about it, Momma."

"Why on earth can you not tell me about this?"

"Because I'm not supposed to tell anyone about this."

"But I'm your mother."

"This is a mission of sorts, one I can't talk about. There would be consequences for both of us."

She stared, searching my face, and a fire rested in her eyes that I well recalled from my teenage years. She was angry, and I couldn't wonder why. This couldn't make any sense to her, and I wasn't even doing a decent job of explaining the information I was able to share.

"Okay, here's the deal. We've all been recruited for an assignment by a branch of government. We've been in training for months and under strict orders to keep this confidential. They're sending us into a location where I'm pretty sure I won't have a way to communicate. I can't say how long this mission will take, but I'll contact you as soon as we're back. I can't tell you any more than that."

"Is this with the military?"

"You could say that."

"Still not good enough," she returned, her voice terse.

"You know I've always been different. I know you realize

Fitz and his family are, too. We're the same type of different, okay? People like us are called to duty sometimes because of our skill sets. You have to accept this because you don't have another choice. And if you can't accept it then you won't be able to see much more of me in the future. Please understand that and what a difficult position I'm in."

"I'm sure we can get you out of this. I wish your father…" she broke off, trying to suppress tears.

"If Daddy was here, things wouldn't be any different," I returned, taking her hands in mine. "He told you a couple of things about a conversation he had with Fitz, didn't he? Right before we lost him."

My mom's eyes widened.

"Look, I don't know what he told you, but… Daddy knew everything there is to know about me, and about Fitz, because Fitz told him everything before he died. There was no danger in him knowing at that point. And if he were here, knowing what he did, he'd tell you that I have no choice. I'm doing what I need to do."

"Oh God, Hadley."

"I know, Momma. It's a lot. And Fitz would be in a ton of trouble for sharing what he did. The same would happen to me if I told you everything now."

"Meaning I just have to trust what you're saying and never expect any more explanation," she finished, her expression flat.

"Pretty much. But what we're about to do – it's a good thing, I promise you that. I'm on the right side of things. I know I can't convince you of that because of how little I *can* tell you, but please... have faith in me."

When we returned to the inn, I nodded to Fitz, answering his silent question. *The* conversation had occurred.

My mother grew increasingly observant, mentally scrutinizing our every move. The longer she watched, the softer her attitude became. Between her observance of our odd group, and whatever knowledge Daddy previously shared with her, she began the work of connecting the dots. She was a quick study. Things were falling into place, and by the end of the night, I was glad I listened to Ann's advice.

*   *   *

I opened my eyes to a sun-soaked room and a life-altering day. Fitz was nowhere to be seen, meaning he was perfectly serious when he said he wouldn't see me prior to the ceremony. I shrugged off the familiar tug of my heart that always accompanied Fitz's absence and descended the stairs in search of coffee.

Jordan, Sarah, Chloe, Isaac, and Molly were buzzing about the kitchen cooking breakfast, running through last-minute details, and briefing the poor woman who appeared to be our wedding photographer. Isaac positioned a large cup of steaming coffee on the table in front of me, miraculously aware that my usual cup of tea was insufficient. He planted a quick kiss on the top of my head, as Sarah deposited breakfast adjacent to the coffee cup.

"Where are the rest of the guys?" I inquired.

"Fishing. Staying out of our way until it's time for Fitz to get ready for the ceremony."

"Isaac," I began. "You stayed here with me?"

"Yeah, of course. I couldn't leave Jordan with all the day-of organization, and I'm team Hadley today. Plus," he added shyly, "Fitz thought you'd be more comfortable with me around."

I squeezed his hand. "Absolutely."

*　　*　　*

I gazed through our upstairs window at the assembly of our soon-to-be ceremony site, nestled under the canopy of a large spruce on the back lawn of the inn. Magically constructed, the rustic trellis was camouflaged in ivy and stood before coordinating rustic benches. Beyond the trellis lay only trees, fields, mountains, and the old barn.

As a child, I found the fog rolling across the neighboring mountain fascinating, and though there were no clouds in the sky, I could distinctly envision the scene, fog sweeping through the deep green tree line like water rolling across stones in a creek.

A knock at the door nearly startled me, and at the sound of my invitation, my mother and Ann walked in, followed by Jordan, Molly, Sarah, and Adalynn. It had been at least a year since I last saw Adalynn, who seemed to have grown up in that short time. Her tall, slender figure bounced through the doorway, her usual exuberance illuminating the entire room. Blonde curls tumbled to her shoulders, framing her storm-cloud eyes.

"Addy! I'm so glad to see you!"

"When I heard your wedding was being pulled together, I thought you might need an extra pair of hands?"

"I would love that!"

"Great! Isaac said he needed another pair of eyes in here anyway. We're besties now."

I climbed into a large chair by the window, the warm glow of sunlight and chirps of happy birds filtering in. My face became Molly's canvas, as Jordan pulled more hair tools out of her duffle than I'd ever seen, setting her sights on my hair.

"Where's Chloe?"

"Micromanaging the men," Jordan replied, laughing.

"That woman loves keeping people in line," Molly said mischievously.

Sarah placed a few items on the bed. "Something old, something new, something borrowed, something blue," she quoted dutifully.

"What's all this?"

"*This* is the hair clip you gave to me when you were, oh, maybe eleven – something old," said Sarah absentmindedly, clearly recalling the child I once was.

"Oh, I can definitely work that in!" Jordan exclaimed, straining for the clip, as she held tightly to a sizable chunk of my hair.

"Something new – this is a wedding gift from us all." She held up a gorgeous pair of earrings. The pearls were held into place by small, sparkling diamonds, and I gasped as Sarah set them into my waiting palm.

"Y'all! They're beautiful! You shouldn't have."

"But we did." Molly smirked, finding my reflection in the mirror.

"Thank you." I grinned, blinking back a tear.

"Something borrowed – to match your earrings," Sarah smiled, holding a string of pearls.

"Momma, these are yours – the ones that were Grammy's?"

"That's right."

"And lastly – something blue. Isaac is forcing you to wear this blue garter. He said he doesn't care if you protest; you are under strict orders."

I cackled loudly, I'm sure to Isaac's immense satisfaction, and decided if he could make all of my wedding wishes come true in mere days, I could acquiesce to his one request.

Ann then removed my dress from the closet, allowing everyone a glimpse of the finished product. Addy deftly tugged at the fabric to steam it, removing the few wrinkles held by the fabric.

With Molly's final brush stroke and Jordan's last pin, I was presented with a mirror to approve my transformation. Molly applied bright red lips and black eyeliner, and I stared at the face reflected in the mirror, momentarily stunned.

Jordan matched her timeless theme, having pulled the long strands above my ears into two French braids. These braids then twisted into the rest of my hair in a large bun at the base of my neck. The hair clip was the final flourish.

Before I could wrap my head around any of it, my look was completed with the dress, jewelry, and shoes, and I found myself rounding the corner to take Ben's arm.

"Please, don't let me trip. Henry will never let me live that one down!"

Ben chuckled lightheartedly, and I tightened my hold on his arm.

CHAPTER FIVE

"Y ou're beautiful," Fitz whispered, closing the door to our room.

I smiled.

"My wife is hot."

I laughed, perhaps my first real belly laugh in days.

"You seem off. What's bothering you?" he asked, taking a seat beside me.

"I can't believe we leave tomorrow for Opimae, and that's honestly tugging at me a little. But tonight is a celebration, and I don't want to focus on the crusade."

"I believe in us. We'll come back together."

"I believe that, too."

"Every force in this world has brought us together. Nothing can part us now."

Fitz switched on the record player that had mysteriously appeared in our room, and Frank Sinatra's rendition of "Something" soon filled the air.

I took stock of my husband, my eyes scanning how his perfectly tailored tux displayed the masculine shape of his body. My breath quickened at the heated gleam in his eyes, as he loosened his tie. He closed the distance between us, placing a hand at the base of my neck before whispering words for only us to know. The air twirled my body around slowly, as Fitz's fingers grazed my waist, eventually resting on the zipper of my dress. He made short work of its removal, and I twirled back to face him, finding his eyes alight with a fire I hadn't yet seen, as we rid ourselves of the final barriers between us. He ran his hands over most of my body, his eyes longingly following their path, taking stock of me. I saw fit to do the same.

Fitz lifted me from the ground and onto the bed, where instinct took control. I arched my back sharply, my mind growing hazy with need, as a surreal urge pumped through my body. I slid my hands across his chest, his back, his taut, strong arms supporting the weight of his body...

Then, sliding a firm hand across my back, Fitz pulled my body toward his. "I'm yours – in every way," he whispered, his voice husky.

"Don't you dare forget that," I replied softly, before tugging at his neck, pulling his face to mine.

CHAPTER SIX

T he journey from the inn to the trailhead for the High Divide was familiar, a route I'd traveled countless times over the years, and memories flooded my mind. Lost in reverie, I was disoriented when the car came to a stop. My energy was somewhere between excitement, mounting nerves, and an acute desire for sleep. Fitz and I dedicated most of the night to studying one another, learning how to be better lovers. But the morning was saturated with the effects of sleep deprivation.

I looked around the vehicle, realizing I wasn't the only creature in somewhat of a trance. Everyone was a bit dazed, and I closed my eyes momentarily, taking in the pops of electricity radiating through the car – nervous energy clashing through the air. Fitz squeezed my hand, for his own reassurance as much as mine, and we jumped from the van, our feet crunching against the gravel parking lot.

The portal was hidden miles into the forest. We hiked all

morning alongside towering trees, damp ferns, and thick moss. It was early in the season for our journey, and snow crunched under our feet in several areas, though luckily our snowshoes were unnecessary. The views were breathtaking, as were the many memories of my father hiking that very path.

Most of us felt at home in the outdoors, and the exercise was good for dispelling nerves along the journey. We stopped briefly for lunch about eight miles in, before trudging deeper into the backcountry.

As we neared the portal I stole a glance at James, who fell in beside me some time ago.

"Do you think we'll succeed?"

"You're asking the wrong question," he countered, a mischievous grin spreading across his features. After a moment's pause, "The proper question is this: are we making a difference?"

"We've started something."

"Of course we have, my dear. Destiny knocked at our door and we couldn't ignore it. We're taking a stand against evil, and you know the wonderful thing about that? Once someone takes a stand, many will follow."

"I'm nervous."

"So am I. I've dreamed about seeing this planet for years, and I'm ecstatic about the prospect of laying eyes on it. But it doesn't then follow that I don't have apprehensions about this journey. This is dangerous… for all of us."

"I've been praying for months. I'm so nervous all nine of us won't come back from the portal in the end. I'm okay if I don't... I don't know if I could bear returning without everyone else, though."

"We're all clear about what we've signed up for, none any less than you. By standing here today, we've declared that the well being of human and witchkind is more important than our individual selves. I can't say we'll all come back, but if we don't, we've fallen for a worthy cause, something none of us could ignore."

"I'm glad you're with us."

He held my gaze a moment more before raising his voice to announce our arrival.

Chills crawled the length of my spine, my second sight awakening to the presence of the portal's power, even as the sun beat down upon the earth, its warmth hard upon my body. I closed my eyes, tilting my face upward, seeking the source of the warmth.

I traveled the rays of light to their point of origin, and I felt the insufferable heat of the sun, its turbulence erupting into the light that it was. I followed a golden ray in the opposite direction of Earth until it met the light of another, and then deposited me onto the soft soil of a new planet. I stooped to the ground and felt the soul of the strange place, my second sight confirming what my intuition already knew – I was standing in the midst of Opimae.

Hearing Fitz's voice in my mind, I wished nothing more than to be reunited with him and opened my eyes to Earth.

"Hadley, where'd you go, my love?"

"Gosh, I'm sorry. I spaced. My mind was in Opimae; it's beautiful," I said absentmindedly. My reverie ended with the pinpricks of four unknown witches standing amongst our circle of friends.

"Who are they?"

"The guard," James answered, his eyes reducing to slits. "You remember discussing this, aye?"

"Oh, yes. Just a little disoriented. It felt stronger than normal."

"It's Lorenzo," one of the guards offered. I only then took real notice of the creatures who guarded the Earth-side portal. They looked young, perhaps college-aged kids out for a summer hike, but I knew better than that.

The creature sported dirty blond hair above mesmerizing hazel eyes, which were intent on my face, searching my reaction. It was apparent he was the leader of the group, and he offered a lopsided grin. Fitz's hand slid around my waist, gripping firmly.

"What do you mean by that?"

"Lorenzo's power strengthens, and as it does, we feel the shifting energy across the portal. It's more difficult to cross now – and to come back."

The guard shivered briefly.

"Don't be alarmed by what he has to say," Chloe added. "This is what you have all prepared for."

I felt the intensity of his eyes upon me.

"I'm a seer, just like James," he added, glancing in James's direction. "I saw Lorenzo speaking with a spirit in his office. It was you, wasn't it?"

My eyes flitted to James, seeking his direction. I exhaled slowly at the quick nod of his head. "Yes."

"I've tried to keep my mind's eye on him. His armor is nearly impenetrable, but I've occasionally found a way in."

"Matt sends any information he glimpses back to the council," Chloe said.

"Tell me what you know."

"He knows your energy. Any advantage you might have – the moment you cross paths, that ceases. He'll know you immediately. Be careful."

"Thank you so much."

"We're all rooting for you guys," he added warmly.

Fitz shook Matt's hand, reiterating our thanks and closing the final crossing details with the guard. I turned to say my goodbyes to Ann and then to Chloe, whose absence was already profoundly felt.

We slowly made our final steps to the entrance of the next world. The naked eye would perceive nothing of importance, only boulders fallen from the mountainside, but I heard and felt the reverberations of energy humming through the air. The energy grew louder and stronger with each step until it grew almost unbearable. One more step would send us into the oblivion of the unknown. My mind's eye scoured the area, granting me as much intelligence as it could possibly find, and I found where our world opened to the next.

I turned to Fitz. "See you in the next world," I whispered.

"I love you."

I gripped his hand tightly, and together we stepped through the unknown, and into the curious world of Opimae.

EPILOGUE

G abriella's heels echoed loudly through the stone hallway. The door hinges of her master's dinner chamber groaned in protest as she turned the large iron ring and pushed the towering wooden door open.

"Gabriella, my darling girl," Lorenzo's thick Italian accent floated on the wintry air. "What news do you have for me?"

She crossed the room quickly, having been the subject of both his impatience and his disapproval of delivering information from across the room. The chill against her bare arms was insufferable. Gabriella couldn't understand why Lorenzo preferred to dine in the cold, damp air of the windowless room.

"Signore, they've crossed over." Gabriella winced as her master's burning gaze rested upon her.

"What have I told you about information?"

"That it should always be clear and concise."

"Would you care to try that once more, *darling*?" he

questioned, a mocking tone resting on his favorite term of endearment.

Gabriella cleared her throat. "A member of Earth's witchkind council has crossed the portal into Opimae. He's brought the team of crusaders with him."

"That includes Fitz MacGregor, yes?"

"Yes, Signore."

Lorenzo turned to his dinner partner, who remained silent. "Alexander, what do you make of this?"

"Things are progressing in accordance with the plan the informant provided."

"We need Fitz to perform his duty."

"And he will."

A soft laugh escaped Lorenzo's lips as he swirled the wine in his glass. Gabriella wasn't supposed to stare at her master, but she couldn't help herself. How could someone be so beautiful... and so cruel, she wondered. She'd promised herself she would escape, but something about Lorenzo was magnetic. Once you joined his ranks, it was impossible to leave – and she hated herself for it.

"You Russians are too straightforward. It's always gotten you into trouble. This is tricky, Alexander, and you better remember that. These are dangerous creatures."

"Of course, sir."

"Gabriella, is the woman with him?"

"Yes, Signore. Had-"

"For God's sake," he interrupted, delivering his strike in a calm, icy tone. "You do not say her name… none of you say her name. Not yet."

His eyes blazed, as his fist met the table with a startling blow. Camille glided through the doorway, holding a tray of Lorenzo's favorite cigars. Gabriella wasn't sure how Camille did it, but somehow she always appeared at just the right moment and calmed their master. She lit Lorenzo's cigar of choice, and his eyes cooled as he exhaled more than the smoke. His lips curled around the cigar, and Gabriella followed his every movement, wondering what they – no. She wouldn't allow her thoughts to travel there, not again. Once the crusaders arrived, she'd be free of Lorenzo's grip – and free of the thoughts in her mind that were no longer her own.

Lorenzo motioned for Gabriella to move closer. He tucked her raven hair behind her ears, his gaze intense. "You know I prefer your hair pulled back." He looked over her appraisingly. "But that dress does make your eyes more green. I like it."

"Thank you, sir. I'm sorry to displease you."

Lorenzo nodded, and she followed his eyes to Camille. Her honey hair was swept on top of her head, a few delicate tendrils escaping along her neck. Camille never displeased the master. Gabriella knew she must learn from Camille if her time in the fortress was to pass without incident. She would fly under the radar as much as possible – it couldn't be much longer, she reasoned.

Gabriella took solace in one belief that she considered absolute truth. Hadley and Fitz would bring one hell of a fight to their army, and she hoped to God that she was just then sitting in the fortress of the losing side.

*   *   *

1662

Esther

I sprang up in bed, my heart racing, my breath ragged, and my energy scaring the living hell out of Hamish.

"Esther! Is something the matter?"

"Aye," I returned breathlessly. "Hamish, I'm sorry."

"What is it?"

"It's Gabriella. I've connected to her once more."

Hamish's sleep ravaged mind finally caught up. "What did ye see?"

"I saw *him*. The witch who's been watching Fitz and Hadley."

"Breathe," he returned, rubbing my back gently. "What more?"

"The crusaders crossed over. Oh, Hamish… he knows they arrived. He's been waiting for them."

ACKNOWLEDGMENTS

This story wouldn't exist without many wonderful people.
A huge thank you:

To my husband, first reader, and president of my fan club, who supported me each time I stumbled. Thank you for the endless encouragement, tough love, caffeine, whisky, making sure I actually showered during writing binges – and countless other things.

To my parents, who told me I could do anything I set my mind to doing, encouraged me to see the world, and pushed me to learn constantly. Your lessons made this book possible.

To my sister for lending her keen eye and witty commentary. We have always been creators, and our joint imaginations cultivated countless storylines. We were children, and our characters were Barbies, but hey, look at me now, Sis!

To my Aunt Elaine, who encouraged me to reach farther than I thought possible and endlessly encouraged my imagination. "till…"

To my friends and supporters. You each know who you are. Your time and encouragement made this book possible. I'd like to say a special thank you to: Bill & Susan Brager for keeping me housed and fed many times during this process, and for some PNW inspiration. The Miller Tree Inn is the most special of inns. Alison McCulloch, Rachel Flink, & Shannon Anderson: thank you for getting your hands dirty reading, editing, advising, and encouraging. You've each left your mark on these pages.

To the agents and editors who influenced my manuscript in various ways. Your advice helped me learn, and your rejection helped me grow. Thank you to William Bernhardt, whose feedback prompted me to make vital changes to my manuscript and to Kaitlyn Keller for finishing touches. This book is better for it.

To Jon Stubbington, who made all of my wildest book cover dreams come true. You breathed life into this cover.

To the people of Paris, London, Edinburgh, & Forks. You made my experience in each location extra special.

And finally, to you. If you're reading this, I've dreamed about this moment for a very long time. When I thought of giving up – when this process seemed too difficult, when I doubted myself – the thought of you reading this book kept me going.

ABOUT THE AUTHOR

M.B. Thurman earned her degree in English from Mississippi State University and has spent her career working as an executive assistant.

She spends her nights and weekends writing books and remodeling old farmhouses. Though her Southern roots run deep, she now lives in the beautiful Pacific Northwest with her husband and opinionated, thirteen-year-old feline, Harriet.

An avid traveler, her book settings are inspired by some of the most stunning places she's visited, specifically areas of the world brimming with the feel of magic and the echo of ancient things.

Summoned is her debut novel, and the sequel is currently in progress.

Made in the USA
Middletown, DE
30 April 2022

64705541R00276